# Human Demon – Cursed Legacy

*Florin G. Vasile*

**MAPLE**
PUBLISHERS

Human and Demon – Blood Legacy

Author: Florin G. Vasile

Copyright © Florin G. Vasile (2023)

The right of Florin G. Vasile to be identified as author of this work has been asserted by the author in accordance with section 77 and 78 of the Copyright, Designs and Patents Act 1988.

First Published in 2023

ISBN 978-1-915996-93-0 (Paperback)
        978-1-915996-94-7 (Ebook)

Cover Design and Book Layout by:
        White Magic Studios
        www.whitemagicstudios.co.uk

Published by:
        Maple Publishers
        Fairbourne Drive, Atterbury,
        Milton Keynes,
        MK10 9RG, UK
        www.maplepublishers.com

# CONTENTS

# Prologue

Every thirty-five thousand years the universe is changing. There are times when entire planets disappear, sometimes everything on the surface of the planet is absorbed inside and becomes part of it, but in some cases, some of the beings populating one planet are moved to other planets. In rare cases magic becomes part of everything. This is the case of planet Xorbia, a small planet in the Milky Way galaxy.

After the last universe "Reset" a lot of the old world was absorbed by the planet with only some of the flora and fauna being left behind. The landforms changed entirely from what it used to be, with new mountains, hills, rivers, seas and deserts forming. Beings from other planets where instantly moved to planet Xorbia and this is how the planet repopulation started.

Immediately after "The Reset", magic started taking over the planet and it began changing things. Plants started changing first, some changed in size, others changed in colour, in a few cases the merged together forming new types and a few rare plants suffered all of these changes at the same time. The plants absorbed magic qualities and, while some became very dangerous, others gained healing effects.

A similar thing happened with the animals, new ones were brought to Xorbia from all over the universe and, influenced by the magic, they started mutating. Some merged, others changed in size, to adapt to the new environment, and some just became magical gaining different features.

Among all these changes a great one occurred. The planet was populated for the first time with civilizations. These were called humans that were brought here from planet Terra and immediately after "The Reset" some of them started gaining magical abilities that they could only dream about before. Some individuals changed entirely becoming new races that might have been considered a fairy tale before "The Reset", others started gaining animal or insect features, few kept their appearance and gained magic powers, while most didn't change at all.

Probably the biggest change caused by Xorbia's magic was that humans started to get memories that seemed to be from past lives, but more about this we will find out in the story that is going to unfold.

# Chapter 1

# Kayro's Early Years

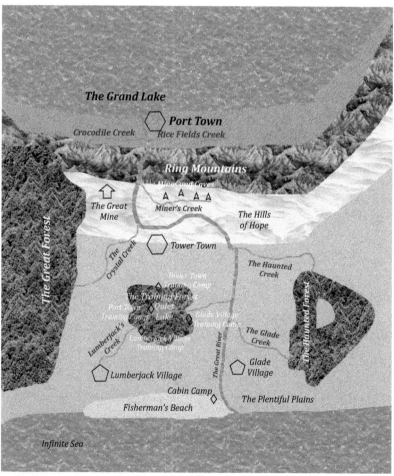

*Median Forests Map as it was known to the people at that time*

# A fateful day and a hateful night

In the year 335 after 'The Reset', in a land called Median Forests, the south-central part of the Ardian Continent, something that would change the fate of the known world was about to happen. While trying to find some herbs and other ingredients to trade at the market, Krysta, a human woman that was forty years old came upon a sound that was familiar to her for twenty years. It was the cry of a newborn baby, a desperate call meant to reach anyone around, a cry that made her move like she was a eighteen years old girl again in order to reach the source faster. Taking almost no time, due to the adrenaline rush given to her by the moment, she came upon what seemed to be a shelter. If she didn't hear the cries she would probably not even notice a place like that as it well hidden past some bushes very close to both The Glade Creek and The Haunted Forest. Lots of leaves were used to cover some twigs and branches into a roof and a door for the shelter. After carefully pushing the small door she was able to enter the small space where she finally found the crying baby. While she picked him up, he slowly began to calm down and even giggle after seeing her smile. As soon as she was out, she noticed some traces of blood the seemed to go both inside the shelter and towards The Haunted Forest.

Looking back at the baby that was now sleeping deeply in her arms she noticed that the cloths covering him had some blood stains. She was shocked at the sight, not as much by what she was seeing, as much as she was from a memory that she always hoped to forget. Almost thirty-four years ago her hands and her own clothes were stained by blood in a similar way. She felt like it was yesterday that everything happened, the hateful day when her own son disappeared and what was left from him was only the cloth he was wrapped in with similar blood stains as she just saw moments ago.

On that cursed day Glade Village was attacked at night by some unknown human-like creatures that left behind lots of blood and tears. That evening everything seemed normal, the local militia was patrolling, the people were heading home after a very long day of work as outside was getting darker by the minute. Things were quiet for nearly one hour after sundown and then suddenly she could hear people shouting while the bells of alarm sounded everywhere. The village law was that the men need to go out and help as soon as they hear those signals and after a few minutes her husband, Klost, was outside with his sword and shield in hand ready to defend their beloved community. She waited for a few minutes and then heard screams very close to her house. Looking outside through the window, she saw some shadows running very fast and her husband along with other men were chasing them. In just moments the world seemed to collapse around her as one of the shadows stopped running and confronted the group her husband was running along with. She couldn't see clearly what was happening, but in just seconds all men were just thrown away one by one as easily as you would throw a rag doll.

Although she feared the shadow, she loved Klost a lot, so she quickly opened the door and started running like crazy to check on him. Just as she reached him her mind felt relief as she saw her husband was still conscious and barely wounded. Even though he seemed fine, the shock of the moment and the impact after being thrown made him dizzy so she had to help him get up. As soon as Krysta turned around, her eyes caught a glimpse of another shadow that was just running out of her house. She was terrified, but her love for her Larp, her son, gave her strength and she left her husband in an instant while running inside the house. Reaching the room where her son was just minutes ago before she went outside, her mind and heart nearly stopped for a second. Her treasure, her main reason to feel happy, her beloved baby was gone. She recovered and went outside shouting his name while the tears nearly kept her from seeing. But this was futile, she couldn't see her son or any sign of him, nor could she see that shadow anymore. Meanwhile Klost started feeling better and at the sound of his son's name being shouted he froze for a second. In no time he was holding Krysta's hand asking what happened.

"Our baby is missing, my treasure is not there anymore. We need to find him before something happens to him. Please, everyone help us look for our son!" she shouted the last words with despair in her tone.

"Calm down, my beloved, and tell me what happened." said Klost trying to comfort her and at the same time find out more.

"I saw it! I saw one of them!" she cried. "It was just coming out of our house as I managed to help you get back on your feet."

"Did you see which way it went? Did you see if it had Larp?" said Klost with tears in his eyes.

"I only saw it from behind as it was running towards The Haunted Forest, but I couldn't see more than that."

"Then let's not waste any time! Let us quickly go towards the cursed forest then!" he shouted as he started running.

A few people from the group followed them, while others went the opposite way to check on their own families. While running other small groups joined them one by one, including some of the village's militia. Soon they got close to The Haunted Forest and noticed under the light of the torches that a trail of blood was leading inside the forest. They feared going inside as spirits were suspected of haunting it and none of those who went in deeper than one hundred meters ever came back. Running in group of at least fifty gave them more courage so they ventured more than that, but the trail of blood had stopped little by little until there were no more drops. At that point everyone realised how deep into the forest they went and started panicking. One by one they started fearing the place they were in as distant howling seemed to get closer, a feeling of being watched and hunted striking at their hearts now.

Despite the wish to find their beloved children, because more than ten had disappeared, the villagers decided to go back and carry on their search during the day. It wasn't something that any of them accepted easily, but without any clues where to go, with the feeling of being in danger they went back to the village.

The next day a village meeting was held, and even though there were more than fifty thousand people there, everyone kept quiet and listened to the village Elder as he summarised what they found out about the previous night. Fortunately, no one had died and some of the children were found as people got back to their homes. Only four were missing now without any lead on where they could be or if they are safe or not.

They formed groups of ten and while some started looking for the children, others looked for ways to improve the security of their village, but unfortunately after two weeks of searching there were no more signs or leads they could follow, so they gave up on the idea of ever finding them, even though their hearts were in constant pain.

Now, after thirty-four years of pain, Krysta found this baby around the area where they saw the last traces of those shadows. She couldn't help wonder if this was some twisted way the universe was trying to give her back some of the happiness she has lost that day and so she rushed back to the village to give her husband the news and see if anyone in the village was missing a baby.

After a few days of searching for the parents, no one in the village had any idea whose baby that might be so Krysta and Klost decided to raise him as if he was theirs. The name they chose to give him was Kayro and little by little they grew to love him as much as they loved their own son Larp.

## Krysta's Family

Every evening after the chores around the house were finished, Krysta was taking Kayro into her arms and started telling him all the stories that were passed on to her by her family. Even though she stopped talking to them long time ago, because they opposed her marriage with Klost, she always treasured these stories as if they were part of her. She didn't hate her parents, but they broke her heart when they pushed her away, just because she fell in love and decided to marry someone that was not rich and more than that he didn't have a family.

Under normal conditions this wouldn't be a big problem, except Krysta's family was one of the richest and most influential families in Tower Town and a marriage like that would mean a huge blow to their reputation. In order to avoid that, they simply decided to make her sister Darma their heir, which not only meant that all riches and lands will be passed on to her, but also the seat that her family held in the Council of Elders. This was almost as valuable as a treasure since it was very hard to get. Most families inherited them from their ancestors, but there were also those families who either distinguished themselves in certain activities or simply earned the seat after another family couldn't produce any heirs.

Having a seat in the Council of Elders was so important that children were simply forced to learn politics at a young age in order to honour their family's name wherever they went. Not only they had to behave in a certain way, but they also needed to take any chance to gain additional reputation for their family. Often the parents would test their child or children in different situations to see if they are worthy to be heirs or if they put the interests of the family first all the time.

As brutal as this process was it was also the only way to ensure that the family will not fall apart in the future, because most of the time when a family lost their seat it meant ruin. Some were banished from Tower Town, others were assassinated in order to prevent them from ever coming back to power. This was the case of the ones that inherited their seat in the Council of Elders for many generations as they were perceived as the biggest threat to power.

Krysta was supposed to be the next heir despite being the youngest child in her family, because her older brother and sister were too selfish and that was considered a major flaw for someone that held a seat of power. It was proven many times before that selfish Elders wanted all the power for themselves and in such cases all the other families would unite against them and wipe them out. This was in fact one of the Laws that were approved when the first Council of Elders was formed just ten years after "The Reset". With Xorbia's magic giving people glimpses into memories from their past lives, all the original Elders agreed that, if they were to have a peaceful society, the power must be shared and everyone must in the interest of the community, not just their own. This law was bent from time to time, but only up to a point that was tolerated by all the other families and as the population grew so did the number of seats.

Elyn, Krysta's brother, despite being the oldest lost the heir title as soon as Darma was four years old, due to the fact that he was very selfish and sadistic. As soon as his sister was born, he viewed her as an enemy and wanted her dead. His parents caught him at one point trying to strangle her, even thought he was just seven years old and his sister a few months old. The look in his eyes was pure hatred, fuelled by people that wanted his family to fall in order to take their place. Often families without any power would force their children to influence the heirs of those who held seats in the Council of Elder. The most common case was when a second child was born in that family, because it was easier to prey on the emotions of the heir. First they would look for children that felt neglected because all the attention their parents used to give them was now divided, more than often parents focusing on the new born too much. In time the older sibling was made to believe that there is no more love left for them so the only way to get that love back was to end the life of the baby and this way the parents will have no choice but to love them again and this was exactly what happened to Elyn. Because Darma was very vulnerable after birth, due to the fact that she was born two months earlier than she was supposed to be, their parents decided to do protect her as much as possible, so they ended up having almost no time for their son. Preying on his pain and insecurity some of their neighbours started putting ideas into his head. They began by showing exaggerate affection to their children in a way that looked equal. Then they showed him affection in order to win his trust before telling him that as long as his sister is alive he will not be loved anymore and also he might lose the heir title which led to his attempt to end his baby sister's life. Fortunately, by this time Darma got better and their parents started focusing on Elyn again, realising that something in him had changed and managed to stop him from becoming a murderer at a young age, but also made the understand that he was not fit to be a good Elder in the future.

Two years after this incident Krysta was born allowing fear into Elyn's heart again. He was even more afraid that his parents will stop loving him, but soon he was proved wrong as they showed no change in how much they love their children.

After some time Darma started reading and writing, so their parents started to 'train' her for the future Elder seat and because she showed great promise the heir title that was held by her brother was given to her. Enraged by that decision, Elyn decided that after he starts the Training Camp he will find a way to go to another settlement leaving behind Tower Town and his family. He followed his heart and after turning sixteen he chose to become a furniture maker and moved to Lumberjack Village where he still lives nowadays.

As soon as Elyn went to Training Camp, Darma became a target for the ones that were trying to take their family down, but it wasn't as easy as it had been with her brother to turn her against her parents since they showed as much love for her as they did for Krysta. Still after Krysta learned how to read a lot faster than her and many other children, being considered a prodigy, she started getting jealous. She would often bully her little sister or make others bully her so that her parents will not change their mind about who the heir of the family should be. But after a short while they found out everything and started testing her to see if she is still fit for the inheritance. Initially all seemed well, but when they found out about the constant bullying that Krysta was being subjected to on Darma's orders, they made up their mind to change their heir again.

Days before Darma was supposed to leave to the Training Camp they finally made the announcement that Krysta is now the heir and confronted their eldest daughter about her actions. She admitted her guilt and related the entire story of how it all started and who exactly tried to make her turn against her kin. More than that she has acknowledged that these were grave mistakes and that she agrees to Krysta being the heir now. She even apologized to her younger sister and swore to protect her and love her no matter what people will say.

Having learned her lesson Darma left with a happy heart and a lot of hope to Training Camp where she patiently waited for her baby sister to arrive in order to help her become the heir that her family deserved, the heir that she failed to be. She kept true to this and as soon as Krysta was there it became her main task to prepare her as best as she could or even get others to teach her things that were essential for a future Elder.

Just before turning eighteen, Darma found out about the love that Krysta felt for Klost and she was very happy for her younger sister. They even celebrated together on the day before she had to go back home and promised that she will support them after they graduate from Training Camp. Unfortunately, after going back and telling her parents the news, she was shocked by their attitude. Instead of being happy that their youngest daughter found a good man and that he loves her as much as she loves him, they were afraid that this love would cause the downfall of the family and make them lose the seat on the Council of Elders. Soon they decided to send news to Krysta, telling her to choose between her family and her lover. The reply was swift, respectful, but also devastating for them, as Krysta said that even though they are her blood, Klost is her future family, that she has chosen him to be her husband and no one should ever make a choice like the one they asked from her. She even told them that while learning how to become better suited for the Elder seat and gain knowledge on how to make the lives of her community better, she also made sure that Klost will have a respectable place at her side by training to be a soldier. Despite his initial interest in becoming a farmer, in order to build a future with Krysta, he changed his training from farmer to soldier just a few months before he needed to go back to Glade Village. Even though in the beginning it was very hard for him, with her support and love, the soldier role started becoming natural to him and the training that seemed hellish was now as much part of him as being a farmer was not so long before.

A week after Krysta's reply, her parents decided to make Darma heir again as she had proven worthy of the title in the way she behaved after they confronted her about bullying her younger sister. No matter how much she tried to convince them that she didn't want the role and that Krysta was the right choice, they simply refused to listen. More than that, they sent news to Krysta that she is not welcomed back anymore and that her future wasn't in Tower Town anymore as long as she considers marrying Klost. The news broke her heart, but she agreed with their choice to make Darma heir again, and decided to start training as a healer in order to move with him to Glade Village.

Klost managed to finish both the soldier training and the farmer training while she excelled in both her training as a possible future Elder, but also as a healer. They returned to his farm in Glade Village and had to work very hard in order to rebuild it as it was abandoned for years since his parents were taken by a virus while he was in Training Camp. According to the Laws as long as he was not moving to another community, it was his property to come back to. Part of the lands were used in order to feed the growing community, but the Laws stated that one year before the possible return they would be left empty to prevent any conflict.

After two years of hard work they managed to get the farm running again and also brought the fruit of their love into the world with Larp being born.

## Stepping into the World

A few weeks after Krysta found him, Kayro took his first steps which made both her and her husband very happy and at the same time a little sad. This was the first time they witnessed a baby starting to walk inside their house, because Larp was too young to do it before he was taken by the shadow, but they decided to move on as there is no gain from staying sad.

Soon he was going with her everywhere, learning how to do all the things she was doing in order to one day help his new parents around the house, at least until he was twelve years old because that is the age when all children are going to Training Camp in The Training Forest. Here they will be trained for six years or less depending on what role they will have in society later. Usually, at the age of sixteen the ones learning different trades would be sent to get qualified while working.

Kayro's appetite for learning was great and by the time he was two years old he was speaking very well and learned the names of lots of plants that Krysta was usually gathering. After a few more months he even started to identify their quality just by looking at them. This made his mother very happy as part of the parent's job in their society was to teach children as many useful things as possible in order to help the growing community. That is why part of the everyday life of all children was learning instead of having no worries and play around all day. They were never forced to learn and always things were taught at the pace they could handle, but the magic on planet Xorbia gave them memories of their past lives, so part of their life essence already knew these things or at least some of them.

With the help of their memories children learned how to read at a very early age. As soon as they were around three years old, their parents started teaching them how to write and read and most of them would be able to easily do it by the age of four. This was the case for Kayro too, and as soon as he started reading and writing properly, Krysta started teaching him everything about plants and about the way you can turn them into tea, food, medicine, poison or antidotes for poison.

Each time they went out to collect plants he appeared to become more interested in what she was doing. This made Krysta very happy as she hoped that Kayro could become a healer based on the way he loved to help all people and on his abilities to learn. Soon she decided to test his collecting skills and started making lists of what they needed to use while she was collecting plants that they could trade in order to offer him better living conditions.

When he was almost six years old she sat him on a chair and said to him:

"Kayro, starting today I will need you to show me if you can take my job as a healer in the future, so take this list of plants that are the minimum required in order to help others or yourself. Some can treat common diseases, others can make injuries less painful and some are they key to making basic antidotes. Your first step is to learn how to properly identify them and their quality. After learning that I will teach you how to prepare them"

"I will do my best, mother, and I hope not to disappoint you."

"You cannot disappoint me, son, in fact you have already surpassed some of the children your age. Now let us go and pick what we need."

On this first 'training' day, Krysta took her son to an area just outside Glade Village close to The Great River, a place where you could easily find the basic plants used by healers. While collecting what she needed to sell she started asking him about his progress:

"Did you find anything, Kayro?"

"Yes, mother, I did. I found an arberry bush and I am now reading which ones I should pick and which ones I should leave."

"Remember, son, you can always ask me for help."

"Well, there is something I am not sure about."

"And what is that? "

18

"If I remember correctly, you can use both the fruits and flowers. I already picked the ten flowers that we need, but the colour of the fruits is making me unsure which ones are the best to pick now. I know that the fruits are green in the beginning and white when they are ripe, but some are mixed."

"Give me a minute to finish here and I will help you see exactly which ones we can get now."

"Thank you, mother."

She quickly finished collecting what she needed from the place she was at and headed his way, feeling proud to see that, even though deciding which ones he could pick was giving him some trouble, his eyes were full of excitement.

"Come next to me, Kayro, and please watch carefully. As you can see, we have the fruits in many different stages here. The best you can pick are the ones that are white all over like you said, but there are some with only a few bits of green left. These we can also pick now and by tomorrow they will be almost as good as the totally white ones. You could even get the ones that are half white, half green, but that would be a waste if you have better ones to pick."

"So, I can just pick twenty that are fully white or some that only have a few bits of green?"

"Yes and no."

"Why yes and no?"

"First of all we have a lot of bushes around us, so if you have the time and from where to choose, it is better to get the fully white ones as they are considered high quality and that is because you can use them as food, for cooking, in a health fortifying mix or to make one of the adult drinks that your father likes so much."

"What about the rest of them?"

"Next, we have medium quality. These are the ones with a few green bits and we can only use them in the health fortifying mix or for the adult drinks, now, and also for cooking tomorrow."

"So that means the half white, half green ones are low quality?"

"Yes, that's true. Those can only be used in the fortifying mix. They would spoil the taste if you use them to make adult drinks or for cooking, and, just like the medium quality ones, they will upset your stomach. Only the white ones can be eaten as they are."

"Oh, I understand. And what about if I can only find one bush?"

"In that case, you will have to choose depending on how many you need, and how long you can wait until you want to use them. For example, if you want to make a fortifying mix one high quality will suffice, five medium or seven up to ten low quality. If you need them as food immediately only get high quality, but try not to eat too many at a time as they are better used for the fortifying mix."

"I understand better now, thank you. And what about goreberries? Are they similar?"

"Goreberries are similar. When they are fully red it means they are high quality, when they still have some green bits they are medium quality and half green, half red means they are low quality. They can be used the same as arberries, but they have an extra use. If you find fully green fruits they can be used to make poison."

"What about muvaberries, mother? If I remember well the quality types are similar. Full purple means high, a few bits of green means medium and half purple, half green are low quality. They can also be used like arberries."

"That's correct. And just like goreberries they have an extra way of being used. When they are green, they can make a paralysis potion."

"If I remember well, there is also a plant called sunberry? How come that one is not on the list?"

"Well, son, that's because despite the name, sunberry bushes grow only in forests since they only need a little or maybe no sun at all. You can determine their quality the same as you do for the other berries, except these are yellow when they are ripe and when the fruits are green they can be used to heal burns."

"That is good to know. Thank you, mother."

"You're welcome. Now, before you finish picking them, I have one more question. How can you identify these berries if there are no fruits or if the fruits are fully green?"

"That's easy, the flowers are the same colour as the ripe fruits are going to be. Usually when the fruits are still green you can find some bits of the flowers left at the base of the fruit."

"I see that you really paid attention to what I was telling you during the times we were out collecting. Speaking of flowers, how can you use them?"

"All berry flowers can be used to make tea, mother, and you can use them all together or separately from each plant."

"Very good, son, very good indeed. Now hurry up, we need to get back home and cook something otherwise your father will starve. As soon as you have everything on the list ready, please let me know. I only have a few things I need to collect myself."

In less than half an hour Kayro was done with the rest of the picking and they started walking quickly towards the village.

The next week, Krysta made a list of useful mushrooms and they went close to the area where she found him as a baby, because they usually grow in areas with a lot of shade and moisture. The Haunted Forest was full of mushrooms, but the best ones grew close to the Glade Creek.

Kayro's task was to identify the three types of useful mushrooms and pick twenty pieces of each preferably good quality ones. These were easier to pick as they only have two quality grades that are easy to tell apart. While he was completing his to-do list, his mother was collecting some mushrooms and other plants herself, including the sunberries that he learned about before.

In less than an hour they started walking towards the village and after they got home, Krysta tested her son about what he learned today.

"Tell me, Kayro, how can you identify the useful mushrooms?"

"By their colour and the shape of their top. Galbana has a star shaped top and it is bright yellow in the beginning, becoming dark yellow as it reaches maturity. Rozia has a round top and it is pink in the beginning, turning red as it gets to maturity. Astria grows as a small cluster of mushrooms with round top. It is blue in the beginning and it starts getting white round spots on the top as it reaches maturity."

"Very good, son. Now, can you please tell me about their quality and what you can use them for?"

"Quality depends on maturity, so they are low quality in the beginning and as they reach maturity they become good quality. When it comes to using them, Galbana is perfect for cooking because it is rich in nutrients and adds a lot of flavour to any dish. Rozia is best used for healing potions making them five times stronger. When it comes to Astria, it is the most powerful enhancer for antidotes, low quality ones making the antidote ten times stronger, while good quality makes antidotes twenty times stronger."

"Well done, Kayro. I am very happy with how fast you are learning. What if you encounter other types of mushrooms?"

"It is best to avoid any other type of mushrooms as most of them are toxic for humans. In the best situation you can end up vomiting, but the worst case means death, so I should only use the ones that you taught me about."

"Perfect answer, my dear son."

In order to make sure that Kayro has lots of practice, but also time to play with other children, Krysta was taking him along only once a week and made sure to rotate the lists that she was giving her son.

## Training years

After a year went by, it was Klost's turn to be a teacher. Since he was a very good farmer, his wife decided that Kayro can learn both about the plants and vegetables that you can grow, but also the process of doing that. This was also a perfect moment to start learning about farming, because it was early spring, a time when sowing began.

"Son, we will now begin you training as a farmer" said Klost, with happiness all over his face, because he was very proud of his job. He had trained both as a soldier and as a farmer, but due to his hind way of being, he enjoyed farming a lot. He probably did this before "The Reset", because the magic on Xorbia showed him lots of memories on how to do it.

"Most of the plants that we grow are exactly the same as we grew in our past lives. Do you have any memories about them, Kayro?"

"I remember them, but I have no idea how to grow them. Probably I had no training for this in my past lives."

"Well, that is not necessarily bad. Even though they are the same, here, on Xorbia, all of the plants that we grow have different ways of being grown than what I remember, so it should be easier to learn without contradictory information."

"I just hope I will not disappoint you, father."

"Don't worry, Kayro. You are still very young and you can take your time to learn. The more you rush things, the harder it is to learn them in a proper way, so be patient and I will do my best to teach you. Before I start showing you around, I need to explain to you how the farming process works in our village."

"That sounds interesting, I cannot wait to learn about it."

"The Council of Elders chooses what exactly we are going to plant and where we will plant it. They summon all main farmers to a first meeting at the beginning of winter, a perfect time for all that was harvested to be checked. Considering the results it is decided if these farmers will be in charge next year or they will be demoted to working farmers. Since the year 100 after "The Reset", when Glade Village was founded, up to this day, none of the main farmers were demoted, they either passed away or retired, meaning that the village always had good harvests. Usually, the main farmers started training one of their children to be their heir and made sure to pass all knowledge to them. In order to avoid the pressure, the heir was chosen based on how much they liked farming and this way success was assured. There were moments when the family had only one child and some tried to force them into being farmers, but soon that changed.

As you may know, one of the most important Laws of the Median Forests land, which includes our village, is that people will be sent to Training Camp when they are around the age of twelve, and once you get there, your abilities are evaluated in order to determine which role will suit you better in society after graduation. That being said, no matter how much the parents insist or what and who they are, the child start training based on the recommendations of the trainers after a series of tests that take place in the first year you will spend there. Of course, they will first test children on the roles that their parents have, and most of the time the experience they gain before Training Camp proves that the child will carry on with the same training as one of the parents was trained for, but there are times when a child will do something entirely different. Sometimes the training gets changed after years of trying another role, or in some cases you can train for more than one role at the same time. Your mother and I both trained for two roles. She started training for the role of an Elder and because she chose to marry me, she ended up training as a healer too. I started training as a farmer, since I loved working the land ever since my father started teaching me, but when I decided to marry your mother, my training as a soldier began. In the end, since her parents refused to accept our love, we moved here to become a farmer and healer, instead of going to Tower Town as a soldier and future Elder."

"That sounds very sad. I am sorry for you and mother!"

"It does sound sad, Kayro, but we found happiness in being with each other. We never really cared about the roles we have in society as long as we have each other. Maybe our lives would have been better, or on the contrary they would have been worse, but now it is too late to think about it. We were ready to help our community no matter where we ended up or which role they would give us, and I hope it will be the same for you when time comes, since this makes life a lot easier."

"Time will tell, just as mother says."

"That is true, my son. Now, let's go back to how farming works in Glade Village.

During the first meeting of the winter, the Elders also consult the main farmers about expanding the fields or about any possible improvements considering the population growth and also the requests from the merchants."

"How exactly do they determine that?" asked Kayro.

"Well, son, depending on the number of villagers and the requests that the merchants receive, as well as the current harvest, they calculate to see if the next harvest will suffice even if the conditions will be poor. When Glade Village was founded, there were only twenty thousand people living here, and in two or three years from now, the Elders estimates it will reach sixty thousand, Lumberjack Village, Tower Town and Port Town have also grown, so the request on the market for food is higher. When my father was your age, Glade Village only had to cultivate about sixty percent of what we are cultivating now. So, unless there are new ways to improve the quality and quantity of what we harvest, we will need to expend again in the years to come."

"Don't they have their own farmers in the other communities?"

"They do, but sometimes that is not enough. Also just like they need food, we need wood, ore, furniture, and many other things they have for trading. Unfortunately our village is too far from the hills and mountains, so there is no ore near us and that is why we get it from Tower Town. At the same time, no one dares to get too close to go inside the Haunted Forest, so we need to get wood from Lumberjack Village. We are getting salt from Port Town since the Great Lake is full of salt deposits and safe for them to get it.

Just like we don't have those, the don't have the lands to grow so many crops on. You see, the crops need a certain type of soil in order to grow and to actually have a good harvest, and sometimes it doesn't matter how much work you put into it, if the soil is not fertile enough."

"I think I understand it better now, thank you."

"You're welcome, son. Now let us carry on. After the first meeting is over, the main farmers meet all of their subordinates, working farmers or helping hands, in order to determine what they can improve. Because of the mysterious way the magic works on Xorbia, some of us get memories from past lives in time, and there were quite a few times when people remembered how their role was done in the past. Sometimes it was only an idea to start with, while on some rare occasions people had a major change on their mind. I remember that my grandfather used to tell us a story of how irrigations were started just a few years before Glade Village was founded. In his story, one of the working farmers, less than a year before passing away, remembered being a farmer in one of his past lives and about irrigation systems. With the help of an artist that could easily draw what you would describe to him, a plan was made and months after the working farmer died, Tower Town had a working irrigation system."

"Did you ever have any ideas that helped, father?"

"As much as I wished, Kayro, I never had one. I guess my love for simply working the fields as well as I can, was always enough for me. But as I said before, my life was and still is a happy one, so that is the most important thing for me. Who knows, maybe I will be just like the man in my grandfather's story and change something just before my death."

"I hope that you will never die" said Kayro with tears in his eyes.

"That is the circle of life, my dear son. And you will have to be brave when that happens, but don't worry, I still have plenty of time to live. Speaking of time, let us waste none and carry on with what we started."

"All right, I will be strong" bravely said the boy while wiping his tears.

"A third meeting follows between the Elder Council and the main farmers. They share information about the previous meetings and decide the plan for next year and if any improvement ideas can be tested or if they need to be planned better and tested the next year. Following this meeting, the Elders summon the engineers in order to estimate the possibility of applying those ideas and to see if they came up with something as well. After this, three people are chosen to travel to Tower Town where each community will be represented in order to see if any improvements were discovered. These three people are usually an Elder, one of the engineers and one of the main farmers.

After a week the meeting in Tower Town comes to an end. As soon as they get back, the three members of our community take a day to rest and spend time with their families, before gathering again. It is now that they decide what will be planted and where, if there will be any need to expand or not, and what the exact responsibilities the main farmers will have. This year they decided to sow everything just like last year. This only happens every thirty or forty years and the results were always very good. Just like last year we will help on the maize fields. I asked the main farmer to allow you to come along one day every week. Your only job will be to pay attention to what we are doing and try to learn as much as possible before winter comes."

"I will try my best, father" said Kayro with burning excitement in his eyes.

The next day Klost took his son to the fields early in the morning. Children were used to wake up as soon as their parents did, so there was no problem for the boy. As soon as they started walking towards the field, Klost started explaining how the day will go on.

"You will stay with me only for a few hours, since you are too young to work and it will get boring after some time anyway."

"I understand, father" said Kayro, with disappointment in his voice.

For the next eight months, Klost showed his son what exactly means to be a good farmer. Every morning they would spend four or five hours together giving the boy a chance to see not only his father, but other farmers doing their best in order for their community to thrive.

During this time, Kayro was also learning how to prepare basic potions and dishes from his mother. She never allowed him to do the entire process by himself, but always gave him a role in it. As much as she wanted him to learn everything before he will have to go to Training Camp, she knew that there is no point to pressure him. Also, there were still a few years for him to practice and learn, so there was no rush.

By the age of eight, Kayro knew everything that a child should know about collecting plants and farming. He still needed experience, but there were still four years left before he had to leave home and train, and at least one year after getting to Training Camp, in order to choose what he will be best at.

Seeing how well he managed on those two potential roles, Krysta and Klost decided to show him what other roles might help their community, so they decided to convince some of their friends to try and teach him about their roles. Most of them agreed to this, and while some requested for their children to be taught in exchange, others simply needed someone to tag along with their own children as what they were doing could become boring for a child.

After the wheat was harvested that year, Kayro started going to the mill in order to see what exactly the role of a miller is. Fargas, one of the three millers in Glade Village was in Training

Camp at the same time that Klost and Krysta were, so he was happy to show their son around and teach him. More than that, his daughter, Allysa, was the same age as Kayro and he wanted to teach her too.

As days passed by, the children started being friends and this made the hours they spent watching Fargas more enjoyable. Soon they started competing with trying to impress the miller with how much they learned and after three months, not only did they learn the basics of his role, but also became good friends. At this point, their parents decided to send them together to the next place where they could learn more about the roles people have in their community. Just as winter was starting, Kayro and Allysa began their journey to learn about baking.

The bakery where they went was run by Rang and his wife Melia, good friends with Klost and Fargas. He was in charge with bread baking, while his wife was making cakes of all sorts. They had a twenty years old son that was running the front shop along with his wife, and six people working in the back helping them throughout the day. This was one of the small bakeries in Glade Village, but it was very close to where Kayro and Allysa lived which made it easier for their parents to trust the coming home by themselves.

Every day both children spent around four hours with the bakers and, while Kayro was watching everything that Rang was doing, Alyssa was closely following Melia. They both seemed captivated by the fast pace of everyone working in the bakery and always exchanged information on their way home.

Winters in Glade Village were quite cold and there was lots of snow, so that made them walk at a fast pace all the time, but at least once a week they stopped to either make snow angels or to have a snowball fight with other children that lived close to their houses.

As the winter was close to ending so was their training at the bakery and that gave them lots of reasons to be sad. The main reason was not getting cake from Melia anymore, but they were also enjoying each other's company a lot and finishing the training would most likely mean that they will not see the other as often as they did now. This is why on their last day, just as they were heading home, Kayro and Alyssa decided to play by themselves. They made snow angels in the beginning, after that they had a snowball fight that turned into a game of tag after a few minutes. At some point they slipped and Kayro made sure that she will fall on top of him in order to avoid injury. That took her by surprise because even though they started being close friends she never expected him to care that much.

As they were both laying in the snow, she blushed and after kissing him on the cheek she said in a soft voice:

"Thank you very much. If I ever marry I hope that you will be my husband."

The words made his face turn red instantly, but after getting up he gave her a hug, a kiss on the cheek and while looking deep into her eyes he said:

"I hope that one day what you said will be true."

After that, there was silence as they parted ways, looking back all the time to see if the other is still there. For nearly a week they were too shy to meet and also they were both busy with their parents trying to decide what they need to learn next.

Klost and Krysta decided that it was time for Kayro to learn about a second part of farming which was livestock and Fargas chose to send Alyssa to the choir since he always liked her singing and she looked like she enjoyed it as much as her late mother had when she was young. Nearly every day, as Klost and Kayro came back from the livestock enclosures they met Alyssa since the hall where she practiced was close to their house. These halls were one of the main means of entertainment in the communities of the Median Forests and every weekend they had a different type of show. Sometimes it was the choir singing, other times it was theatre and at least one a month there was a big dance where folk music was played and all villagers could dance. There were fifty small entertainment  halls in Glade Village and five large ones for artists that came from other communities.

One day, as he was taking his son home, Klost noticed that Kayro was very excited after seeing Alyssa and that he kept looking back waving at her multiple times. Before getting home he sat the boy on a bench and asked:

"Do you like her, Kayro?"

"Yes, I do." said the boy while his face started glowing red and his heart started pounding really fast. Being honest was part of the moral values that his parents taught him and somehow he felt like he also enjoyed in his past lives, but he could still not lift his eyes from the ground.

"But she is just a good friend" he added.

"I understand. And what do you like about her?"

"She is always nice to me, nicer than she is to other children and I always have fun when I play with her. We argue sometimes about what games to play, but we soon reach an agreement that suits both of us. Well, to be honest sometimes I just pretend I agree just so I can play with her and I think that she does the same."

"That is a great friend that you have" said Klost while smiling.

"Yes, she is. More than that, unlike other children who only want to play, we also teach each other new things that we learned since we last met."

"I am happy for you, son. Now let's hurry and get home before your mother gets worried."

As they got home warm food was waiting on the table and while having lunch, Kayro was very enthusiastic about what he was learning, so he started telling his mother about it. After eating, Klost went back to work and the boy helped his mother with tidying up and cleaning. They finished quickly as the houses only had necessary furniture and both Krysta and Kayro enjoyed doing the house chores especially doing them together.

After three months the boy learned a lot about livestock and he was ready to start training for something new, but before that,

Klost decided to see the results of the training, so one Saturday he sat his son at the table and had tea while talking about it.

"Tell me, son, what animals do we breed in the village and how do they help?"

"First, and I think they are the most important, we have the bovri. We use the male bovri as a beasts of burden to work the fields, pull carts, move the grinding wheels on mills or pull trees from the ground, and female bovri for breeding and milk. Most likely, without them, our communities wouldn't have developed as much."

"Very good answer, Kayro. I never saw them as important as you do, but I think I just learned something new."

"I am happy you feel that way, father. Now let us carry one with my number two in order of how important I consider them to be."

"And which ones do you think are second when it comes to importance?"

"Initially I wasn't sure, but now I think that glicks are second, mostly because they are our main source of meat. Male glicks are usually the ones that become food, they are also used for breeding, but you only need one male for ten females, and female glicks are used for breeding and to lay eggs. We also use their feathers, the small ones are turned into pillows and duvets, while the big ones are used to craft arrows."

"This would have been my first choice when it comes to importance, but I think that you generation will start seeing this from a different perspective than mine did. Go on, Kayro, tell me, what comes next?"

"My third choice would be the alpra. Males are usually being slaughtered for food and some are used for breeding, one male being enough for twenty females. Female alpra are used for breeding and milk. We also used the wool from both males and females."

"Is that everything about them?"

"No. I just remembered, both alpra and bovri skins can be tanned and used in different ways."

"Good answer, son. Carry on, now."

"My fourth and last choice are the horgs. They might not be as useful as the rest, but it would sure be hard not to have them. Both males and females can be used the same and they are separated into two races. First we have our faithful guards, the howlers, which are used by the village militia to patrol day and night in order to prevent predators from attacking the village. They are usually trained not to attack human, unless they are being ordered by their master and this happens only in special cases.

Secondly, we have the welx, that are used by hunters. They can alert their master about predators, fetch small animals and birds and they can track both animals and humans."

"Looks like you were paying more attention than I thought you did, Kayro. By the way, you just gave me an idea of what you could start learning next. Of course, we will need to discuss it with your mother, but I think she can agree at least with one of the possibilities."

"That is great. Let's go talk to mother then."

"Be patient, son. We will talk to her tomorrow, so today you can go out and play. Who knows, maybe someone is already waiting for you" said Klost as he winked to Kayro.

It turned out he knew very well what he was talking about. As soon his son was out, not only that Alyssa was waiting with a big smile on her face, but she started running to him. Barely catching her breath, she started shouting:

"Kayro! Kayro! I have good news!"

"What is it? Why are you shouting? Try to calm down a bit, please."

As she realised just how loud she got, she blushed and got silent for a few seconds.

"Alright, now tell me what happened? What's the good news?"

"I'm sorry, I didn't realise how loud I was. I had been waiting for some time to tell you and I guess I got too enthusiastic. The good news is that I am finally allowed to join the choir on stage. The trainer told me that I am finally ready to sing and that tomorrow we will have a show in the entertainment hall."

Kayro hugged her tightly and after that, with a big smile on his face and his voice getting louder, he said:

"That's great news, Alyssa. I am very happy for you. I will tell my parents that we really need to come and see the show."

"Thank you. That would make me very happy. I am a little nervous, but I am sure that seeing my best friend there will help me calm down."

After that she hugged him and gave him a kiss on the cheek that made both of them blush. They played for an hour with the rest of the children and then went home. Krysta and Klost agreed to go with Kayro to the show and that made him very happy.

The next day he woke up very early and started helping with chores around the house moving a lot faster than usual. They finished doing everything that was necessary and had lunch before heading to the entertainment hall. The show was just like any other before, it made people forget about their stress and reminded them that there are a lot of things they can be happy about, but the happiest person in there was Kayro. Despite his best friend being nervous, he was proud of her, he was happy for her and wished that he could sing as well as she did. He was aware that singing was not one of the things that he could actually do properly, but still he wanted to share that with Alyssa.

After two hours, the show was over and people started going out of the hall. As soon as they were out, Kayro and his parents met her and Fargas. While the adults were talking, the children went to close by.

"You were amazing on the stage. I wish I could sing at least half as good as you do it" said the boy with joy on his face.

"I'm not that good, yet. I still need to practice a lot, but I am happy you liked it. One day maybe I will become an artist and sing on stages in all communities. I am aware that I am very far from that, but seeing how people reacted today, I would really like to make them that happy with my singing."

"I am sure that you can do that one day. Just remember to tell me where you next show will be so I can come see you."

"I will do that."

"Looks like it's time to go home" said Kayro after seeing his mother wave at them, and before returning he gave Alyssa a hug.

After getting home, Krysta told her son to change into something more comfortable and join the for tea, in order to decide what the next part of his training will be. Her husband suggested two roles that were related more or less to farming. The first one was training with the blacksmith in order to learn about how the tools for farming were made and at the same time learn about other things related to that role, and the second role was studying trees.

"Which one do you think would be better for you to learn, Kayro?" asked Krysta.

"I feel the same about both, I don't dislike them, but also I am not really interested in one of them a lot, so I think that the choice belongs to you and father."

"Very well, son. In my opinion I think they would both be useful to you, but considering it's summer, the smithy might be too hot for you. Last month of autumn should be perfect to start learning about the blacksmith role and that should give you enough time to learn about trees."

"I totally agree with your mother" said Klost.

The next day Kayro went with his father to Vergast, one of the best trained people when it came to growing trees. The man was born and lived in Lumberjack Village until Training Camp when he fell in love with the daughter of one of the Elders from Glade Village. Since her future role in the community was more important, their parents agreed to have the couple living in Glade Village and find the man a job related to knowledge about trees. After Vergast and his wife, Clara, finished Training Camp, a house was already waiting for them. She started working with her parents in order to learn how to be a proper Elder when the time comes and he was in charge with the orchards and inspection of the wood that was brought to the village. Unfortunately, due to past incidents, the Haunted Forest was off limits for woodcutting, so all wood was bought either from Lumberjack Village or Tower Town. Still, Vergast's role was important and it was a lot easier than what he would do if they moved to his village.

"Kayro, this is Vergast, a good friend of mine since we were in Training Camp. His wife trained with your mother and their friendship gave us a chance to become friends too."

"It's nice to meet you, Mr. Vergast."

"Nice meeting you too, Kayro. Good to see you are doing well, Klost."

"Same to you, my friend, and thank you for taking some time to train my son. I will be working in the fields next to the orchards, so if there will be any problem I will be easy to reach."

"Don't worry. I am not that busy this time of the year and from what I heard your son is quite a good apprentice. Both Fargas and Rang told me how happy they were having someone that paid so much attention to their roles as Kayro did, so I expect us to get along just fine."

The two men shook hands and went to their workplace, with Kayro following Vergast like a shadow. The same as he did when he watched the miller and the baker, he kept out of the way, tried to ask only questions that were relevant and paid attention to all details regarding the role.

The first two weeks, Vergast showed the type of fruit trees they grow in the Glade Village orchards, told him about the vineyards that are grown in Tower Town and described with a lot of passion how wood was harvested and made into different things in his home village. After that, he showed the boy how to collect different types of sap without harming, knowing that Krysta told him about how important that can be for a healer. The boy showed more in more interest in the role that Vergast had and learned the basics quickly.

Two months before winter, big shipments of wood were coming to their village. Most of it was raw, ready to be cut and distributed to everyone in order to keep their houses warm during winter, but some was made into planks. Kayro was watching the quality inspection that Vergast was doing and taking notes. There were not many types of trees, but each type had different qualities and uses and he wanted to be sure that he is learning it the right way. In fact, he used the same journal to write everything he considered important since Krysta started training him.

A month later, Vergast tested the boy's knowledge and to his surprise he learned quite a lot in this short time. He knew that Kayro will never take this role, but at the same time, he was confident that without any other choice the boy could take this role at least at a medium level.

On their last day of training, the man decided to surprise his apprentice and brought him some sap syrup, fruit juice and a fruit cake that was traditional to Lumberjack Village. During their time together he started seeing Kayro as a grandson, and that made him very happy since he could rarely see his own grandchildren, because, after Training Camp, his son moved to Lumberjack Village and his daughter moved to Port Town.

Kayro was very happy about the gifts, not just because he was receiving something, but mostly because he respected the person that was offering them very much. Even if he was hesitant at first, he built up enough courage to speak:

"Thank you very much, Mr. Vergast. I had a good time learning from you and I hope that one day I will get to see all those trees that you told me about, but they grow nowhere close to Glade Village."

"Thank you for being a good apprentice, Kayro, and I hope that, during your lifetime, you will see trees that I haven't even heard of. Remember, if you need any more information or advice you can always find me in the orchards."

The boy went home with a big smile both on his face and in his heart. Out of all people, except his parents, who trained him, Vergast earn his affection and respect on a whole new level. One of the reasons was that as he was growing up he started appreciating people a lot more, but the fact that the man treated him as family mattered even more, because one of the values that his parents taught him was cherish your family or the people that you consider to be your family.

After he got home, Kayro went to help his mother with the chores and told her about his last day of training with Vergast and how much he admired the man. Krysta was very happy that her son found someone that treated him as family and that her boy is growing up holding onto the values that they have been teaching him.

The next day, after Klost and Krysta came home, the three of them started talking about the next step in Kayro's training. They had already talked about having him to learn about smithing, but didn't decide who exactly to teach him. Usually they would choose the closest place to their house, however since the boy was nine years old they decided he can handle going a little further if that will get him a better trainer. Since the village militia was patrolling the streets day and night with their howlers, it was safe for children to walk anywhere in the village by themselves. This helped them gain confidence especially since during Training Camp they were isolated from their parents for a long time, meaning that the faster they become independent, the easier it will be to adapt there.

Klost remembered that a few years ago he trained the son of a blacksmith as a farmer, while Krysta was training his daughter as a healer, and more than that, this man grew up in Tower Town where blacksmiths had to train really hard for their role, because the only way their business would survive was ensuring high quality. Being the first human settlement, Tower Town was the most developed as well, so a blacksmith needed to know how to fix or make all sorts of tools or parts that were necessary for other jobs.

"I guess that Awel is the best choice we can make then. I remember that his daughter spoke with lots of admiration about the way he works, while I trained her." said Krysta in agreement to her husband.

"His son said the same as I trained him. Apparently he was one of the best blacksmiths in Training Camp and he was sent to Glade Village to help improve the work of all our blacksmiths at that time. Initially he was supposed to stay here for five years and then get back to Tower Town, but he fell in love with the daughter of one of the men he was supposed to help. Since she was and only child with no talent for smithing and Awel had three brothers, our Elders had to convince both his family and the Elders from Tower Town to let him stay here."

"It seems like our communities end up limiting freedom sometimes" said Kayro with regret in his voice.

"I hope I will never have my future decided like that. It doesn't seem fair." he added.

"Life is not fair son, you might already know a little about that from your memories of past lives. But we are stronger as communities than we are alone" said Krysta in order to calm him.

"I know that, but trapping people in a place is wrong. The good things are that he made a family here with the woman he loves and he was allowed to keep the role that he enjoys the most." replied the boy.

"That is true, son. As long as you have family and you can do what you enjoy, the limits of communities become bearable." Klost said with regret while looking at his wife. He always felt guilty that she couldn't go back to Tower Town and this conversation reminded him of that.

Seeing his sadness, Krysta decided to encourage both of them:

"Sometimes life will give you the things that you need, not just the things that you want. I consider myself lucky about not getting what I want, because now I have the two of you, my family, my everything. Sure blood is important, but the ones you love and love you back are your true family, even if blood doesn't bind you to them."

Both Klost and Kayro agreed to what she said and suddenly their sadness was going away. They carried on with the conversation and decided that the next morning Klost, on his way to the fields, will go and talk to Awel to see if he can train the boy.

"Tell me father, when can I start learning about the blacksmith role?" asked Kayro before his father even had the chance to close the door.

"Be patient, son. I will bathe and after we all have dinner I will let you know. Now go help your mother set up the table, please."

"All right, father."

After bathing and enjoying a tasty meal with his wife and son, Klost started telling them about the conversation he had with Awel:

"I have good news and also bad news. The good news is that if we decide to send Kayro to Awel, he can start tomorrow. The bad news is that Awel can only train him for four months while usually this training requires at least six months. He said that someone already asked him to train their son before I had the chance to do it, and that he can only have an apprentice at a time. If we want the full training we will need to wait for almost a year. What do you think about it, Kayro?"

"I can do the four months now, father. After all, I just need to learn the basics and I will get to practice in Training Camp anyway. Also, the role I always like was the one that you have, being a farmer." the boy replied.

"And what do you think about this, my lovely wife?"

"I believe that our son is right in this case. Four months should be enough to get an idea about the role and he can learn more during Training Camp if he starts liking it. Or he can even train for two roles like we did."

"Then it's settled, tomorrow I will walk you to the smithy and introduce you. Be ready to sweat a lot and drink a lot of water ,son" said Klost.

"And make sure to keep a safe distance from sharp or pointy tools and from the fire" Krysta added.

"I promise to do as you ask" said Kayro.

Since nearly a week has passed without any training and because he was thirsty for knowledge, Kayro slept only a little that night being very excited. The next morning finally came and after getting to the smithy, the boy got even more excited. Klost left quickly after introducing his son to Awel and reminding him about the promise he did on the previous day. The deal was that Kayro will train for five or six hours with a small break to eat. This was the first time they needed to pack food for him, because even he was just watching and learning, the heat would still take a toll on someone's body. All the workers in the smithy had breaks to eat after every three hours of work, so this was part of the blacksmith role anyway. As Kayro learned in his first day, both the blacksmith and his helpers were working for three hours, then took a fifteen minutes break to eat, followed by two sessions of three hours of work with a half hour break to eat an rest between.

Just like he promised he drank lots of water and made sure to stay far from things that could endanger him. After feeling the heat and listening to Awel's stories about all possible accidents he realised that his parents were right to make him promise, as any wrong step in a smithy could cost your health or maybe even your life. Still , Kayro was eager to learn about the role even more than before, because he viewed it as an art. The final result depended strictly on the smith's skill and knowledge. Sure all the roles he trained for before this included that, but the precision needed by blacksmiths seemed on an entire new level compared to the rest.

Farming, collecting plants and trees were influenced by nature a lot, while milling and baking had lower a level of required skill.

The idea of creating something with your own hands or by using tools to directly create it, had always been wish of his. Most likely it had something to do with the memories from past lives, but that was a big part of who he is.

On his second day, Awel started teaching him about different types of ore and the known places they could be mined. Unfortunately Glade Village had no way to directly get ore so they had to trade for it with Tower Town. Luckily, the smith had a good relationship with most ore traders as his family had been trading with them for a long time, so the quality of goods that he received was always good or superior. Despite that only a few types of ore were affordable to villages, so no choice but to work with that.

"Kayro, always remember, the better the quality of the ore, the less time you need in order to separate the metal from rock and thus not only you can do your job faster, but you can also obtain more objects. Let's say we are trying to make a plough, since your father is a farmer. If you use low quality ore, you need one hundred kilograms of ore and twenty hours to separate the metal. When it comes to good quality you need only fifty kilograms of ore and ten hours to get the metal, while using superior ore takes the time down to five hours and the quantity to twenty-five kilograms."

"That is a big difference, so why don't we use just superior quality ore?" the boy asked.

"Unfortunately, that is not something we can do. First of all, the better the quality, the higher the cost. Second, the ore deposits are randomly formed so you cannot choose which quality you take. We have people trained as prospectors to decide the general direction of the mining, but even with their knowledge they are not able to find only superior ore. And another important factor is one of the Laws of the Median Forests, which states that we should use as much as possible from the things we take from nature. So even if we get low quality ore, it should still be used."

"But doesn't that make you work a lot harder?"

"My work directly, no, since by law, the low quality ore should only go to smiths that are creating tools that are not necessarily vital. For example, I am making farming tools and weapons, which are needed by every community in order to survive or to ease the work of farmers, and soldiers in towns or militia in villages. A few streets to the north you will find a blacksmith that makes tools that you mostly use in the kitchen such as knifes, spoons or forks. Those are not needed as much as the ones I make and require small quantities of metal, so using low quality ore is the best option. The law offers them lower trading prices for the ore and a fair trading price for the objects they create."

"Now it makes more sense. Thank you for explaining that to me, Mr. Awel."

"I am glad that you understand, Kayro. You see, you don't always need the best materials in order to get the best results and the same goes for people, since you don't need a genius to do my job. Now let's go and check the other types of ore quickly before we start melting them."

"Are you using many types of ore in this smithy?"

"I am using the three types here. What I showed you earlier is the main ore used in my smithy. That one is called sparus and it is the most common metal. All smiths use it for everything they create because the price of trading is low and the objects they use it for last enough time for people not to complain about.

The second ore and metal that I am using is called horbium, which is rare to find. Blacksmiths use this one in a mix with sparus, one third of horbium and two thirds or sparus resulting in a metal that can be used to create the same objects, but with a longer durability. This is the standard combination used in Tower Town, but it is very expensive to use in villages, so only a few people will ask for tools or weapons made from it."

"What about the horbium ore, is it the same as sparus?" asked Kayro.

"Quality and quantity obtained from ore are similar, but the colour is different. While sparus is yellow, horbium is blue, which means that when they are mixed the colour will be green."

"I see. Easy to remember then. What about the third type of ore?"

"The third type is maxor, which is considered a luxury or better said a precious metal. I only use it in very small quantities to customize my creations and that happens rarely at the request of my clients. I buy small quantities and always just good quality, never low or superior."

"And why is that, Mr. Awel? Since you don't need that much, wouldn't it be better to get the low quality?"

"Good question, Kayro, but you see, while I only use small quantities, my wife is a jeweller and what I don't need she will use. In fact, I you can choose one day to go earlier and stop by her shop. After all, that is part of metalworking too and who knows, maybe it would be something you will be interested to do in the future."

"That's a very good idea. I will go tomorrow and check the jewellery shop, since today I want to focus on what we started. Going back to maxor, I assume it is different from the other ores. Can you, please, tell me what the differences are?"

Seeing the passion in the boy's eyes made Awel remember his years spent learning from his father and reminded him of how much he loves his role. After a few seconds he replied:

"As I said before, maxor is considered a luxury and there are two reasons for that. First of all, the ore deposits are very rare and very deep inside the mines. More than that you only get half the quantity of metal after melting, compared to what you get from sparus or horbium. When it comes to colour, maxor is red, almost like blood. Now let us go an inspect the remaining ore so we can start melting."

"I'm sorry if I wasted time, Mr. Awel. I get very excited when I'm learning new things and forget about anything else." said Kayro while looking at the ground.

"Don't worry, boy. I was the same when I started learning. In fact, I'm sorry I didn't ask more questions at that time."

The blacksmith's words cheered him up quickly, so they were able to finish inspecting very fast and even managed to see all three types of ore being melted. Awel asked the helpers to melt a part of each so that he can show Kayro the process, because this way they could focus on more important things in the future.

The next day went by very fast and even though he didn't want to leave, the thought of learning about maxor and jewellery got him excited, so an hour before he would normally leave he signalled the blacksmith about going to the shop. In a few minutes he arrived there and just by watching the displays from outside, he felt like he stepped into a different world. He never paid attention to jewellery before, not even the ones that Krysta was wearing, but now, seeing so many types with or without crystals to decorate them, left him staring. After a few minutes of awe he decided to go inside and made his ways to the counter. There was no one there, so he rang the bell, and a woman with lots of jewellery on her came from the back.

"Hello, boy. How may I help you?" she asked with a polite smile.

"Oh, wait, I know. You must be Kayro. Awel told me that you will drop by today before going home. My name is Lana and that is the only way I accept people to address me, unless they are my family, of course." she added before he had the chance to speak.

For a moment, the boy panicked, because Krysta told him to always show respect when addressing someone older than him, but soon he realised that respecting Lana's wish was the proper way to proceed:

"Hello, Lana. My name is Kayro, just as you said. Your husband told me that I really need to see the jewellery shop in order to know more about metalworking."

"That's right. Even though he is doing the hard part along with the helpers, my job is to turn maxor into the wonderful jewellery that you can see displayed. In fact I was just working on something with my new apprentice and you are free to join us."

She opened a small door to allow him inside the counter and then they stepped behind a curtain to get to the backroom. As soon as he was inside the room he froze, because to his surprise Alyssa was there. Lana gave him some time to recover after seeing his reaction and then asked:

"I assume that you have already met my new apprentice before, haven't you?

"I did, she is a good friend of mine if not the best" said the boy with his face reddening.

At the sound of his it was the girl's time to freeze for a few seconds now, but soon she came to greet him. Lana smiled again and gave them a few minutes before getting back to work. She explained to Kayro that she just started training Alyssa that morning and about the jewel that she was about to create while they watch and learn. With one eye on what the woman was doing and one eye on his friend, the boy didn't realise when time passed.

Two hours after he arrived Lana reminded the children that it's time for them to go home otherwise their parents will get worried. On their way home, Kayro and Alyssa started catching up to what they learned since they last trained together. They saw each other a few times a week, but they only had time to play, so they didn't talk much. Now that they trained so close to each other, they decided to go home together every day and this way they could talk and play a little before getting home.

The next morning, Awel proposed that in order for Kayro to learn even more about metalsmithing, he should finish early once a week and then stop by the jewellery shop and join Alyssa in learning. Apparently, his wife, Lana suggested that during last night's dinner and they both agreed that it was a good idea. The boy was happy that not only he gets to walk home with Alyssa, but also spend time learning together, which always helped him focus, because they got competitive.

The four months went by very fast and the children learned what they needed, maybe even more, so now it was time to see what followed in their training. But before that, they spent the last three hours with Awel and Lana in the jewellery shop. The couple decided to show the children together how to make a ring from ore to finished product and that made Kayro think about how nice it would be to create one for his mother when he got older. Who knows, maybe he can do that during Training Camp since they were allowed to practice there, not just watch.

As a token of their training, Kayro received step by step instruction on how to make daggers and swords and Alyssa on how to make different types of jewellery. Seeing how he looked at the instructions that Alyssa received and knowing about his wish to make a ring for Krysta one day, Lana gave him a copy of the instructions for that.

The following day, after Krysta and Klost finished doing their jobs and the chores around the house, had a conversation with Kayro about the next step in his training. The decision was hard because they wanted to give him as many possibilities to choose from when he went to Training Camp, but they soon agreed that learning about fishing would help the boy a lot in the future. This wasn't really an important role in Glade Village, but it would be a great survival skill for the future. Also the training was going to be short since there were not so many places to fish with only the Great River and Glade Creek being close enough for children to train.

After two days Klost finally found a fisherman that lived close to their house and also was willing to teach Kayro about fishing. His name was Ermin and his grandfather grew up in Port Town, so he knew a lot about what a fisherman's role is in a fishing based community.

Since it was the beginning of spring, when river fish start reproducing, the first month was spend just on theory. The first lesson was about reproduction times depending on each environment, after that Ermin showed the boy what tools can be used for fishing, how to use them and when exactly they can be used. Another lesson was about the types of lure, which environment they are best suited for and the potential fish that will bite.

"Even if the lure that we use is just a small part of the fishing process, people tend to underestimate it's importance. For example, if you use a swamp-type fishing lure in a river, the chances of a bite decrease a lot. More than that, if you use the proper lure with the wrong type of rod you can end up with a broken rod, because you can have a very big fish biting, but the material the rod is made is not strong enough or not flexible enough." Ermin explained.

"I totally understand. To be honest, I never thought fishing would be this complicated, but I realise that I was wrong." said Kayro.

"Unfortunately, nothing is as easy as it looks and this is why we need to learn and then practice a lot in order to get better at it."

The next month, the fisherman took the boy two times a week to watch how fishing is done both by groups and by individuals. Glade Creek was better suited for individual fishing using a rod, because it was narrow and the water was not so deep, while the Great River was perfect for groups in smaller or bigger boats. On the days that they didn't go fishing, Ermin was teaching the boy how to craft fishing tool and lures.

Time went by quickly and on the last week of training the fisherman was mostly testing the knowledge that Kayro acquired during their time spent together.

"Can you please tell me how many types of river fish are known to our communities and give me some details about them?" asked Ermin.

"There are four types. To begin with, we have the smallest called chrib. We can identify it by its multicoloured scales and it can grow up to two kilograms. They are usually found in shallow water and sometimes can be tricky to catch. It is best to keep the ones that weigh at least one kilogram and throw anything smaller than that back. Since they are long and slim, they rarely get caught in nets.

Next we have two similar fish abruza and scorm. Both are considered medium-sized and grow from three kilograms up to fifteen. The main difference between them is the colour of their scales, blue for abruza and red for scorm. Apart from that abruza has a bigger head in proportion to the rest of the body.

Last we have the falmo, one of the biggest fish that live on the Ardian continent and the biggest that can be found in rivers. It can be found in deep water mainly in the Grand River, growing from five kilograms up to fifty and has golden scales."

"How about the types of fish that you can find in swamps, Kayro?"

"There are two of them. First we have orma that is a small-sized fish, with green scales and that can grow up to four kilograms. The second one is called marg, a big-sized fish with black scaled and can grow from seven kilograms up to forty." replied the boy.

"Well done. What about the fish types in lakes?"

"In lakes there are three types of fish that you can catch. The smallest one is called trum that can grow up to seven kilograms and that can be identified by the sliver colour of its scales.

The second type is reggia, a medium-sized fish with purple scales that is usually weighing between three and twenty kilograms. They can also be caught in the sea close to shore.

Lacrom is the third type of fish that can be found in lakes and his orange scales make it easy to be identified. The same as reggia, it can be found in the sea and it can grow from ten kilograms up to one hundred."

"Remember that these are only the ones we are certain about and there might be lots of others out there. Also these are edible for sure, so if you ever discover a different type, try to test if it is not poisonous. I heard some tales about people that were scratched while fishing in the Grand Lake that had to be rushed to see the healers and while some recovered, others ended up dead."

"I will definitely remember that, thank you."

On his last day of training, Kayro received a fishing rod and some lure from Ermin and after he thanked the fisherman he hurried home to show his presents to Krysta an Klost. While they were having dinner, his father revealed that he also has a surprise. Not only he will start teaching the boy how to swim, but in two weeks, the next day after Kayro's birthday, they will go and spend five days at the seaside, swimming , fishing and relaxing.

The news made the boy very happy, but also a little sad that his mother will not go. This would be his first time not seeing her for more than a few hours, but it was also a chance to test himself, considering that in just two years he will have to go to Training Camp and he will be separated for at least four years from his parents. Krysta and Klost were very proud of his attitude regarding the trip, and, even if they felt a little sad that their son is growing up so fast, it made them happy that he was becoming more mature by the day.

As promised, for two hours after finishing work, Klost was teaching the boy how to swim. This was not a hard task since most remembered how to swim from their past lives, one of the biggest advantages of the magic on planet Xorbia, so in just one week the child was swimming without any help from his father or the jacket that they used in the beginning.

The days were gone fast and Krysta organised a small birthday party for her son. She invited a few neighbours from their street and the people that trained him along with their children. Some were not able to come, but Kayro didn't really care, because his best friend, Alyssa was among the ones that came. They had a barbeque party during the day which ended with a surprise cake sent by Rang and Melia, who were too busy at the bakery, but still wanted to be a part of the boy's celebration. After all the guests left, Klost told Kayro to get plenty of sleep because even with the cart pulled by their fastest bovri, they will need almost a day to reach the cabins on Fisherman's Beach. That evening, the boy hugged Krysta tightly and said his goodbyes, barely managing to stop the tears in his eyes.

## A trip to remember

The next morning, they woke up so early that there was still a little dark outside, but Klost wanted to make sure they will get to their destination before sunset. The journey was not that easy even during the day, but at night predators could show up and make it even harder. As they were getting out of Glade Village, other carts were joining them on the road to the beach and seeing them made Kayro very curious.

"Father, how come there are so many people on the road. Are all of them going with us?" asked the boy.

"Yes, son, they are all going to the beach. We have a tradition in Glade Village that is shared by the people in Lumberjack Village. During the summer months of each year, fathers take the children that are aged ten, to spend five days in the beach camp, also known as Cabin Camp. A list is made during the winter to make sure that people go there by rotation and not at the same time, because there are only twenty-four cabins." replied the man.

"Why are there so few cabins? Why not build more?"

"Well, they will probably need to build more in the next few years, but at the moment that is all they can have. These cabins are only used during summer to help children make a step forward growing up. Ten of them are for people from Glade Village, ten of them are for people from Lumberjack Village, one is for trained militia, another for their howlers, and the last two are a storeroom and a big kitchen with enough tables for all people that are staying there. The kitchen also has a room where they smoke food to make longer lasting provisions. The twenty cabins that people use can fit maximum four people inside while the one the militia is using can fit forty people."

"Why do we need militia and howlers, father? Is it going to be that dangerous?"

"Not necessarily, but they are there to make sure that everyone will be safe. Also they pair freshly trained militia with experienced ones in order to give them more confidence while patrolling the villages. Usually, after Training Camp, the new militia will take turns and guard the Cabin Camp. Each squad will stay there for one month and then go back to their village."

"That sounds very interesting. Can you please tell me more about it and how come you know so much?"

"I know so much because after finishing Training Camp, I was there for a month. Remember, I didn't get training only as a farmer, but also as a soldier or militia for villages. Regarding the other part of your question, same as Glade Village, the Cabin Camp has a fence all around, but there are only two access gates compared to the four that our village has. The militia are guarding day and night, with two mean on each gate and two teams of three men patrolling. Every day they are being rotated in order to learn how to work with different people, but each militia always have their own howler, since they start bonding with them immediately after Training Camp."

"This sounds like a good way to train adults while training children at the same time." live

"It is, yes. The Elders are always trying to find ways for resources not to be wasted, including human resources."

"Why are they doing this only during the summer, why not all year?"

"That is a good question, son, but the answer is very simple. The Cabin Camp is used like this in order to prevent overfishing and overhunting. You see, this area is quite poor, the fish are usually reproducing in spring and also they need some time to grow. Since there are no forests close to the beach, there are only a few animals around and that makes hunting very hard. Basically, the militia men that are training here wouldn't have enough food if there were parents and children here all year. During summer they get part of the fish caught by the children that come here and their fathers, some of that fish they eat fresh and some goes into the smoking house and stored in the cellar after being properly cured. Along with what they are able to bring from the villages that food will have to suffice. In the winter, since there are only militia men here, the rotate to go out hunting and some of the meat they will eat fresh while some of it will be cured and stored in the cellar."

"Are these the same reasons why they didn't build a village here or maybe a town similar to Port Town?" asked Kayro.

"These are some of the reasons, but the main reason is that our communities were not able to properly explore the Infinite Sea. In fact, the Cabin Camp was supposed to be the start of a settlement, but we didn't have boats advanced enough to explore. All attempts that were made in the past ended up with the boats disappearing along with the ones that were using them. Some say there are giant creatures in the sea that could swallow even the big boats that we build, others say that the people who went exploring simply found a better life somewhere else and decided not to come back."

"And which one do you believe to be true, father?"

"To be honest, son, I am not sure. All I can say is that I hope during your lifetime the people in the Median Forests area will finally be able to know the truth about what our world really looks like. Who knows, maybe one day you or your children will travel across the Infinite Sea."

"That sounds exciting. Being able to explore our world, seeing new places, meeting new people" said Kayro.

"Were you ever tempted of going into the world, father?"

"I did, a few times when I was a child, but it wasn't something for me. I love working the fields too much, I knew this since the first day my father took me out to show me what he does. I guess you could say being a farmer was in my blood and the only thing that could have made me give up this was if you mother's parents accepted our marriage. If they did that I would probably be a soldier in Tower Town right now instead of a farmer in Glade Village" replied Klost while he seemed lost in thoughts about how his life might have been.

"Do you think that living there and having a different role would have made you sad?"

"As long as I was with your mother, it wouldn't matter where I was and what I was doing. I love farming, but compared to the love I have for your mother is like a drop of water in the sea. From the moment I fell in love with her, until now, I only felt happier with each day."

"I am happy to hear that father and from what mother told me, she feels the same as you do."

"Sometimes the bond between two people can be stronger than anything else in the world son. While many people dream of having bigger houses or lots of jewellery, others find true happiness in the people they share their life with. Having you and your mother, makes me feel like I am the luckiest and richest man in the world."

"I feel the same way having you and mother. I couldn't have asked for better parents even if I could choose."

"It makes me happy to hear that, son. Now, please try and get some more sleep before we get to the cabins."

"I will father."

Kayro fell asleep quickly as he was too excited and sad at the same time to get much sleep during the night. He was very happy about the trip and the time he was going to spend with his father, but his mother's absence weighted heavy on him. After a few hours they reached Fisherman's Beach and Klost gently woke him up.

The next hour was very busy, seeing people quickly unloading the carts, rushing in all directions, trying to get as much done as possible before sunset. After all the carts were emptied and the animals were stabled, it was time for everyone to have a meeting in order to get acquainted. While most fathers have only been here as children, some had more than one child and have visited in the last few years, so they were used to the Cabin Camp. They shared their knowledge about fishing spots and areas where it is safe to swim, as well as some ideas on activities they can do in groups. Nearly three hours after the meeting started all families were already getting ready to sleep in their cabins.

"It feels very strange to be away from home. Not seeing mother, not having my bed, but it is quite exciting, makes me feel like a grown up."

"I know it's hard son, but we cannot always stay in the same place. We need to grow, not just physically, but mentally and this is one of the steps that are part of that growth. It was hard for me too when I came here with my father, but after those five days, I felt stronger, better prepared for the world."

"Did you have a good time, father? Did grandfather teach you new things while you were here?"

"I don't remember that much since it was long time ago, but I do know that at that time I was happy to be here. My father loved the sea and fishing as much as he loved being a farmer and he tried to teach and show me all the things that he enjoyed. Coming here with you makes me feel closer to him, as close as we were at that time and I am happy that I finally get to experience how he felt knowing that his son was growing up."

"I wish I could have met grandfather" said the boy in a sad voice.

"I wish for that too, son, but it seems that life had other plans for him and my mother. It's been too many years since they were taken away from me by that cursed virus that hit Glade Village and made me wish that I never left to Training Camp."

"I am sorry to hear that, father. It must have been hard for you."

"It was at first, but having your mother in my life gave me hope and made me realise that we can only look to the present and future and that no matter what we wish or want, the past will always be behind us. I do wish that they were still with us and often think about how much I regret the fact that they couldn't meet the love of my life, but that is simply how life works and there is nothing we can do about it."

"Mother told me once that she regrets not meeting them. She said she wanted to thank them for raising such a wonderful man. If I ever have a wife, I hope she gets to meet you both."

"I hope so too, son, but only time will tell and you are still very young" said Klost surprised by his son's thoughts.

"Now, let us try to get some sleep, it's late and we need to wake up early tomorrow and take advantage of the few days we get to spend here. Goodnight, son!"

"Goodnight, father!"

They woke up early in the morning, just as the sun was announcing its presence. The five days included both individual activities and group activities. Breakfast, lunch and dinner were part of the group activities, and everyone had to help prepare the meals. While the adults did most of the job, children helped setting up the tables and bringing different ingredients from the storeroom.

During breakfast, all parents had to decide on a plan for daily activities. Between breakfast and lunch they had a few hours for individual activities, after lunch they had group activities for three hours and then individual activities for three more until they started preparing dinner. Some chose to stick together in smaller groups even during the individual activities, while others, including Klost, decided to spend more time with their child. As soon as they finished eating and cleaning, every family went to their own cabin to pick up the tools and provisions necessary for their activity and then went outside the Cabin Camp.

Klost decided to take his son to the seaside to do some fishing. The day before he remembered his father's favourite fishing spot on the beach and decided to show it to Kayro. They took two fishing rods each and two types of lure and quickly made their way to the location.

"This is the exact place where your grandfather brought me on our first day here, many years ago. Apparently it was a tradition that started in the family since the first time that the Cabin Camp was used for this purpose. It is a little far , but it is also very quiet since most families stay as close to camp as they can. For me it is more relaxing not having so many people making noise, this way we can talk to each other freely without being disturbed or disturbing others."

"I agree. For some reason I don't really enjoy being around too many people" said Kayro.

"We will go with others during the evening, after all you are here to learn how to socialise with people that you are not familiar with, but most of the time it will be just the two of us during individual activities."

"Alright, father."

The hours went by very fast and productive. The fish they caught would be enough for everyone in the camp at least for two days. It seemed that choosing to go further than all the other families paid off and to their surprise it was nearly double the amount that anyone else managed to catch.

A small part of the fish that everyone brought back was used to cook lunch, while the rest was left in the smoking room to ensure provisions for the militia.

After eating and cleaning the table and the dishes they started the first group activity. On this first day, they had different games that could be played in father and son pairs, each game testing and training different skill as well as team work. Despite his introverted personality, Kayro had more fun than he expected and also learned a few new things. He enjoyed seeing thing from his father's point of view regarding other activities than farming, it made him feel closer to Klost.

As soon as the group activities ended, all fathers decided to go as a group and show their children the hunting grounds where they will go on the last day to get the meat for the Farewell Feast, which was their last meal in Cabin Camp. The place was not so far, next to the Great River, an area with lots of shrubs and tall grass.

"What animals can we hunt here, father?" asked Kayro after they got there.

"Unfortunately, not so many animals live here. It's mostly turen, some orren and rarely there are miskra passing by. When I was here with my father, they managed to hunt two miskras, one was cooked for the feast and the second got smoked . Everyone was happy that day, especially the men in the militia, because they rarely get miskra meat here."

The group needed half an hour to scout the area and they only managed to see a few turen while doing that. The group activity for the next day was to plan the hunt and repair or make new traps. In order to avoid any incidents it was decided that only traps will be used during the Farewell Festival hunts, after long time ago someone was injured by an arrow while a miskra was being chased.

As soon as they got back to Cabin Camp it was time to cook dinner and this time they only used vegetables. On the first four days only fish and vegetables were used for lunch and dinner in order for the children to understand the importance of using resources according to their availability. Even if they were not so happy about this, the bits of memories from their past lives helped them accept the situation easier.

After dinner, as usual, everyone helped with the cleaning and they all went to sit by the campfire that the militia prepared. The fathers shared their own stories about the Cabin Camp trying to help their children get more comfortable and that helped a lot, because up to now they just saw the parental side, while now they could see them as friends, as someone who has been in their shoes and experienced the same things as they do now. Since it was getting too late and everyone was getting up early, the parents decided to postpone some of the stories for the next evenings.

The next morning, after breakfast and cleaning, Klost took his son to a fishing spot located where the Great River meets the Infinite Sea. Same as before, this was a traditional spot in his family.

"Kayro, the reason why this fishing spot was a favourite for both my father and I, is because there is a chance to catch both river and lake fish. Most of the time you can catch very big ones with the water being very deep and there is a small chance we might even see new types of fish. It seems that the magic on planet Xorbia not only makes them grow big, but sometimes also mutates them into a mix of two species."

"Is that what happens to all life here, father?" asked the boy.

"I am not sure, son. I was never curious about these things, but I certainly the instructors from Training Camp will have more answers for you when you will finally get there. In fact, the first year is based on teaching you about this world and everything that is happening in it, so I don't want to give you wrong or old information."

"I guess I will just have to wait until then. Thank you, father. Just as you said, it is best for me to learn from the instructors about it" said Kayro with disappointment in his voice.

Klost was sad that he cannot share more information with his son, but for some reasons, the Elders in all communities decided that all information regarding Xorbia, magic, other lands and a few other things should be kept a secret from children until they get to Training Camp. They said the main reason for this was that the world was changing too fast for that information to be accurate, and it was better no to fill the children's memory with wrong information.

Just as the man said, they managed to catch both river and lake fish and each of them was bigger than the ones caught on the previous day. Having their cart was a very useful and again it would help the Cabin Camp future provisions a lot. As they were going back, Klost told Kayro that these catches are normal during this month, but on most months you can barely catch half of what they managed to do now.

Just as it was decided a day before, after having lunch and cleaning, they all started fixing traps and even build a few new ones. The children were really excited about this even if it took them until dinner to finish with the traps and planning. Kayro was one of the most curious in the group as he didn't really want to hurt any other being if possible, but also knew that this is an important survival skill at the same time. Dinner time and the campfire stories passed by really fast and the camp fell silent as everyone except the night patrol was asleep.

The next day, after having breakfast, Klost decided it was time that they join other people, so along with everyone from Glade Village went to swim in the Great River. This was a chance for all children to practice and encourage each other as most of them recently learned how to swim. There were a few that learned a year before and that boosted everyone's confidence.

Klost was trying to give his son as much freedom as possible while keeping an eye on him from the distance. He knew how important learning how to be independent was for a child's future, especially with Training Camp being less than two years away for Kayro.

After getting back to camp, preparing and eating lunch, cleaning the tables and dishes, it was time for the group activity. Today the children were working in smaller groups and went patrolling with the militia. Each hour they swapped places in order to make sure that they get to know each other better while doing an activity together. Following that, the captains explained how the camp was used, how they take care of their howlers, but also how their normal role in the villages work. Kayro was happy to get more information about the militia roles, even if he already knew some of the basics from his father. Hours went by very fast and soon the Cabin Camp was silent again.

On the fourth morning, Klost went with Kayro to the seaside again. For an hour they were swimming in the Infinite Sea and after that they went to the fishing spot from their first day. This time someone was already there, Jung and his son Zodar, a family from Lumberjack Village. They were surprised to see someone else come this far away from camp and explained how it was a tradition in their family to use this spot. The two families started being very friendly to each other after finding out about this common tradition and managed to catch a lot of big fish before going back to camp.

The afternoon was spent getting ready for the hunt, since it will be a full day outside camp. They prepared their traps and provisions along with bows and arrows, just in case some predator ends up coming to the area. By the time they finished packing and reviewing the plans it was already dinner time. The children were already thinking about not having to eat fish again next evening and even some of the adults agreed that some other meat would be a good change in their diet.

In the morning everyone woke up before sunrise and got ready to travel. In less than half an hour they were already leaving camp and two hours later they started setting up traps according to the plan. In just two hours the managed to capture ten turen and one orren, but the three hours after that went by without even a sign of animals.

That was going to change soon, when very loud sounds came from two of the larger traps and, as soon as they went to check them, it turned out that each trap was barely holding a big miskra. Just like the wild animals that were caught earlier, the miskras were given food that contained powerful sedatives in order to keep them quiet. It took fifteen minutes for them to fall asleep and the hunting grounds became quiet once again.

The group decided to have lunch since it will probably take some time for animals to come back to the area. One hour past lunch there was a loud sound coming from the traps that were set closest to the river and after reaching them everyone was amazed. Two of the bigger traps had miskras inside and inside the smaller traps they found six more orren and twenty turen, but the biggest surprise was that one of the miskras had babies trapped inside with her. Everyone in the group decided to let the mother and babies go, along with the smallest turens and orrens, because every community in the Median Forests respected nature and one of their laws was to never waste anything, especially food, which was one of the most important resources.

After setting them free, the group realised that they already have quite a big catch and decided to return to Cabin Camp. The militia men were alerted by their early arrival thinking that something might have gone wrong, but as soon as the group got close the worry on their faces change to joy. One miskras, three orren and five turen were enough for the Farewell Feast, which meant the rest of the animals will be smoked and turned into provisions just like the extra fish from the past days. Soon the camp turned into a slaughterhouse, but they did try to do everything as less painful as possible. Since the animals were still sedated, they were sacrificed easier and faster and after that people were going in all directions. The children helped with firewood and water, also they deposited bones in the smoke house while the howlers could feel the taste just by looking at them.

Just before sunset the feast was ready and people started celebrating the end of their time in Cabin Camp. Some were singing, others were dancing, a few were close to falling asleep while eating. As soon as dinner was finished and the tables and dishes clean, the parents were enjoying fresh beer next to the campfire, while the children were playing close by only stopping to drink some fruit juice.

As everyone was getting tired Kayro decided to talk to Zodar before saying goodbye. He got close to the boy from Lumberjack Village during their fishing trip and the hunt, close enough to consider him a friend. They were both sad about leaving and promised to send each other letters before they will meet again in Training Camp. After two hours the camp was silent again, with everyone sleeping deep after a very busy day.

Next morning, just before leaving each family received a small pack of provisions to share with their families since both fishing and hunting went so well. Everyone said their goodbyes one more time and then started the long journey to their villages. Half way on the road they met the new groups that went to the

Cabin Camp and wished them good luck and just an hour before sunset they were home.

Two streets away from their house, Kayro asked Klost's permission to get out of the cart and run home to his mother. As soon as his father approved, the boy started running like some predator was chasing him and soon he was at the door. After Krysta opened the door he jumped into her arms holding her so tight that she needed to catch her breath.

"I missed you so much, mother. It is good to see again and it makes me happy to see that you are well" said Kayro while tears were streaming from his eyes.

"I missed you too, son. Welcome home!"

## The moment of truth

Minutes later Klost arrived home too, hugged his wife and after kissing her, he said that they need to talk after their son will go to sleep. Krysta prepared a delicious dinner and after they finished eating Kayro started telling her about everything he did in the Cabin Camp. After one hour he started feeling sleepy and he went to bed, but not before he promised his mother that he will finish telling her the rest about his trip.

As soon as they were sure the boy is sleeping, Krysta and Klost sat at the table and started a conversation that was postponed for a few years.

"What did you want to tell me, my dear husband?" asked the woman nervously.

"Oh, my beloved wife, I am afraid that the moment we kept trying to delay is close. During our stay at the Cabin Camp, Kayro started being very curious about a lot of things and even if he shared some of his thoughts with me, I fear that some he kept for himself, but that made him a little distant sometimes."

"Do you think he knows?"

"I think he suspects something. He didn't say anything about his thoughts, but I could see him trying to study everyone around. I guess being a lot older than the rest of the parents that were there made him think about the huge age gap between us and him."

"That makes sense. Until now he mostly spent time with us or other adults, never really saw lots of families together. Do you suspect he knows that we are not his parents or he is simply wondering about why is there such a big age gap between us and him?"

"Honestly, I'm not sure. My guess is that he has questions about the age gap and he is afraid to ask in order not to hurt our feelings, but he is getting smarter by the minute, so there is a high chance that he will start thinking if he really is our child."

Krysta gasped and tears started running from her eyes. She was afraid of Kayro's reaction after he will find out about them not being his real parents. Part of her was terrified that he will reject them and she will end up losing another son. Seeing her like that, Klost hugged her tightly and kissed her forehead while reassuring her that everything will be all right.

"I'm sorry, light of my heart, but I think it is best that we tell him the truth before he will realise it by himself. Knowing him and his heart, I think he will be happy to hear the truth and I am sure he will understand why we kept the secret for so long."

"You're right, my brave husband. He will probably be shocked in the beginning, but he is strong and loving, so everything will be fine after a while."

"I'm glad we agree, my beautiful wife" said Klost before hugging and kissing her lips.

A few moments later, they calmed down and carried on with their conversation. Soon they agreed that they will tell Kayro the truth after next evening's dinner and for that they will get the boy's favourite cake and syrup, hoping the surprise will give him some comfort. Since the decision was made, they decided to go to sleep and get some rest.

Next day Kayro woke up late being very tired from the long journey and found a note from his parents next to the breakfast that was waiting for him on the table. In the note they told him to get some rest and if he has energy to try and do some of the chores around the house before they get back.

After eating his breakfast, the boy went around the house and garden to see what needs to be done and seeing that most of the chores left for him to do were easy, he divided them in two parts. He will take care of the first part, after that he will go and see his best friend Alyssa and tell her about his trip, and after that he will get home and finish everything before his parents will come back. In less than an hour he finished the initial part of the chores and he started walking towards Alyssa's house while singing and dancing. He was happy to share his adventure with her, but more than that he was happy that he can see her after what seemed a long time since they saw each other.

Luckily, the girl was just coming outside to play after finishing her own chores and as soon as they saw each other started running like predators were chasing them. Seconds later they hugged like it was years since they last played, not just a few days. After two hours they shared everything they did while being apart and realising how much time has passed, decided to go home and finish the rest of the chores before the parents get home.

Minutes after Kayro finished, Krysta was home with everything they needed to prepare dinner and something else that was a surprise. After the woman took a bath they started cooking and half an hour before they finished Klost was home too. He finished his bath just as his wife and son finished preparing dinner and they finally revealed the surprises they had for the boy. Like always, the deal was that first they have a meal and then dessert.

After they ate both dinner and dessert, Krysta made some tea and they sat around the table telling each other how their day went by. It was something that they did every evening before going to sleep and sharing always made them feel closer. As soon as everyone finished telling how their day was and what they did, Kayro was ready to get out of his chair and go to bed. Just as he got up, Klost asked him to wait because they have something more to talk about.

"What is it father? Did something happen?"

"Everything is fine, son. We just need to tell you a secret that we have had for a long time and hopefully you are now ready to hear it" said the man with tears in his eyes.

"Father, what is wrong, are you well? Mother?" the boy asked.

"Just as your father said, Kayro, everything is fine. We just need to confess something" replied Krysta.

The same as Klost tears started flowing from her eyes, but she managed to calm down and start talking again:

"I hope you will not hate us for keeping this away from you, Kayro, but you see, and there is no easier way to say it, even if we love you as a son, you are not our child" said the woman before starting to cry again.

Seeing that the boy was in shock, Klost went to him and hugged him, while confirming his wife's words:

"I am sorry son, but what your mother said it is true. We feel bad for having secrets, but we were always afraid that the truth will hurt you and make you hate us."

"Father. Mother. You have absolutely nothing to be sorry for. I always had a feeling that might be the case and as time went by, I started suspecting it, but even so, you are my parents no matter what happens or what anyone else says."

Krysta and Klost wrapped their arms around the boy and each other and fell silent for a few minutes. His words made them feel loved and soon they were able to go back to their conversation.

"Please, forgive us, son. We always wanted to tell you, but never found the right moment. And even if you were not born from the two of us, I consider myself your mother" said Krysta.

"Just as I consider myself your father" added Klost while kissing his wife forehead.

"Everything is well, I am your son and will always be. Even if I could choose my parents, I couldn't get someone as good as you are. In fact all I can do is thank you for raising me and loving me even if I am not yours. More than that I really appreciate that you tried to protect me from the truth until I was ready to face it."

Klost and Krysta hugged the boy again and kissed his forehead, before telling him the story of how and where the woman found him. Kayro was disappointed that no one knew where he came from or who his parents were, but deep inside only the man and woman in front of him were regarded as real family.

After he asked how come they didn't have any children, tears resurfaced and made him bad for asking, but, before going to sleep, his mother and father told him about their lost son Larp, about the evening when he disappeared and about the lack of courage to have another child until Krysta found Kayro.

Finding out about him being found close to the place where the shadows that might have taken Larp made the boy curious. In fact he ended up thinking about that for at least an hour after getting into his bed. Was that fate, was it simply a coincidence, was it the universe trying to balance the loss that his wonderful parents had, and many other questions went through his mind.

# Hunting is not a sport, hunting is for survival

In the morning, before leaving to do their jobs, Klost and Krysta had breakfast with Kayro and seeing how nothing changed made their hearts feel lighter. The woman left him a list of extra chores and they told him that after dinner his next step in training will be discussed.

As soon as they left, the boy started doing his part around the house and quickly finished most of his chores.

One of the extra tasks that his mother asked him to do was go to the bakery and buy some bread, so Kayro decided to stop and play with Alyssa, let her know what his parents confessed and then buy the bread before going back home. The girl was shocked to hear his story and admitted that there were some rumours about Krysta and Klost not being his parents, but she didn't care about rumours and that is why there was no point in mentioning this before.

The journey home, after his conversation with Alyssa, seemed like years instead of minutes for Kayro. Moments of his life kept coming to him mixed with the ones from his previous lives. He couldn't wait until someone will finally explain how these things worked and how they were connected. Despite all of these thoughts he knew that in his heart Klost and Krysta are his parents and they will always be, even if his real parents will show up one day in front of him.

After getting home, he quickly finished the rest of his chores and impatiently waited for his parents in order to see where his training will take him now. He didn't have to wait long and two hours later, after having dinner, everyone sat around the table with some hot tea in their cups. Kayro always liked talking to his parents like this, because it made him feel included in the adult life. Lots of children had their future decided by parents, but he was always included in the discussions and asked about his opinion. That made him think of how much he appreciates Krysta and Klost not just as parents, but also as friends. These thoughts were soon interrupted by his father's voice:

"Son, we were thinking about two options for you next training step and they are both related to our trip from Cabin Camp. The first choice is for you to start training with Jabix, one of the best hunters in the village and the second is training for a militia or soldier role. For the last one you can start training with me and then I have some friends that are working in the local militia and they could give you a proper training."

"So, which one do you think suits you better, my dear boy?" asked Krysta.

"They are both very important, so to be honest it is a difficult choice, but I would like to train as a hunter now and keep the second choice for next year. It might not be a big difference, but when it comes to that role I would like to be more mature when learning about it."

"We are glad to hear this, son. Both your mother and I have reached the same conclusion as you did and it makes us admire your way of thinking."

"Now that this is decided, we were also thinking about the next step that is related to the role you chose, Kayro. The hunting training will last from the end of this month until the second month of winter begins and we were considering that training with the tanner and weaver would be a good way to see how the hides and furs from the animals that the hunters catch will be used. What do you think? Will that be something that you wish to learn?" asked the woman.

"That sounds perfect and it is a very logical way to learn things" replied Kayro.

"Well, since we reached a decision, I will confirm to Jabix that you will soon start training with him" added Klost.

Days went by fast and it was finally time for Kayro to start training with the hunter. His father took him to the cabin that Jabix was using and introduced the man to his son quickly before going to the fields. After Klost left the hunter was the one to speak first:

"I heard a lot of good things about you from some of you previous trainers. Everyone agreed that your appetite for learning is amazing and they are all happy with how respectful you were regarding both their role and person. That was the main reason why I accepted to train you and the second was the way both your parents love their roles in the community."

"Thank you for the kind words, mister Jabix!"

"I'm sorry, Kayro, but I need you to forget about the 'mister' part. I don't consider myself old enough to be one and I also want you to think of me as a friend, not just some boring adult."

"I apologise, mi…"

"You don't need to apologise, you just need to call me by my name, dear boy. I understand and appreciate that your parents taught you to respect the people around you, but in my case I feel respected more by dropping the titles."

"I never thought of it that way, Jabix. Most people like to hear those titles even when they are being addressed by another adult."

"As you will see soon, I am not like most people and I hope that will apply to you in the future to, Kayro. You seem like an unique individual which is one of the biggest qualities someone can have."

"Thank you very much! I hope I will live up to that" the boy said with joy on his face."

After that, the hunter showed him around his cabin. The main room was quite big with a fireplace that seemed very useful during cold days, a massive table where the man crafted everything that was necessary for his role and a small table with some chairs that he used to eat on. Aside from that there were three more rooms, a small room where bows and arrows were kept and two large rooms. One of these was used to store the traps that were ready and the second one was used to store the materials needed for crafting.

"This seems like a lot of work. Are you doing all of this by yourself?" asked Kayro.

"I'm only doing part of it. There are three of us using the cabin. I am considered the main hunter and I have two apprentices, one just came back this year from Training Camp and the other one is waiting for a main hunter role to open. If it was up to me, he should already be doing that job, but we have a limited number of hunting cabins and there is no opening."

"Why are the people in the village not building more cabins then?"

"It is not that simple, Kayro. You see if we build too many cabins and get too many hunters we will end up not having anything to hunt in the future."

"And why is that?"

"Just like any other resource in the world, wild animals are finite too. So if we catch all of them, there will be none to re-populate."

"Now I understand why last month, during the trip at Cabin Camp, the adults decided to allow a miskra and her babies to go."

"That is a perfect example, especially in that area. As my father and his father before said, hunting is not a sport, hunting is for survival. Which means we shouldn't try and catch or kill things just because we can, we should do that only when needed."

"How exactly do we do that?"

"Just like all the other roles in the communities, the hunter role is directly controlled by the council of Elders."

"So they give you orders?"

"It is not that simple, Kayro. Everything is part of a larger system. To begin with, I am sure that you heard this before, from time to time Elders from all communities in the Median Forests meet and share information. Part of that information is represented by our reports regarding the density of each species in the area, the species that live where the hunting grounds are, the possibility of extending or the need to reduce hunting. Depending on all that information and also on how much the livestock has increased, the Elders start making plans for each community making sure the hunting grounds will be plentiful. On some occasions the hunters are tasked with getting rid of a certain number of predators that live close by, maintaining a balance while making sure all species survive in optimal numbers."

"Wow! That complicates things a lot. I never thought of things this way. To me hunting was just going out to get food and I believed that the more animals you catch the better it will be."

"I'm afraid it is not that simple, Kayro. All our actions have impact on the world we live in, and we can try to respect it and keep a balance or we will end up destroying it. The problem is that not everyone understands the fact that we need the world to survive, but the world doesn't really need us to go on. In fact, no matter how much we will destroy, it affects our future as a race, but the world will carry on using our remains to rebuild itself, especially on a planet with magic like Xorbia."

"I don't really know what to say, but I promise to always respect the world we live in."

"I think that is enough talk for today, dear boy. Let me show you the types of traps, bows and arrows that we use and during our time together I will teach you how to use them and explain when you should use them."

"Sounds, great. I cannot wait to learn about it."

A few hours passed as if they were minutes and it was time for Kayro to go home, but before that, Jabix took him to the back of the cabin ad showed him the welx kennels. Just like the militia had a howler to help with their role, hunters had a welx as an aid. Only one of the kennels had an occupant and it was a strong female inside.

"Her name is Alana" said the hunter.

"She is beautiful and it looks like she is very happy to see you. Is she yours?" asked the boy.

"Yes, she is the one that does the hard part, while I just tag along and get the credit."

"This is my first time seeing one and I never imagined it will be like this from what I heard."

"I know the feeling. I was your age when I met my first welx. It was Alana's mother and she belonged to my father. He was always telling me about her, but unfortunately I had to wait until it was my time to train in order to meet her. But my biggest surprise came after I got back from Training Camp when I went to the kennels to check on the welxes and found a new one that looked very young. My father said that as soon as I give her a name she will be mine and since that day I knew that all my hunts will go well. I'm sorry, Kayro, but it is getting too late and you should already be on your way home. I promise to tell you more about welxes and of course about my lovely Alana during your training."

"I cannot wait to hear more. See you tomorrow, Jabix!"

Since he was ten years old now, Kayro could spend eight hours on his training every day, so he got home the same time his parents returned. They each took a bath, started preparing dinner together and after eating they relaxed by drinking some tea and sharing about how their day went. Kayro asked to be last to share since he will need a lot of time to tell them about his new adventure.

At the end of their conversation, Krysta and Klost couldn't be happier about their son's desire to learn and how excited he was every time he had the chance to learn something new. They all went to sleep smiling and looking forward to the next day.

The first training month Kayro spent inside the hunting cabin learning about bows and arrows, how to use them, when to use them and how to craft them. His training with Vergast made it easy to identify the different types of wood used in the crafting process. Since the hunters were taking turns at going out, Kayro learned from all three and to his surprise each of them had something extra to teach apart from the information the other two had. Jabix was a very good general hunter and his skill was best used with the help of his helpful companion Alana, Lien, the experienced apprentice, had a lot of knowledge about hunting predators and because of that his skill, regarding using and crafting bows and arrows, was the best in Glade Village, while Erno, the new apprentice, was an excellent trap maker.

During the second month Kayro went out with each of the hunters and learned about tracking and laying traps. He was surprised that all three, despite being interested in different things, were working the same way. They all taught him the same steps and showed him the same way of laying traps. One day, after getting back to the cabin, he decided to have a conversation with Erno:

"How come all of you choose the same way of placing the traps and follow the same steps when tracking? I was thinking that being better at different things will change the way you do the job" asked the boy.

"Honestly, I think that going out with Jabix for the first three months after coming back from Training Camp made us copy his way of doing things. You see, he likes to teach people in a logical way and he always chooses the optimal solution. Being able to do that, his style of hunting most likely got imprinted in our memory" replied the young hunter.

"So, that means you're doing everything the same way he does it?"

"Up to a point, yes. But as you know, all three of us have different specialisations. For example, when it comes to traps, I make mine sturdier than Jabix and Lien, also, after hunting with them for a while, I convinced them to try the baits that I developed during Training Camp and since then we are using the same type. When it comes to hunting predators, both Jabix and I had a lot to learn from Lien. Apparently the year before he finished Training Camp, there were lots of predators going into the Training Forest and everyone had to work harder on that aspect of hunting, otherwise the balance between predators and the rest of the wild animals would be broken. When it comes to Jabix, he very skilled in training welxes, apart from everything else. To be fair, without his help, both Lien and I would have needed years instead of months to train them properly."

"Oh, I think I understand better now. Everything seems the same because you are simply a good team and always learn from each other."

"More than that we also trust each other. Of course we each had to prove our worth before being trusted" said the hunter.

"I have always seen the three of you going separate ways. How did you manage to get so close if you don't hunt together?" asked the boy.

"There are only a few months every year when we hunt alone and it just happens that you came during that period. This is a result of very low predator activity on the hunting grounds and we use it to become better as individuals in order to make an even stronger team after that."

"Thank you for telling me all of that, Erno."

"You're welcome, Kayro. It is nice to have someone that is actually interested in your role, so any questions you have I will try to answer. The same goes for Jabix and Lien, as all of us enjoy this role."

The first half of the third month was dedicated to learning about making and using different types of bait, while the second half was all about welxes and their training. During this time, Kayro realised just how much he likes animals and that one day he would like to have one as a companion.

The fourth month it was time to learn how to hunt using a bow, so on the first week Kayro went with Erno to learn how to properly kill a turen. The week after, it was time to see how a orren can put down with an arrow, with Jabix being the tutor, while on the third week Lien taught him how a miskra can be killed. As winter was getting close, predators started coming to the hunting grounds. Luckily it was only a three gurmas and since they hunt alone it was the perfect occasion for the three hunters to teach the boy how to hunt predators. Before the hunt, they mapped the areas where the felines usually go and made sure they will be far away from each other when the hunt will take place.

After hearing about hunting a predator, Krysta and Klost were a little worried, but Jabix and his apprentices promised that nothing will happen to their son. The main hunter and his experienced apprentice would normally go alone to hunt a gurma this size, but now all three along with their welxes will guard the boy while showing him how to take the predator down.

Just as they promised Kayro was safe during the hunt as Lien took the gurma minutes after they reached the hideout that was prepared on the previous days. Despite everything happening so fast, Jabix decided to have a word with the boy.

"I hope you will not imagine that taking down a predator is always this easy. As we told you parents, both Lien and I could have done this without a hideout or help, in fact Lien is so good that along with his welx he could kill two of them, but it is always good to have a safe way of doing things and only use a direct approach if there is no other choice. I'm sure Erno can confirm that even with a hideout and aid from his welx, he would still risk being injured."

"I understand. I prefer a safe way of doing things anyway" said Kayro.

"My advice is to always weigh you options, as sometimes the safe way is not the best. If you overthink and waste too much time preparing and following the animal, you might end up giving yourself away and become prey, but I trust your judgement and I am convinced that during Training Camp you will learn what actions are required depending on the situation."

"Thank you, Jabix. I promise that one day I will make you proud of my hunting skill."

After the hunt, Kayro was sad to hear that his last month will be spent inside the cabin since he hoped to take part in more hunts, but more predators got closer to the hunting ground and the three men, no matter how skilled they were decided not to risk a child's life. He already learned a lot and now he just needed to imprint the information in his memory and practice when he will be in Training Camp.

Days went by very fast and it was time to end the hunter training. Kayro spent his last day with all three men at the cabin since there was a violent blizzard outside which made hunting impossible. Before going home he thanked them and wished them good luck in the future.

# The richest family in the Glade Village

After his exciting training with the hunters, the boy was feeling sad, so Klost and Krysta decided to prepare a special dinner that evening. They roasted a whole turen, bought his favourite syrup and even got a small cake. These surprises cheered him up and after eating and cleaning it was time for the usual family discussion.

"Kayro, we have another surprise for you" said Krysta after taking a sip from her tea.

"What is it, mother?" asked the boy impatiently.

"You next training will not only be with the tanner and the weaver, it will also include some time spent with a butcher and a tailor."

"In fact, son, you will be learning all of these from a big family, one that everyone calls the richest in the village" added Klost.

"I'm happy to hear that, but how come one family can teach me so many things?"

"It's a long story son, but to make it short, the butcher's son, who is a tanner, married the tailor's daughter, who is a weaver. They have been friends and neighbours for their entire life and as close as brothers, so when their children fell in love and got married it turned them into a big family" replied Krysta.

"That sounds nice and complicated at the same time, but how come they are seen as the richest family in the village?" asked the boy.

"That is for you to discover, my dear son, and I am certain that at the end of your training you will know the answer" replied his mother.

"It's just as your mother says, son. Some things are better left for you to discover and decide upon the answer yourself" added his father.

The next morning, as always, before going to do his job, Klost took Kayro to his next training place. As soon as they arrived there, the boy was awed. Not only did the family have two beautiful big houses, the two shops between them, a tailor and a butcher shop, but after passing a gate to get to the back of the properties he was left speechless. The land they owned was huge, in fact he could barely see where it ends, and in this massive backyard he could see more buildings. The closest was another house, which he found out later it was built for the tanner and weaver by their parents as a wedding gift, there was a big wooden building, that turned out to be used for storage and two workshops. The first one was close to the tailor shop and it was the weaver's workplace, while the second one was the tannery and due to some powerful smells they decided to build it at the far end of the property.

Klost started introducing the families by their last name, which, just like his, 'Farmer', was meant to reflect their role in the community. In most cases, the wife was taking over her husband's last name and if their child would have a different role than the father, then his last name would be change according to that.

"My son, meet your new trainers, the Butchers, the Tailors and the Tanners."

"It's nice meeting everyone. Thank you for accepting to teach me about your roles!"

After the introductions were over Klost went to the fields and Kayro was left with the younger family. Brand was the tanner and his wife Jera was the weaver. They decided to spend the morning having tea at their house where Kayro can also meet the other children that came here to learn. As if there were not enough surprises on that day, as soon as they went inside the guest room, the boy saw a familiar face, Alyssa was here too and just like him it was her first day. The Tanners excused themselves since there were two more children to arrive:

"It seems like the two already know each other which is good. Unfortunately there are two more trainees to arrive, but we will be back as soon as they get here and we can all have a conversation before the training starts" said Brand.

"Make yourself comfortable and have some fruit juice or cookies from the table, please" added Jera.

The children were happy to be able to spend time together again and they quickly started talking about the huge property they were on before their hosts get back.

"I wish that I can have at least half of this one day. It would make me feel like a princess in her castle" said Alyssa while imaging her future.

"It is too much for me. I would like a bigger house than my parents have, but not too big."

"So I assume that you don't want to have many children?" asked the girl.

"I never really thought about that to be honest. We are too young to know how our lives will be by the time we are old enough to have children. I'm not sure if I want to have any children" replied Kayro.

"You might be right, it is early to know where life will take us."

Just as she finished her sentence, the Tanners were back with the other trainees and after everyone got acquainted it was time to talk about how the training will proceed. During the first day, because it wasn't a busy time for them, Brand will show the children the butcher's shop and the tannery and for the second half of the day, Jera will give them a tour of the tailor shop and her weaving workshop, with a break to have lunch before changing tutor.

All children were scared at first when they entered the butcher shop's back rooms. If the storage room was just full of dead animals and gave them chills, the slaughter room was full of bones, animal parts and blood which made the trainees feel afraid and a little sick. Luckily, the Butchers started showing them around and explain the process and that made the children relax and see things just as they were. Brand's parents were both very patient and kind, so they made sure to quickly distract the children's attention, from the horrific part of the butcher shop, to the importance of having it. As soon as Madam Butcher explained about the variety of meat they sell and about the dishes it can be used for, the trainees went from being afraid to being hungry.

Following that, Brand started explaining how important his father's role was for him. Without a good butcher to skin the hides properly they will end up in average or poor quality and that would be a waste. Just like everyone else in the Median Forests, he disliked wasting anything. In fact after coming back from Training Camp, he had some ideas that helped his father save even more from the animal parts.

Initially the butcher shop seemed very quiet, but as soon as the customers started showing up everyone started getting busy. Up to that moment, the children didn't even notice the two helpers in the front and the three in the back of the shop. After making sure that they were given a proper presentation, Brand decided to take the children to his workshop. The walk was quite long, but, as he explained, it is better for the tannery to be far from houses due to the bad smell that can occur sometimes.

Despite him not being here there was activity inside and as soon as the door opened the children saw three men that were working inside. Brand explained to the children that, considering the amount of orders that they get, hiring helpers was needed. Not only he was tanning hides for his mother-in-law to turn into clothes but he was also doing it for other tailors that were able to buy cheap hides from the merchants.

After a few hours just as everyone was finally getting accustomed to the smell inside the tannery, they had to go and have lunch. It was time for the trainees to have another surprise as lunch was being served in a big canteen where both the entire family and all hired hands were gathered. More than that, in the room there was a separate smaller table where six younger children were eating. Two of them were the Tanner's family descendants and the rest had parents among the hired workers.

It was at that moment that Kayro started thinking about the meaning of a family. Was it all about parents and their children or could that extend to friends or people that you work with. He soon forgot about that thought as he received a plate with food that looked very delicious and a glass of fresh fruit juice.

After lunch Jera took the trainees outside and showed them the pasture where they have the sheep and the cotton field. Unlike other weavers she was using her own raw materials instead of buying it from merchants or farmers. The family had hired people to take care of livestock and the field for them and even had two experts in livestock and cotton coordinating them.

Seeing all of that, Kayro was thinking that when he grows up he might enjoy getting a bigger land, build a house and the rest of it would be turned into a farm where he can work along his father. It was a dreams that made him smile without realising.

As soon as they reached the weaving workshop, they realised that, just like in the tannery, three hired workers were here too. This time it was two women and a man who worked in harmony as a team. After two hours of explaining and showing them around, Jera took the four children to the tailor shop.

The front of the shop was managed by madam Tailor who was helped by two women that the family hired, while in the back mister Tailor was working along two other hired people, a man and a woman. During the remaining hours, Kayro and the other trainees discovered that everyone in the shop could work on the standard clothing that was always available, but when it came to special orders madam Tailor was making the women's clothing herself, while her husband was taking care of the men's custom orders.

That evening Kayro and Alyssa walked home together continuing the conversation they started in the morning and catching up to what they did in the last few months when they barely met. Since there was not enough time to finish, the children decided to walk back home together every day until they finish the training.

Next morning the two of them were paired to spend six hours training with the tanner and the last two hours they were learning about the butcher shop. They will have this way of training for the next two months and after that, they will swap with the other trainees and spend four hours in the weaving workshop learning from his wife and the other four hours in the tailor shop learning from his in-laws. Both children were happy to be paired for the training, since this way they can spend more time together.

Before starting to show them what he does, Brand told the boy that he has a surprise for him. The hunters decided to send the gurma hide to him and paid him and the Tailors to make some clothing of his choice. Kayro was very happy to hear that, because this was a good was to always remember his time spent with them and not only that but he could choose what the leather will be turned into after being tanned.

The two months went by very fast and Brand was pleased with how much the learned and with the fact that they always wanted to learn more than the other. The competition between them when it came to learning was fierce, but also motivated the more than anything else could. His father, the butcher shared the same opinion when it came to the trainees.

The same happened when Kayro and Alyssa trained with Jera and her parents which made the trainers admire how much thirst for learning the children had and, at the same time, enjoy teaching them. During the training with the Tailors, Kayro requested them to make a belt and a vest out of the gurma's tanned leather, but a few sizes larger, because he wanted to wear them in Training Camp and maybe even after.

The evening after finishing his training period with the Butchers, Tailors and Tanners, Kayro had a long discussion with his parents, as always sitting around the table with a cup of tea after dinner.

"What do you think, now that you spend some time with the richest family in Glade Village, son? Why are they called that?" asked Krysta.

"I think that I was wrong to judge their wealth just from their possessions" replied Kayro

"And why is that, my dear boy?" asked Klost.

"Because everyone working there was treated and acted like a big family. Some of the workers were husband and wife, they even had their children spending time there and eating with Brand and Jera's children. More than that, there was a young couple that had to leave from Lumberjack Village, because both their families opposed to them getting married, after finishing Training Camp, and everyone helped them train for different roles than were ready to take."

"Very good answer, my beloved son. That was the main thing that both your father and I wished you could learn from them" said Krysta.

"Lots of other people could teach you about the tanner, weaver, butcher and tailor role, but very few could teach you what you just learned" added Klost.

"That is true and I am happy that even for a short while, both Alyssa and I were able to share the feeling of being part of the richest family in our village."

The next few minutes the conversation was focused on the girl and there were a few times when Kayro blushed. Lucky for him, it was getting close to sleep time, so Klost decided to change the topic.

"As we talked before, son, starting tomorrow I will teach you a little every day, for the next two months, about the soldier or militia role, after I come home and in the morning your mother will teach you about the healer role at her workplace for a few hours daily."

"I am happy to hear that, father. I always wanted to learn more about the second role that you chose in Training Camp and of course about going to see exactly what mother's role really looks like apart from picking the necessary materials."

"I am glad to hear that, son. Most boys dislike the healer role and they prefer to learn how to fight and hurt others instead of helping someone get better. I remember quite well that your father was like that the first time we met. Farming and fighting were his favourite things to do, but in less than a year I helped him see things from a different point of view."

"Is that true, father?" asked Kayro.

"More or less, son. More or less. Farming was indeed my first love, but that was before meeting the love of my life. After that I had to fight, not because I liked that, but because I loved her."

"Yeah, yeah. Always looking for a way to sweet talk me, just like you did back then."

"There you have it, son. Not only that I had to fight for her attention, but also had to fight other boys that wanted to be with her and I always got blamed for it. "

Krysta started laughing, followed shortly by her son and husband and then she replied:

"That only happened because you were too blind to see that you were the only one I was interested in, or maybe you had dirt or grass in your eyes from working you beloved fields."

Kayro was happy to see them tease each other like that and could see how much love was between them even after so many years of being together. With the night ending in a happy manner, all three went to sleep.

## Last year in Glade Village

The next morning they walked together for a short time after leaving home and then Klost went his own way. After reaching the healing building, the boy was amazed by how many people were there and by how calm all the healers were no matter what the problem was. Knowing how relaxed his mother was, he never imagined that her workplace could be so busy.

"That's how it always looks the first time you come here, son" said the woman after seeing his reaction.

"And how does it look to you, mother?" asked the boy, while looking in all directions to see what is happening.

"This is just a normal day, my dear boy. We have days that can be quiet from time to time and rarely we have days when everything you see now will seem like peaceful. But at the end of the day, we feel good for being able to help someone, no matter how crazy the day was."

In that moment, Kayro started admiring his mother even more, because it assured him that she was the good person he always believed she was. A few minutes after they entered the room where Krysta was healing people, there was a knock on the door and after it opened the boy froze for a second. His best friend, Alyssa, was here and he was afraid that something happened to her, but soon his mother explained that the girl will be training with her for the next six months.

The two months they talked about passed by very fast and Kayro learned a lot from Krysta and most of the theory that his father wanted to teach him. The boy always preferred experience over theory, but his father knew that and tried to find a way to simplify the knowledge he wished to pass on, which helped a lot.

After his eleventh birthday, the real training about the militia role started. Klost asked four of his friends to teach his son and they all agreed to have him tag along for a few hours daily. This way the boy received eight hours of training daily, two hours with each of them and they could properly do their role for the rest of the day.

There were also days when Kayro was spending all day in the barracks watching the new recruits train hard to reach the same skill level in combat as their seniors and to his surprise and joy, some of them proved to be better already. That made him think about his future and how much he wanted to make his parents proud after coming back from Training Camp.

Just like most of his training before, he was only allowed to watch and that made him feel a little sad. The older he got, the more he wished he could join, but Krysta and Klost always made sure to remind him to be patient because he will start practising more than he wishes in less than a year.

Five months went by quickly and Kayro was happy with the things he learned about howlers, fighting techniques, the importance of patrolling despite it being boring and many other things that will probably be very useful when he can finally practice.

When winter came and his militia training was over, Krysta decided to teach him about cooking. Every day she left him a list of ingredients that they needed to buy and a recipe. At first she had him use very small quantities, but after two weeks she allowed the boy to cook all meals. Even if they didn't taste very good, he was improving with each day and at the end of winter he could make decent basic dishes, as his confidence improved.

With only six months left before Training Camp began, all children were allowed to act freely, enjoy playing with others, spend valuable time with their family and only to think about the things they were taught during the last few years without training anymore.

Like most children, before going to Training Camp, Kayro started writing a journal about what he learned so he can use that knowledge in the future. This was a method used by people for many years in order to remind themselves about the roles they were taught until now. The boy found it very useful as, during his last six months at home, he managed to remember key details from all his days of training, things that he knew very well while he was learning them, but without doing them daily, he partially forgot, being focused on the new things he was learning. From time to time he was comparing things that he wrote to the ones Alyssa wrote and this way they could see everything from different point of views.

After three months he decided to make a second journal about his memories from the past lives. Unfortunately they were all vague so he had to treat them as a great puzzle.

"Could they be all tied together, are they just random glimpses or should he consider them as being lessons to help him in the future?"

These were just some of the questions that went through his mind and hopefully during the next few years he will receive answers that will help clear things out. He often tried to see if his parents knew more, but every time he was told that he needs to wait until Training Camp as the known facts keep changing and only the village Council of Elders has access to that information.

He even tried comparing information about these memories with Alyssa, but she didn't really care about things that were not affecting her everyday life. Initially he was disappointed by her answer, but he learned to accept that people are different and as long as she was happy it didn't change their friendship in any way.

The six months were gone very fast and on the day before going away, Klost and Krysta didn't need to work, so they can enjoy the last day in many years to come that they can spend with their son. Both reminded the boy of how important it is to always look forward to the future, to stay humble and safe, to try not to hurt others unless he had to defend himself or someone close to him, and many other things that they considered a decent human being should see as rules to live their life.

"I promise to do my best and make you proud with the way I behave and that I will come back being an even better person" said Kayro, trying to comfort them.

"I am sure you will, my beloved son. We both know how much potential you have and believe that if you reach at least a quarter of it that would make you a great man."

"Thank you, mother, not just for these words, but for raising me, teaching me and loving me throughout all these years."

Klost went to hug his wife seeing her burst into tears after hearing their son's word, while he nearly had the same reaction as her. In order to prevent the tears that were forming in his eyes, he started talking:

"We are already proud of you, my boy, and we look forward to one day having you back, no matter how things will go. You might not be our biological son, but we never taught of you as not being part of the family. It was a pleasure for both your mother and I to raise you and I am sure she will agree that while we were teaching you, we also learned a lot from you."

Kayro went over to his parents, hugged them and despite his attempt to stop his tears they started flowing form his eyes. He wished to avoid that in order to encourage his parents, but simply couldn't help it. After a few minutes of crying, they were all back in their seats around the table sipping tea. The boy broke the silence:

"I will write to you every month and let you know how things are going and tell you about the new friends that I will make there. From what I heard once a month, a cart of supplies will be delivered to each camp in the Training Forest, so we can still communicate even if it will not be as close or as much as we did it over the years."

"We will write to you as well, son, and if they allow us we will try to send you gifts on your birthday. Speaking of, if you ever need anything or you wish for something specific for your birthday, let us know and we will do our best to send it to you" said Klost.

"And never forget, Kayro, it is fine to make new friends which can become your family. Just as you saw when you trained with the Butchers, Tailors and Tanners, people actually work better as a family, than by trying to do everything themselves. I know it's hard for you to get close to others, but make sure to try and give people a chance before deciding to avoid them" added Krysta.

"I will remember all of that. Thank you!"

Their conversation carried on until late, probably later than they ever did before and, after getting everything off their chest, everyone went to sleep.

The next morning Kayro said his goodbyes and once again thanked his parents for everything before going to the caravan that was taking all children around twelve years old to Training Camp.

## Chapter 2

# Training Camp

### The Glade Village Camp

After travelling for a day and a half, the caravan finally reached its destination. Situated on the eastern side of the Training Forest, the camp that all children aged twelve to eighteen from Glade Village were using as a temporary home, was similar to a small village.

The camp could easily be considered a farming village with lots of fields that already had crops and a few large livestock enclosures. Apart from those, the camp had a builder site, silos and other storage buildings, a healing site, a meeting hall, a small trading post, barracks, a bakery site, a butcher site and the residential area. All the buildings looked old, but well maintained and the arrangement seemed to follow a certain logic, nothing was there at random.

After the caravan stopped some of the instructors came to greet the new trainees and one of them had a welcome message:

"Hello everyone, my name is Zoss, and I am the head instructor in Glade Training Camp. We are happy to have you here and hopefully after a few years you will also be happy that you were here. I understand that your journey was long and tiring, so today we will show each of you where you will live while attending Training Camp, or at least while you are learning about the roles available at Glade Camp. Today you can settle in and get to know each other, because as you will see in the future team work will be very important and the better you know someone, the better the team will function. I will see you all tomorrow morning in the meeting hall where you will receive more information about the camp. See you all tomorrow and welcome to Training Camp!"

Following Zoss's speech, the trainees were divided into two groups with the girls on one side and the boys on the other side, and then into one hundred people groups. Each hundred followed one of the instructors to their living quarters which were buildings big enough to fit the entire group inside or maybe even more. The same as before the boys were taken to one side of the living quarters, while the girls were taken to the other side.

The trainees discovered that all these buildings were organised the same way. As soon as they entered there was an open space with a reception desk for the militia that was guarding the building on the left side and a lot of water barrels stored on the right side next to the stairs that could take you to the first floor. Behind the open space were forty doors out of which twenty-five were toilets and fifteen were shower cabins. On each of the other three floors there were forty small single rooms that only had space for a small wardrobe, a bed with a storage box under it, a foldable desk that you could use while sitting on the bed, a lamp and a small window.

Kayro found the room perfect as he never did need much space. He only needed half of the wardrobe for his belongings, the desk was big enough for him to have a few books opened at the same time and the mattress was hard, but comfortable at the same time. From what his parents described, he was thinking the room would be even smaller, or who knows maybe the living quarters were rebuild.

After everyone was given a room, the instructor told them about the activities they can do to relax for the rest of the day and of course each day after training. They included playing different sports in the designated spaces behind the cabins that were used as living quarters, borrowing books from the library located inside the meeting hall or simply going to the small park that was built in the middle of the camp. Hearing about the possibility of reading other book than what he had at home made him feel happy. Unfortunately the only community that had a public library was Tower Town while everywhere else only some people wanted to read so they had to buy them from the merchants.

Since it was only the first day, the boy decided to explore instead of reading, after all there were six more years left to do so, unless he chooses a role that requires him to go home early for training on the job. First he went to see the designated spaces for sports, but he left quickly as he wasn't really interested in playing any, then went to see where the library was located and ended everything with a walk in the park.

As he was walking, someone came from behind and covered his eyes.

"Guess who it is?" a girl's voice asked.

"That's easy, Alyssa. You're the only person that could do that" he replied.

"Are you sure? Maybe I am a secret admirer."

" Well, I heard there might be some creatures that can mimic human voices in the Training Forest, so maybe you are one of them."

After saying that, the girl smacked him on the back and started laughing, before hugging him.

"So I was right, there is a creature that can mimic human voices. Never expected to meet one so quickly, but I am happy to see you."

"I am happy to see you too, annoying boy."

Kayro and Alyssa went for a long walk sharing their first impression about Glade Training Camp and their journey here. While the boy was satisfied with everything, the girl was complaining about having to use common showers and toilets, about how small the rooms were and how she already used up the entire space of the wardrobe.

"If everything was at least double in size I wouldn't complain, but now I feel like I can barely breathe in there" she said on a sad and angry tone.

"For me it's enough. Not too small. Not too big, I still have plenty of storage space left and having a desk where I can read was unexpected."

"You always settle with a little, I have no idea how you can do it. I don't want a palace, but at least something that doesn't make me feel too big. I bet that all the other camps have bigger rooms for their trainees."

"We will find out one day, but until then, this is the situation and there is little we can do to change it."

"I guess you're right. Who knows, maybe our parents had even worse conditions than we have now. Speaking of parents, how do you feel about being so far away from them?" asked Alyssa.

"I miss them a lot, but just I cannot change anything about the room, I cannot do anything about that either. They are always in my heart and that is what is important" replied Kayro.

"I am glad that you're not sad. I know how much you love them."

"They have been preparing me for a long time for this moment and trusted me to handle it, so I wish to respect that. How about you, Alyssa? "

"I miss them so much, but I promised to be brave like my mother and strong like my father."

"I am happy to hear that. I know you didn't get to spend a lot of time with your mother, but your father was there nearly every time we met. Anyway, don't forget that you have me, your best friend, here with you."

"You're right. Having you here is like having part of home here. Maybe we will not be spending too much time together after the training starts, but we can always meet and take a walk in the park."

She hugged him tightly and they decided to walk back to the living quarters. They made some new acquaintances while walking back and now they were ready for their first night away from home.

Before going to sleep, Kayro decided to start writing two journals about life at Training Camp. One would be about everything he learns and the second will be about his personal life.

The next day at the meeting hall head instructor Zoss informed the trainees about how everything will proceed from this day until they choose a role for when they go back to their community, or decide to get married in a different one, and they learn everything that can be learned about fulfilling it.

The first seven months will focus on the history of the Training Camp, of each community and of each role that can be taken after graduation. Following that there will be a month when trainees, with the help of instructors that will act as counsellors, will choose the roles that suit them the best and then during the next four months they will learn about the role that one of their parents has in their community, since most of the time children tend to choose that one for their future as well.

After the announcement, the children were given a tour of the Glade Camp. In order to avoid overcrowding they were divided into fifty persons groups and led by an instructor to different parts of the camp. Training groups were not separated by gender, so Kayro and Alyssa ended up on the same one.

First, they went to the healers site which was the closest to the meeting hall, it was quiet despite the big number of people they could see. Inside the big courtyard there were two buildings, a smaller one built only with a ground floor which they were told it was the treatment building and a five floor building that could be used to teach up to five hundred people at the same time about the healer role.

Next, the trainees were taken to the builder site. The courtyard was smaller than before, but there were three big buildings this time. Together they could fit in more than one thousand people at the same time. The instructor informed the children that two of the buildings were used for practice and one was used to teach theory.

The trading post was next on their tour and by far had one of the smallest courtyards out of all training areas. The main building was organised as a shop and storehouse and there was a stable for bovri and carts built on the opposite side of the courtyard, close to the livestock enclosures. The instructor informed everyone that everything traded inside was made by the children that are training for different roles, also the ones running it are also trainees and there is one of them in each community's Training Camp. More than that, as they start learning things everyone will receive credits which can be used to buy what they want from the trading posts.

Next on the tour were the livestock enclosures, two for bovri, four for alpras and three for glicks. Next to them silos and storehouses were built to make it easier to feed them and behind them were the farming fields that spread across a large area all the way to Lumberjack Creek.

After that they went to the closest barracks, the ones on the eastern part of Glade Training Camp. In order to keep everyone safe the camp had a tall wooden wall build around with an access door in each of the four cardinal points. Next to each door they build barracks for easy deployment of troops in case something might happen. The instructor informed everyone that each of them was built the same way, with a big training yard in the centre, an archery range, a building that was used to train and shelter howlers, and living quarters for the militia instructors and trainees.

While going back towards the camp centre they passed by the butcher site which was a lot bigger than expected. Since Glade Training Camp was the only one out of all four to have livestock this was the only place to have a butcher site. Almost everything that was caught during the hunts or fishing was sent here in order for children to train. The courtyard was small, but there were lots of buildings. One was used a living quarters, another was used a smoke house, three were used for storage, one for teaching theory and three for practising.

The next step of the tour was the bakery site which was similar in size to butcher site. The main building was used as living quarters, five small buildings were used as mills and next to each there was a silo were grain was stored, a big building was divided into several bakeries and a medium-sized one was built for teaching theory.

Going further with the tour they stopped for a short time at the meeting hall to show the trainees the library and register them so they can borrow books, then they walked through the park and finally reached the last point of interest, the special areas designated for sports and recreation that were next to the living quarters.

Before dismissing them, the instructor informed the children that next morning they will be assigned to different guidance counsellors who will help them during their entire stay in the Training Forest and that for the first month head instructor Zoss will spend eight hours with them, four days a week, in the meeting hall to teach and answer questions about the history of Training Camp.

As soon as the instructor left, the children started forming smaller groups to discuss about their day. This reminded Kayro of his evenings with Krysta and Klost sipping tea around the table. After nearly an hour, one by one the trainees started going back to their rooms until only the boy and Alyssa were left.

"I wanted to stay a little longer with you, after seeing that you felt sad" the girl said.

"Thank you. I saw you feeling the same as I did and hoped that everyone will go so he can chat."

She smiled and hugged him.

"What was that for?" he asked.

"Thank you for being a good friend. It was really hard to fall asleep far from home last night and even harder waking up without seeing any familiar face, but you made me happy by waiting until everyone left instead of leaving first as you usually did when there were too many people around."

"I couldn't leave like that. You're the closest to family that I have here, so I wanted to spend some time just with you, but it wouldn't be polite to ask you to go away, so I waited until all the other people were gone."

They decided to go for a walk and then just lay on the grass in the park while talking about the tour they were given during the day and after two hours it was time to go back to the living quarters.

# The first year of Training Camp

As the instructor told them, the next morning, each trainee was assigned to a counsellor, who was the same gender as them in order not to make them shy about certain topics that would be discussed in the future. Kayro's counsellor was a farmer named Monta, a man that seemed similar to his father after seeing how his hands looked. This was confirmed as soon as they had the chance to talk to each other and turned out to love working the fields as much as Klost did.

"I am glad they assigned me to you. Your attitude when it comes to farming is very similar to my father's and it makes me feel closer to home" the boy said.

"I hope I will be able to help you just as a father would, Kayro. I know I'm not him, but when I was here as a trainee I had the luck of being trained by someone that I still see as family even now."

"That is great. Just as my parents always taught me, family doesn't always mean being related by blood."

"I can only say that I couldn't agree anymore with that. I met lots of people that proved to me that your parents are right."

After a few minutes, the boy excused himself, as it was nearly time for the lessons with head instructor Zoss, but not before promising to continue the conversation when they will both have some free time.

The first day was a general introduction to the importance of Training Camp, about the main reason to build it in this forest and why it was divided in four with each community having separate camps. Zoss also answered some of their questions regarding what he taught them that day and promised to do the same as they get into details.

To make sure that they will not need to keep up with too much information at once, it was decided that each week, the second, fourth and sixth day, the trainees will use for recreation. Kayro was mostly using these days to read and a few hours before evening he was spending time with Alyssa. Sometimes it was just the two of them, other times they joined different groups in order to get to know each other better. Every week he also had a one or two hours chat with Monta in order to see how the new information he gained fits with his future plans.

After each day spent with Zoss, the boy was writing everything he found useful in his training journal and the questions he would like answers to in his personal journal. To some of those Monta was able to give him the answer, but the head instructor seemed to have more information than anyone else in the Glade Training Camp.

As the first month was getting close to the end, the counsellor told Kayro that he managed to get him some time alone with the head instructor and hopefully he will be able to get the answers he was seeking. He wouldn't push this much for any student, but something inside him deemed the boy worthy of going that far.

It was the fourth day of the week when Zoss summoned Kayro to his office in the meeting hall, with only one day of training with him left after. The boy was excited and he started feeling more relaxed as soon as he got to the waiting room and found out that other trainees requested a meeting with the head instructor. After waiting for fifteen minutes, it was his time to go in and hopefully to find answers to at least part of the questions that he wrote in his journal.

"Welcome, boy. Take a seat, relax and ask the questions that you are seeking answers to" the man said.

Intimidated by his presence, Kayro had a few seconds of silence. Zoss was a very tall man that looked young for his age, he seemed to be trained in different roles, probably an expert regarding all training sites within Glade Village Training Camp, but more than that he had the air of a fighter. His hands showed signs of hard work and a few visible scars made the boy realise that the man was more likely experienced as a soldier, not as militia. Realising the moment of silence he started talking.

"First of all I want to thank you for taking time to see me, sir. I know that being in charge of the whole camp gives you little time to spare."

"Don't worry, son. The instructors here are capable of managing without me a few hours every day. In fact having one on one meetings with trainees relaxes me and teaches me new things."

"I am happy to hear that. Hopefully our meeting will do at least one of those two."

"So, what brings you here, Kayro? I noticed that you always pay attention and I was surprised to see that you still have questions after hearing about the books that you've read since you started Training Camp."

"Unfortunately books don't always have answers, in fact they can sometimes bring new questions to light. Out of all of them I guess the most important is how come the Training Forest is so safe?"

"I'm afraid that I can only partially answer that, son. Maybe in the future, depending on how you perform, I will be able to say more, but right now, all I can say is that apart from all the militia that reside in each of the four camps, we have some groups of adventurers that patrol between camps to make sure nothing dangerous gets too close" the man replied.

"I read something about that, but there was only a little information. Can anyone join those groups?"

"I'm sorry to say, but no. Only people that prove to have very good survival skills during the first five years can join them for the sixth and last year."

"So, as long as I get better at surviving I can get a chance to join them?" asked the boy.

"You don't just need to get better, you need to be among the best and most of the roles that you will train for need to be related to survival. For example fishing, hunting, crafting tools or weapons have higher chances of helping you than training in jewel crafting or as an artist."

"I understand. I guess I will need to choose everything wisely then. Are there any roles that involve exploring the world, sir?"

"There is one, actually called 'Explorer', but for that you will need to train as a cartographer and then prove to be an excellent adventurer" Zoss replied.

"Why is that not mentioned in any book or by any instructor. I have never heard of it."

"Because these roles are usually proposed to the fifth year trainees that are very good when it comes to survival skills, and rarely someone accepts them. You see, most people are happy leading a life similar to the one their parents had, quiet, inside a community choosing one of the roles their parents have, instead of risking their life."

"Still, there are some people who would like to go out there and discover more."

"I agree and we have a lot of people in all camps that ask about these roles just like you are doing now. The problem comes when they need to prove that they are worthy of it. Most trainees change their mind after their first trip between camps inside the Training Forest, others fail to learn the minimum required skills about surviving, and from the ones that go forward to the survival test each year, only one or two, out of nearly a hundred, decide to settle as adventurers. Every ten years we finally find someone that goes through as an explorer, but no one has ever seen one get back."

"After hearing all of this I think I understand better why some roles stay hidden. They might be attractive as an idea in the beginning, but after learning more about them it scares people."

"I am happy that you understood that, Kayro, and as I said, if you do decide to follow through with being an adventurer or explorer, you will need to be prepared to work hard and later have your life in danger constantly. Do you have any other questions?"

"No, sir, that was all. Thank you for giving me part of your precious time and I promise it was not wasted. I will try and figure out a proper way of training before my last year with Monta helping me and hopefully I will at least become an adventurer if the explorer role proves to be too much."

Zoss shook the boy's hand before he left and wished him luck. It was the first time in years that he felt someone is determined enough to try the explorer role.

On his way back, the boy started thinking about the conversation. He was hoping that once he gets to Training Camp everything or at least almost everything could be answered, but even now it seems like there are things meant to stay hidden from the public. His guess was that after starting to train for one of the risky roles he might be able to get more information and decided that he will do everything he can to become an explorer when Training Camp will be over.

Just before getting to the living quarters he met Alyssa and had a conversation about everything that was said in Zoss's office and his decision to take on a high risk role for the future. As always, she tried to convince him to forget about that and focus on what he already has, a wonderful family. Kayro disliked arguing with her, so he pretended to agree, just before going back to his room, but the fact that only a few people try going for those roles motivated him even more.

As he was growing up his curiosity about the world got bigger and now he was certain that risking his life would be worth it if that meant discovering more about the magic that gives people memories from their past lives and also what else or who else is out there besides the human race. When he got to his room he started writing everything that was going through his mind in his personal journal and after the conversation with the head instructor he decided to make a hiding place for it. For some reason, someone didn't allow the public to have access to all the information available at higher levels.

His mind was very busy that evening and the thoughts wouldn't let him fall asleep. Part of him was thinking that Alyssa is right and having a loving family might be enough, but there was a thirst for knowledge deep inside that seemed stronger than anything.

The next morning, he was feeling tired, so he was close to being late on his last day of Training Camp history with Zoss. Usually he liked to arrive at least fifteen minutes earlier, but this time it was just as the man was starting his speech. Hours went by and just before dismissing the trainees, the head instructor informed them that in two days they will begin learning about the history of Glade Village for a month, using the same schedule as they did for the last month.

As everyone was getting ready to leave Zoss came to ask the boy if he has an hour to spare, because he would like to talk about their conversation from the previous day. It seemed a little strange, but Kayro accepted, so they went into the office. Monta was already waiting for them and that surprised the boy, but he had a feeling he could trust the man. After everyone was seated, the head instructor started talking.

"I'm sorry for not telling you someone else will be here, son, but if you want to pursue one of the roles that we talked about, then you will need Monta's advice too."

"I understand, after all I will need his guidance for the next few years."

"I am happy you feel that way, Kayro. We didn't want to make you feel uncomfortable, but there are some things that we need to discuss" the counsellor said.

"You both seem very serious. Did I do something wrong?" the boy asked.

"Everything is all right. We just need to clarify a few things that will help with your future training and keep you safe at the same time" Zoss replied.

"Unfortunately, for some reason, most Elders think we should not encourage people who wish to take the role of an adventurer and try to stop the ones that wish to become explorers, so we came up with a solution to hide the fact that you are going for one of those two" added Monta.

"Then why are we talking about it and how come you will allow me to do it?" Kayro asked.

"Because, son, we are working for our community first and then for the Median Forests. You see, just like you, we are curious about this world, and even a few of our Elders share this idea, but every time someone openly goes for these roles, people from the other camps always try to convince them to back down. We are not entirely sure why this happens, but we have a few theories and that is why we will need your help as much as you need ours."

"Just as the head instructor said, there are a lot of complications. The main problem is that when we tried to train a lot of adventurers or explorers, a representative of the Tower Town Council of Elders arrived here without any notice and they told us to try and convince the trainees to give up their choice. Apparently this happened in each of the four training camps and, after that, all instructors stopped talking about these roles. More than that, any trainee that had approval from his own camp was made to reconsider his choice after going to a different camp to train. We are not sure if this happened as a result of loyalty to the Council of Elders or if they simply were afraid the children were sent as spies."

"This sounds very bad and honestly it only makes me more curious about everything. So, how come we are talking about it since you are supposed to prevent me from choosing one of those roles?"

"Your determination and curiosity at such an young age makes you the perfect candidate for any of those roles. We also had time to do some research about your family and even if they are not your natural parents you seem to have inherited part of their traits. We learned that even though your father is one of the best farmers in the Median Forests he was very skilled and determined when training for the soldier role and that your mother was initially supposed to be one of the future Tower Town Elders, but chose to carry on as a healer out of love when her own mother disowned her" said Zoss.

"While all of that is true, how can it help?" asked Kayro feeling proud about everything that was said regarding his parents.

"Because you will officially train for all four roles that they did until the end of your fifth year. After that, if you decide to go on with one of those we will support you and if you announce that you wish to become an adventurer or explorer it is too late for anyone to change your mind" Monta replied.

"As you counsellor said, you will have to hide your real purpose and while you are away from our camp, if possible, find out what reasons the other instructors or head instructors might have to prevent trainees from choosing these roles. We know it will not be easy, but some of the Glade Village Elders are really worried about all the limits that are being imposed on the Training Camp as well as on our community" Zoss added.

"Well, I guess this can work. What about the other instructors? Don't you think they might suspect anything?"

"Even if they do, I will be the first person they will inform and assure them that you are only doing the same training as your parents did" the head instructor replied.

"We will all need to work as a team for this plan to succeed, but this is the first time in the last five years that I feel we can do it. Unless something really urgent occurs, we will not meet like this again in order to avoid any suspicion" the counsellor added.

"I only have one question before leaving. Are there other trainees doing the same thing as me?"

"Of course, son, during their first year lots of boys and girls are curious about the world and wish to explore it, but most give up in time. Every year their number seems to go down and we suspect it might have something with some of the mentors they had before coming to Training Camp" Zoss replied.

"It is best that we don't tell you who they are in order to protect all of you from any outside influence, and for extra safety we will have these initial evaluation meeting with all the new trainees" said Monta.

"That's about everything I wanted to ask. Is there anything else you wish to tell or ask me?"

"All we had to say now was said, son. We will stay in touch with your counsellor's help."

Both men shook hands with Kayro before he left and there was hope in their eyes as he walked out. The boy felt the same hope and that made him smile as he was finally on the path that had been calling him for years. As promised he will not talk to anyone about their conversation, in fact, no matter how much he wished to, he decided that he will not even write about it to his parents or in his journal in case someone else might open the letter or find his journal.

In order to prevent anyone from finding out about his true wishes, that evening he went to Alyssa and told her that he was just being silly last time they talked and with the help of his counsellor he decided to follow the steps of both his parents, with the final choice being made at the end of the fifth year of Training Camp.

Hearing this made the girl so happy that she hugged him and even gave him a kiss on the cheek. Both of them blushed after that and quickly change the conversation topic to get past the moment. Before going back to their living quarters they went and watched as others were playing different sports and at that moment Kayro decided to try and play some of them in the future as they could help him build a better physical condition. More than that, he decided to try and practice some of the moves he saw during his militia training in Glade Village, but he needed to find a quiet place for that.

For the next month he practised every evening and played sports at least three times per week while during the day he learned about the history of his home. Most of the information he already knew from Krysta and Klost and only some unimportant details were new. During this time he was spending at least one hour talking to Alyssa before sunset which always made him feel like being around the table sipping tea with his parents.

The day before leaving to Lumberjack Camp to learn about their village and its history, Monta asked him to have a meeting. The counsellor told him to be careful on the road to each new camp and also about the instructors he will meet there. Kayro agreed that it's best to be cautious and promised to be convincing when asked about the roles he chose to train for.

Just as Zoss said, the roads looked dangerous, but the patrols made of militia and adventurers seemed ready for any challenge. Luckily you could reach any camp within a few hours when travelling by carts that were pulled by bovri, so throughout the entire journey they had daylight to chase any fear away. The caravan that left on this learning tour included both trained and trainees militia along with their howlers in case any wild animals might get too close.

After reaching their destination, Kayro was sad to find out that he couldn't meet his friend Zodar, because he also went on the same tour, but being able to learn more about the place where he grew up made him feel better. The instructor that was teaching the Glade Camp trainees seemed very interested in their choice of roles which made the boy suspicious, so he tried to limit interacting with the man during his stay. Before leaving for their next destination he approached the instructor, but only to ask if he can leave a letter for his friend in which he apologised for not being able to meet now and that they will surely see each other in the future.

The next two months, the boy had the same routine, learning about the history of the assigned community on the first, third, fifth and seventh day of each week, play any sport he could, training his fighting skills in secluded areas and talking to his best friend, Alyssa. With each day he started seeing her more and more as family, but he couldn't decide if he considers her a sister or maybe something more. He always admired the love between Krysta and Klost and hoped that one day he might find someone to share the same feelings with, but he never had the time to consider exactly what the girl meant to him. Even now he was too focused on training, ignoring his personal life completely.

After their history learning tour was over, it was time to decide on the exact steps for the next years of training. Each trainee had one month to choose with the counsellor's help in order for all camps to find a way not to be overcrowded. As soon as Kayro got back, he had a meeting with Monta, who handed him a letter from someone that called him a friend. To his surprise, Zodar had the same idea of leaving a letter behind with the promise to see each other again, hopefully soon.

"I am happy to see you smile, son. I guess that boy really is a good friend just as he claimed."

"Apart from Alyssa he is the only other person my age that I ever got close to. It was during a trip at Cabin Camp when we were ten years old and after that we wrote to each other often. Chances are that he will train for the same roles that I am."

"That is exactly what he told me. After he gave me the letter, we had a short conversation and he revealed his plans. It seems that some of the instructors in Lumberjack Camp have a similar plan to ours and if the man that is his counsellor wasn't a close friend of mine, I would have suspected Zodar to be a spy."

"I think it was the same person that taught us about the history of Lumberjack Village. He seemed very interested in our future role choices so I avoided him as much as possible."

"That was a good thing to do. Unless you had a reason to trust him, you chose the best solution. Going back to your friend, he said that one of the instructors in Port Town Camp shares our concerns regarding the wishes of the Elders to hide things. As he was learning about Port Town, the instructor approached him and gave him a letter for his counsellor and asked him to give one to an instructor from Glade Camp, if they seem trustworthy."

"What did the letter say?" Kayro asked.

"It said that he will probably be imprisoned soon for seeing something in the middle of the Quiet Lake and that we should be warry of all instructors from Tower Town. Apparently there was a meeting on the lake between one of the Elders from Tower Town and one of the instructors from their camp. There are no details as he probably wanted to avoid evidence about how much he knows, but it seems serious."

"And what does head instructor Zoss think about this? Does he believe it to be true?"

"He's not sure. Currently he is trying to find out if any of the instructors in Port Town Camp was imprisoned, but it will probably take some time, because he will need to figure a way that doesn't lead back to him."

"I remember hearing about some instructor going missing after we arrived there. If you want I can ask some of the other trainees to confirm and this way we can avoid getting the head instructor's name involved."

"That is a very good idea. Make sure to find at least a few people to confirm it."

"I will, sir. If there's nothing more, then I should be on my way."

"Kayro, wait a minute, please."

"Is something wrong?"

"No, it's the opposite. You proved yourself trustworthy and both the head instructor and I decided to answer a few more of the questions you asked him in his office after your first month here."

"Hearing that makes me very happy. So which ones can you answer to now?"

"One of your questions was about how come there is no religion in the Median Forests. Well that was voted out in the beginning. Apparently, when humans suddenly found themselves on planet Xorbia, they had access to some of their past lives memories and while a few still believed in deities, most of them felt how the universe randomly changed everything during 'The Reset'. In order to avoid fighting, since there was only a small number of people in the area, they voted if any religion should be created or not."

"And what happened after?" the boy asked.

"The majority decided that religion would only divide people, so none will be created, but if anyone feels like praying or worshipping, as long as they don't try to create a cult that wishes to impose their beliefs on others, they are free to do it."

"Did everyone respect the vote?"

"Unfortunately, no. Because of that a small part of the people were banished from the lands where the first human settlement, Tower Town, was formed."

"What happened to those people? Did they build one of the other settlements?"

"No one knows for sure. Some say that another group went after them and slaughtered everyone, while others say that they simply vanished."

"How can a group of people just vanish like that?"

"Two groups, son. A second group did leave shortly after the others were banished and it's been more than three hundred years without any sign of them."

"That sounds very strange. I would expect at least a few to survive."

"I agree, but even if there were signs, someone is hiding them very well. Enough about that, I have the answer to a second question that you asked and it is related to the first in a way. You said that some of your memories from the past lives showed you that people hated each other for their skin colour and asked Zoss how come there is none of that hate here."

"That's right. I have multiple memories where people were marginalized because of the colour of their skin. As I was growing up I was happily surprised that there was no such hatred."

"That also goes back to the first humans on the planet and the issue is similar to the lack of religions. Some even say that the problem was solved before 'The Reset', that after thousands of years people learned to accept each other for exactly what they were, and that is humans. Other say that it was the other way around, that in the beginning of their past lives everyone was seen the same and in time they started being divided by their skin colour, but the most important thing was that everyone on Xorbia agreed to the equality of people as an unwritten law, one that hopefully will always be respected."

"It seems that the initial humans wanted unity more than anything."

"From what I heard the first five years were crucial. Initially, people were disoriented by their memories of past lives. Some thought they went crazy after seeing the environment they woke up in, thinking it's a dream or an illusion, while others simply accepted the new reality, but the beasts that started attacking them made them stand together."

"Were these beasts that strong?"

"According to the stories some were strong enough to take out up to twenty people by themselves, but most were acting just as predators usually do. At that time, the most dangerous were wolves that didn't suffer any mutations. As you know welxes and howlers are part wolves, probably there are a few more animals like that, but some simply carried on in their initial form and that made them stronger."

"How did the humans manage to survive then?"

"They learned from the wolves that a pack is stronger than any individual. At one point they got attacked at once by a pack of wolves and one of the strong beast that I told you about earlier. Since they didn't want to share, the animals started to fight each other and the pack easily won. After witnessing that, people started forming packs of their own and drove the wolves away."

"That was a smart thing to do."

"Yes, it was. Also that is the moment when most humans decided to have a vote about religion and understood that we are all the same species no matter of the skin colour."

"Thank you for the answers, counsellor Monta. What about my third question that was left unanswered?"

"I'm afraid that neither the head instructor nor I have any answer to that. We simply don't know how and why the magic is affecting humans except that it brings them memories from past lives. While it also seems to affect animals and plants, we have no clue to where or what the source might be. What we do know is that the Elders from all communities forbade people to look any deeper into that."

"Is that why you need someone to push through and become an explorer?"

"That is correct, boy. I'm afraid that no matter how qualified we are at other things, we need to train someone even harder for that role and hopefully one day find out more about our planet. The main issue is that the Elders insist on making our settlements stronger, take on roles that are meant to support the growth of each community and find new and easier ways to improve work. The claim that if we start exploring the humans will start to divide."

"Well, they do have a logical reason, but I doubt that the Median Forests will start to divide just because we start exploring."

"Once again, thank you for the answers, counsellor. I will do my best to be discreet when I ask about the Port Town Camp instructor and as soon as I check more sources I will inform you of the result."

"Thank you for your support, Kayro. While you are busy with that, I will try to find the best choices for your future training.

Hopefully next time we meet everything will be ready for you to check and tell me your opinion about the planning."

The boy decided to wait until next day before he will ask any questions about that instructor. He wanted to make a plan that will make people believe that is only a personal curiosity, not an information that can prove to be very important if confirmed. Since the weather was good, he decided to go to the park and relax while thinking. Just as he entered the park, his eyes got covered by a set of hands. Like always, it was Alyssa trying to surprise him, even though they both knew that she is the only one to do this. The children decided to take a walk together and admire the beauty of nature while sharing thoughts about what roles they will train for.

Kayro felt guilty for not being entirely honest, but knowing her, it was the best decision he could make. He was also considering the fact that most of the information regarding his choices would place her in danger and he never wanted to get people into trouble, especially not his best friend. As they sat on a bench both shared opinions about their learning tour and when it got to the Port Town Camp she confirmed the rumour about the missing instructor. The boy was surprised and speechless for a few seconds, but he needed the information, so he broke the silence:

"And what makes you think that story was true?"

"Because I heard it from one of my cousins that is training there."

"You have a cousin that doesn't live in Glade Village" the boy asked.

"Yes, my father's uncle moved to Port Town after he graduated Training Camp and his granddaughter is two years older than us and she told me that her counsellor disappeared recently without any clue."

"I thought that was just a story. I heard a few of our colleagues joking about it."

"I heard something like that too. Some said that the man had enough of his students so he decided to run away, but my cousin told me that he had a great relationship with all trainees, not just the ones he was guiding. In fact, some of the boys that you usually play sports with can confirm what I just said, because they also have family in Port Town and some of their relatives are in Training Camp now. Did you think that you are the only one that writes to someone from another community?"

"Well, no, but I never bothered about any family outside Glade Village and as my parents told me so many times, sharing blood doesn't necessarily make you a family. Speaking of, have you always known that you have relatives in Port Town?"

"I did. My father used to tell me stories of how happy grandfather was when talking about his brother, so, as soon as I could write properly, I sent a letter to Port Town to check if he had any children. Two months later I received a reply from my cousin and since then we sent each other a letter at least five times every year."

Their conversation lasted until evening and the boy was surprised at how little he knew about her, but also about how little he cares that his mother has family in both Lumberjack Village and Tower Town, people that he never felt the need to connect with, not even before finding out that Krysta and Klost were not his real parents. After they went separate ways, Kayro went to do his fighting training, as always in a place where no one can find him. During his first month in Training Camp he found a few potential such places and after scouting them for some time, he chose five that gave him privacy.

After going to his room, he made a plan on how to approach the people who could confirm Alyssa's story and then went to sleep. It took him a week to get to each person to check what they know and, just like the girl, everyone told him a similar story. He decided to write most of the information in a third journal in case he might be discovered, but before that he made a hiding place just outside camp, close to where he was doing most of his evening training.

The next day he met with Monta and told him the story and about the hidden journal, since both his counsellor and the head instructor won his trust. After hearing everything the man decided that all three of them need to meet again and they will use the training plan for the next years as an excuse. While each student and his guide were the ones coming up with the plan, it still required approval from the one in charge of the camp and this was a perfect cover up for their meeting.

Two days later Kayro went to Zoss's office where Monta was already waiting. To make sure there was no suspicion, the counsellor took a few other trainees to have their training plans approved and Kayro had to spend some time in the waiting room before going in.

"I'm happy to see you, Kayro. It's been some time since we last met and talked." said Zoss as he was shaking the boy's hand.

"Happy to see you too, sir."

"I was glad to hear from your counsellor that you managed to quickly find the information we needed, even if I hoped it will not turn out to be true."

"I didn't have to do much, since it was luck that helped me find out that fast."

"Luck or no luck, you managed to do it quickly and without the head instructor having his name tied to it" said Monta with pride.

"That is true. I will probably need to use my connections another time when will need information. So, you did a very good job, my dear boy."

"I am glad I could help, sir."

"Despite all of that, sorry to say, but I have some news that will make our plan harder. The Elders cannot allow us to train you directly for their job, since none of your parents are currently doing that role, but since your mother trained for it, you can do it as a back-up, so we had to change the plan that you and Monta came up with."

"As long as I can reach the final step and be able to choose the explorer role, I don't see any problem."

"I made sure that each training you will undergo will be from two points of view and since the head instructor vouched for you, everyone had to agree. As you know, the normal training was following the same schedule as before with days one, three, five and seven of each week being considered as learning days, while the other three were your free days. In addition to those four days, you will get to see things from the point of view of an Elder on the fourth day. It will mean less free time for you, but it was the only solution that everyone approved."

"I've always had a thirst for learning, so now I can learn even more."

"Here is a copy of the final plan, Kayro. If you want anything changed just let me know, because now it is the last chance to do it."

The boy took the document and started reading out loud:

"The remaining of the first year includes three months of building training and three months of farming training both to be done in Glade Camp.

During the second year I will spend two months as a butcher and two as a baker in Glade Camp, two months as a weaver and two as a tanner in Lumberjack Village Camp, two months as a tailor and two as a cook in Tower Town Camp.

For the third year I will spend two months learning how to craft fishing boats, one month crafting fishing tools and lures, and one month improving my swimming and learning how to use fishing boats, all three in Port Town Camp, followed by two months of fishing practice on the eastern side of the Quiet Lake next to Lumberjack Creek with the trainees from Tower Town. After that there will be three months of woodcutting and three of learning how to make furniture in Lumberjack Camp.

The fourth years seems very simple. It begins with healer training in each camp for a month, followed by four months of military training in Tower Camp and to the end I will have practice as militia or a soldier in each camp for a month per camp.

The fifth year looks busy: one month mining in a cave on the north-western part of the Training Forest, then it's two months jewellery crafting and three for weapons and armour crafting in Tower Town, followed by two months crafting woodcutting and farming tools, and two months crafting hunting tools and traps in Lumberjack Camp, ending with two months of hunting practice with the Lumberjack village trainees south of the Quiet Lake.

The sixth year, 'Personal choice training', is left as blank to be filled in at the end of the fifth year."

"Is everything in there all right with you?" asked the counsellor.

"Considering the limits imposed by the Elders, I cannot think of better choices. I guess everything is settled now" replied the boy.

"Not really. I saw you looking at the scars on my arms during our first meeting and I would like to confess that what you thought was right. As much as I tried to hide it anyone can see that I am not just an instructor. In fact I have been doing this only for the last ten years and before that I was an adventurer" the head instructor said.

"What happened after that?"

"Well, to be honest, aging doesn't really help when you do that, but the main reason is that I started wishing I could go do my role outside the Median Forest. After hearing that, the Councils of Elders gave me a choice, either become head instructor here or lead the Glade Village militia."

"So what made you choose this?"

"It was freedom, Kayro. You see, even if this place is not so big, at least the Elders are not here every day. Sure they have some people that send them reports, but it is not the same as them personally watching you."

"That makes sense. I sorry that they didn't allow you to follow your wishes, but at least they didn't try to imprison you."

"In a way, they did imprison me, son, but at least this prison is of my choice. Also when they made me choose I realised that something is wrong and I hope that before my life ends I will find out the truth."

"I will do my best to help with that" said the boy.

"I will try to lend a hand too" added Monta.

"Before you go, Kayro, I have a surprise for you. I heard that you are training by yourself every evening and it is hard to find a place to do it without being seen. I have a room in a cave just outside our camp where I train sometimes and I want you to have a key for it as well, maybe even teach you some things when we meet there. On top of that, every month, when they come to Glade Camp, some adventurers use it for training too, so I will tell them about you and ask if they can help you improve."

"Thank you very much, head instructor Zoss. I learned as much as I could in Glade Village from watching the militia and my father taught me a lot of theory, but I need some practice too."

"You're welcome, dear boy. I just hope our help will be useful on your way to becoming an explorer."

"I'm sorry that I cannot aid you in any way, but my fighting skills are so bad that a turen could probably easily defeat me" said Monta with sadness in his voice.

Kayro left the office very excited, but soon he remembered that he cannot share the good news with anyone. Writing to his parents about everything would be too risky and despite how well he got along with Alyssa, the girl would just tell him he needs to be happy with a lesser role and forget about being an explorer. That made him feel lonely for some time, but in the evening he went to the cave and found a huge room with lots of training equipment. Not only he could use the dummies to train his skills with weapons, but also there was equipment that could help him build a better physique. After a good training he went back to the living quarters, took a shower and went to bed early.

With one week left before starting the building training he decided to do some reading while he still had time, so he went to the library. As he was coming out with the books, Monta called out his name and told him that he has a private collection of books that might help with his desired role. The counsellor promised to make a list that will include short reviews of each book and then the boy could choose the ones he wants to borrow. After three days, Kayro decided to take two books related to hand to hand fighting and using those he made a training plan to improve even more. Monta was happy to be of help, even if it he wasn't doing it directly as Zoss and the adventurers will do it.

The boy tested the routine that evening, writing in his third notebook about things he could improve or use differently. Also, realising that the people who wrote the books were all adults, he decided to find a way to adapt everything for his size and strength. Since it was late and the next day his building training started, he chose to go back to his room, after hiding the notebook, and get some rest.

As soon as he entered the building site, Kayro could barely hear anything. There were different noises all over and people had to shout to understand each other. Their instructor for the role barely managed to get everyone to follow him to the cabin that was used to teach theory and he was able to do that by using his hand instead of his voice. After getting inside all that noise from before was barely noticeable and that was because of the way the cabin was built as the man explained to the trainees. He told them that by the end of the three months they will spend together, everyone should at least know in theory how to build anything related to their community and most will know in practice too. Just like every other role learning, the building training was scheduled with theory days on the first and third day of the week and practice on the fifth and seventh.

When the day was over, Kayro met Alyssa and as usual they went for a walk in the park and talked about their first day of learning the roles. The girl started training in the bakery camp first since her father was working as a miller and was very happy that her instructor praised the skills she acquired before coming to Training Camp. One of the things they both found strange was being separated into smaller groups after the first six months when they did everything together with everyone their age that came here from Glade Village.

"I hope you're not being a 'ghost' like always" the girl said even if she knew that was the case.

"That is how I am and chances are this will never change. I just don't like getting close to people."

"How come you go and play all those team sports and get along with everyone during that?"

"Because I find teamwork as something useful in life and also gives me a chance to improve my physical condition. I get along with them because I learned about them from the distance and I knowing how they will act makes it easy to co-ordinate with them."

"So, they are not your friends?"

"No. I only have two people that I can call friends, you and Zodar. The rest are just acquaintances."

"I was hoping that you can finally open up to other people and not see you alone nearly all the time" said Alyssa with disappointment in her voice.

"Well, unlike you, I like to be alone. More than that I only choose people that I feel I can trust to be my friends. I don't want a collection, I just want to be around people that I can count on."

"I understand your point of view, so as long as you are happy I will respect your choices."

The boy was glad to hear that, because he really cared about Alyssa's advice, after all she was his best and closest friend. He gave her a hug, thanked her for caring and then they started walking to the living quarters.

The three months went by quickly and, just as the instructor promised, everyone learned the basics about building. Some had a real talent for it and saw it as a role they want to have in the future, others were very good at theory, but lacked when it came to actually doing it, and Kayro was average on both. He saw it as a useful skill, but seeing it from the point of view of an Elder, every fourth day of each week, made him realise that he will only use it if there is no one that can do it better.

After his last day of building training ended, he met with Alyssa and told her that he is excited about the next part where he can learn about his father's role even more and he hopes that by the time Training Camp finishes he will come up with an idea to make Klost's work easier. The girl was happy to hear that and supported his idea. She told him that after graduating she will bake a cake for him and his family using the training she was receiving now. Moments later she started blushing, because her thoughts went as far as imagining herself in their kitchen and that made her realise that maybe Kayro was more than just a friend in her heart. In order to shake that feeling she made up an excuse and left quickly. With his mind unsure of what happened, the boy decided to go to the room in the cave to train his fighting skill and to his surprise Zoss was there. It was the first time since he received the key meeting the head instructor here.

"This is a nice surprise, sir. I was looking forward to seeing how you train."

"As a gift for finishing your building training, I decided to come check your fighting skills and see if I can help you improve."

"Thank you very much, head instructor!"

The boy started showing him his training routine, the ideas he wrote for adapting everything he learned from watching the Glade Village militia and from reading Monta's books. After a careful thought the man broke the silence:

"I'm sorry to say this, but you are pushing yourself too hard and it will only make it more difficult for you to learn. My advice is that you should learn things one at a time and then try to mix them. For example, the best thing to do at your age is to learn how to fight without using any weapon. Some of the beasts you might encounter as an adventurer have really thick hide or sharp claws and both of those could easily break your weapon, so you need to learn how to attack and defend without it."

"That makes sense. I guess I was too focused on learning how to gain skills instead of learning about possible opponents. Thank you for your advice."

"Don't thank me yet, that was just the beginning."

"What do you mean by that?"

"I mean that I will try and make a fighting skills training schedule for you. I have been working on one for some time with the adventurers that keep the roads in the Training Forest safe and I would like to share it with all that wish to train for the role and earned my trust. Just like you have a journal, I also made one based on personal experience and talking to other fighting experts. In fact it has always been hidden in this room, so I will show you where to find it, but before that, I want to see exactly how you are practising now."

The boy started doing his best to impress Zoss and combined everything he wrote in his journal, but just as the man said, it was too much for a child. Reading the disappointment in Kayro's eyes, the head instructor decide to encourage him, but only relating to true facts.

"Parts of what you just showed me are flawless and I would like to add them in my journal, but the routine is not suited for you yet. Still, I am convinced that by the end of the six years of Training Camp you will perfect it."

"Thank you, I will do my best. So, how would the routine I just showed you work against what the adventurers meet in the forest?"

"Honestly, you would need a lot of luck to escape alive from an encounter with any angry adult wild animal, but considering your age, I think only those that came from military families would be slightly better."

"I was hoping for more than that, but I guess it is not that easy."

"Well, don't forget that you are training for survival, not for defending others, so you will be alone. That is why you can always save yourself by running and then hunt down the beast that made you run."

"What if I need to defend someone at some point?"

"That is why you will have the healing and military training in your fourth year. When you learn about healing you will also learn about which areas of the body must be protected and the militia or soldier training helps in defensive cases, of course with the howlers at their side, working in groups."

"So what you are saying is that wild animals are better fought with a group?"

"I'm afraid so and even then you have a chance to get hurt. That is how I got most of my scars, by fighting gurmas along with my group of adventurers and militia while making the roads safe."

"Was that just in the Training Forest?"

"No, it wasn't. After graduating from Training Camp I was patrolling the road between Glade Village and Lumberjack Town for a few years, then between Glade Village and Tower Town for some time, before being sent to be an adventurer here."

"You sound disappointed, sir. Why is that?"

"Because, just like you, I wanted to explore the world, not to have my freedom limited, but my desire to go out there was noticed and each mistake made, small or big, while patrolling the roads between communities, weighted me down until I was ordered to be an adventurer in the Training Forest and then the head instructor in the Glade Training Camp."

"That seems very bad."

"It is worse than you can imagine, but as I said before, I still have more freedom here than being stuck in Glade Village or any other community. Also that is the reason why I am being very careful about the explorer and adventurer role and pretend to follow the orders from the Elders. Any big mistake now would probably put me in a bad situation that might even end my life."

"I am sorry to hear that, head instructor. I guess I never thought of things from your point of view. As trainees, we think that most people enjoy their roles and I was under the impression that you are too."

"I do enjoy my role, son, but only to a point. If I could go back in time, I would probably run away from the Median Forests instead of accepting to come here. You see, for me, freedom has more value than any role that someone might offer me."

"I think I understand that more than others would. I like being practical and might be happy to accept a role in society if I have no choice, but my mind would still wish to go out there. It's like something has been always calling for me to go outside the Median Forests borders."

"It seems that I was right about you. Anyway, it's getting late and I need to go back before my absence is noticed. I will try to come here from time to time and see your progress."

"Thank you for everything, head instructor Zoss."

After the man left, Kayro started studying the schedule and realised that this was probably the best way to carry on with the training, learning each way of fighting separately and then combine them. Just as Zoss suggested, the boy decided to start with hand to hand skills. Following that, he would use the short sword, then add a shield and use both, spear training would be next, testing both the long version and short one, and after training as a hunter he will add a bow and arrows to everything. Realising it got late, he rushed back to the living quarters to get some rest before starting the farming role practice.

Despite going to sleep late after spending a lot of time thinking of his future fighting style, he woke up rested and got to the farming training area. Here they were informed that the first month will be focused on working the fields, the second month they will learn about orchards and during the third month they will be learning about livestock and breeding horgs.

Kayro enjoyed the first month a lot, because it made him feel closer to his father, but he didn't like the role as much as Klost did. He got the chance to use some new tools that were being tested at Training Camp to see if they will make the farmer role easier and during his training from the point of view of an Elder he witnessed one of those tools being approved to be mass produced and sent to the communities. Seeing that made him very happy since his father's work will get easier and old age was starting to make it harder for him. He was so happy about it that he wrote a second letter to his parents as soon as he got back to his room that evening. Usually he was writing to them only one letter every month, but he already finished that one the day before finding out about the approval of use for the new tool.

The second month of farming training was less exciting than the first one, but everything he learned about trees from Vergast earned him the praise of the instructor. In addition to learning how to grow and care for the trees, the trainees were also taught how to make fruit juice, syrup and even the alcoholic beverages that some adults enjoyed so much. As the month was coming to an end he received the monthly letter from his parents and to his surprise Klost wrote nearly all of it. Usually it was Krysta who wrote about how things are at home, but now the man was so excited to hear about the new tool and the boy's training on working the fields that she barely had the chance to write much. Reading the letter made Kayro very happy, because he could feel his father's joy just by doing that.

During his last month of farming training, the boy learned how to ride a bovri, how to care and train both races of horgs and the similarities between them and wild animals. When it came to the last part he focused mainly on learning about each animal's weaknesses and strengths, something that could prove useful to his fighting training. When it came to the Elder point of view, the last two months showed him just how well connected the three farming branches were and how practical the system used by all communities was.

As he finished his farming training, Alyssa finally finished learning about the miller and baker roles, so they decided to celebrate by having a picnic. The boy prepared made some fresh syrup and fruit juice, while the girl baked a delicious cake. This celebration reminded them of the time they spent together in Rang and Melia's bakery which seemed like it happened during another lifetime. Talking about that made them miss home, but it was only for moments as they quickly encouraged each other to be strong, since the first year in Training Camp was over and there are only five left.

After celebrating with her, Kayro went to the cave to train and this time both Zoss and Monta were waiting for him. They both wanted to congratulate him personally, since he was beginning to be like family to them, and give him some gifts. The counsellor gave him a book written by an adventurer from Tower Town on all known wild animals and the head instructor hired a smith to make a custom short sword out of horbium. The boy viewed each gift as something precious and he apologised for not having enough words to thank them. Deep inside he wished he could share the joy of receiving them with his parents and Alyssa, but that was not possible. Before leaving the room in the cave, both men watched him train and the progress made by the boy in hand to hand fighting proved that it was the perfect time to receive a short sword and begin the next step in his training. Just as the head instructor suggested and wrote in his journal, training each fighting style one at a time proved a lot more effective than combining them from the start. After getting back to his room, Kayro felt ready for his second year of training to begin.

## The second year of Training Camp

Starting the second year felt more like crossing a mental bridge for Kayro, since there was no actual break, but, as always, getting the chance to learn about more things was more important for the boy than having a long break. As soon as he got to the butcher training site, the boy noticed that now the training included older trainees as well and not all of them were from Glade Village.

On the first day, the instructor tried to get them familiar with the site and told them that the training will be divided in four. For the first two weeks they will learn about butchering livestock, the next two will be about butchering game that is brought back to camp by hunting teams, after that there will be two weeks when they will be taught about butchering fish and the last two weeks will be dedicated to trading meat and other animal part either inside a butcher shop or with other communities through the Trading Post.

While walking around the site, Kayro's attention was drawn by two of the students from the other communities. One of them was a girl named Takya from Tower Town and the second one was Laren a boy from Port Town, both being very skilled when it came to different parts of the role, in fact it looked like they were doing it even better than the instructors.

After the first two weeks went by and he finished learning about the livestock part of the role, the boy met Takya as they were both training on how to butcher game. Seeing her skills up close determined him to know more about the girl and find out how she got so good. She promised to tell him more after the training day is finished, because she is too focused on learning and doesn't like to talk much while practising. As soon as everyone cleaned their workspaces Takya came to meet Kayro and apologised for sending him away earlier. The boy told her there was no need for that, because he has moments when his mind works the same way.

They decided to go for a walk in the park and met Alyssa on their way there, who initially seemed mad about something, but that was something he will have to ask about later. She was important to him, but he was too focused on learning how the girl from Tower Town got so good. While talking, they found out that she was two years older than them and she wants to be a cook just like her father, only she wants to specialise in cooking game and this is why she is so focused on learning how to get even better at butchering it.

"My father told me that the best cook needs to also be a butcher. By taking apart an animal yourself you can already imagine what you can cook with each part and this way you will end up using more than what a regular butcher will. I don't mean that in an offensive way, but I've seen it done by too many."

"So what made you choose game as a specialty?" the boy asked.

"For some reason I always enjoyed its taste, even if my father is very good at using livestock when cooking. Also, as I was trying to gain experience before coming to Training Camp, I got the chance to see a few butchers taking game apart and it made me unhappy. They were wasting too much of what could be used and some didn't even have the smallest idea of how hard the hunters worked to get it. I never had the courage to say anything about that, but I promised myself to learn more while practising here and then when I get the chance to teach other how to make the best out of it."

"What made you think that they were not doing it properly or didn't care about the work that was done to get that game?" asked Alyssa.

"Nearly all of the butchers that I watched were familiar only with livestock since the hunting grounds around Tower Town are not that productive, so when they received game, they just tried to quickly finish butchering it as they were uncomfortable. Luckily one day I met an old lady that was saving a lot more from each animal that ended on her table. She told me that from her family had been taking the butcher role for years since humans started working as a community and built what later became Tower

Town. All that knowledge and the importance to use as much as possible out of everything was passed down by her family, but as the communities got bigger and they started to raising livestock, only few were interested in her 'old ways' of doing things."

"That is very sad. My parents always taught me to use as much as possible out of everything because that is the only way to respect nature and yourself" said Kayro.

"I'm happy to hear there are still people who teach their children about that. I'm sorry, but we will need to continue our conversation another day. It is getting late and I promised my friends to meet them today. It was nice meeting both of you and I hope we will see each other around before I go back to Tower Town Camp."

"Before you go, Takya, I have one favour to ask. Can you please teach me how to butcher game the way you do it?" asked Kayro.

"I cannot promise, but if I get the chance I will gladly do it" replied the girl.

After she left, the boy saw that Alyssa was feeling better, so he saw no point in asking her what happened and this way he considered that he avoided making her mad by reminding her of what happened. Little did he know that she was jealous after seeing him with another girl, but, after talking to Takya, she understood that he wasn't looking for a friend or a partner, instead he was just interested to learn from someone he considered very skilled.

The next day, as he started practice, Kayro found out that all the new trainees will work with a senior during their two weeks of practice and more than that he was paired with the girl from Tower Town. This gave him the chance not only to learn from her, but also make a new friend, which made Alyssa happy, because she could never imagine him coming out of his 'shell'.

As he was starting to learn about butchering fish, they boy was again lucky and he got paired to practice with Laren for a week before doing this on his own. Unlike Takya, he focused better while talking during practice and that gave them the chance to get to know each other quickly. He was a year older and despite his family being known for their skills as fishermen, he wanted to become a butcher. He learned part of that from his mother who was always making sure that what her husband caught was being used properly. At some point in their conversation, Kayro built up the courage to confess his admiration:

"I have to admit, I was hoping to get the chance and see your skills up close and maybe even learn from you a little."

"I'm glad you like it, but I still have a lot to learn before I will be happy with myself. There is someone even better visiting Glade Camp and her skills are simply fantastic. I wish I had the chance to learn from her, but we are rotating to learn about all three way butchering specialisations and I will always do something different than she is."

"Are you by any chance talking about Takya from Tower Town?"

"Yes, that is exactly who I am talking about. How did you know that?"

"Because I felt the same way you did about her skills and was lucky enough to practice with her for the last two weeks. If you want, I can introduce you to her when the training day is over, since I am meeting her and my best friend in the park."

"That would be great. I only had the chance to see her work from the distance and it looked like she enjoys it so much. Also I heard that she is the daughter of one of the best cooks in Tower Town and I was curious to see what makes her so interested in butchering."

"Sorry to disappoint you, but to her, butchering is just a step in learning more about cooking, still as you said, she is enjoying that and the reason is that she is already imagining what she could cook with that."

"So, basically, what we see as a part of an animal, she already sees as a dish."

"That's right. She said that by learning how to properly butcher everything, she can make better use of each part while cooking."

"I have to admit that she is even more amazing than I thought. Now I really have to meet her and at least get some tips from her."

With their workplace being clean after a busy day, Kayro and Laren headed to the park. Once again Alyssa was happily surprised to see him make a friend and just like in Takya's case she found out it was all about learning from someone very skilled. After the introductions it turned out that both trainees from outside Glade Camp wanted to learn from each other and they decided to start as soon as possible. Even if they didn't get the chance to practice together, they both promised to write down the most important instruction about the way they work and to keep in touch even when they get back to their camps.

The two weeks of fish butchering were gone and Kayro managed to learn a little from Laren, but he also made copies of what instructions the boy from Port Town and Takya wrote for each other. Since both of their training periods in Glade Camp were finished, all four decided to celebrate with some cake and juice promising to keep in touch.

Out of his last two weeks of butcher role training, Kayro spent one in the butcher shop and one in the Trading Post. If the first part was familiar from that time he spent with the richest family in Glade Village, the second one was something totally new, but he adapted quickly and learned the most important parts of it. Also, he was happy to learn that some of the other camps are sending requests for animal parts that are not usually used in his community. This made him understand Takya's point of view even better.

Two days before he finished learning about being a butcher, he wrote a letter to his parents telling them about his new mentors and friends from Port Town and Tower Town. On that evening he also had a visit from Monta in the cave room.

"I am happy to see how you performed during these last two months and I hope that those two trainees that I paired you with were able to teach you at least part of their skill" the counsellor said.

"So it wasn't just by luck that I got to train with them?" asked the boy.

"They were here for some time and the instructors were impressed. After seeing them in action I shared the same opinion and knowing that you will soon train as a butcher made me realise that you might enjoy learning from them."

"Thank you very much, sir. It was a pleasure to practice with both of them. I know I could never reach their level, but seeing how passionate they were about all aspects of the roles they wish to take after graduating made my desire to become an explorer even bigger. Speaking of exploring, I have a question for you."

"Ask away."

"For some reason, in the memories from my previous lives I believe that time was measured a little different. If I'm not mistaken, there were more than three hundred and thirty-six days in a year."

"That is true, but a few years after 'The Reset' people mostly remembered that there were seven days in each week and four weeks in each month, so they voted on keeping it simple. Now we just count the days from one to seven without giving them any name, the weeks from one to four and months from one to twelve. Apparently, the days and months had different names to different people and that produced some misunderstandings in the beginning, which made the Elders ask for a vote on the current way we are counting."

"I see. Honestly it makes more sense like this."

"I am happy I could answer that for you and I'm afraid it's time for me to go back."

"Thank you very much for your help with the training and for answering my question."

"You're welcome."

After the counsellor left, Kayro started his training routine which was beginning to look better with each passing month. As usual, the first step was training his muscles by using the weights available, followed by hand to hand combat and finished with short sword practice. Since there was not much space available inside the cave, he was still regularly playing sports to improve both his stamina and team work. Even though the explorer role will not be done as a team, there will be occasions when he will need it, like being able to blend in while he will be away in the other camps.

Every time his training was over, he would leave the cave quietly making sure that there is no one around to see him and then sprinted to the living quarters. He was always taking a shower after training and used running as a cover for disappearing when he was training. After starting his second year he had to move around a lot since all campsites had their own living quarters for smaller groups. The boy considered this part of his training since an explorer would rarely sleep in the same place for a long time. For the same reason he never really wanted to own too many things, so everything he had could easily fit in his backpack.

The book he received from Monta was part of those things too and each night, before going to sleep, he made sure to read at least ten pages. There were times when he was absorbed by what he was reading and ended up staying late, but usually he made sure to rest properly. From time to time he was also writing in the two journals that he kept in his backpack, but it wasn't as often as he did when he started Training Camp.

After his last day of training for the butcher role he decided to ask Alyssa for advice related to the baker role. The girl told him that in his case it will be a lot easier since it was for a shorter period than she trained for, but he will know the basics at the end for sure. Just as she said, at the end of the two months in the baker site he knew the basics about milling, about baking different types and sizes of bread, also how to make various cakes, as well as running a baker shop or selling the baked goods through the Trading Post.

"I told you that it will not be so hard" Alyssa said.

"You were right, I did manage to master the basics, but I could never do even half of the things you can."

"Well, I will do it for you then."

Realising what she just said the girl's face turned red, but quickly went away as she noticed the boy didn't realise what she meant. She has been seeing him as a future life partner for some time, but they were too young to think about things like that yet.

"I could always eat the delicious cakes that you make. The ones I made wouldn't even classify as edible."

In order not to give him enough time to think about her previous words, Alyssa quickly changed the topic to something that always got his attention:

"So, what did you like the most about baked goods?" the girl asked

"I was happy to see that there are ways, just like the butchers use for meat, to preserve them for a longer time and that means there will be less waste. Also, seeing both roles from the point of view of an Elder, I realised that the quantities produced are always close to what is needed, never too much or too little. That seems like a huge difference from my memories of past lives when lots of the goods were mass produced without a proper limit, so they ended up as garbage instead of being consumed."

"It is way better as we do it now. Sure, you limit the freedom of the makers, but this way almost anything created will be used."

"Just as my parents always said, by respecting nature, we respect ourselves, even if this means doing certain things according to limits that are set by others."

Following the conversation with Alyssa, Kayro went to train in the cave room. Since he was going to leave the Glade Camp for a long period, both Zoss and Monta were waiting for him.

"Son, with the way your training is scheduled, you will be away for a year. Please make sure to stay safe and try to never let anyone know about your real purpose. I am certain that you already knew that, but we just want to see you come back safe."

"Just as the head instructor said, you will need to be very careful and everything should be all right. You can always write to me, but only about the things that you are supposed to be doing, the rest will have to wait until we meet again" added the counsellor.

"I promise to do my best. I am determined to reach my goal even if that will mean I cannot train as much as I want."

"Regarding that, since we last saw each other, I spoke to some of the adventurers and it turns out that all camps have some hidden places where trainees go to learn from them about the adventurer roles. I will give you a pendant as a proof that you can be trusted, so if you meet them, this will gain you access into those places. It will probably take some time, but that is the best I can do to help with your fighting skills training" said Zoss.

"Thank you very much, sir! That will help a lot and hopefully by the time I get back I would have learned how to use the short sword in combination with a shield."

"Don't forget to keep up with reading too, Kayro. I heard that all the other camps have bigger libraries than we have here, so you should take advantage of that. Just make sure not to take too many on subjects that might give away your goal" Monta said.

"I had no idea about their libraries being bigger. I should be able to find a lot of new books there. Thank you for the good news!"

The conversation carried on for a short while and ended with both instructors wishing him good luck and to return safely.

The next morning, Kayro met Alyssa early so they could travel together to Lumberjack Village Camp. Both were training for the weaver role there for the next two months which them happy. Everything was quiet on the road and they got there even earlier than expected. The boy hoped to meet his friend from Lumberjack Village that evening, but after arriving they were taken on a tour of the weaving campsite and by the time they got to their rooms it was already very late.

After their first day of practice, Zodar was waiting for them just outside the training site and he gave them a detailed tour of the camp. Even though they were here before it was a long time ago and usually the instructors were just moving quickly. He showed them the different training sites, the park that was similar to the one from Glade Camp, the areas were sports were played each day after training by those who still had energy left and of course, the library which put a big smile on Kayro's face.

Just as he expected, Alyssa and Zodar were able to quickly become friendly, which made him very happy. In fact, they even decided to spend as much time as possible before they will need to separate again. After a few days of training, the boy from Lumberjack Village took them to a field where they could play his favourite sport and after they finished he asked Kayro to talk in private when they get the chance.

"I will tell Alyssa that I need you to help with something in my room and since girls are not allowed in the same living quarters as boys, we will talk then."

"Sounds good. There is no need to rush, but I would prefer if we did that today" Zodar said.

After apologising to the girl, they went to the room and the conversation started.

"I'm sorry for asking you to talk like this, Kayro, but during the game I saw something on you that got my attention and chances are that Alyssa doesn't really know what that is."

"What exactly did you see?"

"That pendant that you have attached to your necklace, can I please have a closer look? It is similar to the one my cousin has."

Initially Kayro panicked, but then agreed to his request. For some reason, ever since he met Zodar, he knew he could trust the boy from Lumberjack Village.

"There you go. Is it the same as the one you've seen before or does it only look similar?"

"It's the same one, but I am surprised that you have it. You see, my older cousin is an adventurer and he told me to check if any of the new trainees that come to our camp have it. Apparently, only those that wish to train as adventurers should have it and he explained to me that I will have to keep this as a secret from anyone else around which is why I wanted to talk in private."

"You're right, Alyssa doesn't know about my real choice of role, so it was a good decision. Is your cousin in the camp at the moment?"

"Not right now, but he should arrive tomorrow evening. It is best if just the two of you meet at the park's entrance, I will let him know to wait for you there. Also, you don't need to worry about me telling anyone, because he told me that lately only a few people each year dare to choose the adventurer role, since for some reason the Elders are trying to discourage anyone who wants that."

"I'm happy that at least I have a friend I can share my real choice with and honestly I'm going for the role of an explorer, the adventurer training is just a step to get to my real goal."

"I was thinking that might be the case, ever since we met, I noticed your curiosity about what's beyond the Median Forests borders."

"Thank you for being a real friend and please make sure that no one will find out about you helping me with this as it could get you in trouble."

The next evening, Kayro met, Wux, Zodar's cousin and he was given a key to the hidden training room used by the adventurers and the trainees that wished to become one. It was easy to get to it without being seen because it was hidden underground in the huge training site used for teaching the children about the woodcutting role. After a quick tour the boy decided to go meet with Alyssa because she will get worried if they didn't have their usual walk in the park and the conversation about how their day was or what's going through their mind, and very soon they will not see each other for a few months.

After the last day of weaving training, they had a picnic to celebrate before being separated. Zodar was happy to finally be able to train alongside his friend as they were both scheduled for tanning training during the next two months, but the fact that Alyssa will go to Tower Town for the next year made everyone feel a little sad. They will meet there for some time as both boys will go to learn about different roles, but for Kayro it felt strange not to be able to have their usual routine after a training day.

The next morning he woke up very early in order to say goodbye before she left and gave her a token that he was working on during their weaving training. After tightly hugging him, she gave him a similar one and then joined the caravan that was taking the trainees to the Port Town and Tower Town Training Camps.

Shortly after the caravan left, Kayro met Zodar and they went to the tanning site. Just like all the other trainings it started with a detailed tour, followed by one of the instructors informing the children about their schedule for the next two months. Both of them were happy to finally have the chance to practice together and by the time the two months ended became even closer than before. Despite having different goals they had similar ways of viewing the life around them which was the reason they bonded on their trip to the Cabin Camp.

Now it was time to separate again with Kayro going to Tower Town Camp, while Zodar was going to Glade Village Camp , but after four months they will meet again and train together in Port Town Camp. Before they parted ways they wished each other good luck and once again promised to keep in touch through letters.

Soon after arriving at his destination and finished the tour of the tailor training site, the boy went out to find Alyssa. He promised to meet her at the camp's park entrance and moments after he got there a familiar gesture took him by surprise. As she did so many time before, the girl covered his eye with her hands, making him guess who it was even if they both knew that she was the only one to get this close to him. After a long hug they started talking about everything that happened while they didn't see each other and, despite the letters they wrote, the conversation lasted a few hours, which was still not enough to discuss all details. As they talked, the girl showed him the fields were sports were played and where the library in Tower Town Camp was.

It took Kayro a few days to find some quiet places to train his fighting skills, but soon everything felt just like it was back in Glade Camp, learning about the tailor role during the first part of the day, meeting Alyssa for a walk and a conversation in the park, playing sports and late in the evening improving his fighting style. Despite all of that the boy felt like he is somehow barely making a difference in getting better, so he decided to check the library in case he might find an answer there. The decision turned out to be very good, because the library had twice as many books as the one in Glade Village Camp and he was able to find a lot about survival, wild animals and even a few about fighting skills.

By the time the two months of tailor role training were over, he had improved his knowledge a lot towards achieving his goal, but he knew that it's one thing to read the theory and completely a different one experiencing the things he read about.

On his first day of cooking training, two things made Kayro very happy. The first one he already knew about for some time and it was the fact that he will learn how to be a cook at the same time as Alyssa which meant he could spend more time with his best friend. The reason why he was so happy was that, after this training was over, they will not see each other for four months. The second thing that made his day better was meeting Takya who was invited by the instructors to display her cooking skills showing the new trainees what a prodigy could do in just a few years of practising at Training Camp.

Just like the day they met, he waited until training was over to talk to her . She was happy to see both of them here and after some time asked Kayro to talk in private when they get the chance. Despite finding that strange, the boy agreed to meet her next morning in the library, since there was no training and he wanted her opinion on some books about cooking anyway.

"That is a very interesting pendant you have there. Can I please take a closer look at it?" Takya asked.

If anyone else from Tower Town Camp asked that, the boy would probably not know how to react, but, just like in Zodar's case, something about her made him think he can trust the girl. As always, his instincts prove right:

"There is someone who would definitely like to meet you and as soon as possible. Don't worry, I know what the pendant means and I will keep your secret, in fact the person I was talking about could help you."

"And who is that person?"

"She is my older sister, Synia, and just like you she is secretly training to be an adventurer. Well, that will not be such a big secret anymore in two months when she will officially make her choice for the last year of Training Camp, still I bet the two of you can help each other."

"I heard that some girls are going for that role too, but I didn't really believe it. Someone told me that even if that is a rare thing to happen, having a girl in the team usually helps a lot when it comes to safety. Apparently the teams that have only boys or men always take more risks not considering all points of view."

"Now I'm sure that my sister will be happy to meet you. I will bring her later to the park when you go with your friend for a walk and find a way to distract Alyssa and give you time to talk. That is unless she already knows about you."

"Unfortunately I cannot tell yet. She has a different was of viewing life and also I don't want her to know information that might affect her future. I will probably tell her some time before I make my decision for the sixth year of training official."

As they agreed, the meeting took place while he was having his usual walk with his best friend and Takya found the perfect way to distract her and learn something new at the same time. She asked for help with pairing up some cakes with the dishes that she is usually cooking, knowing that Alyssa was very good at baking.

Since it was the first time meeting another person that was secretly training, Kayro felt nervous, but Synia, just like her sister had something that made him feel she is trustworthy. The quickly talked about meeting later so he can show him a hidden room where he can train and then went over to Takya and Alyssa.

Later that day, just outside the camp, the boy discovered that the secret training room was nearly twice the size of the ones from Glade and Lumberjack Camps. More than that he had the chance to meet a few other trainees from Tower Camp that wanted to become adventurers, which gave him the perfect chance to finally test his skills by sparing. He had some short fight with boys and girls of different ages finding out that he still has a lot more to improve. For some reason, he never managed to excel at any of the roles he trained for up until now, but he at the same time he adapted very well to all of them.

During the two months he had left to train in Tower Town Camp, he learned that, just like Zoss, the head instructor was worried about the way the Elders were making some decisions, but he could never do something about that since his father was one of them and his older brother was next in line for the role. All he could do was make sure that no one will find out about the trainees training in secret.

Kayro also managed to learn about some new fighting styles and about new beasts, making sure to write everything in one of his journals. Sparing with others proved to be very helpful and that made him improve faster than practising by himself. Occasionally he had a bruise or a cut and, every time Alyssa asked about them, he made it look like he was just too clumsy while learning how to cook.

At the same time the cooking role training was over, so was the second year of Training Camp. To celebrate the end of the year, Kayro and his best friend joined Takya and her sister for a last dinner together. Just as many other trainees, Alyssa was shocked about Synia making the decision of becoming an adventurer official, but since they were not close it wasn't something to bother her as it would in the boy's case.

The dishes prepared by Takya were perfectly matched by the cake baked by Alyssa and all four of them enjoyed the dinner. When it was over they said their goodbyes as everyone will be in a different place starting the next day. Kayro was going to Port Town Camp, Alyssa was staying in Tower Town Camp, Takya was scheduled to train in Glade Village Camp and Synia was off to Lumberjack Village Camp.

# Years three, four and five of training

On the road to Port Town Training Camp, Kayro felt sad and happy at the same time. Being away from Alyssa always made him feel down, but knowing that he will meet Zodar and Laren again made him wish he could reach his destination faster. Since they kept in touch he knew that both of them will be there during his training.

After the usual tour and getting a room in the living quarters of the fishing site, the boy went to meet his friends. As he got to the fields that were used to play sports he noticed a third person was next to his friends who turned out to be Laren's girlfriend, Etra. The girl was there to support her boyfriend while he is playing his favourite sport and waited for them until the game was over.

Having a girl in the group made him think of Alyssa and as he looked at Etra he noticed that the girl was staring at him. He smiled thinking that maybe some mud got on his face and then started talking to the boys. While were walking towards the living quarters they decided to meet again the next days for a walk in the park or to play some sport again.

The next morning Kayro went to the library in Port Town Camp to check what books might be useful and as he was looking at the ones about fishing, he heard someone calling his name. To his surprise it was Etra with a boy that looked older than they were.

"I apologise for startling you, but I saw you here and I wanted to introduce you to my older brother, Nous. I saw that you were wearing a pendant that was similar to the one he usually wears and after telling him that he asked if he could meet you."

The boys shook hand and in order to go talk privately, Kayro told the girl that he needs her brother's help to choose some books about fishing. Just as he thought, Nous was training for the adventurer role and this was his sixth year at Training Camp, so they decided to continue their conversation later preferably somewhere with no people close by.

Since it was a hot day, they went for a swim in the Quiet Lake where Kayro learned what exactly happened to that instructor from Port Town Camp who gave the letter to Zodar two years ago.

"Unfortunately there were two reasons that lead to his disappearance. The first one was a rumour about where our secret training room was and that Rigu, who was also my counsellor at that time, was suspected of trying to get trainees to join us there, and the second thing was that during one of his trips on the lake he saw the head instructor from Tower Town Camp kneeling in front of an Elder from their community."

"And that was enough for what followed?"

"It wouldn't have been, but Rigu didn't know that the Elder was the head instructor's father, so he panicked and started rowing very fast to get away from them thinking he saw something he shouldn't have seen. More than that, when he got back, he went straight to our head instructor and started telling him about what he saw and that was the moment when they came up with a plan.

According to it, Rigu will set the secret training room on fire to make it look like he is covering up his actions, but he was actually just making sure that no one would find out which trainees were using it, then he will disguise himself and be taken in by the adventurers that come to our camp from time to time, leaving everyone to believe that he ran away before they managed to catch and question him.

The problem was that the Elders already had someone on their way here to investigate the rumours and they arrived before the adventurers could take my counsellor away. Seeing them here, the head instructor decided to change the plan. He asked Rigu to write two letters warning the other camps about the meeting on the lake and give them to a trainee from Lumberjack Camp knowing that they will go to Glade Camp before going back to theirs and this way everyone will be informed.

Since my counsellor was already in trouble he agreed in order to make sure that no one else could be blamed, so by signing that letter he would be the only one considered guilty if it falls into the wrong hands.

After giving the letter to a boy, he decided to run to the Cabin Camp where his brother was at that time and he could help Rigu hide or find a way to start over. I hope he got there unharmed, but, unless I get to meet him again by chance, there is no way to know that for sure."

"Now I understand everything better."

"From what the head instructor said, if he just greeted the Elder and his son on the lake, instead on rowing away so fast, Rigu should still be an instructor here. There was a plan to make him look like found out where the secret training place was and he set it on fire to serve as a warning for those who used it. But I guess that life doesn't really go according to plan and now we have to go into the forest to train our fighting skills, at least for a few more years before another hidden room can be built."

"That explains why I saw so many people going there in the evening and why it was so hard to find a quiet place for myself."

"We try to go in small groups and practice by rotation, always having four people on the lookout. Feel free to join us any time you wish.

"Thank you very much, Nous, both for inviting me and for telling me what happened to Rigu. I hope that one day you will meet him again."

After that conversation, Kayro joined the trainees from Port Town every day and rotated sparring with them. Just like in Tower Town, this proved to be very effective and he improved a lot by the time the four months of training here ended. During this time he also learned about properly building and using a fishing boat, new species of fish and what lures he can use to catch them, became a lot better at swimming and got to see the importance of fishing from the point of view of an Elder. It was now time to say goodbye to his friends, but he was happy to meet Alyssa soon. More than that, he could finally talk to Monta and Zoss after being away for a year, because he had so many things to tell them.

As soon as his caravan got back to Glade Camp, he was surprised to see that the girl was waiting for him. She looked very happy to see him and hugged him before he even had time to greet her. After two months of fishing practice the boy will go to Lumberjack Camp and they will not meet again for six months, so she wanted to spend as much time as possible together.

After their usual walk in the park were they could catch up to what happened while not seeing each other, Kayro went to the hidden room in the cave where both the head instructor and his counsellor were waiting. They were happy to see him and noticed that he improved a lot physically. After telling them about everything he learned while being away, including the story of the instructor from Port Town, he showed them how much his fighting skills improved.

Zoss admitted that for a fourteen years old boy he was good, but just like in anything else he was just above average, so there was still much to work on. Both him and Monta agreed that most trainees were simply focused on one role they wish learn and that made them get better results, but, while they got very good at something, they barely managed to learn about other roles. Opposite to them, Kayro was becoming a jack of all trades, which would be very useful when he will finally become an explorer and go into the world.

"Before we leave, there is one more thing that we would like you to know" said Zoss.

"And what might that be, sir?" asked Kayro.

"Thanks to that letter, I secretly planned a meeting with the head instructors of Port Town Camp and Lumberjack Village Camp, where an unexpected guest came. Confirming everything you told us earlier about how things work in Tower Town Camp, their head instructor came to propose an alliance between the four of us, in order to push the influence of the Elders away. Initially we will keep everything a secret, but in a few years we will all demand at the same time, that trainees will be allowed to openly choose the adventurer or explorer role from the beginning."

Hearing that made the boy happy, knowing that being able to freely train for that would help a lot more than doing it secretly. He was hoping that will be possible before he graduates.

For the next two months he had to wake up very early to go to the designated fishing place on the eastern side of the Quiet Lake just where it meets the Lumberjack Creek where they joined the trainees from Tower Camp. Each group was travelling with adventurers and some militia which were patrolling the area while they were fishing. Once a week, by rotation, they were using the fishing boats that were built by trainees to go on the lake, but they always stayed close to the shore.

Even he was a little tired, he would still make time to meet with Alyssa and also practice his fighting skills. For the first time since he came to Training Camp, he met other trainees from Glade Village that were using the hidden room in the cave. It was only six of them, two were younger from the first year group and other four were from the fifth year group and he found out that somehow they were never in the same place at the same time which is why they have not met yet. Having partners to spar with was always giving him extra motivation, so he was very happy.

The day before leaving to Lumberjack Camp to train for the next six months, he met with the head instructor and his counsellor in private.

"Kayro, I will go to Glade Village to visit my parents and I will stay there for a few weeks. If you have anything that you want me to tell your parents or if you wish to inform your parents on your real goal, I can personally take the letter to them. I know it was hard not being able to tell them and this is the perfect opportunity to do so" said Monta.

"I totally agree with the counsellor's idea and I am sure that your parents will support your choice" added Zoss.

"That is great news, thank you. I will have a letter ready by the end of the day. It will feel a lot better knowing that my parents are aware of my real goal when it comes to choosing a role."

The boy wrote three letters, one for each year since he came to Training Camp, and they were all very thick. His face looked a lot more peaceful after writing them and Monta was happy to see that. The counsellor promised not only to deliver the letters, but also to spend a few hours with his parents to see how they react.

As the caravan that Kayro was on set for Lumberjack Camp, Monta was leaving for Glade Village. That made the boy both nervous and happy at the same time. He was waiting for so long to finally be able to share his real goal with his family and now it was only one more person he wished he could tell. Unfortunately Alyssa will have to wait until their fifth year, because she would see this as something bad and try to convince him to give up on his dream and that will surely lead to them arguing, a thing that he was not prepared for. Despite making new friends which actually knew the truth, he still saw the girl not just as a best friend, but as family.

After reaching his destination, the boy took the tour of the great lumberjack training site and then met with Zodar. They will not train together, but they will play sports and go for a walk as often as they can. During one of their walks in the park, the boy from Lumberjack Village told his friend that the next year will be his last in Training Camp. He was now sure that woodcutting was the best role for him and he can start doing it after finishing the fourth year.

Despite being sad, Kayro encouraged his friend and promised that one day he will visit his village and hopefully see him fulfilled by the choice he made. In fact, if he or his family will need wood, they will request it from Zodar's family.

After three months of woodcutting and three of furniture making practice, Kayro was ready to go back to Glade Camp. They will get to meet each other two more time, but only for a short period. They were both unhappy about that since their bond only got stronger while spending time together, but life always has to go on and they will always be writing to each other.

Just like eight months ago, Alyssa was waiting for Kayro as he got back to their training camp and she was very happy to see him. Even better, they will also spend the next four months together training for the healer role. The boy realised just how much he missed her and this time it was him hugging her immediately. They promised to go for a walk after the healer site tour and as always give each other details about everything that happened while being apart.

The next morning, the boy went to meet his counsellor who gave him very good news about his parents being very supportive of his role choice. They were a little concerned by the fact that it has to be done secretly until the sixth year of Training Camp, but they agreed it suits their son the best. Everything Monta told him was confirmed by the letters he received from Krysta and Klost, who decided to each write their own from their point of view. While his father was very happy about his fighting skills practice, his mother was still more excited about him being able to train for the Elder role, even if he was just doing it as a backup. Still they both agreed that whatever choice he will make in the end, it is the best one.

After a few days, Zoss decided to come to the hidden room in the cave and watch the trainees sparring to see how much they improved. By now, Kayro already started using the short spear and he even found a way to use it at the same time with a short sword, not just with a shield. What impressed the head instructor even more was that unlike the older trainees that quickly chose a certain weapon and style, the boy was always trying something new and got good at doing it. At this point he really looked forward to seeing the end result which will probably be revealed during the sixth year of Training Camp.

The month was over quickly and it was time for him to go away again for nearly a year, one month training as a healer in each camp, followed by five months of military training in Tower Town Camp, then a month of practice as militia in each camp, with Glade Camp being the final point. As always, before he left, Monta and Zoss met him in private.

"After you start the military training, please remember that you will need to show only a fraction of your fighting skills."

"Fortunately, your father's past training is known to all and, if you somehow end revealing too much, the head instructor from Tower Town will be able to cover that by using this information. Still, it is better to be careful" added the counsellor.

"I will do my best not to show too much. I guess it is handy not to be an expert in any type of weapon. I will also try to focus just on the long spear which is commonly used by the militia in Glade Village and it was next on my list to train with. Hopefully, this way I can learn about it without revealing my true potential."

Both men agreed with that and after wishing him good luck they left the cave. Before going, Kayro took a look at Zoss's journal about fighting skills and to his surprise there were a lot of new pages written, some of his ideas being included in it, along with the ones from adventurers and other trainees. He was hoping that one day this might be the base theory of training groups of explorers.

Three months went by quickly and not only he got to spend every day practising alongside Alyssa, but he got to meet his other friends as well as the people who helped with his secret training, while visiting their camps. He felt sad after she had to go back to Glade Camp, because they were now closer than ever.

Since the healer role training had Tower Camp as a final destination, he had some extra time on the first day of military training, so he went to the library to make a list of the books he could borrow during his six months of being there. After he finished, Kayro realised that he had to give up on a lot of them, but he will try to read them the next time he trains there.

Just like he told Zoss and Monta, the boy tried to use only a long spear when training with a weapon and held back a lot during the hand to hand practice. The militia training campsite had a lots of means that helped build muscle mass, so he took advantage of being able to do that without hiding. By the end of the five months of training he was not happy with the way his body looked, but still had time to work on it before his last year in Training Camp.

The three months of practice in Tower Camp, Port Camp and Lumberjack Camp were gone and he finally got back to his own camp. As always, after getting his new room he went out to find Alyssa. They hugged each other tightly and he realised just how much he missed having her next to him and no matter how close he got to his other friends she will probably be the most important to him all of his life.

After he finished talking to her, he went straight to the hidden training room in the cave where his counsellor and the head instructor were waiting. He tried to tell them about all of his experiences without too many details in order to save time and then sparred with one of the older trainees to show his improvement. He was moving a lot faster than before despite gaining extra muscle mass, his strength was greater and he was able to combine different styles and weapons a lot easier than nearly a year ago.

Zoss and Monta were both impressed, but as always the boy was just above average at what he was doing and felt bad for not being able to excel. The men explained to him again that you don't always need to be the best at something to get better results in life and that being good at many things will give you more options to choose from.

What made him finally understand that they were right was when they started talking about his training from the point of view of an Elder. During that, he learned not just about all those roles, but also about how they work together in each community. In fact, excelling at something meant sacrificing your freedom of choice, since one of the laws of the Median Forests was to take on the role that you are the best at. While that helped society by making sure the productivity will be highest this way, it limited the individuals a lot. Sure, there were cases like his father or Zodar who simply loved the roles they were given based on their skills, but freedom was more important to Kayro.

Before going away, Monta gave the boy a pack from his family which contained the gurma leather vest and belt who were made years ago.

"Your parents gave them to me when I visited the village and told me to hold them for you until they fit. After seeing how much you grew when you arrived today, I realised it was time for you to have them."

The boy thanked him and while trying them on saw that the man was right. Despite being able to wear them, they were still a little loose and that meant he will probably be able to use them even after graduating from Training Camp, just like he wanted.

For a few moments his mind went back to the time he spent with Jabix, Lien and Erno, and to his parents. This made him feel sad, but also happy at the same time, since he knew that in nearly two years from now he will be going back home and return as a young adult instead of a child, just like his friends Zodar and Takya will do in less than a month.

A day before the militia practice in Glade Camp was finished, Kayro celebrated the end of their fourth year just like they did some time ago, with cake, juice and syrup. After that, he met with Monta and Zoss who wanted to congratulate him on his overall performance and give him some advice regarding training he will do during the next ten months when he will be away.

"If you want to craft something good when you will train for the smith role, the best thing you can do is to try and get yourself a small amount of maxor, a decent amount of horbium and as much sparus as they allow you to. After you start crafting practice, try to learn how to shape and refine by using the most common while saving the rare ones for your final days. When it comes to jewellery, I cannot give you any advice, since they never helped me in combat against beasts or humans, but after you get better at crafting weapons try to make them fit your style."

"What do you mean by saying that, head instructor?" asked Kayro.

"You see, standard weapons are made nearly identical in shape and weight, and they can prove too light or too heavy for the one using them, so if you make it yourself it can be properly adjusted. By having a bigger quantity of sparus you can use it for practice and since horbium weighs the same after they are both melted, you can save that for your final attempts" said Zoss.

"Many will try to use everything from the beginning, but they don't understand just how hard proper smithing is. Since my grandfather was a smith and I watched him a lot as a child, I can only say that the head instructor's advice is what you should follow" added Monta.

"Thank you very much. I am certain it will help me end up with a better quality product in the end."

The conversation carried on for a few minutes and then, while Kayro went back to sparring with the other trainees, the two men left. An hour later, the boy went back to his room and started getting his backpack ready for travelling.

Two days later, Alyssa came to see him early, just before he left, and they were both happy that it will only be a month until they meet again. While on the road, the boy was already thinking about his next months of training and started day dreaming about finally being able to create some jewellery for his mother and maybe some tools for his father. Soon he realised that this was the perfect opportunity to make something for his best friend too and give it to her as a gift after finally graduating from Training Camp.

Just as Zoss advised him, Kayro focused on getting the maxor and horbium first, managing to get good quantities during his first week of mining and then he got plenty of sparus by the end of the month.

As they started training for crafting jewellery, Alyssa was surprised to see that the boy was using the low quality metal instead of maxor, but after he explained the logic behind his decision, she chose to do the same.

After the two months of training were over, he showed Alyssa the ring and bracelet he managed to craft for Krysta and she was impressed by his work. Maybe he wasn't the most skilled out of the trainees, but he was a lot better than her and she could see the jewellery reflecting the boy's love for his mother. Part of him wished to give the girl the bracelet he made for her after seeing how much she admired those, but he decided it was better suited to wait until Training Camp was over.

Still he prepared a new syrup for her from a recipe that Takya gave him last time they saw each other and gave that to Alyssa. He tested the recipe a few times since then, but this was the first time he was happy with its taste. The girl was happy with the taste, but knowing that she will not see her best friend for seven months made her sad, despite getting a gift from him. After she went back to Glade Camp, Kayro focused a lot on crafting weapons and armour and the advice from Zoss and Monta proved to be very valuable.

By the end of the three months of practice he ended up not only with a short sword and a short spear which helped improve his fighting skill a lot, but also with some great boots that could be part of his future explorer armour. After making them, he understood better what the head instructor meant when he said that custom made objects can help a lot more than the standard ones.

Going to Lumberjack Camp made Kayro feel sad since Zodar was not here anymore, but getting the chance to craft a tool for his father cheered him up. Since he saved some of the horbium by not using it from the start, he was able to make a very good quality tool for Klost which should help a lot. Even the instructors were amazed by the way it turned out, so as soon as he got the chance he arranged for it to be delivered to his father.

The next step was training to craft hunting tools and the advice from his counsellor and head instructor helped Kayro to end up with a kit of horbium tools that could be used to hunt and skin animals of any size. During these three months, he also added using a bow to his fighting skills training and that made him feel closer to reaching his goal.

After getting back to Glade Camp, Zoss and Monta were very impressed with his work and told him that this is exactly what a kit for an adventurer or explorer should look like.

"Those are the right tools to survive in the wilderness, Can we please use borrow them for a while so we can get more sets done?" the head instructor asked.

"Of course you can, but wouldn't that get attention from the Elders?"

"You don't have to worry about that anymore, Kayro. We finally managed to convince them to allow us to openly train adventurers and explorers next year, so everyone you age will need to take a test of survival in the Great Forest for three months before you can graduate from Training Camp."

"More than that, they promised we can ask the trainees that will choose the military and the healer roles to join you during this test" added Monta.

"Does this mean that now everyone can be honest about their real choice of roles?"

"We will try to keep the first and second year trainees a secret just in case, but, yes, you can freely say that now. The training room in the cave will also be kept as a secret and you will be able to use the militia rooms and equipment to train as well."

Their conversation went on for an hour and after it was finished, the boy went straight to his best friend to finally tell her the truth and about the next year's test. Despite not liking the idea of him being in danger, Alyssa supported his choice and told him that she would like to join the test as a healer. Kayro was surprised to find out that she decided to take on the healer role, but he was happy to hear about being able to take the test together.

For the next few days, other trainees decided to reveal their interest in becoming adventurers. A few military and healer trainees requested permission to join the survival test and even a few of the ones training as hunters.

Everyone was informed that the decisions will be made during the next six months and then a list with everyone else besides the adventurer or explorers ,chosen from all four camps, will be made public.

The first two months after the news, Kayro practiced hunting south of the Quiet Lake with trainees from Lumberjack Camp during the day and met a few of the ones that will join the test at the end of next year. During this time, a schedule for the trainees who chose the adventurer or explorer role was made and Monta revealed it to the boy as soon as it was approved.

"You will start by studying cartography in Tower Town Camp for three months, followed by learning the theory about survival and crafting the necessary items for two months, then you will spend a month in each camp to train at crafting them and learning about different types of environments and everything will end with the Survival Test in the Great Forest for three months where only one instructor from each camp along with a four trained adventurers and twelve trained militia will join the group of trainees."

"Will that be enough, sir?"

"Each month we will send some adventurers to scout the area where the camp will be set and make sure there are no large groups of predators or any major beasts. It was decided than anything else could be easily handled by the group of trainees."

"Hopefully everything will be well and after we pass the test, more will choose those two roles."

After their conversation Kayro met Alyssa and told her about everything which made him feel free. There were too many times when he wished he could share these things with her, but couldn't and now he was happy to be totally honest with her.

As the fifth year of Training Camp ended, they celebrated not only the end of it, but also finally being a year away from going home.

## Sixth year of training and the Test of Survival

Kayro started the year by going to Tower Camp at the same time Alyssa did. While he will be learning cartography, the girl will learn advanced methods of healing. Unlike him, who will be there for six months, she will only stay for two months and a week before going to Port Town Camp, Lumberjack Camp and then to Glade Camp for the same period to learn about the different methods or treatments that they are using.

After the boy was able to tell her the truth about his role choice and not only she decided to support him, but also join the group that was taking the test at the end of the training year, they got even closer than before. While the girl knew for some time that she wishes him as a future partner, his feelings for her were still unclear, but he did think of her as being family.

When she had to leave for Port Camp, both of them were sad, but the fact that they will spend the last four months of Training Camp together, and then finally go back to Glade Village, made it easier.

During his lessons as a cartographer, Kayro learned that all the known maps of the Median Forests were updated every ten years, excepting the cases when a new settlement was built, when that will be immediately added and the updated maps will be sent to all the communities. There were always two people making maps, the main cartographer and an apprentice who was trained to take his place when it was time to retire.

From what the trainees were told, the two of them would travel accompanied by a group of very skilled adventurers within the borders of the Median Forests from spring to autumn and then spend the winter in Tower Town working on the new maps. This year they had to take a break from their travels to come and teach the ones who wished to take on the roles of adventurers or explorers.

At some point they were asked about exploring the entire Ardian continent or maybe the entire planet and they replied that as long as there is no planning for a new settlement, there is no point in going beyond the borders, since it would be a waste of resources.

By the end of these three months, Kayro managed to get good at the theoretical part, but, when it came to drawing, he was not doing very well. Still, his overall skills were above average, so he could easily travel without getting lost. The boy felt sorry that he could not train from the point of view of an Elder after starting the sixth year since he chose to go on and become an explorer. Usually when doing that he was always getting some extra information which proved very useful when it came to most things that he was taught before.

The next two months, which were focused on the survival theory skills and crafting, went by very fast and it was now time to practice crafting. Kayro was now going to spend one month in each camp starting with Tower Town camp, followed by Port Town Camp and Lumberjack Village Camp, ending in Glade Village Camp, before going to the Great Forest for the Test of Survival.

Since his friends in each camp already went back to their communities, Kayro spent most of his free time training his body and fight skills. It was strange not meeting them, but, in less than a year he should be able to write to them or even visit their community and that thought made him feel free.

After getting back to Glade Camp he finally saw the list of people who were going to take the Test of Survival. It was a total of one hundred people, with fifteen adults, five healer trainees, fifteen adventurer or explorer trainees and sixty-five military trainees.

He was happy to see the names some of the boys and girls he met while training for the healer and military roles, but more than that, Alyssa's name, because having her next to him for the final step of his journey meant a lot. When it came to adventurers , he was surprised to see that none of the ones he met were on the list, and more than that, except the head instructor from Tower Town

Camp, there were no other instructors going along with the group, so he went to talk to Monta and Zoss.

"Unfortunately, this was a decision the Elders imposed on us. They said that only by choosing impartial people, they can confirm if they will allow this kind of training to go on in the future" the counsellor said.

"How about the head instructor from Tower Town Camp?" Kayro asked.

"He made sure that no one knew he was supporting the adventurer and explorer roles training and even then hardly managed to convince his father to allow him to join" replied Zoss.

"They motivated everything by saying that any of the people who supported you will try to help instead of just observing you" added Monta.

"So, basically, they want us to fail?"

"Yes, because this way, they can prove us wrong about asking to train people for these roles without them requesting it" replied the counsellor.

"We are sorry about this entire situation, but you will have to be strong. Since I met those adventurers before, I can guarantee that they will be fair while observing and protect you if needed."

"That is good to know. Most of us trust our skills, but it's one thing to know the theory or to craft something related to survival while protected by the walls of a camp, and a whole different thing to do it out there in the wilderness. Since the Training Forest is always patrolled there aren't really any dangerous animals, but while we were practising hunting we still had difficulties, so going to the Great Forest, even after the area where we will camp was scouted, will be challenging."

"Regarding that, the Elders decided to change the location as well. Initially it was supposed to be west of the Training Forest, but now it will be somewhere close to where the Great Forest will meet the Hills of Hope, which can be more dangerous since a lot of beasts are known to live in the hills and mountains" said Zoss.

"Well, sooner or later we will have to face them anyway, so it might be better to do that while having so many adventurers with us."

The conversation carried on for some time with Kayro asking about how everything on the known map got its name and the two men answering his questions in turns. This was something he wanted to ask while training as a cartographer, but the instructors made him feel uncomfortable, so he chose not to.

One day before the Test of Survival all the trainees participating were called in for a meeting with the head instructors and their counsellors. Everyone had words of encouragement for the young adults and wished them good luck.

It took the caravan two days and to get close to the designated location and as soon as they got there a meeting was held to decide on the tasks each individual will have starting the next morning. For the test to succeed it was agreed that the adventurers and the head instructor from Tower Camp will remain with the caravan just outside the Great Forest, taking turns in watching how the children perform, while the trainees will go nearly three kilometres inside and set up their own camp from what they can find around.

Making the decisions was easier than normal since most of them had trained together at some point even if they came from all four camps. The ones training as healers would starts looking for plants, berries and mushrooms. After that, they will all meet and decide what they will gather immediately and what will be left to be used in the future. Hearing about this part made Kayro remember his time spent with Krysta identifying and gathering things.

When it came to the military trainees, some were divided into groups of four to protect each of the healers, others into groups of two that will be acting as guards for the adventurer or explorer trainees, while the other fifteen will act take turns to watch the area where they plan to make camp.

When it came to the ones training as adventurers, they will be rotating in doing various tasks until they manage to get some shelters built. Four of them, along with their guards will go look for places where they can hunt or fish, one will look for a water source, while the remaining ten will look for materials to make shelters and fires.

On his first day, Kayro went out to look for water source and he was lucky to quickly find one a kilometre away from camp. While he was doing that, the fires where ready and he could start boiling it to make sure it is safe to drink it. Everyone else was successful with their tasks, so by the end of the day, they had a small shelter to smoke meat and fish, a bigger one where they can butcher and cook the game and fish that they catch a big recipient full of drinking water and fires to keep them warm during the night.

The next day, the boy was helping build shelters that looked more like small houses. Since they already knew where to get materials, they managed to build three shelters that could fit around twenty-five people each.

On the third day, they made three more, one for the camp guards, who could fit ten people at a time, one that will be used by the healers to store everything they collect, to make their healing mixtures and treat whoever gets sick, and a very big one to be used as a multipurpose crafting workshop.

Since all the shelters they needed were ready, they decided to start changing the tasks. Some of them went to the hills to find some ore, others started building a smithy to make better tools, a tannery and a loom to make better clothing and to improve their sleeping conditions.

By the end of the first month, the camp started looking like a small village. They managed to make improvements in everything they were going to use while taking the Test of Survival and they only had to work a little now, compared to their first days. Along with the other adventurers, Kayro could now start training his fighting skills again, when they were not going for a hunt or exploring.

The healers were the least busy trainees in the camp as they already stored everything they needed and there were no serious injuries among the members of their group. The military trainees didn't have much to do either except follow the adventurers around when they left camp, or to be ready to act if anything happened while the adventurers were crafting something.

On the days when he wasn't tasked with doing something around the camp, Kayro was going out exploring as much as possible, but always made time to spend with Alyssa. Both of them were sad for not being able to send letters home, but it was nearly time to get back soon which mean they could finally see their parent after such a long time.

Starting the third month everyone realised that more predators showed up close to their camp and that made the trainees nervous for some time. Soon they realised that this was normal and as long as they stay alert the wild animals will not be able to harm them.

They had a few nights when they needed to chase some wolves away because they got too close to the camp, but they were always alone, not as a pack. In fact, the ones that scared them the most were a group of miskras that ran into their camp after being chased by a gurma, but there was only little damage done and no one got hurt. After that incident it was quiet until one evening when something unexpected happened.

With one week left until the end of the Test of Survival, a pack of seven gurmas came and attacked the camp, which was the first sign that something strange is happening since gurmas are solitary predators. Everyone was awake, so the ones that had armour and weapons quickly got ready to fight.

The trainees intended to wait inside the shelters, but that didn't help as the predators could easily get rip apart the walls that were made mostly out of grass. This was the second sign that made them think something is wrong, because they never heard of any animal trying to get inside and attack people, but after everyone was forced to get outside an image that seemed from a scary story was waiting for them. A gurma that was three times the size of the other ones was growling in all directions, making it look like it was giving orders.

All the trainees made a big circle with the healers in the middle, followed by layers of military and on the edge were the adventurers. They considered this to be the best way to defend themselves.

Since there was no sign from the adults that were usually watching from the distance, they decided to separate into two groups. A small group would slowly go away trying to get to the caravan and bring back help while the ones staying behind will distract the predators, giving them time to get away unnoticed, but as they started walking the unusual gurma faced them and growled. This made the rest focus on the small group of humans and they soon started walking towards them.

Seeing that, Kayro realised that the only way to get help was in danger, so he decided to act by himself. The boy told the ones next to him that he will try to act as a decoy and get the attention of all the predators. Initially they tried to convince him out of this plan, but soon had to admit that this was the only way, especially since Kayro seemed to be better prepared than they were and probably the only one brave or crazy enough to act by himself.

After being frozen for a few seconds, he slowly started moving in the opposite direction of the small group which confused the gurmas. They never expected prey to get closer to them, so there was no reaction except turning to face him. Even the abnormal beast was surprised my his actions and started growling, which made all the small ones go after him.

The boy knew that going back to the group would be impossible now, so he took out his short sword and shield. To make sure the predators will not ignore him and try to chase after the small group again he started making noise by banging them against each other.

The leader of the gurma groups growled again and one of the small ones went after Kayro. Despite being afraid, he stood his ground and blocked its claws as it started attacking him. This confused the animal and gave the boy enough time to stick his sword in its neck. Although he managed to kill it, getting the sword out was harder than expected, so while he desperately tried to pull it out, another gurma came at him. With just a meter between them left, the animal was struck by three arrows, one of them dealing a lethal injury.

As the trainees were cheering, the abnormal gurma growled loudly sending the four remaining small ones to the large group. Having their shield ready proved very useful and the trainees only had some small scratches after repeated attacks. Inside the circle, the healers were getting their tools and mixtures ready to treat the wounded, but fortunately none needed that.

With the distance being too small, the military trainees could not use their bows anymore, so the only way they could help was by having their shields ready and changing with the adventurers from time to time, but no one could deal a killing blow to the animals.

After getting back his short sword, Kayro decided to reunite with the others, since the small group managed to get away. It proved to be more difficult than he imagined, but soon he was standing next to the others helping them to defend the ones inside the circle.

For a few minutes the adventurers and military trainees kept changing places in order not to get too tired, but that was all they could do. During this time, the boy started talking to the others and they came up with a plan that was voted as the best choice they have to survive. According to it, the remaining ten adventurers will form a group that will keep distracting the gurmas and hopefully kill them, while the others will start backing up, far enough to be able to shoot arrows.

The plan was working and while being undecided which group to go after, one of the gurmas had a short spear going through its head. The reaction of the rest was quick and in just a few seconds, two of the adventurers couldn't stand up anymore. The wounds were not very deep, but still they were out of the fight. Luckily, at the same time arrows started flying and another gurma was now fatally injured.

Seeing that, the adventurers gained confidence and now six of them were attacking the animals while two of them carried the injured to the main group so they can be treated. A few minutes later, the remaining two small gurmas were dead. One was hit by five arrows with the last one piercing its heart, while the second got stabbed by short swords and spears multiple times until it stopped moving.

Being the only one left, the abnormal beast started growling louder and louder and it seemed like it went mad. Soon it started charging towards the main group and after a very high jump that surprised everyone, it landed between them.

Before the trainees managed to get away, two of the healers were injured. Having four people to care for made the group split into two which made them easier targets.

As soon as he saw the healers being attacked, Kayro forgot about everything and started rushing by himself madly. With Alyssa being in danger, he forgot about anything else and just went after the beast. His actions surprised it and gave everyone time to start running away. His blows with the short sword were landing on the abnormal gurma, but its hide seemed a lot thicker than the small ones had, so he was just scratching it. In less than a minute, his shield was thrown away after receiving a very hard attack from the animal's claws and as it landed it broke into pieces.

The boy immediately took out his short spear and used both weapons for attacking and defending at the same time. Initially he was doing well and if that was one of the normal animals it would certainly be dead by now, but the one in front of him only had a few scratches. As he was fighting it, the adventurers that were unhurt, along with a small group of military trainees and Alyssa standing in the middle of the circle they made, came to help him.

Everyone else started going very fast towards the caravan where the adventurers and the head instructor from Tower Town Camp were. As soon as he saw that most people managed to escape and now he had help, Kayro gained more confidence that, not only they will survive, but also take down this ferocious beast in front of him.

Unfortunately, in less than two minutes, half of the people around him was down as the animal seemed to get enraged. He shouted at the ones that were left standing to take the wounded in different directions and hide while he will do his best to keep there long enough for them to be safe. The plan worked in his favour for a short time, but soon both his short sword and short spear were easily flicked away by the gurma's huge claws.

Even without a weapon, the boy decided to stand in its way even with the price of his life. The abnormal beast pounced on him pinning him easily to the ground and, to his surprise, instead of killing him straight away, it just stared in his eyes and growled.

When it tried to bite him, Kayro punched its teeth which saved his life, but also left his hands bloodied. Before it could try to bite him again, the gurma was struck by arrows, but they broke as soon as hitting its body. Alyssa was the one shooting them from inside a hollow in a tree trunk and while she managed to save him, also made the animal go after her.

Seeing the beast run towards his beloved friend gave the boy strength and he started chasing it and shouting to get its attention, but there was no reaction. After getting close to the girl, it started walking slowly which gave him enough time to get close enough to kick it, which probably hurt him more. A few seconds later he was the one receiving and attack which sent him away.

As the strange gurma was trying to reach Alyssa inside the hollow of the tree trunk, Kayro, who barely had any energy left, kept swinging his fist from the distance in the predator's direction. Suddenly he had a strange feeling as if something was happening inside his body. Moments later, blades started flying from his bloodied hands towards the animal's back which made it turn away from the girl. Despite more and more blades hitting it, the gurma slowly started getting close to the boy. They both noticed that there was not much damage done by those, so the beast got confident and started running. After a few seconds, Kayro had a huge paw on his chest, pinning him to the ground, but he was still swinging his fists. Seeing how helpless he was, the feline decided to play with him, torturing his prey before the kill, by repeatedly striking at his chest with her claws, but the vest that the boy was wearing as a reminder of the people who trained him as a child protected him from most of the damage.

Each strike made Kayro angrier and soon his mind went into rage and his first instinct was to catch the paw and bite it really hard and then fainted for a moment. Seeing him down made the gurma think he is nearly dead and it decided to go after Alyssa again. With the beast distracting itself, the boy had enough time to get back on his feet. He had a strange sensation like an aura surrounded his body, and then he started growing fangs and claws which scared him, but at the same time made him feel stronger. While the boy was experiencing these changes, the gurma was making its way to the girl trying to kill her quickly.

Kayro saw its intention and despite his blood feeling like it was boiling, he started running to save his friend. As he was doing that, he realised for the first time that his feelings for Alyssa are stronger than he thought and now he saw her as a potential partner. For some reason his body started moving even faster than before, and to his and the gurma's surprise he ended up blocking the animal's way.

Seeing how confident the boy was, the beast started to get angrier and soon a shadow-like aura surrounded its body. That made it look a few time scarier than before and it seemed a lot stronger as well, but he decided to protect his friend with the price of his life.

As the gurma started it's attack he took a grappling position and waited for the right moment to catch it with his arms, but the feline was too stronger now and with a hit from its paw and claws the boy was sent a few meters away, exactly in front of the tree where the girl was. Anger made Kayro go berserk for a moment and he quickly got up waiting for the animal to strike, only this time he was in an attack position, seeing that as the best way of defending in this case.

Seconds later the abnormal animal started running towards him, making the boy the boy feel just like a cornered animal. That made him growl and at that moment his instincts kicked in harder than before, making his fangs and claws grow even bigger. He grabbed the feline as it leaped and somehow managed to pin it on the ground slashing its exposed belly. Still the fight was not over, as the gurma managed to somehow throw him away which made him lose conscience for a few moments.

While he was knocked out, the animal tried to get the girl again thinking that this time he was surely dead, but that proved to be a big mistake. After getting on his feet, Kayro let out a growl even louder than before and started running towards the gurma leaping on its back before it got the chance to react. From there, he started punching it head which made the animal dizzy long enough for him to jump in front of it.

Another growl from the boy made the beast feel like prey now and while he was trying to punch with all his might, the blood on his hand formed a huge spike that went through the gurma's skull. After the spike melted, the boy kicked the feline very hard and his instincts made him bite its neck to make sure it is dead.

Kayro could hear the sound of blood moving after sinking his teeth in, but he wasn't sure if that is his blood or the beast's. His body suddenly felt stronger than ever despite all the damage it took during the fight and with the gurma being dead he started walking towards the hollowed trunk to check on his friend, but the blood loss made the boy collapse half way there.

Realising that the fight was over, Alyssa started running to see what happened to him. Seeing him like that she started looking inside her healer bag for something to help him heal. After cleaning some of the blood that was covering his body, she understood that the boy was in grave danger and noting in the bag could really help, but her strong feelings getting more intense by the moment made her trigger a strange hidden magic inside her body and somehow she started healing his wounds. After nearly half an hour she had to stop as the magic was making her feel very tired and she didn't want to pass out in the middle of the forest, especially since no one was around to help.

She remembered that there was a cave nearby and dragged him inside where she could apply some healing paste on the wounds that the magic didn't close. As a healer, she always carried lots of bandages, twine, a needle and the healing paste, so the boy's remaining wounds were sewn and wrapped quickly, giving her time to collect some leaves to make a bed and some wood to make a fire. The cave was still too cold even after doing that, so she decided to use the clothes they were wearing as cover while she laid naked next to him to keep his body warm. Being very tired she fell asleep quickly, but not before kissing his lips for the first time.

The next morning, Kayro woke up before her and blushed after realising they were naked next to each other. Since he was nearly fully healed and the girl was deep asleep, he dressed up and went to the gurma's body to get some meat for breakfast. Predator meat was not that tasty, but it was their best option for an easy meal. After getting there, he was amazed at the size of the beast, a thing he didn't really notice while fighting, but he quickly found a way to drag its body back to the cave.

Before Alyssa woke up, the boy butchered the carcass using his experience from when he trained as a hunter and butcher, making sure to keep the pelt, fangs, claws and bones in good quality while taking the meat off. As the girl opened her eyes she saw him cooking the meat and after realising that she was still naked, so she shouted and made him turn around until she can get dressed. A few moments later she joined him near the fire with her face being all red from embarrassment and she barely managed to find the courage to talk.

"I see that you are feeling very well despite everything that happened last night. Please make sure that you don't move too much to avoid breaking the twine I used to sew them and open them again."

"Thank you for your concern, but I only have some scars left. By the way, how did you manage to heal them so well? I'm certain that stitches, healing paste and bandages cannot be this effective."

"Seeing you down, barely breathing, bloody all over triggered something in my body and a blue light started coming out of my hands. Soon it was all over your body and started closing some of the wounds."

"Wow! That's amazing! You're amazing! I didn't know that was even possible, but I guess that this planet has a lot more surprises for us."

"I can say the same thing about you killing that horrific beast. There were a few times when I thought you are dead for sure, but somehow you managed to get up and fight it again."

"Honestly, I was ready to die from the moment the attack started, but I wanted to make sure that as many people as possible will survive, so I had to fight, otherwise all that fighting training I did would mean nothing."

"Weren't you scared?"

"I was very scared, but my biggest fear last night was losing you."

As he finished saying that, Kayro kissed her passionately and the girl responded the same way. The feelings they had for some time were out in the open now, and with no sign of anyone around they went inside the cave where they made love. They were almost eighteen years old now, with no experience, except some fragments of memories from their past lives, but the passion between them was very intense.

Both felt a little ashamed when it was over and remained silent for some time, until the boy started talking about what they should do next.

"I'm sure that the best thing we can do now is wait here and surely the adventurers will find us soon. While I was training they told us that this is the best thing to do in case people end up running in all directions."

"Are we going to be all right until then? Do you think any of those beasts might still be around?"

"From what I've read and heard about gurmas, they never act this way. Even if there are a few in the same area, they never attack together. I'm sure that the strange one was controlling the small ones somehow. Chances are that most animals including predators ran away last night considering how dangerous the group that came after us was."

"Hopefully you are right" said the girl before kissing him again.

A few hours later, Kayro and Alyssa started hearing people shouting their names and quickly answered. A big group led by the head instructor from Tower Town Camp reached their cave in minutes. After getting back to the caravan, they found out that everyone survived, but some had some really bad wounds.

All this time the boy carried a big pack on his back and only now, after finding everyone and reaching a safe place, the head instructor noticed.

"What is that thing that you are carrying?"

"I took the big gurma apart and kept everything I could as a trophy. I want to take them home with me and use them to craft some items."

"You actually killed it? How did you manage to do that? The other trainees described the beast to us and we were afraid it might still be around and come back after dark."

Kayro and Alyssa both started telling everyone about what they remembered from the fight and all people around started cheering and congratulating them. To take on a normal gurma and survive was hard enough, but to kill an abnormal beast like that seemed impossible, but after the boy opened the pack on his back, the huge skull and hide were proof that it was dead.

After finishing their story about killing the feline and how come they looked unhurt, everyone was stunned. Even the most experienced adventurer in the group had no words, but knowing about the magic planet Xorbia, all agreed that it was possible to gain this kind of power.

A few days later, after all trainees were treated and even the most injured were ready to be moved, the caravan left the Great Forest behind and headed back to Training Camp. The journey was quiet with everyone trying to rest as much as possible after a night they will never be able to forget even if they wanted.

All the trainees in the sixth year along with some of the instructors from all four camps getting ready to hold a graduation ceremony in Tower Camp, as soon as the group that took the Test of Survival was back. Since one of the adventurers came back earlier, everyone found out about what happened in the Great Forest, including some of the Elders who came to see the ceremony.

After the group finally reached their destination, everyone started cheering and applauding for them, including Monta and Zoss who couldn't wait to check on their trainees, especially Kayro after hearing how he managed to slay the abnormal beast.

As soon as they had the chance, they took the boy away to have a private talk. They both shook his hand and gave him a hug and then a quick conversation started.

"As happy as we are to see you, there are also some bad news you need to hear. The Elders wish to talk to you and Alyssa in order to find out more about the magic you both claimed to use" said Monta.

"If it seems like something unusual for us, they seemed to think of it like being something normal. Just tell them everything you remember and try not get them angry. They already seem displeased with the fact that the Test of Survival was a success and we can now train adventurers and explorers without having to hide anymore" added Zoss.

"Thank you for telling me and most of all for the chance to train. Without that, I would probably be dead in a situation like that."

"As useful as the training was when it came to the normal gurmas, what happened with the big one was all down to you being able to use magic or whatever that was. I just hope it doesn't get you into trouble with the Elders" said the head instructor.

"Even if it does, there is nothing to be done. What is in the past cannot be changed."

Both Monta and Zoss agreed with the boy and after congratulating him again, they wished him good luck at the meeting with the Elders.

A few hours later, the ceremony was over and the sixth year trainees were preparing to go to their own camp for a last day before going back to their communities. Just as the counsellor and head instructor told the boy, an aid of the Elders summoned both him and Alyssa to a meeting, before leaving Tower Camp.

They were taken to an office and after being questioned about everything that happened, one of the Elders told them that they have one month to spend with their parents before they will have to undergo some special training in a location that will be later revealed to them.

Hearing that made Kayro and Alyssa unhappy, but they had no visible reaction trying to avoid angering anyone, just as they were told by the instructors. As soon as they could leave, they went to take their backpacks and in Kayro's case the big pack which contained the remains of the abnormal gurma.

Unfortunately, by the time the meeting was finished, everything was taken away under orders from the Elders with only some smaller bones and the hide being left behind for him. Despite being angry about that, he knew there was no point in asking for the items to be returned, so he quickly joined the caravan that took them to Glade Camp.

On the last day he talked to Zoss and Monta about what happened the day before and they both looked worried.

"I heard that there might be some secret training place on the Ardian Continent, but I thought it was only a rumour. I honestly have no idea where it might be or what exactly you will do there, but try to be careful. When it comes to what they took from you, it's best to forget about it. In fact, you were lucky they allowed you to take anything" the head instructor said.

"Despite going to an unknown place, please try to keep calm at all times and don't show them you are afraid or angry. I know it will be hard to stop yourself from showing your real feeling, but until you know if it's safe or not, just assume the worst" added the counsellor.

"Thank you both for the advice and most of all for helping me become someone that my parents can be proud of. I will try to send you the information about the secret training place if I can."

After finishing their conversation, Kayro went to see Alyssa. He told her everything the instructors said while they took a last walk in the Glade Camp Park and as the sun was ready to set, they went to their rooms to get everything ready for next morning when they finally get to go back to their parents.

Before the caravan left, Monta joined by Zoss, came to congratulate all the sixth year trainees for the last time and wish them a long and healthy life.

On their way back, Alyssa and Kayro travelled together and revealed to everyone that they were now a couple. No one was really surprised by that, because they spent a lot of time together all these year, but everyone cheered and shouted after hearing the news.

A few minutes later, it was total quiet again and that is how it stayed until the caravan got back to Glade Village.

# Chapter 3

# Blood bonds and Mage Island

## Last month in Glade Village – the truth is finally revealed

Even though six years had passed, the village looked just like when they left to Training Camp, but somehow smaller at the same time for Alyssa and Kayro. Maybe it felt like this because of their experience from the Test of Survival, or just because they went away as children and came back as young adults, but there was one thing they knew and that was they were happy to finally see their parents and home again after such a long time. Just as everyone started going their own way, the two of them kissed one more time and promised to wait until the next day to reveal their relationship together to their parents.

Since the exact day or hour of their arrival was not known, after getting home Kayro knocked on the door and surprised his parents. Despite the major changes that went on with his body and not seeing him for such a long time, Krysta and Klost immediately recognized him and hugged him tightly for a few minutes without saying anything.

They had no idea what happened during the Test of Survival since he couldn't send any letters, but they were speechless for some time after the boy told them the everything. They were happy about the man he became, but also very sad that he will only be home for a month before going to train again in a place from which he might not even be able to train. Still, unlike Zoss, they trusted the decision of the Elders and were happy to hear that their son was chosen by them for special training.

Since it was late, they decided to carry on with the conversation the next evening, so everyone went to sleep. The boy was very excited about being back and happy to see them again, that he barely slept. On top of that, he couldn't wait to tell them about him and Alyssa being together.

In the morning, after his parents left, he went to meet the girl and they visited the people who trained them in the past. Everyone was happy to see them after such a long time and congratulated them on both their graduation and their new relationship. After a few hours the couple went to the mill and revealed to Fargas that they are now together. Since he had no words initially, he chose to embrace them tightly. After a few minutes he admitted that he was expecting that to happen after seeing them so close as children and the fact that they will go together to get special training made him feel better.

Two hours later, Alyssa and Kayro went together to the boy's house and told his parents about the relationship as well. Same as Fargas, the confessed this was something they could imagine it was going to happen sooner or later, and just like the miller, knowing they will go together to train at the request of the Elders, made them happy.

For the rest of the evening the conversation focused on all the children experienced during Training Camp. As they got to the story about the last night of the Test of Survival, Krysta gasped.

"What is wrong mother? Did we say something that bothered you?" asked Kayro.

"You both just said that at some point, the beast had a shadow-like aura. That made me remember the night when my baby was taken away from me. There were some very fast moving shadows in the village that night. It made me think that this might be connected to those."

"That's right. Now I remember you telling me about that years ago. I had a feeling that made it look familiar, but I just couldn't remember where I heard about it before."

Klost intervened and told them that all of this can be just a coincidence. There were too many years apart from the incidents and also they took place on opposite sides of the Median Forests.

Everyone agreed with him and they chose to change the topic of the conversation. Since it was getting late, Kayro walked Alyssa to her house and then quickly came back, but what his mother said about that shadow-like aura was still on his mind.

After two weeks went by, a strange cloud could be seen over the Haunted Forest and the wind was bringing it to Glade Village. Since it was late, almost everyone was inside their houses, so they were not bothered by it as it passed through and went away. Less than an hour later, loud noises could be heard outside. That made Klost and his son get up from their chairs immediately to check what was happening.

As they looked through the window, there was not much to be seen, but the noises got louder with each passing second. While Klost took his shield and opened the door, Kayro went to his room to get the horbium short sword that he made in Training Camp. He wished he had it during the Test of Survival, but they were not allowed to bring weapons or tools, so he made himself new ones out of sparus. As he was getting out of the room, he heard Krysta shout:

"Klost, get back. It's the shadows again. Quickly, come inside."

As soon as he got back, they were all looking through the window and couldn't believe what they saw. A group of miskras was running around and the one leading, just like the gurma from the Test of Survival, was three times bigger and covered by a shadow-like aura.

They were not damaging anything, and since no one could be seen anywhere, they couldn't hurt anyone. They were making a lot of noise and a few minutes later vanished heading towards the Haunted Forest.

"Mother, father, I'm sorry, but I need you to close the door behind me and stay safe. This is too much to be just a coincidence and if there is any chance to get information about what happened to your son so many years ago, I need to go after them."

They knew it was dangerous, but the young man in front of them was not a child anymore and they were not so young anymore which meant going with him would only make it worse. After he got all the equipment made with his own hands during the last few years, along with the belt and vest made for him long time ago, Kayro stepped outside and started running in the direction where the miskras went.

Just as he got close to the Haunted Forest he saw the shadow-like beast going deeper inside and he chose to ignore everything he heard about the things that happened to people who enter it. As he was advancing, he could see green shapes of what could be called ghosts, but since none of them was getting closer, he continued his search.

A few minutes later he reached an open area that seemed to be scorched long time ago and while the smaller miskras disappeared, the abnormal one looked like it was waiting for him. He could clearly see the shadow-like aura that was covering the beast and it looked somehow more powerful than the one he saw on the gurma not so long ago. Something inside him was telling him that this miskra was stronger, but at the same time, he knew that killing it would not be a problem.

After pulling out his short sword and short spear, Kayro started running at the wild animal, but there was no sign that it will move or do anything. After swinging his sword he was sure that will wound it, but his attack was easily blocked by its tusks.

Even after that, he was still confident, and to the beast's surprise he put his weapons away. After focusing for nearly a minute, the young man managed to get out the claws that he grew during the fight with the abnormal gurma, but they were not as long as before. Despite the difference in length, Kayro started his attack and the miskra was now pushed back, barely being able to defend.

His moment of dominance was brief, because the massive animal decided to fight back. With visible anger in its eyes that looked red, just like the strange gurma had, it started using both horns and tusks to injure him, but there were no results, since the young man was simply blocking the attacks and seemed to get stronger with each passing second.

Soon the beast got angrier and pushed him back, making feel cornered with no chance to escape. As his instincts kicked in, Kayro growled, his claws got longer, the fangs appeared again, his blood felt like boiling and his rage was growing. Feeling stronger than before, he started pushing back the massive miskra which made him feel confident.

Forgetting about the weapons he had, he focused on using the claws and his feet to attack. The horbium boots proved to be very resistant and they inflicted some damage, but it was not as much as he expected. Still, in the next few minutes he managed to pin the miskra down and using his to bite its neck finally killed it.

Just like last month, after biting the gurma, he felt a surge of power go throughout his body. Somehow he felt stronger, so he decided to test this on a boulder that was close by, and to his surprise both the kicks and punches easily damaged it.

His mind started to calm down and he was thinking that in some way he managed to 'steal' this power away from the beast he killed earlier. That made him curious, so he decided to go back and check its lifeless body. When he was just a few steps away, a human figure with the shadow-like aura came out of nowhere and attacked him.

For some time it was easy to block the punches and kicks, but soon claws similar to the ones he could grow were being used against him. All he was able to do now was defend, because everything was happening so fast that he had no time to think about a plan to attack. In fact, even defending started to look harder as time passed.

At one point, feeling like a cornered animal, Kayro exploded with rage and felt like power was overflowing inside him. His claws grew longer and somehow stronger which allowed him to parry easier, but still that was not enough. Since there was no time to think of a solution to win the fight, he decided to abandon himself entirely to his instincts.

As soon as he did that, things started to change, with his speed and strength improving a lot. Not only that, but now he was able to dodge the attack that not so long made him struggle to defend. This didn't feel like being his limit, but he had no idea how exactly to break past them. Then, in a moment of pure rage, he growled and cut himself on the fists. Without realising it, he was now throwing small red blades like in the fight against the abnormal gurma.

When that happened, he was expecting his attacker to back down or at least be surprised, but the humanoid figure covered by a shadow-like aura was acting like nothing changed. He was forced to defend himself now, but that was something he could easily handle.

For a minute or two, it looked like a fight without a winner, but then things drastically changed. Kayro saw how his opponent's eyes turned crimson and a wave of power hit him. Following that, the attacker was driving him back just like in the beginning of the fight. As a reaction to that he used the claws to make cuts on the dorsal side of his forearms and the blood that was coming out turned into spikes. Even that was not enough to push his opponent away and that made the young man's anger and blood boil. Soon his own body was covered by the shadow-like aura and despite being scared, he could feel more powerful than ever.

After a minute of intense fighting, something unexpected happened. His opponent's aura was suddenly gone and the man that was now in front of him shouted:

"Enough!!!"

Kayro froze for a few seconds and his own aura disappeared.

"I apologise for pushing you this hard, but I wanted to test you and make sure that you inherited that aura. Now, if you have some time, I would like us to have a talk about who you really are."

Still being a little shocked from seeing a human in front of him now, instead of some creature, the young man could barely find his words.

"All right. Let's talk."

"First of all, let me introduce myself. I am R'mal and I was sent here to guard you, and, when the time comes, tell you who you really are."

"If you are supposed to protect me, why did you attack me?"

"I needed to confirm that you possess the demonic aura. This was a fight to test your power."

"Demonic aura? What is that? Have you been watching me for a long time? Where the hell were you when I was fighting the beast in the Great Forest and nearly died then?"

Kayro was so angry that he could barely stop asking questions and give the man a chance to answer them, but R'mal was patient and gave him time to calm down. It took some time, but now he could finally answer.

"I understand that you have so many questions, but we need to have this conversation with your adoptive parents present. What I have to tell you is related to them too, so I would prefer to do this when everyone is present."

"How do I know that you are not tricking me and you will not attack them as soon as you get the chance?"

"What I have to tell you will answer that as well, so let us go back to your house and continue this talk there. You should go in front since you cannot use your aura properly and I will follow making sure that no one can see me and that we are not being followed."

Kayro agreed despite having more questions to ask, but he realised that the sooner the can continue the conversation, the better for all involved. As he was walking back, he saw the spirits of the Haunted Forest again and didn't know if he should be afraid of them or not. He chose to ignore them, since getting answers to his questions was more important, so he rushed home.

As soon as he got back, he quickly told Klost and Krysta about R'mal and what happened in the Haunted Forest. Since they were having a guest and there was going to be a long conversation, the woman prepared some tea. They were warry about the man who would arrive shortly, but, as her husband said, if he wanted to hurt them, they would probably be dead already.

About ten minutes later, a human figure covered in a shadow-like aura was opening the door and coming inside. Even knowing about that, Krysta was still scared and angry at the same time, remembering the night her son, Larp, disappeared.

Seeing her reaction, R'mal quickly made his aura go away and apologised to everyone. He was invited to sit around the table and drink some tea and as soon as all of them sat down, he started talking.

"I know there are many questions you might want to ask, but to save us time, I will try to tell you everything from when it all began up to this point, and then happily answer if there is still something you wish to ask."

They all agreed to his proposition as it seemed to fastest way to obtain information, so the man began to tell his story.

"First of all I want you to know that I am here to protect all of you, since you are all blood related to the ones I serve. I know it might sound strange, but you will understand soon."

"What do you mean we are all blood related to someone you serve?" Klost asked.

"It's your son, sir. Your real son, Larp, is alive or at least he was last time I heard. What happened many years ago was a total failure on my race's behalf."

"Are you referring to the night he was stolen from me by you beasts?" Krysta shouted at him.

"I am afraid so, madam. You see, the plan was for the representatives of my race to come and convince you to move with him into the Blood Lands, our home which is basically the continent south of yours across the Infinite Sea, but everything went wrong that evening and they had to take him away quickly without harming anyone."

Hearing all of that made Krysta burst into tears just like the night her son was taken away if not worse. She was happy to hear that he is still alive, but her anger at herself for not being able to protect him resurfaced.

"I understand how we are related to the one you claim to serve, but how about Kayro? What does he have to do with our son?" asked Klost while comforting his wife.

"Larp is the boy's father and our princess, V'rca, is his mother. Nearly eighteen years ago they were coming to you to clarify everything and introduce you to your grandson, but again something went wrong, only this time it ended worse. As we were approaching your village we were attacked by a group that opposed the royal family, so a battle began inside what you call the Haunted Forest. Since we were overpowered, the princess had to hide her son in order to be able to fight. Unfortunately, the fight was lost and both her and your son were caught and imprisoned.

Seeing that the odds were against us, they told me to run away and protect the child, but when I got there he was gone. I tried looking for him in the vicinity, but there was no sign of the baby, so I decided to go and check what happened to the princess and her husband. By the time I got back to them, they were chained and transported back to be imprisoned along with a few of us that survived, so the only thing left for me was to look for their son.

As soon as the sun set, I could finally enter the village without being seen and found the boy at your house. Knowing who you were, I decided to stand back and watch over him from the distance, after all you seemed to love him even without knowing who he really was."

Finding out they were actually blood related made Kayro and his parents very happy and they got up embracing each other.

R'mal gave them some time to enjoy the moment quietly and after they sat down again, he was ready to continue his story. Before he got the chance to do that, Klost wished to get a question answered.

"You said that you are a different race. What do you mean by that?"

"We are demons. Or at least that is the name given to us. As far as I know, we used to be humans when everyone got to Xorbia, but some experiments changed us into what we are now. We kept most of the human features, but as Kayro can confirm, we are able to grow fangs, claws, cover ourselves in a shadow-like aura, called the demonic aura, and also steal abilities from strong opponents that we kill."

"That might explain why I am now able to see in the night after defeating the abnormal gurma. Speaking of that, where were you at that time if you are meant to protect me?" asked Kayro.

"Unfortunately, that incident is related to the ones that created my race, so I will start with that and then tell you what exactly happened during your Test of Survival."

"Very well. Carry on."

"As you might know, not all people wanted to stay together in the beginning and some of them ended in places where the magic of the planet had a high concentration and that gave them magic powers. Some can control the elements, while others can move things with their mind and who knows what else they might be able to do. Unfortunately, that was not enough for them and they started looking for new ways to increase their power and they found some mines all over the planet that contained crystals infused with magic that could do that.

Not knowing if there might be any side effects, the mages, began to experiment on humans. At first they only did it on a few by tricking them, but soon they would start to press people into doing that on a large scale. In our case, they made use a potion using the crystals, had us drink it and somehow merged us with spirits just like the ones you can find in the Haunted Forest.

With the new gained powers, and becoming a stronger race than humans, we managed to push them away, but even now they still imprison some of us to work in their mines all across Xorbia and they limit our possibility to travel."

"That sounds impossible. We never heard of anyone like you or the mages you talk about, and I lived a long life" said Klost.

"Well, it is exactly what they have been preventing you from finding out for years. You see, everyone in the Median Forests thinks that the ones leading you are the Elders and their Councils, but in fact, they are controlled by the mages. I know it might be too much to believe, but Kayro will get the chance to confirm that soon as he will be taken to meet them."

"What do you mean my son will meet them?" Krysta snapped at him.

"I am afraid they mistook his blood magic for ice magic. As he probably told you, he is able to turn his blood into blades and spike, at least for the moment, before he will master his powers, and after he killed the gurma controlled by the assassin they sent, they think he might be one of them."

"Assassin? What are you talking about? Our group was attacked by a pack of gurmas, there was no one there."

"If you remember, earlier, a group of miskras came to your village and the one you killed was abnormal, just like the gurma that you killed in the Great Forest. Well, it was abnormal because I used my blood magic to control it and get your attention. That is how the assassin was doing it during your Test of Survival."

"So why didn't you do anything? Why did you allow them to hurt me and the other trainees?"

"Because I was busy looking for the one controlling them. I was afraid he found out about you and came to kill you. Also, I have been watching you and seen you train which made me certain you can handle those lowly felines, including the abnormal one."

"Lowly? We barely survived?"

"Those are the weakest felines you could ever meet, I am sure you will find that out sooner or later considering your choice to become and explorer, well at least after convincing the mages that you are indeed one of them, but we will get back to that later.

Going back to what happened in the Great Forest, after I finally managed to find the assassin, I had to torture him to find out why he was attacking the trainees and it was all requested by the mages. Since people, just like you, are getting more curious about what's beyond the borders of the Median Forests, they came up with the plan and told the Elders to allow training adventurers and explorers with one condition, taking and passing the Test of Survival.

To make that impossible, they hired an assassin from my land knowing that we can control beasts and get him to hurt the trainees, making them look like the training was useless and that no one could ask for that again."

"Why would the Elders want to stop us from exploring outside the borders? I never heard my parents talk about such a thing" Krysta intervened.

"First of all, your Elders have no say in this, they are just doing what they are being ordered to. Secondly, from what I know, we are not the only ones who ended as experiments of the mages. There are other humans who ended up being used by them in their quest for obtaining more power, but we don't have much freedom of movement except inside the Blood Lands, so I cannot say for sure in what way the others were changed, but preventing anyone in the Median Forest from seeing the results is what protects them.

Just imagine if everyone knew about the mages and their power and also everything they put other humans through. I am sure you can agree that people will rise against them and losing control over you will leave them without important resources such as clothing, weapons, food, basically anything than can be produced in the Median Forests."

"If that is the case, then we cannot let Kayro meet them" said Klost.

"Especially now after finding out that all this time he was really our grandson" added Krysta.

"I partially agree to what you said, since my duty is to protect him, but there is a reason why he needs to train with them."

"You cannot be serious. What could be so important for us to risk his life?" Krysta snapped at him.

"As I said before due to the experiments, we became a new race and some years ago, one of the demons gained the ability to read the flow of magic, which is in fact part of the universe. While doing that, she could see that in the future, a boy will get not only our blood, but also the blood of mages. However, the accuracy of who will that be or when it will happen was uncertain. All the was clear is that he will have you blood Krysta and Klost.

Knowing that, the former royal family in the Blood Lands, sent an envoy to convince you to join us and live in our country along with your baby. As they were getting close to Glade Village, the envoy was attacked by the mages who have barriers in more places of the continent which can sense the presence of anyone or anything passing through them. The Median Forests borders are actually part of those barriers and that is how they knew we were coming. During the attack, the former king was badly injured, but the queen managed to run away with her personal guard and steal the baby from you. She was ashamed for having to do that, but it was the only way to get him. As a distraction, she had other members cause a disturbance in the village and even take some other children which they released safely."

"I remember that other children went missing, but they were found soon after the search groups went out looking for them" Krysta said.

"They did their best not to harm anyone and since there was no time to talk to the two of you, the only solution not to get you involved was stealing Larp. To avoid the fight, the queen ran through the Haunted Forest and her guard gave a signal to the ones involved in the battle with the mages the objective of our visit here was achieved.

Since the mages thought we were planning to attack Glade Village, they allowed us to run away. More than that, they made sure no clues of our existence or theirs were left behind by burning the ground where the battle took place, turning all the victims into ashes."

"So what happened then? Was out son the baby you were looking for?" asked Klost.

"For some time that is what we believed, because usually both the demonic and mage power awaken when an individual turns eighteen. While waiting for Larp to get to that age, the royal family made sure he was treated well, so he was raised and trained as if he was their son. After he completely healed, the king tried to get to you a few times, but the mages were waiting at the border and the members of each group that was supposed to come to you was either imprisoned or killed, which made him give up on that idea.

As years passed Larp became one of our most skilled fighters and despite princess V'rca being older than him they ended up having feelings for each other, but after his nineteenth birthday we were sure that he is not the one from the so called prophecy. At the request of the king he went through some trials for a year, but no magic or demonic powers surfaced.

Unfortunately, the ones opposing the monarchy used this to try and make the royal family give up on the throne. They wished to change to Councils of Elders like you have in the Median Forests, but the king made a bold decision. Seeing that his daughter and your son were in love, he allowed them to get married and, during the ceremony, as they exchanged blood, Larp became part demon.

With half of the prophecy being true, he asked his subjects to be patient and surely soon everything will turn out just like that woman saw years ago. And they did, but that was only for a year when everything in the Blood Lands changed.

Since many years had passed from the time Larp was taken and Kayro was just born, princess V'rca convinced the king to allow them to visit Glade Village so you can meet your grandson, of course with their guard, which I was part of, joining them as they travel across the border.

Initially, everything seemed peaceful, there was no sign of the mages, but as soon as we got to the Haunted Forest things changed. Not only did we get ambushed by the mages, but half of the royal guard turned against us. Later I found out that at the same time, the ones opposing the monarchy were working with the mages to being down the king and his family and take the power for themselves. Apparently it was planned for years, but with the princess and part of the royal guard gone, it was the best moment for them to act.

Seeing that the fight was going against us, princess V'rca decided to quickly hide her son so she can join the battle since she was one of the strongest fighters just like her husband. We managed to keep both mages and demons busy while she did that, but even with her help, after she returned, we were slowly losing. Knowing that no one will bother with a guard, they sent me to take their baby and run as far away as possible, making sure at least he will survive.

As I told you earlier, when I got to the place she used to hide him, there was no sign of Kayro. After quickly searching for him on a two kilometres radius without any clues about his whereabouts, I was certain that someone from the village found him and took him away.

Being covered in blood and with him being away from the battle, I decided to go and check how things were going on, but it was too late for me to do anything. Larp and V'rca were already in chains along with a few of the survivors, while the demons and mages who attacked us were mocking them as they were being thrown into metal cages.

Seeing that, I stayed hidden as the last order I received was to protect the baby, and as they went towards the Infinite Sea, I went to the Glade Creek to clean myself up and start looking for Kayro again to make sure he was safe. After nightfall, I covered myself in the demonic aura since it makes me faster and at the same time harder to see and sneaked inside the village.

It was easy to find him here since your house is close to the eastern entrance and seeing him in Krysta's arms made me think that watching what happens next from the distance was the best way to protect him. I was afraid that the mages might come look for him, but I guess no one cared about a baby.

Since the area where the battle took places was burned away by the mages, along with the bodies of those who died, they probably didn't know that I survived, so I dug myself a hideout inside the Haunted Forest in order to be close to the village and I have been around watching from the distance, making sure he is well."

"What about my parents? Where are they? Are they still alive?" Kayro asked.

"They were taken to a mining prison on the Blood Lands territory, and last time I had news from there they were alive. One of the royal guards that stayed behind with the king pretended to join the uprising so he is able to send me messages from time to time and go to the prison once every six months."

"Would we be able to rescue them?"

"Unfortunately as we are now and with only the two of us, there is no chance. This is one of the reasons why you need to train with the mages."

"How will that help? I am not even sure I have any power like that. And what about my demonic power? Are they not enough if I start training them?"

"Honestly, no. We will both get killed as soon as we cross the border. Your demonic power is unique, but it is only part of the solution. After hearing what happened in the Great Forest and seeing you fight in the Haunted Forest, I realised that the woman who could read the flow of magic was not wrong. Only instead of your father, you were the one whose birth she felt at that time. The blood blades and blood spikes are a combination of demonic and magic power and I am sure that is just a small sample what you are really capable of doing."

"Can't you start training me now so I can get stronger faster?"

"That would be a wrong step in you reaching your true potential. Basically, if your demonic power gets too strong, you will end up using it when training with the mages and that will get you killed or imprisoned. What I can do is show you how to hold it back so you can use just the magic. You see, the blades and spikes are actually ice and you should be able to make them without using your blood. They will not be as strong, but that should allow you to get to Mage Island."

"Mage Island? What is that?" Klost asked.

"It's an island situated in the middle of the Grand Lake. Apparently that is where all mages from the Ardian Continent live."

"And how come the fishermen from Port Town haven't seen it in so many years?"

"As I said before, the mages have many powers, including making barriers. Just like they have one for detection on the borders of the Median Forests, they have one around their island which makes it invisible from the outside."

"So if they are that powerful, is it wise for us to send Kayro there?" asked Krysta.

"I wouldn't say it's wise, but at the moment, he is our only choice. They are the only ones who can train his magic powers. Being able to combine them with the ones given by his demon blood, will make him on of the most known powerful beings on the planet. More than that, he will be able to pass as a demon or as a mage and that will be very useful when the time will come to release his parents."

"Mother, father, or should I say grandmother and grandfather, I think that R'mal is right and this might be the only way to get them out. I don't remember them, but they are my parents and I cannot allow them to stay imprisoned for life."

Klost and Krysta could see that the child who left for Training Camp six years ago, was now quickly becoming a man and they couldn't be any prouder. Since he already made a choice, they agreed that the only thing to do now was offer their support.

R'mal started teaching Kayro how to suppress his demonic power and after a week, the boy was able to make ice blades without having to cut himself and use blood. They were not as powerful as before, but still it was enough to earn him a place to train on Mage Island.

They were only able to do this after nightfall in the Haunted Forest, since they needed to avoid anyone finding out about it, so that gave them only a little time every day. As they agreed in the beginning, despite hating to keep secrets from his girlfriend, Kayro didn't tell Alyssa about anything that happened after that evening.

Since everyone was put to a deep sleep, by the cloud R'mal created on the evening when the miskras came into the village, including the militia that were patrolling and their howlers, there were no witnesses to what happened and that made it easy to keep the secret.

Kayro found out from him that this was the same way the adults were put to sleep in the Great Forest during the Test of Survival, making it impossible for them to come to the aid of the trainees, before the gurmas attacked. He was hoping that one day he can learn how to do that, but that will have to wait until he comes back from Mage Island.

On the last day of the month R'mal met with the family again to talk about his plans for the time when the young man will be away.

"Since there might be barriers of detection along the Grand Lake, the best thing I can do is stay here and make sure your grandparents are safe. If something goes wrong I promise to take them away to a safe place, but hopefully that will not be the case."

"I agree. Knowing they have someone to protect them will help me focus on my goal of learning and practising magic."

"I know it is hard for you not to tell Alyssa about your origins and power, but please try to wait until you get back or there is no other choice. Chances are that despite her feelings she might get scared and reveal your true identity to the mages and that is the last thing that you want, since it will put the both of you in danger."

"I understand. I hate myself for doing that, but I have done something similar in the past to protect her."

"And remember that you don't need to become the best mage, so try not to push yourself and reveal your demonic power, especially not your aura. Just learning the basics and testing how far you can get should be enough."

"I will do my best, thank you again for showing me how to suppress it."

"Sir, madam, before I leave, if you ever need my assistance leave a lamp next to a window all night and I will come to you as soon as possible, without making my presence known."

Krysta and Klost thanked him as he was leaving and then started talking to their son on his last night home. Part of them was still worried about what might happen, another part was hoping that R'mal was exaggerating and part of them trusted that their grandson will be able to succeed.

The next morning they said their goodbyes to both Kayro and Alyssa and waited in one place until the caravan that was taking them to Tower Town couldn't be seen anymore.

It took three days for them to get close to their destination and the sight in front of them was shocking. They heard, learned, seen images of it, but nothing could describe the greatness of the town. As the access gate opened, it seemed like something that came out of a fairy tale to them. Lots of tall houses, shops and people were all around them and as they were getting closer to the centre it only got more crowded.

It took one hour to reach the great hall where the Council of Elders was holding meetings and they were glad to finally be able to stretch their legs. Getting down from the cart they couldn't help but feel small when looking at such a dominant building. Remembering his training as a builder, Kayro tried to imagine the effort and numbers it took to build the town and everything inside it. More than that, he was surprised about the details that turned the stone from something rough into something as beautiful as the view in front of him.

Just like him, Alyssa was amazed by everything around, which made her wish that one day she might move from Glade Village and live here. Before today this was not something she might think possible, but that is just how imposing Tower Town was.

Minutes later a man came out and escorted them into a massive meeting room where Elders from all four communities were waiting. Aside from them, there were three other people in the room and one of them was the first one to talk.

"Children, it is nice to meet you. We are here to confirm if what we were told about what happened during the Test of Survival was true, so we prepared a test for each one to demonstrate your abilities. You don't have to be afraid and we understand if you cannot use your power as you did at that time, but we have to see a sample of it in order for you to come with us to the location of the next training."

Kayro and Alyssa confirmed that they understood and they were encouraging each other before the tests. First to be tested was the young man and his goal was use his skill on a training dummy that was brought to the room. With the pressure of hiding his demonic power, he froze for a few seconds, but after concentrating they way R'mal showed him, he was able to throw ice blades towards the target. Despite only a few of them hitting the target, everyone was impressed.

It was now the young woman's turn and as a test one of the three unknown men used a dagger to cut his hand before asking the girl to demonstrate her power. It took a few seconds, but the blue light started coming out of her hands healing the cut very fast.

"I guess that settles it. We will leave for Port Town in one hour. Until then we have prepared a meal for you to enjoy while we finish our meeting."

Kayro and Alyssa were taken to another meeting room and offered a delicious meal along with juice, syrup and one of the alcoholic beverages they learned about in the past. It was not the first time trying it, but this one seemed a lot different and with a more pleasant taste than what they had before.

As soon as the meeting between the Elders and the three men was over, they were invited to join the caravan that will soon leave from Tower Town. In less than an hour they arrived at the dock where the boat taking them to Port Town was waiting. Just like they learned during Training Camp, this was the only way to reach the town between the mountains, or at least the safe way.

It took them two days to reach their destination and, from what the crew told them, they were lucky not to feel any sign of sickness. Despite not being as imposing as Tower Town, Port Town was still greater than Glade Village. Unfortunately they didn't get the chance to visit it since they only stopped to change to a bigger boat.

"You will definitely see it after your training is over children, but for now we have somewhere else to go" the man who cut his hand during their trial said.

After another two days, what R'mal told Kayro and his parents about the barrier who made Mage Island invisible from the outside, was confirmed. Both the young man and his girlfriend were shocked when out of nowhere an island appeared in front of them.

Their boat stopped at a dock that was very small and quiet compared to the one from Tower Town and a cart was waiting to take them to their next step of the journey. After a few hours, they reached a small pier where a small boat was waiting to take them to their final destination, which was the Mage Institute, a complex of buildings built on a small island situated on the lake at the centre of Mage Island.

"Here we are, children. The place which will be your home for the next two or three years, maybe even for longer. As you will see, there will be mages of all ages and with different abilities" the man whose hand Alyssa had to heal said.

"Since we are finally here, let me introduce myself. I am Ghilod and just like the young lady, I have the power to heal. The ones that we travelled with are Lurmand, the grandmaster mage of the institute" he said while pointing at the man who stayed quiet all this time, "and Frigus, our best ice mage" said Ghilod while pointing at the man who spoke first in the meeting room from Tower Town.

Kayro and Alyssa bowed their heads as a sign of respect and then they were taken to the living quarters where a room will be assigned to each of them.

As soon as that was done, Ghilod told them that he will become the young woman's counsellor, while Frigus will be the young man's.

## Mage Island and the Mage Institute

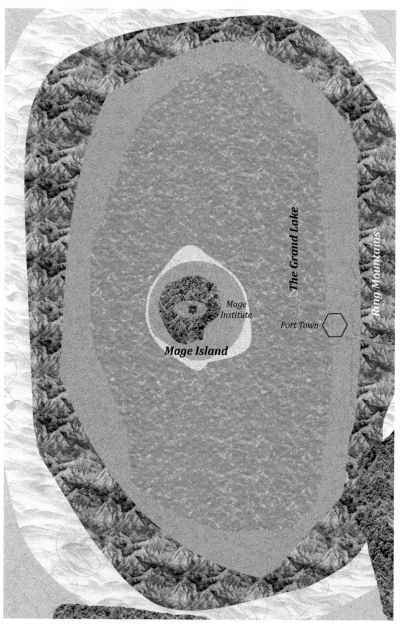

*Map of the Mage Island as it was known to Kayro at that time*

An hour after the mage left, a man that looked just a little older than them, came to take Alyssa and Kayro on a tour of the Mage Institute at the request of the master mage.

"Welcome! I am Sidius, a fire mage, and I was sent to show you around. Tomorrow morning you will meet your counsellor and they will give you the schedule that was prepared for both of you for this year."

After the introductions were over, he took his time to give them details about each building they passed and as soon as the tour was over, he excused himself and went back to his room.

While Kayro was happy to see the enormous library and the training rooms where he could train his fighting skills as well as his body, Alyssa was impressed by how clean everything was, but the greenhouses impressed her the most. Both of them were happy to see that even here they had a small park where they could go for a walk and talk about how their day went on, just like they did during Training Camp.

After hugging and kissing each other, they went to their rooms and started writing letters for their parents. They were told not to give any information about where they are and who and what abilities the people around them had, which didn't leave much to write about, but they still managed to write a few pages, especially about how great Tower Town was.

The following morning, Kayro had meeting with his counsellor, Frigus, who told him that the first day of the week will be focused on answering some of the questions the new trainees have and for the next six they will be tested to check if they possess other powers apart from the one which got them recruited.

"When did the mages start living on this Island, master Frigus?" the young man asked.

"We are not certain of that, but what I do know is that the Institute was built nearly one hundred years ago, so probably the first mages got here a few years before that" the man replied.

"Are we using only the grounds of the Institute for training?"

"Of course not. Most of the novices cannot properly control their power, so you will only be taught theory here. When it comes to practice, we have the Mage Island divided for different abilities and even a few areas where wild beasts are allowed to roam."

"Are we going to fight those beasts, master?"

"In time you will. But there are a lot of steps before that. First you will need to learn the theory about your ability or abilities, then it's time to practice against non-moving targets, followed by a test against other mages when you must prove your fighting skills and only then the trainees will be tested against the beasts."

"Are these animals that dangerous that you need a group to fight them?"

"I think that, based on the experience that you have from the gurma attack in the Great Forest, you should know just how dangerous animals can be. Since we have barriers preventing them from leaving their areas, they are now acting like it's their territory. They only allow beings that pose no threat to them to live there."

"Does that mean that only one species of predators is left?"

"If we didn't separate the predators, that would probably be the case."

"That means there are areas all over Mage Island which these beasts see as their territory. Are the barriers that strong to hold them inside?"

"They never failed. The magic that holds them in place is as strong as the one which makes the entire island invisible."

"Earlier you mentioned testing our fighting skills, does that mean we can use weapons?"

"I'm afraid that is not allowed. Since you are getting trained as mages, you will need to prove use your powers in order to succeed, but you are allowed to wear any armour you wish. In fact, some we have an entire department who studies and creates magic armour."

"Is that even possible, master Frigus?"

"Lots of things are possible in this world. Who knows maybe you might even be able to imbue your magic into armour as well."

"Speaking of this world, no one was able or allowed to tell me exactly how humans got here and why do we keep seeing memories from our past lives."

"I'm afraid you will first need to prove yourself worthy to receive that information. Only after you become a full mage, by joining a group and defeating at least one type of beast that lives on Mage Island, will anyone be allowed to share that information with you."

"I understand, then I must work hard to develop my powers."

The conversation lasted for another hour and then the ice mage took the trainee for a walk around Mage Institute. It was basically a tour like Sidius gave him and Alyssa the day before, only this time there were a lot more details.

After nine hours passed, Kayro was happy that he got the chance to find out some of the things that Frigus was allowed to tell him, but this was still not enough. There were too many questions left unanswered, some which he didn't even dare to ask, and great steps to take in his training before being allowed to get the information.

Just as they planned in the morning, he went to meet Alyssa and then walked around the small park talking about what they learned from their counsellors. Since the girl was not as curious as him, she barely had any information that might answer his questions, but seeing how happy she was about training here made him forget about everything.

For the rest of the week both of them were tested to see if any other powers might surface. While Kayro proved to be able to control water and air, just as Frigus expected, the young woman didn't show any sign of having any other ability than healing, but she was able to take that one step higher than she did in the Great Forest no so long ago.

After a month spent at the Mage Institute, not only did he learn the basic theory related to all three of his elements, but Kayro was also able to improve his ability to control them. At the same time, since she only had one power, Alyssa was able to use her healing power for a longer time and close wounds that she could barely attempt to heal before.

Three months later, it was time for the young man to finally test his fighting skills against other mages. With the counsellors acting as witnesses and referees at the same time, and all healers present, to quickly take care of any injury and test their skill this way, random battles were held for a week.

On the first day, each of the trainees was asked to use only the power they feel more confident about and it proved difficult for Kayro. With each of the elements that he was able to use, he hit the same wall as he did during Training Camp while learning the roles, which was the fact that he could only get above average, never being able to fully master it.

Despite that, the following day, when everyone was able to use all elements, he proved once again that being a jack of all trades can pay off. Still, this was not enough to defeat trainees that had more experience and more than one power, so he decided that after the week of battles was over, he must go to the library and find new ways to take his magic fighting skills at least one step higher. After all there were a lot of questions that he needed answers to, and becoming a true mage was the only way to get them.

At the end of the week, the young man was happy about his overall results. Even Frigus congratulated him on being able not to win nearly half of the fights, but also managing to sustain only a few small injuries even while he lost. Alyssa was impressed and happy about the last part as well. Since she was assigned to heal a group of five trainees she has seen winners taking more damage than Kayro did after losing.

On the first day of the next week, he decided to spend all his free time in the library looking for a solution to make himself stronger. As he was going from section to section of the library, he accidentally bumped into another trainee. After apologising, he realised the person in front of him was quite short and thin compared to him. Thinking about the moment of impact, he remembered that somehow he was the one being pushed away despite such a big difference in size, so he decided to ask the other trainee about his power.

"Once again, I am sorry for bumping into you. I was just looking for some books on the top shelves and didn't realise that someone was next to me. My name is Kayro and it's nice to meet you."

"My name is Allgos and you don't need to worry about that. All my clothes are imbued with magic to sustain physical shocks, since, just like you, almost everyone fails to see me until it's too late. When they first brought me here, I was barely able to use my power, but ending up on the floor every time someone couldn't notice me, I started being more motivated until one day, with the help of some of the books in this section, I created my first shirt that allowed me to stay on my feet as people were bumping into me. After that I managed to add that effect to all my clothes and even to some armour that is being used by mages while they test themselves against the beasts on the island."

"That sounds impressive. If you don't mind, can you please tell me which books helped you? I want to try and see if I can imbue magic into clothes and armour, but I need to learn the theory first."

Allgos picked a few books from the shelves and told him that the information inside should be sufficient as a starting point, of course if the imbuing power was part of him already. After thanking his senior trainee, Kayro started reading and learning from the books every time he had spare time.

During the next month, he found a way to spend time with Alyssa while training his three elements and read about magic equipment and the power to make it. As soon as he felt confident, he went to Allgos's training workshop and, with some advice from his senior, Kayro was able to imbue his old but helpful gurma vest and belt with magic. The only difference was that the objects were now able to sustain damage from the elements he could control, instead of physical damage.

Although he was a little disappointed, it was a step forward to getting stronger and that motivated him to read more on the subject and experiment as well.

The next day, he went to talk to his counsellor and request permission to reduce the number of training hours spent to improve controlling the ice, water and wind elements, in order to focus on creating magic equipment. Seeing how despite his efforts and time spent break his limits, Kayro was barely making a difference when it came to his already known powers and happy about his new ability, Frigus agreed that this was the best choice.

In just a month, the young man learned how to add physical protection to clothes and armour. Not only that, but he could also randomly add protection against the elements that his powers were weak against. Meanwhile, Alyssa proved to be a prodigy and now she was able to use her power ten times longer than she did when she healed Kayro during the Test of Survival. More than that she could heal nearly fatal wounds without leaving any scars, if she was treating them immediately.

Their skills were not the only things growing stronger since they got to the Mage Institute. Spending a lot of time together made their feelings stronger than ever. Alyssa already started thinking about marriage after graduating from Training Camp, but only now, six months since coming to Mage Island she dared to tell her boyfriend about it.

"I know that you have other curiosities, Kayro, but it's been some time since I started thinking seriously about us, and I would like you to think on the idea of us getting married after we finish our Training here."

"My dear, no matter how curious I am about the world and about magic, you are more important. The moment I realised my true feeling for you, I knew that I also want to marry you. I will need some time after we get back to Glade Village to settle a few things and after that we can finally have a wedding."

The young woman was shocked. Despite his numerous ways of showing affection and being there for her all the time, she was not expecting him to think about marriage. After a few moments of silence she finally replied:

"You have no idea how happy you just made me. Ever since we were children, all I knew is that you want to explore, learn and get answers to questions that most people don't even bother to ask. More than that, choosing the explorer role during Training Camp, made me think that you will leave the village in order to see the entire planet, so I never really thought that you will want to marry me. I'm sorry for being so wrong about you. I love you, Kayro!"

"I love you too, Alyssa!"

As they hugged and kissed, all he could think about was the guilt of not telling her the truth about his origins, but his feelings were real, his intention of marrying her was too. That was exactly the reason why he was pushing harder and harder to become a mage, get the information he was looking for, gain the skills that will help him reach his future goals and get away from Mage Island as soon as possible.

The next day, after arriving at the magic equipment workshop, Kayro saw a new face for the first time since he started going there and he asked Allgos who that man was.

"That is Badar, my counsellor and the master when it comes to imbuing objects. He was away visiting his family for a few months and came back yesterday evening. Let's go and introduce you to him."

As they were introduced by his senior, something felt different about the man, but Kayro was not sure what exactly that can be. He could sense that the master craftsman was no ordinary person, but had no idea what set him apart from others. When

Badar stared into his eyes, the young man could feel the fighter behind his appearance , but at the same time he felt no threat.

The moment of silence was soon broken by the older trainee who suggested that they should start working on making leather boots just as strong as the ones you can make out of sparus. During this trial, Kayro was able to see the skills of the master and he was simply amazed. Not only did the man achieve the exact results he intended to, but he was doing it quickly.

"We will not be able to do it as quickly as he does it and the reason for that is Badar's lack of magic. You see, he is using crystals charged with magic by very strong trainees and sometimes by the masters of each element. He lacks magic, so his only choice is to channel it from those crystals, but that can be quite expensive as they are rare and he usually ends up paying the mages charging them as well."

Kayro remembered that R'mal's said something about these crystals and understood why they were so expensive, but he was not expecting them to be so powerful. Despite the fact that they came from prison mines, the young man wished he could get his hands on at least a few and make himself a strong battle outfit.

During the next month, with help from the master craftsman, Kayro improved a lot. He even managed to make himself a battle outfit which would soon be put to test. Since both him and his counsellor agreed that he reached his maximum potential when it came to all three elements that he was able to fully control now, and also managed to make himself something to wear during battles, Frigus decided it was time for the young man to join a group that will fight against beasts.

With his first and main element being ice, he was allowed to join a group that was going to the eastern side of Mage Island where there is an entire habitat, on the beach, dominated by flacaras, the fire breathing lizards. A day before the test against them, Kayro was called by his counsellor for a meeting to inform him about the trial:

"They might be the least powerful animals that you can face on the island, but even so, normal ones are the size of an adult human and some can grow two or three times bigger, so be careful. As you know, with your girlfriend being one of the best healers that we ever had, she will join the group as well. I understand how important she is to you, but the task given to all of you, which is to take down five flacaras, comes first, so you will need to focus on that."

"I understand, master, and so does she."

"Very well, just remember that you must act as a whole, not separate into smaller groups. I need you to protect yourself and the others just as you would protect her. I am certain that everyone will act the same, especially since a few of the ones in the group have failed this trial before."

"I promise to treat everyone the same, sir. I would sacrifice my life for Alyssa, and, if needed, I will do so for anyone in the group."

"Let's just hope you don't get pushed that far. You are still one of my best students and I think that one day you will become a great mage."

"Thank you, master Frigus. Your words mean a lot to me and I will do my best to prove that you are right to have such high expectations."

After finishing their conversation, Kayro went to see check the equipment that his girlfriend will be given to wear during the trial. He was surprised and happy to see that the one who made her outfit was Badar, the master craftsman. They had a short conversation and, at the end of it, he thanked the man for giving her such precious equipment.

"I know you said that he was very skilled, but I have never seen you appreciate someone's work so much. Is this really that valuable?"

"Maybe even more than we think. The crystals used by him are adding a lot of value, but his skill is what makes it better than something crafted by someone else. He told me that this is something he created for the first time and it should have increased protection compared to the ones he usually makes. Basically you are testing it for him and I am sure it will prove to be exactly what he claims."

"If you trust him and his work so much, then I will too. This makes me wish you had one like mine as well."

"You don't have to worry, my dear. I tested mine with Sidius's help and it will definitely handle anything the flacaras might come up with."

After a short walk in the park, each of them went to their rooms and made sure to rest properly for the trial. Early in the morning, the group was taken to the main island by boat and then close to the area of the trial by cart. They set up camp for the night and in the morning, the group went crossed inside the barrier that kept the animals inside. The beach looked a lot like a desert if not for the lake in the distance and there was no sign of life except some plants here and there.

As they were walking, rodents started showing up, but there was no sign of flacaras yet. Kayro remembered that the fire lizards often bury themselves in the sand to cool down or just to set up an ambush. The others had the same information, but even the ones who experienced this before were not able to see any sign of it. Minutes later they could see one flacara running in the distance and they cautiously went after it.

Suddenly one of the trainees that failed the trial before remembered that this was the way his group was ambushed, but it proved too late. As he was shouting to inform everyone, nine flacaras surfaced from the sand. Eight of them were positioned in pairs of two on each side and a bigger one that was most likely the leader was facing the group of young future mages.

Shortly it was confirmed that the big lizard was indeed the leader, because, as soon as it started making some strange noises, the others slowly walked towards the humans. One of the trainees was able to master barriers, so, when the next sound from the leader made the smaller flacaras breathe fire, he was able to protect everyone. As impressive as his ability was, the goal of the trial was to kill five of the lizards and bring back their tongues as proof, so they couldn't just wait inside.

It took the trainees a few minutes to come up with a plan and then they started acting. Since it was only eleven of them, they left the healer, which was Alyssa, with two men behind. One of them was the most experienced and his role was to watch from the distance and help whoever needed help the most and the other one was the man who was able to conjure barriers. To avoid wasting his power, as soon as everyone was ready to act, he started shrinking the one that he created earlier, up to a point where at least half might fit in if they needed to run back inside.

Since he already had experience from fighting the abnormal gurma, Kayro decided to distract the leader of the flacaras making it easier for his colleagues to each face one of the smaller lizards. Covering himself in ice, he was able to quickly run through and get close to the big one. This got the animal's attention and soon a breath of fire melted his cover.

By using his wind element he threw sand at the reptile which gave him enough time to create two orbs of water nearly as big as he was. Before the dust settled he threw the orbs at the flacara's mouth which immediately put down the fire in its breath. As soon as he saw that, he threw ice blades at the leader's eyes blinding it for long enough to make two ice spikes which he then used to impale the big lizard in the head.

Before falling to his feet, it made a horrible sound and the other flacaras were looking to run away. Since they only needed to kill five, the other trainee mages coordinated by the one inside the barrier acted in groups of two and while one was acting as a distraction, the second in each group took down the reptile they targeted.

To make sure that there will be no surprise, they quickly slit the tongues of the lizards and started making their way back to camp. Only after they stepped back into the safe area, the trainees finally celebrated, but they did so for a short time.

As soon as they got back to the Mage Institute, all the masters including grandmaster Lurmand, came to inspect the proof of passage and the state of the ones who were part of the trial. They were surprised to see that no one suffered any major injuries and the ones they had were healed up to a point where you could barely see any scar. This was proof that Alyssa was almost ready to become a full mage.

The trainees that stayed next to her were also congratulated, one for being able to create the barrier which protected everyone and used as a shelter later and the second for his leadership skills. Going on with the inspection, everyone, except Kayro, was congratulated and advised to train more before taking on the next trial. The young man was told to stay behind while the rest were dismissed.

"I apologise for singling you out and at the same time I congratulate you on doing such a good job. Still we have some extra questions since not only did you manage to kill a bigger flacara by yourself, but also have no major injury considering the marks on your outfit" Lurmand said while shaking the young man's hand.

"It is quite a feat to impress the grandmaster, son, but I have to admit that we are all curious on how you managed to do that so easily " Frigus added.

Before Kayro could say anything, Badar started talking:

"I think I know the reasons why he was able to do that. I might not have any power, but I am sure that if you test his ability to control fire again, you will find out that he can do it now. Along with the protection from the outfit that he imbued with his magic, it should be enough to protect him from any fire lizard's breath."

"That would explain a lot, honestly" grandmaster Lurmand said.

"Let's just test the boy already. As his counsellor I am ashamed that I didn't think of that, but while I trained him there were no signs of it."

To make sure that no one could be hurt if Kayro lost control of his potential new power, they had the mage who was master when it came to conjuring barriers set one up and then asked the young man to try and create flames. As he was trying to do that, each of the other elements came out in turns, but on his tenth attempt a small flame orb came appeared. Usually any element would show up during the first week of tests when the powers of all new trainees are checked, but on rare occasions it might manifest after or during certain events in the mage's life.

Having an answer it was decided that the young man will train for a week only on learning how to control his fire element and then he will join a group that is set to face a group of animals that are more powerful than the flacaras were.

With nearly everyone gone, Kayro went to Badar to thank him for realising what exactly happened, knowing that without his intervention he was definitely in trouble.

"Master, I cannot fully express my gratitude for seeing what was actually happening with my powers."

"I'm afraid it's not that simple. I cannot say more now, but meet me later in the crafting workshop, because we really need to talk."

The young man agreed, but he was afraid of what the master craftsman might want to say. Still, avoiding public meant that he didn't intend to expose his opinion. A few hours later, making sure that no one followed him, Kayro entered the workshop. As soon as he saw Badar, he was getting ready to speak, but the man told him to be quiet and led him to the basement of the building where he opened a secret room by using a secret lever.

"Before you say anything, I need you to know that I am on your side and I want you to promise that everything we talk about or you just saw will stay a secret."

"I promise, master."

"First I would like to properly introduce myself. My real name is B'dar and just like you I am a demon. Well, at least half of you."

213

"I have no idea what you're talking about and if this is some sort of test, I find it to be a really bad one."

"You don't need to worry, Kayro. Just like R'mal I used to be loyal to your parents and I wish to free them or at least help do that."

"What is a demon doing here?"

"Spying, learning, and now helping you."

"Why should I trust you? Even if you know R'mal or my parents, the mages will not simply allow a demon to live on their island."

"You are partially right, my prince, but you see, as skilled as they are with magic, they will never be able to craft equipment as powerful as the one I am. In fact, that is how I convinced them to bring me here."

"Tell me more and then I will decide if you can really be trusted."

"Since I was not travelling with your parents when they went to visit Glade Village, just like many others I pretended to join the ones who took down the royal family. It took me five years to prove that no one else could imbue clothes or armour as well as I did, and one more to make armour for all the mages on this island. Only after they tested each one, I was allowed to show my face and become an apprentice in the crafting workshop."

"Even with your skills they made you an apprentice?" asked Kayro.

"The former master was very skilled for a human and the mages still didn't fully trust me, but still needed me to make clothing and armour. While I was good at imbuing, my crafting skills were not so good, and that is why they had him train me on customizing everything. Four years later, after he passed away, I was made to take a trial and after that swear that I will only be loyal to them, even if they start a war against my race."

"So, how were you able to convince them?"

"For the trial, they brought some demons from the Blood Lands, and grouped me with the trainees that were ready to take their final test before becoming mages. In order to prove my loyalty and pass, my task was to make sure that no human will die, while all demons must be killed and at least one of them by my hands."

"Wasn't that hard for you? Especially since you were going against your own race?"

"I knew them from before and none was loyal to your family. More than that it seemed they could not control themselves anymore, they were just like any wild animal. With that in mind I had no problem taking any of their lives. It was not easy, but I killed them all by myself while the humans could barely defend themselves "

"And how did you managed to kill one without magic or weapons?"

"Since the mages tested me lots of times and saw that I had no magic power, they allowed me to use weapons. They don't know about this, but you can infuse weapons with magic too."

"You can? I have never heard of that?"

"It is not easy, because apart from charged crystals you need remains from an animal that was stronger than the normal ones. The stronger the beast you have the parts from, the higher the quality of the weapons you can craft."

"How exactly does that work?"

"As you melt the metal and pour it inside the mould, you add bones, claws or fangs from a powerful animal and then start to work on it. But you must be careful, because if you do it too early, they will simply be burned. After the weapon is ready you transfer magic from a crystal or from yourself, which will increase durability a lot, you will never need to sharpen it and it will easily pierce even the thickest hide. It might be able to do more than that, but since I don't have any magic and I refuse to allow the mages to find out about the possibility of making magic weapons, I was not able to fully test one."

"I can try that for you if you want."

"Unfortunately, I was not allowed to carry weapons anymore after the trial, not even when they allow me to travel to the Blood Lands. Instead they just cast a protection barrier on me."

"And that is enough to keep you safe?"

"Along with my magic imbued outfit, it's more than enough. Since my skill is very important to them, the grandmaster is the one casting the barrier and I have never seen it break. I was attacked by demons, humans, beasts that are a lot stronger than any you have faced and they were easily repelled. Anything trying to get closer than a metre to me gets pushed back and the stronger the impact is, the stronger the push will get."

"Are they able to track you or hear what you say while you are covered by that barrier?"

"No, they can only sense if I touch another barrier. For example, when I leave or get back to Mage Island, when I enter or leave the Median Forests. Starting the second year, after they allowed me to visit the Blood Lands, I had some conversations with people that still support your family, which would definitely cost me my life, if I was seen or heard doing that, but nothing happened. In fact, that is how I learned about you being here. When I was on my way back from the Blood Lands, as I was getting close to Glade Village, R'mal stopped me and told me everything about the recent events, your new powers and the fact that you might be brought to Mage Island and trained here. After getting back, I have been watching you to confirm if what he was saying was true and now I am certain that you are the one who our race was waiting for ever since that woman was able to read the flow of magic."

"Speaking of the flow of magic, Frigus said that as soon as I become a mage I will be able to get answers to some questions. Are you able to give me any of those answers?"

"I'm afraid that no one is sharing any other information with me aside magic clothing or armour. Some still see me as an enemy and if Lurmand wasn't protecting me I would have probably been killed as soon as I got to Mage Island. You will need to pass the remaining three trials and hopefully after that, they will share some of the information you seek."

"Hopefully I will be able to do that soon. I am afraid that any moment the mages might find out what I really am and have me killed."

"Even if they find out what you are, make sure that who you are is not revealed. The blood of your family is very powerful and they might fear it enough to kill you, but if they think you are just common demon they will send you to a mining prison and you will be able to escape from there in time."

"I will do my best to hide who I am."

"Regarding that, you will need to control your demonic power better and stop yourself from healing so fast. Lucky for you that your girlfriend was not experienced enough to notice your ability to self-heal yet, but any other healer mage would have."

"I always forget about that, since I am focused on stopping my other demonic powers from coming out, but I will be more careful."

"You did a good job at hiding those considering that you recently started using them."

"I'm sorry, but it's getting late and I need to meet Alyssa soon. She will be worried if I don't get there in time and I am already hiding too many things from her, so it is best if I go now. Once again, thank you for saving me!"

"Before you go, my prince, if you ever need to talk to me, just come to this room and leave a note for when you wish to meet. Outside this room you should keep as much distance as possible from me, when possible, because the mages might suspect something if they see us talking too much."

"I understand. We will meet in the workshop from time to time, but I make sure that Allgos or at least another craftsman trainee will be there."

Kayro went to meet his girlfriend and after their usual walk in the park they went back to the living quarters. With each day he was feeling more guilty about hiding things from her, but he couldn't find another way to protect her.

At the end of the week, Frigus called him for a meeting to inform him about the next trial. The counsellor told him that this time the group was going to face a swarm of zumzi, giant insects that could fly and attack very fast. What made them even more dangerous was their sting which was poisonous. Despite their size, they only released small amounts of poison, but being stung by a few and not taking an antidote could prove fatal.

This time, the task was to kill an entire swarm which meant ten zumzis and bring their stingers back as proof. The place where the trial will take place was on the northern side of Mage Island, in the forest, and the group will have a total of twenty members. There was also an additional condition to pass this second trial, which was that everyone must be alive at the end of the day.

Just like a week before, the group was taken to the main island by boat and then by a cart pulled by bovri close to their destination. They set up camp for the night again and early in the morning Kayro's group crossed the barrier inside the territory that was dominated by the zumzis. Since there was no mage with the power of conjuring protective barriers everyone was walking slowly expecting an attack at any time.

After nearly half an hour of wandering around, the trainees heard the sound of flapping wings. All of them reacted quickly taking defensive positions, but that didn't help as much as they were expecting. Just as Frigus said, despite their size, the zumzis moved at incredible speed.

Even if they were taken by surprise, the future mages were calm and they started making a plan. They quickly cut some weeds and tree branches, piled them up and as soon as the sound was flapping wings would get close, the one that can control fire would set the piles surrounding them on fire. The plan worked very well, but everyone was aware this solution was good to defend, so they had to think of a way to kill the insects. Because of the additional condition, no one could act as decoy, but one of the more experienced trainees came up with the idea of making clay dolls and dress them up to get the attention of the zumzis. While everyone who could control earth, water or fire was working on making the dolls, the rest used some vines they found close by to make nets.

As soon as everything was ready, the fires were put out, the smoke was blown away and the trainees were hiding in the trees ready to ambush the insects. Despite being nervous after they heard the sound of flapping wings get close, everyone had quick and precise reactions, trapping the entire swarm under nets. Without giving the chance to move too much, the future mages started a merciless attack. Orbs of fire, blades of water, rocks, bolts of lightning, spikes of ice, were overpowering the insects.

After quickly taking their stingers, the group was on the move again. Fearing an ambush from a second swarm, they made some torches and wrapped plants and leaves around them to cover their retreat with smoke. Again, the plan worked perfectly and after the healers inspected and treated everyone it was time to head back to the institute.

Since there were no extraordinary events and the group worked as one, Kayro's secret was safe. Only two more trials and he could finally become a mage and return to Glade Village. As he was going to meet Alyssa and give her the good news about easily passing the trial, he heard a voice calling his name from behind. It turned out to be grandmaster Lurmand and he requested the young man to meet him next morning for breakfast.

Although he was surprised, Kayro accepted immediately and after bowing as a sign of respect, he started walking faster to meet his girlfriend and tell her about the trial and what just happened minutes ago.

"I see that once again you managed to survive without a scratch, my dear. If you keep this up I end up thinking that I made you invincible after healing your wounds in the Great Forest."

"We were simply lucky. All those years of playing sports helped me fit in without really knowing any of the other trainees, and, as a team, we managed to pass by combining our magic powers."

"That is good, I am happy to hear that for once you didn't have to play the hero and act as decoy."

"I was close to doing that, but thankfully, one of the more experienced members had a great idea about making clay dolls and use them instead."

"Maybe this will make you use your brain more instead of your muscles."

"It sure will, but if we didn't have mages that could control the earth element, we would probably be in bed receiving treatment."

"Well, at least you learned that there are alternative ways of dealing with dangerous beings."

"That is true, and speaking of them, the grandmaster asked me to join him for breakfast tomorrow. I would rather face the flacaras and zumzis altogether by myself than being so close to him. He doesn't seem bad, but he is rather cold and it's difficult to know what he is thinking about."

"I think I know why he asked for that. Master Ghilod told me today that they wish to make me a mage as soon as possible. He said that I exceeded their expectations and I can do the job as good as any other mage with healing powers."

"That is great news. We need to celebrate."

"Not yet. I asked the grandmaster to postpone giving me the mage title until you get yours. If I accept it now, I would be forced to leave Mage Island and become a healer for all the Elders. Since I will need to travel a lot between the communities, I got his approval to make you my bodyguard and travel companion, but only after you pass all four trials."

"I understand now. He probably wishes to officially inform me about that. I'm sorry to make you wait, my love."

"It's all right. I can study some of the ways they grow plants in the greenhouses and also practice my healing magic, hopefully not on you."

After finishing their conversation, the couple sneaked inside the living quarters and went to Kayro's room where they made love. It was not forbidden to have a relationship, but they were not allowed to live together yet, so once a month at least they were forced to sneak around.

In the morning, the young man dressed in his best outfit after taking a shower and headed towards the grandmaster's office. Lurmand was happy to see him and after they finished eating, a conversation started.

"I think you might know already why I wanted to see you, son."

"If it's about Alyssa's choice, grandmaster, than you are right. I know what she asked for."

"It was unexpected for someone to make a request like that, but I fully understand that the feelings which bind the two of you are strong and you could prove the ideal guard for her. Hearing about your actions during the trials you passed, knowing about you Test of Survival from last year and adding the love you have for her, I can imagine you could become a one man army if she is ever in danger."

"That is right. I would face all the beasts on the planet in order to protect her."

"It makes me happy to hear that, Kayro. Her role will be one of great importance. We already have a mage doing that, but he is getting old and having help from Alyssa would ease his work a lot. Since you already passed the test to become an explorer I imagine travelling across the Median Forests will be easy, all you need to do is become a mage by passing the last two trials."

"That is my intention, grandmaster. I feel sorry for holding her back, but if I am to properly protect her, then I need to get a lot stronger. I haven't heard of flacaras or zumzis being seen in the Median Forests, but after facing them, I understand just how dangerous it would be to face such animals without being fully prepared."

"As long as you stay inside the borders, you should be safe, dear boy. We have barriers surrounding our land and nothing should be able to enter. Even if, by chance, a creature could pass through, we can sense it and immediately dispatch a squad of mages to take care of it, but that never happened since I was named grandmaster."

"That is good to know. I was afraid that my parents would be in danger after seeing the creatures from my first two trials."

"Speaking of trials, son, I convinced the masters to allow you to join a group for your third one in a month, but we have one condition, which is for you to learn how to control the fire element as well as the others you possess. Since we are all aware that is not an easy task, you have permission to focus only on that, setting everything else aside."

"Thank you very much, grandmaster Lurmand. This will make Alyssa very happy since we will be one step closer to going home and for her to start the new role."

"Don't thank me just yet. Not only you need to pass this trial, but also prove how much you improved. Based on that we will be able to decide when you will be allowed to join the final step in becoming a mage."

"I promise to do my best in order to pass both of them quickly and prove that I am worthy of becoming a mage, as well as Alyssa's protector."

After saying that, they shook hands and while the grandmaster went back to his office, Kayro headed straight to the area where fire element mages train. He was barely able to learn how to control that during the week between trials, so he chose to ask Sidius for tips on how to improve.

With his senior's help, he was able to make a training schedule that was his best choice of controlling fire as good as he was able to do it with the other elements. Happy about how his day went, Kayro went to see Alyssa and share the good news. The young woman was concerned about him needing to push so hard for her sake, but it also made her understand just how much he loved her. As they walked she started thinking about the future and being next to him all the time, something that she could only dream about a year before.

The month he was given to get his control of the fire element on par with the others passed, and he managed not only to meet the condition that was set, but also find a way to combine it with the wind element, making it stronger. As agreed, he would join the group that was facing the third trial, and, just like before, his counsellor asked for a meeting to inform him about what he will be facing and the tasks that must be completed to pass.

"This time the trial will take place on the western side of Mage Island and you only need to kill one animal, but your group is reduced to five people. It will be something you need to do at night and again everyone must survive. The animal which you need to take down is a ghetera, a feline that is a lot faster than the zumzi and with its black fur can easily hide in the night."

"This one sounds quite hard. How will we be able to face a pack of that?"

"There is no need to worry about that, Kayro. They are solitary creatures and only hunt alone. They rarely allow another of their species to get close and that is only when they are mating. Still do not underestimate how dangerous it can be."

"I definitely will not do that. After seeing the flacaras ambush us during the first trial, I learned that any beast could easily outsmart us."

"It is good to hear that, because you will not have much protection. The group is not allowed to have a healer or someone who could conjure a barrier. More than that, you will need to be careful with fire attacks too, since we don't want the entire forest burned. I know that you trained hard to improve your fire controlling skills, but try to use it only as a last option. "

"I understand, master Frigus. I will do my best to complete the task by working with the rest of the team and I am sure they will also try to protect the forest. What exactly do we need to bring as proof of killing the beast?"

"You must bring the entire carcass, so my advice is to try not to fully use your energy while fighting it. This way the group will be able to carry it back into the safe area."

"Is there any time limit for the trial?"

"You have two nights and two days to kill the ghetera and get to the safe zone. Since they only come out at night, that is when you must fight it, but you're free to wander in the forest during the day if you think that will help you in any way."

"Thank you for the information, master. Hopefully we will see each other after."

"Good luck, son. Try to come back without too many wounds."

After talking to Frigus, the young man went to see Alyssa and tell her about the trial. She was concerned about his safety, but this was the only way to move forward for them. After hugging him tight and kissing him with passion she wished him good luck, before going back to the living quarters.

After getting next to the barrier, the group had a meeting and they decided not to go in straight away. They will sacrifice the first night, go check the area during the day when gheteras usually sleep, maybe set up some traps and, after sunset, try to lure one of the felines and easily pass the trial.

Since he trained as an explorer and also learned a lot about hunting, Kayro was able to track the areas where the predators might hunt and also find the best suited place to set up the traps.

Since none of the predators had hunting grounds close to the safe zone, they decided to have the one who was physically stronger out of the fight, so he could carry the carcass back without stopping.

A few hours later they built the traps, found some turen and orren to use as bait and then went to get some rest before nightfall. The group slowly made their way to the area where they set up the traps, but there was no sign of any ghetera, not even sounds in the distance.

Just as they planned, the group separated, with the strongest staying behind, well-hidden to make sure he will be rested enough to carry the predator after it's dead. The remaining four formed two-people teams, each consisting of a man and a woman, and slowly started walking towards the area they considered to be the closest hunting grounds of a ghetera.

Kayro stopped himself from using his powers to see in the dark, knowing that one of the other trainees might notice, and that made him feel vulnerable. Even so, he had no choice but to carry on with the plan and find one of the beasts before trying to lure it into a trap. As they got closer to the area where he found tracks during the day, a feeling of danger took over him. His instincts were trying to let him know that something was lurking close by, but, without being able to use the power of his eyes, there was not much he could do.

As he was thinking of a way to make the ghetera expose its location, he remembered that the woman he was forming a team with could control the earth element and asked her to move some rocks in front of them , but the further she could do it, the better. Just a few seconds after she did that, they could hear the sounds of running and growling, and the scary part was they were coming from behind.

As the feline went past them and got to the rocks that were moved earlier, they saw the other team trying to get its attention. A second later, they started running as fast as possible in the direction of the traps keeping some distance from each other in order to confuse the predator. It worked for some time, but then the ghetera stopped and started sniffing the air. Since the other team already managed to get to the hiding places they set up during the day, Kayro knew that they were the target now and this was confirmed soon when the feline turned its head facing them. He signalled his team mate to start running as soon as he moves and then quickly sent four fire orbs in different directions.

While his decision allowed the girl to start running, he could also see that the beast was now going after her. Without any hesitation he rushed in her direction while shouting to act as a decoy. His plan worked, but the animal proved a lot faster than he thought and managed to get very close to him quickly. Now there was only one option left, and that was to run as fast as possible and make follow him to one of the traps.

Despite running in zigzag, which slowed the ghetera a little, he knew that it was getting closer with each step, but the traps and the hiding places of his group members were only a little further. Being in such a dangerous situation his instincts took over for a few moments, but he was able to calm down without revealing any of the demonic powers.

Unfortunately, that distraction proved to be enough for the feline to reach him and as it leaped at him, the others started shouting. Thanks to his reflexes from when he was training his hand to hand combat skills, he only ended up with a scratch on his arm. Despite the minor injury he was worried about his instincts kicking in again as he could feel his claws and fangs growing. Once again he was able to calm down, but the price was receiving a full claw attack on his back. If he wasn't wearing the gurma leather vest which he imbued with magic some time ago, the same one which saved him a year ago in the Great Forest, he would be almost dead now, but, with most of the attack being cancelled by it, he managed to sprint just as the others began their attacks.

Since he was able to distance himself enough, it was time to join them and try to finish their task. Still, the ghetera look unharmed, managing to take the magic attacks as if they were nothing. Remembering his fight with the abnormal gurma, Kayro realised that its hide must be even thicker and the only option was to impale it. While running towards the predator, he formed two ice spikes that were thicker and sharper than any of the ones he conjured before, and thanks to the continuous attacks of his team mates, the beast couldn't dodge his furious attack.

Seeing how close he got, the others stopped attacking, waiting to see what exactly happened. As the ghetera seemed to move they were ready to start over, but soon realised that Kayro was the one pushing it away. With its last breath, the predator forced one more attack trying to bite his neck, but luckily it failed to do so. If not for his demonic healing powers, the young man would probably be severely injured, but he was almost healed. As soon as he noticed that, he forced his power to stop, otherwise his powers will be questioned again.

After the rest of the team reached him, two of them helped him to get to one of the hiding places, while the other three took the ghetera carcass to the second hiding place and made sure there was nothing in the area that could attack them. With a few hours left before morning, they waited impatiently for the sun to rise. An hour after that happened, they started walking at a fast pace towards the safe zone and managed to get there without an attack occurring.

Since they had no healer, the group quickly made their way back to the Mage Institute to get Kayro treated. As soon as Alyssa saw him being carried she feared the worst and rushed to check on him. Fortunately he was just asleep, being too tired from pushing himself too hard. At least that is what everyone believed, when in fact his body needed the rest after healing itself.

Seeing the minor injuries, she took of his vest and top, and started using her magic to heal any minor wound she could find on his body. Despite being amazed of how little his body was hurt after hearing what happened, she kept quiet about it and pretended that she used a lot of magic to heal him.

When the young man woke up the next day, he was invited to join the meeting which would determine when he was allowed to join a group for the last trial. His girlfriend refused to leave his side as he walked there and she was even allowed to be a witness to the meeting.

While some of the masters were praising his actions, the others claimed that he put everyone in danger with the way he chose to end the ghetera's life by getting close and using the ice spikes, which made it impossible for anyone else to attack without hurting him as well.

After two hours of debating and checking the carcass of the animal again and again, as well as any marks on his body and equipment, especially the vest, the masters reached the same conclusion as he did. The only way to take down the beast was an attack that could pierce its thick hide. Even so, it was decided that he will have to train for three more months before being allowed to take part in the final trial.

Despite being unhappy about the decision, both Kayro and Alyssa chose not to protest and as soon as the meeting was over, they went for a walk in the park to talk about what just happened.

"I wish we could get away from here faster, but I think they are right about you needing to train more. I am still surprised on how you only had some small wounds after hearing what happened during the trial."

"I guess my skills when it comes to crafting protective equipment got better. Except the gurma leather vest, I crafted and imbued everything with magic just a week before the trial. Since I got stronger the protection clearly improved."

"I still think it's not normal, but I am happy that you came back without any severe wounds."

"Who knows, maybe I have some hidden power that I don't even know about yet."

"Hidden power or not, please promise me to train hard and find or craft even better equipment before the final trial. I really don't want to lose you, especially now that we are so close to finally going back home."

"I promise, my love" said Kayro while kissing her forehead and hugging her tighter than ever before.

Starting the next day, the young man was training so hard that everyone was wondering where all his energy comes from. After a month he was already able to combine the power of all his elements, but his skills were still just above average.

He had an idea about using bones, claws or fangs from the ghetera, but B'dar advised him not to. That might give the mages ideas of how to create weapons which would make them even more powerful. As a way to gain more protection, the man suggest to Kayro to make himself some rings and before the metal gets too hard, he could add some of his own blood to it.

"That is how I can sometimes imbue even more magic into objects, but I only used the technique for what I wear. It was used by some of our blacksmiths in the past and my guess is that only a few demons still know about it. Even so, none would reveal this to humans, especially not to the mages."

"Sounds like something I could try. Can I please use your secret room to do this?"

"Of course. I was thinking about the same thing. I will try to distract Allgos and the others in the crafting workshop and while you get inside, just let me know when you want to do it."

"I will, master. Thank you for all your support."

# The proposal and the last trial

A month later, Kayro asked B'dar to distract everyone in the workshop and he quickly made his way into the secret room. It took him hours to create three rings, but once the sun set the master craftsman gave him the signal that he could safely come out.

"I will wear these two and test them during my last month of training before the trial" said the young man while showing the rings he had on the middle finger of each hand.

"What about the third one? Is it a spare?"

"No, master. This will be the ring that I am going to use tomorrow when I will officially ask Alyssa to marry me. I have been thinking about making one for her even before you gave me the idea, but now it will really be a special one. I will keep the secret of my origins from her for a while longer, but at least I will feel less guilty by giving her not just a token of my affection, but also something that will keep her safe."

"That is a good idea, my prince. It will surely make her happy and keep her safer than any other magic imbued ring could."

Happy and nervous about what he planned for the next day, Kayro returned to his room and wrote a letter to Krysta and Klost informing them about finally asking his girlfriend to marry him. They already knew about his intentions, but up until now he was not sure when exactly to do it.

Without being able to sleep much that night, the young man came up with a plan to propose, but in order to prepare he would have to take a day off from training, so he went to talk to both his counsellor and the grandmaster. Since his progress was better than expected, they agreed with his request and even offered to help, so Kayro asked them to find a way to keep her busy while he will get everything ready, a task that proved to be easier than expected, because a group of trainees failed their second trial and ended up with a lot of wounds that only the master healer or someone with Alyssa's power could fully heal.

Initially, the young man wanted to come on the stage that was used to congratulate the trainees who just passed a trial, after their small ceremony ended, but since the they failed and ended up getting treated, he had to adjust his plan. With the help of the mages who were in charge with the greenhouses he decorated the stage with beautiful flowers who were planted in pots. It took some time to get them there and move them around as they were heavy, but that also gave his girlfriend time to finish healing the wounded.

While getting the stage ready, he took a few minutes to go see Lurmand and tell him about the rest of the plan. Kayro's idea was for the grandmaster to pretend to hold a short moment where he would thank Alyssa for doing such a good job at healing the wounded that took part in the trial, but, instead of that happening, he will be the one coming up on the stage holding the ring and asking her to marry him.

"I'm afraid I cannot agree with your plan, dear boy. Both Ghilod and I decided some time ago to publicly praise and thank Alyssa for her hard work and skill, so you will have to wait until we do that and then get up on the stage and ask her."

"That sounds even better, grandmaster. Thank you very much for your help."

As soon as the young woman finished healing the wounded, her counsellor told her about the ceremony that will take place later, so she went back to the living quarters to clean herself and change into something more formal. To her surprise, as she got close to the stage, there were a lot more mages than usual present, so she got a little shy. She couldn't see Kayro anywhere, but there was no time to look for him since Lurmand called out her name and invited her on the stage.

Ghilod was the first one to speak, followed by the grandmaster and after they finished praising her skills and help, they officially announced her future role as a healer for all Elders in the Median Forests. She was given time for a speech and when that was finished everyone started cheering, but only for a short time since her boyfriend quietly got on the stage, came behind her and kneeled while holding the ring.

Seeing that everyone instantly froze by whatever was going on behind her, she turned around only to see her boyfriend kneeling. She forgot about the crowd, the beautiful flowers and everything that was said by her counsellor and the grandmaster, and after a few seconds of silence accepted the proposal. As soon as that happened, small orbs of fire and lightning were being sent above the crowd by some of the most experienced mages, while the ones who could control wind or earth elements were making a rhythmic noise to make the moment even more memorable.

After years of training his body, Kayro gently and easily took Alyssa in his arms and started walking away from the people who gathered to celebrate with them and were still cheering. He took her to his room in the living quarters and took advantage of the silence to tell her exactly how much she means to him.

"I know that for many years I only saw you as my best friend, but I think part of me fell in love with you on the first day we met as children. I guess that was the reason why I always felt to prove my worth by competing with you, in order to show you that I am good enough to be your future husband. As years passed, my thirst for knowledge and my curiosity about the world we live in, took over my mind, but all this time you were in my heart. I'm sorry that it took so long to realise what I felt for .you, but now I ready to love and be fully honest with you until the day I die."

Before he got the chance to say more and reveal the truth about his origins, the girl started passionately kissing him and they made love several times before they fell asleep in each other's arms. After waking up, they made love one more time while taking a shower together, forgetting about the rules of the Mage Institute. Since there was no time to talk before starting his training, Kayro decided to tell her the entire truth later that day.

While he was training on combining all the elements he could control to develop a fighting style, just like he did with the weapons and techniques learned during Training Camp, the young man was visited by Frigus.

"I have some good news for you, son. Considering your engagement to Alyssa and your progress when it comes to controlling all the elements of power that you awakened, at Ghilod's proposal, all the masters agreed to allow you take your final trial tomorrow."

"That's wonderful news. Thank you, sir!"

"You will not be so thankful after I give you the details about it. To begin with, there was one condition that made everyone agree and that was for you to have only your fiancé as a partner, which will mean that you have to do the work of four mages. You see, there are usually five people in a group for the final trial, four that have very good fighting skills and can control their magic very well and a healer, but in your case an exception was made based on your future role as Alyssa's guardian."

"That sounds very dangerous for her. Is there any chance for me to take the trial alone?"

"Unfortunately, you must prove that you can keep her safe by yourself, so you will need to risk your life and make sure that she never gets seriously wounded. That is going to be the main task of your trial, but there will also be an additional one, which is to take down a pack of wolves from what used to be a safe area a few days ago. It was supposed to be a group with a lot more experience to receive this task, but the masters think that you should suffice with help from your fiancé."

"How many wolves are there? And what area did they get to?"

"Their number, as well as how they passed through the barrier is yet to be confirmed, but it shouldn't be more than eight, and the area is on the southern part of Mage Island including the road that connects the Mage Institute to the small dock where the boats that can take you to Port Town are."

"What you just told me worries me a little, but, if that is what it takes to finally become a mage and go home where I can marry

Alyssa, I will get rid of the wolves and make sure that she will come out without any serious wounds, if not completely unharmed."

"I believe that you will be able to succeed. Since you don't have much time left before the trial, it is best to finish your training quickly. After that, please go see the grandmaster as he wishes to talk to you and then use the rest of the day to prepare yourself."

"Thank you for everything, master Frigus. I will do my best to prepare and pass the trial."

An hour later, the young man felt mentally and physically prepared, so he ended the training and went to see Lurmand. The grandmaster told him to be very careful during the trial since he had no idea how the barrier failed to keep the wolves from the safe area and promised that after he passes, a lot of his questions will be finally answered. He also admitted that he was pressured into allowing such difficult conditions, but he can only reveal more information after the young man will pass the test.

After finishing his conversation with the grandmaster, Kayro went to talk to Alyssa, but she was nowhere to be found. While searching for her, he was told that she is undergoing special preparations before the trail with her counsellor and master of healing, Ghilod. Since he had no idea when his fiancé will finish, he decided to go to the crafting workshop and get B'dar to check the equipment they will wear during the trial.

The master craftsman inspected everything and offered to give him new outfits that he personally made for both him and his future wife. He wanted to give that to them as a wedding gift, but with such a difficult task ahead, there was no choice but to start using them the next day. Kayro thanked the man, while making sure to keep the distance, and, after everyone wished him good luck, he went to the living quarters to shower and rest.

Soon after the sun set, Alyssa came to see him and he felt that something was different. Thinking it might be a result of getting nervous before the trial, he chose to ignore his instincts and showed her the outfits that B'dar prepared as a wedding gift. She seemed happy about receiving them, especially after hearing so many good things about the man's craftmanship and ability to imbue protective magic. More than that, the colours and style were a perfect fit for her taste.

After she was done trying her outfit and inspecting it, the young man decided it was time to finally tell her the truth. While he was taking about R'mal, B'dar, being a demon and his powers, his instincts stopped him from revealing who his parents really were. He decided that was enough information for now and, as soon as they left Mage Island behind, she will hear the rest of the story.

Alyssa kissed him before going back to her room and insisted that they both need to get as much rest as possible before the trial. Being aware that he needs to be in his best shape for what waited, he agreed with her and went to sleep.

Both of them woke up early and, as soon as they were ready, a boat took them to the small pier south of the Mage Institute. Since it wasn't a safe area anymore, the two of them were the only ones who got out from the boat, while their counsellors went back. Before leaving, the two masters wished them good luck one more time and gave them a magic crystal which would act as sign that they need a rescue team if smashed.

"I will leave that crystal with you, but I am certain we don't really need it. Since it's nearly night we should find a safe place to rest and tomorrow I can track the wolves and hopefully kill them quickly, so we can finally go back to Glade Village."

Alyssa agreed and they found a place to spend the night safely. Again she insisted that they need to have as much energy as possible the next day, so they went to sleep after adding some wood to the campfires around them. They chose to make a few, not only to keep warm, but also to keep the wolves away, and Kayro woke up twice to add more wood.

At dawn, after putting the fires out the couple started tracking the animals. With such a big area to cover, they kept to the road and three hours later finally found a sign of the pack being around. After searching the area quietly, the young man heard howling in the distance and realised that this was only one of the hunting grounds used by the predators. After studying the tracks better, he reached the conclusion that there were ten wolves in the pack with one of them, most likely the leader, being a little bigger in size than the others and surely stronger.

With Alyssa help he managed to make some traps and then went around looking for bait. They were lucky enough to find a miskra close by and Kayro was able to quickly kill it by using an ice spike. They kept part of it as food for the next days, not knowing exactly how long it will take to kill the entire pack, and the rest was used to make bait. For the rest of the day, the couple decided to build a safe place on the higher branches of two trees that were close to each other.

As the sun was setting they started hearing the wolves getting closer. Soon Kayro was able to see them using the demonic power which allowed him to see in the night. Alyssa was a little shocked to see his eyes changing their colour from brown to crimson, but he didn't notice, being too focused on the predators. As soon as five of the animals stepped into the traps, he used his wind powers to close them inside and jumped to the ground.

Seeing that the wolves considered him an easy target, he allowed them to get close and then conjured fire orbs to distract them while creating ice spikes. Three of the wolves, including the leader ran away, just as the he was using his wind magic to make the spikes pierce the heads of the other two. For a few minutes he searched using his demonic power and as soon as he could confirm there was no threat around, went to each trap and killed the trapped wolves.

While Alyssa was watching from the safe place in the trees, being afraid to come down until sunrise, Kayro was taking the predators out of the traps. After that, he started using his hunting kit to take their hides, teeth and claws to use them for crafting something in the future. As soon as he finished storing the part in his backpack and made more bait from the meat on each carcass, he climbed up next to his fiancé and they went to sleep.

For the next two days and nights there was no sign of the remaining wolves, so the couple decided to go after them. They were given five days to kill the pack, otherwise a group of mages will be sent to do it, meaning that the task will be considered failed and Kayro will need to wait longer until becoming a full mage.

A few hours after sunrise, the young man was able to track the three wolves and decided there was not enough time to build traps. He found an area that would give him some advantage while fighting three opponents and placed the baits to lure them here. As soon as all of them were in the positions he wanted them in, he will leap from his hiding place and quickly take out two, leaving the last wolf for a one on one fight, while Alyssa will wait in a safe place, away from reach or any danger.

His plan worked well and a few hours after the sun set the wolves were in position, so Kayro quickly started his attack. Taking them by surprise, he was able to kill the small ones very fast, making the leader of the pack his last opponent. Before the young man had the chance to turn around and face it, the beast disappeared inside the tall grass. Since he was expecting an immediate attack, the actions of the leader confused Kayro, but he chose to act as bait and wait for the predator to show itself.

A few minutes later, he heard Alyssa shouting at him to turn around fast and, as he did that, the wolf was already too close, easily pinning him to the ground. The protective outfit made by B'dar and his old gurma vest, saved the young man's life, but he was in great danger. Even so, he shouted and told his fiancé not to get involved because he cannot guarantee her safety, and then started thinking of a plan to escape.

With the beast trying to bite his neck, Kayro formed an ice spike with one hand while using the other to defend himself. Unfortunately, the pack leader was moving too fast and its hide proved to be too thick, so the ice spike broke instead of going through. The bite and claw wounds on his arms and chest made his instincts kick in, which activated part of his demonic powers.

The grown fangs and claws along with the strength stolen from the big miskra he killed in the Haunted Forest, allowed the young man to push the beast away, but not before it managed to bite his neck. Luckily, his self-healing abilities were working fast, so moments later there were no bite marks left. Apparently, his body could identify what was life threatening, because the claw marks on his arms were healing a lot slower than the rest, but that proved to be useful.

While forming another ice spike with one hand and a fire orb with the other, Kayro added some of the blood coming out from his wounds to the magic changing their colour to crimson and making them a lot stronger than before. He threw the fire orb towards the wolf, but the animal managed to dodge that fast enough to only get small burns. Still it was a perfect distraction and gave the young man enough time to send the ice spike at very high speed by using his ability to control wind. This time, it easily penetrated the wolf's hide, but it didn't hit a vital spot, so the fight was still on.

Seeing that the pack leader was slowed down, the young man started to form two more ice spikes, but soon he realised that might not be enough. As he could see a shadow-like figure in the distance, the pack leader's body started being covered by a demonic aura. Not only did that make the beast grow bigger and stronger, but also it gave it a scary bloodlust.

Despite the changes of the wolf's body and strength, Kayro could feel that the figure in the distance was more dangerous, so he covered himself in the demonic aura as well. By doing that, his fighting ability increased a lot, allowing him to move at incredible speed. Using two blood covered ice spikes and this newly gained speed, he was able to impale the beast's front paws into the ground and bite its neck.

As the pack leader was dying, the young man could feel a surge of power. His aura, body and demonic abilities were getting stronger, but there was no major change like the times when he killed the abnormal gurma and miskra. Just as the wolf gave its last breath, the shadow-like figure in the distance was trying to escape and that made Kayro very angry.

He quickly formed two fire orbs adding his blood to make them more powerful and threw them in the direction of his foe who managed to dodge them. Still, with his ability to see in the night, the distraction created by the orbs and the speed given by the demonic aura, Kayro caught his opponent, who proved to be a demon. Remembering what R'mal said about the assassin from the Great Forest, he started questioning his captive.

"Who sent you and who is your target?"

Since he refused to answer, Kayro used his claws to cut one of the demon's arms.

"Before I totally lose my patience, you should start talking. By attacking us you endangered the life of the person who I love the most, so unless you start talking, your head will be the next thing I will take off."

"No matter what you do to me I am unable to give you answers. There are spells that prevent me from revealing anything. All I can say is that I wasn't told my target would be another demon and more than that one who could use magic."

"Still, I need at least some clues from you and then I can spare your life. That information could help me protect my fiancé, so it would be worth letting you go, despite the fact that you might come back one day to finish your job."

"There is nothing I can tell you, prince."

Seeing no reaction on his capturer's face, the assassin carried on.

"Yes, I know who and what you are. You..."

Before he could finish his sentence, Kayro bit his neck and then used his claws to decapitate him. Seconds later, the young man was thinking about his actions, but this looked like the best choice he could make. He was afraid that others might know about who his parents were, but at the same time maybe the assassin was here only to confirm that.

As soon as the demon was dead, he went back to Alyssa and she sent a signal meant to let the mages know that the task was completed. With a few hours left until morning and little energy left after using his magic and demonic powers for such a long time, Kayro joined her in the hiding place and he fell asleep before they could talk about what just happened.

Two hours after sunrise, a group of mages led by Ghilod came to take them back to the Mage Institute. Since the young man was still recovering, he was carried by some of the trainees, while others took the dead bodies of the demon and the pack leader.

With so much energy used during the fight, Kayro was asleep for two days, until he was suddenly awaken by people shouting. Just as he opened his eyes, Allgos entered the room he was placed in to recover and fear could be easily read on his face.

"Good, you're awake. You need to dress up and run away. Ghilod imprisoned Lurmand and Frigus and he sent a group of mages to capture you as well. Quickly now, I have an outfit prepared by master Badar"

"What do you mean capture me? For what? And why did he imprison my master and the grandmaster?"

"Apparently some told him about a demon living in the Mage Institute besides my master and they told him it was you. As soon as Badar heard about this, he gave me this special outfit to bring to you, since he was suspected of bringing you here, and said that you could use this to hide the fact that you have magic powers. He told me that you must convince the mages who come after you that you are just like any other demon and the equipment made it look like you can control the elements, in case they manage to capture you.

"And where is he now? Is he still alive?"

"The grandmaster and your counsellor helped him escape and promised to do their best to get you out too, but, as soon as they managed to get him off the island, Ghilod was waiting for their return and imprisoned them for questioning."

"Ghilod did? What gives him the right? And how did he manage to beat two of the strongest mages?"

"Apparently, all this time he was hiding his real powers, pretending to be just a healer, but he was easily able to overcome the grandmaster and his followers outnumbered master Frigus allowing them to capture him."

"Are they still alive?"

"They are for the moment, but I'm not sure for how long. They told me to come and get you out of here as soon as possible, so it is best for us to go."

"I will not leave them behind. They risked their lives for both B'dar and me, so I cannot abandon them."

"All three said that you are too important to be captured, Kayro. So let us go now, before the group of mages that was sent after you will get here."

Just as Allgos finished his sentence the doors of the building were broken. Ghilod was leading ten other mages who were ready to attack at any time. Seeing the trainee craftsman there angered the healer and he ordered the group to attack. Just as fire and lighting orbs, along with ice blades and other elemental attacks were sent their way, Kayro covered himself in the demonic aura and managed to block most of them.

"Get behind something" he shouted at his senior. "I cannot fight them and defend you at the same time."

Realising he was right, Allgos quickly got behind a wall, which allowed Kayro to start his attack. He growled loudly at the mages before using his demonic speed, and, seconds later, five of them were laying on the ground unable to fight any longer, after he used his claws to incapacitate them.

Ghilod ordered the ones still standing to use stronger attacks, but their opponent was able to easily dodge or block them. More than that, as soon as he got the chance, he started taking them down one by one, until the healer was the only one left.

Confident from taking out the ten mages, Kayro was trying to go after the master healer, but as he got close to the man Alyssa jumped in front of him. Shocked by her appearance, he barely managed to stop himself, but that was enough for Ghilod to trap him inside a barrier and send multiple lightning orbs inside to put him down.

Later that day, he woke up in a cell of a prison he never knew existed on Mage Island and just as he was regaining conscience he heard the voices of the grandmaster and his counsellor.

"Grandmaster Lurmand, master Frigus, are you all right?" Kayro asked.

"We are for the moment, son, but I don't think this will last for long" the elder mage said.

"They will probably come and question all three of us soon and chances are they will use torture" the counsellor added.

As soon as he finished his words, the door big door at the end of the corridor of the dungeon opened. To his surprise, Kayro saw Alyssa coming followed by two guards. Each had a bowl of food and some bread for the prisoners and while his fiancé gave that to his, the guards gave the ones they carried to Lurmand and Frigus.

Before getting the chance to say anything, the young man was shocked by the words coming out from Alyssa's mouth.

"This is the last time you will see me, evil creature. I'm not here to say goodbye to you, but to find out what your intentions were. So, when did you start using me, you fiend?"

"My love, what are you talking about?"

"Don't try to use tricks on me, because they will not work. I was lucky enough to find a man who broke the control spell you cast on me."

"Control spell? What are you talking about? Even if I knew how to cast one, I would never use it on you."

"Lies, lies, and more lies. And here I was believing that you were keeping secrets from me in order to protect me, just as you said. But now I know the truth, you used me to get here and gain the trust of the mages, maybe even control some of them, before killing everyone and going after the humans in the Median Forests next."

"Are you out of your mind, Alyssa? Krysta and Klost might not be my real parents, but I love them as if they were, so I couldn't harm anyone in Glade Village. I also have dear friends in the other communities and I have you."

"Had, you HAD me. To be specific you had me fooled and controlled, but not any longer. Now I am free from your evil spell and I can clearly see you for the creature which you are. If master Ghilod didn't fall in love with me, he might have not noticed these things, but luckily he saw through them and released me from whatever you did, spell or not."

"So you were the one who betrayed me? I cannot believe this. You were the only person on this island who I could fully trust. Sure I kept some things secret from you, but that only to protect you. The less you knew about me, the lower the chances for anyone to try and get any information out of you."

"Again you are lying. Even with the truth revealing spell which my future husband placed on you, I can see that you can still spout your nonsense."

"Future husband? Truth revealing spell? Who are you? Where is my beloved Alyssa?

"Beloved? Yours? Don't make me laugh, evil creature. I'm sure that my real beloved will find out how you controlled me and what exactly it is that you want by the end of the day, but I guess part of me wanted to believe that you actually cared, at least enough to tell me the truth."

Before he got the chance to say anything else, the one who was his everything left. Kayro was too confused and too angry to react in any way. He was simply frozen, until a voice called out to him.

"I'm sorry son, but there is no time for you to cry or be mad. It seems that whatever spell Ghilod might have to try and make us talk is not working on you, so your blood might be blocking it. Both Frigus and I know your real identity, which is why we helped Badar escape and intended to do the same with you before your former fiancé betrayed all of us. The only way for us to resist that spell is to ingest your blood, so please send some to each of us by controlling it with your wind magic."

The young man grew his claws for a few seconds to give himself a cut, then used his wind magic to get some blood to the grandmaster and the counsellor.

"Do you think that will be enough?"

"I'm not sure, Kayro, but as grandmaster Lurmand said, this is the only thing we can do."

A few minutes after that, Ghilod came to see them followed by twenty other strong mages. He muttered some words and then started asking each of the prisoners the same questions. Thanks to the blood from Kayro, Lurmand and Frigus were able to hide the truth about him, but not getting the answers he wanted angered the master healer.

"Very well then, if you found a way to cancel my spell, then I will need to use more drastic measures."

He ordered the guards and the mages to get all the prisoners in chains and take them outside. Thinking that it was only him, his counsellor and the grandmaster, that were imprisoned, Kayro had a surprise when he saw Allgos being dragged along with them. The young trainee was barely able to walk and he had severe wounds all over his body.

"This is your last chance to tell me the truth!"

Since everyone kept quiet, Allgos and Frigus were taken aside and executed by the group of mages, which made both Lurmand and Kayro scream in anger and pain.

"What do you want to hear? We already answered you questions and just as your future wife, as she called herself, you have a spell that forces us to tell you the truth. What else can we say?" the grandmaster shouted.

"So, you still claim that you told me everything. In this case, I will make you slaves in the prison mine and ask you again in the future, maybe one year or longer in there will make you talk."

As he finished his words, Alyssa arrived with a metal tool. One of the fire mages used their power to heat it up and the young woman used it to brand, both the grandmaster and her former fiancé, as traitors to the Median Forests.

"Tomorrow morning, you will be sent to what I hope will become your grave and along with everything you will suffer there, the thought of being responsible for the death of your friend shall haunt you. Take them back to their cells and don't waste any food on them until they reach the prison mine."

After he finished saying that, Ghilod walked away holding Alyssa's hand, while Kayro and Lurmand were taken back to their cells where the mages started punching and kicking them. Even with the chains on, the young man managed to knock down a few of their attackers forcing them to leave the old man alone.

A few hours passed and Kayro finally woke up.

"Are you still alive, grandmaster?"

"I am son, and thanks to your actions I got away easily. I was afraid they might kill you, but I see that you are indeed quite unique when it comes to self-healing. I know that your demonic powers are able to heal you and I saw that happening some time ago after your first trial, but never expected them to keep you alive after the beating they gave you earlier."

"It seems that they are getting stronger and stronger as I kill powerful opponents or at least the ones that posses magic in any form."

"Well I guess that what I heard about you I true then. You are indeed the one who all demons have been waiting for."

"You know about that? Do you really believe they could read the flow of magic?"

"Not only I believe it, but I am certain, son. Since we have a lot of time to spend together before being sent to the prison mine

245

and you have earned your right to be called a full mage by passing the last trial, I can now answer your questions. Well at least up to a point. Feel free to ask anything you wish."

"What made you help me and B'dar? I thought all mages wanted to kill the demons."

"As I said before, I heard the story about the woman who read the flow of magic and predicted your arrival. More than that, even the mages were able to sense the same think, but, just like the demons did, we made a mistake too. In their case, it was believed that the one with both demon and mage blood will be your father, and in our case we didn't know who it will be, but that this new being will want to kill all mages and steal their powers."

"What makes you think that will not happen, especially after all the recent events?"

"You just proved that earlier, when it was so easy for you to let the mages hurt me, but you made sure they will all want to hurt you. Also, the moment B'dar came back from the Blood Lands, he told me about R'mal and who you were, and the way you behaved all your life. I'm not sure if being raised by Krysta and Klost changed what the magic flow told the mages or if you were always meant to be who you are now, but I can guarantee with my life that your purpose in not to seek and take all power."

"Thank you for your kind words, grandmaster. Indeed I don't care about getting all the power in this world. I don't want to be the strongest, but I want to be strong enough to break all the borders set by the mages and free my parents."

"I'm sure you will manage that one day, dear boy, but first you must get stronger and learn more about this world we live in. As I said before, I will be able to give you some of the answers, but there is much you will need to learn by experiencing life."

"So what exactly is this magic and why are we able to use it now? Why don't I remember anything about it from any of my past lives? Speaking of that, why do we have any memories of that?"

"Everything is part of the universe, but the energy particles are different all over. If you have any memories about 'The Reset', you should know that everything changes after a long period of time. From what any mages were able to feel through the flow, this happens every thirty-five thousand years and the changes are random. In Xorbia's case, not only did new beings, including humans get transported here, but also the concentration of particles grew giving everything on the planet a certain amount of magic."

"Then why are we not all as strong as the mages?"

"Because no one was supposed to be that strong. You see, only a very part of the humans, plants and animals on this planet received a higher concentration of particles as they came to existence, but after the magic crystals were discovered, the humans known as mages started experimenting to make themselves more powerful and become the rulers of this world. They began by using the crystals on plants, but without seeing great results, since nature doesn't really allow anything to control it. Then they started using them on animals which allowed some to become fearsome beasts unlike any you have ever seen."

"You mean there are animals out there stronger than the ones I already encountered? Even than the ones controlled by demons?"

"Indeed there are, dear boy. Some will make the beast that you took down in the Great Forest look like a pet. Fortunately only a few gained that much power and they prefer to live alone, in areas where humans cannot easily go."

"Is that why the mages are trying to stop the people in the Median Forests to explore the planet and why the keep people caged within their barriers? They want to keep them safe from these beasts?"

"I'm afraid that is not the truth. You see, no matter how strong the mages get, they still need someone to produce goods for them. Using our magic is not enough to maintain this lifestyle and that would mean wasting time instead of finding ways to get stronger. Basically, the humans are simply slaves that supply the mages with whatever they need. Of course, they are not allowed to find out about magic, so the Council of Elders was forced to believe that everything we do is for the protection of the human race."

"Are all the mages on Xorbia living on the Ardian Continent?"

"No. Only a handful. In fact they sent the weakest one here. Basically the ones outside the continent bullied the rest of us to bully the humans into being slaves without their knowledge."

"So, how big is Xorbia and do you have a full map of it?"

"I am afraid that someone as weak as me was not allowed to know that. All I know is that there are three four more continents apart from ours. One to the north, one to the east, one to the south and another one to the west."

"Are there humans living on these continents?"

"Well, I am not entirely sure. As you know, in the south, there are demons living on the continent they call the Blood Lands, but apart from that, I have no idea what else might be out there. I suspect there might be other humanoid races since there were a lot of experiments on humans during the first one hundred years after the discovery of the magic crystals, but I have no certainty of that."

"Thank you very much for helping me and B'dar and for answering my questions. I think it is best for us to rest since there will be no food to help us recover our strength and when we get the chance, we will carry on with the conversation."

Lurmand agreed and they went to sleep in order to recover.

# Chapter 4

# The Desert Mine Prison and the way to a new beginning

## The journey to the Desert Mine Prison

Kayro and the grandmaster were suddenly awaken by orbs of cold water splashing their faces and bodies, and, after their chains were checked, a group of mages started punching and kicking them again before throwing them on a boat. They passed out from the beating and woke up the next morning inside a metal cage that was placed on a cart pulled by bovri which was going north judging from the sun's position. Apart from theirs, there were two more carts and each of them had four mages and five guards, with one of the guards acting as a driver.

Just before sunset they reached a port similar to the one on the southern side of Mage Island and they were moved inside a cage of a big boat. Since they didn't have any food for a few days, Kayro's wound were barely healing, but he was still in better shape than Lurmand. Even so, after receiving another beating they both passed out and woke up the next morning.

"Grandmaster! Grandmaster! Are you still alive?" the young man was shouting while everyone around them was laughing at the old man's poor condition.

"I am not going to die so easily, dear boy, but I have to admit that these might be the worst days in my entire life up to this one."

"As soon as the guards and mages fall asleep, I will cut myself and give you some of my blood. Maybe it will help heal your body just as it worked to negate that truth revealing spell" said Kayro after getting close enough to make sure that no one can hear him.

"Are you sure about that? You lost a lot of blood already and it might not even work. This will surely endanger your life."

"I will risk my life if that means saving yours."

"You really are totally different from what the ones reading the flow of magic said you will be."

"We never know how life changes us, grandmaster. Maybe in order to save my parents I will need to become what the mages feared."

"And that is why you must make sure that none of them find out who your parents are."

"I will do my best not to reveal my identity, sir."

Since they barely had any energy left and the mages still refused to give them any food, both men agreed to sleep as much as possible. Every two or three hours some of the mages were throwing water orbs at them, waking them up, but they always found a way to keep calm and, as soon as they had the chance, go back to sleep.

As it was getting closer to midnight and there were no mages around, Kayro used his demonic power that allowed him to see in the dark and checked to see if they were being watched. As soon as he was able to confirm that no one could see what they are doing, he grew one of his claws, made a small cut on his forearm and told the old man to drink some of the blood before the cut heals.

Initially there was no reaction, so they gave up on that idea and went back to sleep to save energy, but, in the morning, after being awaken by the water orbs thrown at them, Lurmand noticed that most of his wounds were a lot smaller than the day before.

"It seems that your blood is unique. I heard about mages experimenting with demon blood before, but there was no effect to either drinking it or adding it in different potions."

"I have no idea how and why mine works, but I am happy to hear that it's healing you, grandmaster."

"Still, I am surprised that your wounds are healing so slowly. I was expecting you to be fully healed hours after each beating you took."

"If I allow my instincts to take over, I would probably heal even faster than that, but it uses a lot of my energy and also I want to avoid showing the mages my full power. To prevent my body from doing that, I am supressing my demonic power and my instincts as much as possible."

"That's a good idea. They will probably turn you into a test subject and perform experiments on you until you die, if they ever see the full extent of your abilities."

"I just remembered that you said something about being sent to the Ardian Continent. Where did you come from?"

"I was born and raised on the Blood Lands territory. Both my parents were mages and we lived in a small community protected by barriers. Just like everyone the humans in the Median Forests, we were not allowed to go outside the barriers, but this was for our protection. In fact, to make sure that no demon could ever find out about our community, a barrier of invisibility was created and maintained around the area where we lived."

"Is that even possible? I could barely believe that someone was capable of creating a barrier around Mage Island, so I cannot imagine how powerful someone has to be in order to cover a bigger area."

"It was possible just because of the magic crystals and with the sacrifice of the mage who conjured the barrier. He was my ancestor and probably with similar abilities as mine, but the Council of Magic ordered around one hundred mages, who were able to create barriers, to transfer their entire power into magic crystals. They were able to get nearly five hundred fully charged crystals at the cost of everyone losing their magic."

"Council of Magic? What is that? And how exactly did your ancestor die?"

"Be patient, dear boy. I will answer all these questions one by one."

"I apologise, grandmaster, but my curiosity always gets the best of me."

"Well then, let me continue with my story and answer your questions. As I was saying, with the cost of losing their magic, one hundred mages were able to store their power into magic crystals and those were used as amplifiers for my ancestor. He was told from the start that, as soon as the barrier will be created, he will surely die, but he simply wanted to protect his friends and family, especially from the most dangerous creation of the mages which is your race, the demons.

Just as he was told, when the barrier was finished, all life drained out of him along with his magic and the five hundred magic crystals are keeping that barrier in place even now and will probably do so forever."

"Was he that strong? I can barely hold control over the elements for a short period of time, let alone create one that would last at least for an hour."

"No. He was just a little above average and that made him expandable. If one of the members of the Council of Magic would try the same thing, he would only have a low chance of dying, but they are too selfish to risk anything unless it makes them directly more powerful, so they just sacrificed a pawn."

"I am sorry to hear that, grandmaster. It must have been hard on your family."

"Not really, dear boy, or at least not at that time. Since they knew from the start what the outcome of conjuring such a powerful barrier was going to be, everyone was ready for his death and saw him as a hero. Only when my father, while training as a mage, discovered that more powerful mages managed to create similar barriers with no risk, he started looking into what exactly made my ancestor accept his death that easily.

Apparently, the Council of Magic found out that my ancestor discovered how exactly the demon race was created and he was going to tell everyone about that. I know this might be shocking to you, but many of the mages still have no idea that your race was the results of greedy mages trying to become more powerful.

Going back to what happened, my forefather was forced into accepting the task and basically be executed. By making him a hero, the Council of Magic made sure that no one will see it as an execution, but as an act of love towards his friends and family."

"I am really sorry to hear that, grandmaster. So, what exactly is this Council of Magic? How come they were able to get away with that and why do they want to hide things that much?"

"They are all direct descendants of the first mages and they are bred for taking that role."

"What exactly does that mean?"

"With only a few strong mages in the beginning, the male and female who were the strongest at controlling one element, were told to make children and then hopefully the child was going to be stronger than each of them at using that power."

"What about the next generations? Since their children would be the strongest, will they need to have babies with their siblings?"

"Fortunately that was not the case. Only one of their children in each family was able get stronger than both parents, so they had to look for a partner from another family, with the same power level or close to it. Still the power was passed down and I could confirm that any of the current members of the Council of Magic are as powerful as monsters compared to their ancestors."

"That sounds quite bad. I hope I will be able to free me parents without having to fight one of them."

"I am afraid that you will need to fight at least a few of them. Since I am too weak as a mage, I was never told exactly how many members the councils has or who they are, but I suspect that at least one of them is here, on the Ardian Continent. I am not sure if he is hiding among the people of the Median Forests or maybe in the Desert Prison, but this land is too valuable as a resource to be left unguarded."

"I guess we will see that in the future."

Seeing them talk for too long, the mages and guards started beating them up again until both men passed out. Kayro was getting angrier and angrier every time they were assaulted, but, without eating, he only had enough energy to slowly heal his wounds.

They woke up after sunset and after making sure no one can see them, the young man gave Lurmand some of his blood again.

"Thank you very much, dear boy. I would probably be nearly dead if it wasn't for your blood."

"You're welcome, grandmaster. I just hope we will survive long enough to eat again and recover properly. Do you have any idea how long it will take us to reach the Desert Mine Prison?"

"Probably four or five more days. We left the Grand Lake and now I think we are on the Great Northern River which passes through the desert."

"Hopefully we will still be alive when we finally get there."

"So, do I, son. So do I."

They went back to sleep to forget about the hunger and they woke up in the afternoon of the next day. The cold air from the Ring Mountains was making the shiver, and it felt like this might be the end of their lives. A few minutes after they woke up, the mages threw some blankets inside their cage.

"It seems they need us alive" Kayro said.

"Not really. They are trying to keep us alive so we can be tortured for a longer time. You see, the ones that are transporting us to the Desert Mine Prison are just some low mages and they have no idea what made me choose to betray the mages. They simply see us as the worst criminals and probably, as Ghilod surely suggested to them, they think we are working with the demons to kill all humans, including the mages."

"I guess I would react in a similar way if my family or friends were in danger."

"Me too, son. That is why no matter what they do, I cannot react. These people are simply being used by that cursed Council of Magic."

"I am aware of that, but if we want to ever escape, we must be prepared to harm or even kill some of them."

"I know and I will hate myself when that happens."

"What made you take our side, grandmaster?"

"I was raised to strive for peace between all races that live on Xorbia. Especially after my father found some information about the experiments made during the early years. Also, as I grew up, I realised how the mages could help the normal humans and improve the quality of life even by using just a little of their power."

"I was wondering why they are going so far to keep their existence a secret. While training on Mage Island, I could think of so many ways that my powers would make my grandparent's work a lot easier. Even the ones with a little magic could help more than tools or livestock are able to."

"That's true and, after I came to that conclusion, I asked one of my superiors about working together with the regular humans.

Initially he told me that normal people would be afraid or jealous of our abilities and they will try to kill us, and, when I insisted about at least trying to see how it works, I was almost killed. Up to this day I have no idea if that man was brainwashed or he saved my life by not allowing me to talk to anyone else about my ideas."

"Why would you think that? After all, he tried to kill you."

"He seemed sad as the other novices were punishing me in a similar way that our escort is doing to us. And I will never know for sure, even if we manage to escape the Desert Mine Prison, because a few years after that incident, the man took his own life."

"Well there's nothing that can be done about the past, so we will have to focus on the future. I cannot promise you that we will get away, but I will do my best to do so."

"I am happy to hear that, dear boy. As long as we don't lose hope, the future will wait for us."

Getting warm under the blankets and still tired from being hungry, they fell asleep again.

The next morning they could see the Ring Mountains behind and the Hills of Hope around them, which meant that they were getting closer to the desert. Two days later, after passing through a forest, they could see the great sea of sand. It would probably take them a day or maybe even more to get there, but that meant they are very close to their destination.

Feeling weaker with each passing moment, both Kayro and Lurmand, decided to stop talking and just sleep. Their stomachs were growling and they could barely keep their eyes open, so the mages and guards stopped torturing them making sure they will not die before getting to the prison.

Three days later orbs of water woke them early in the morning and in front of them were some animals that the young man has never heard of, let alone see before.

"They are called 'crafa' and it looks like they are the best way to move around in the desert. I have never seen one, but I heard that they can last for a long time without water and, with their long, but thick legs, they can easily pull the sleds which are used instead of carts."

"We will soon see if that is true."

Just as Kayro finished his words, the mages and guards opened the door to their cage and started dragging them towards a massive sled that was pulled by two crafas. As much as they wanted to see the how the wonderful animals were doing, the lack of energy made the men fall asleep.

A little before sunset, they reached the entrance of a huge cave. It was so big that it made the crafa look small and they were at least two times taller than most humans.

"I guess that we are finally here, grandmaster."

"Looks like it, dear boy. Now, let's hope that we will get some food soon, because I feel like this might be my last day."

As they were talking, one of the mages shouted.

"Keep quiet you cursed traitors! And say goodbye to daylight, because this is surely the last time you will see it. Tomorrow morning you will meet the warden of your tomb and you can start by thanking him as soon as you see him."

"And why should we do that?"

"Because he ordered us to feed you, get you cleaned and let you rest properly."

Kayro and Lurmand suddenly felt alive again, just at the thought of eating something again. They were very weak, but happy to be alive after enduring a long journey, surviving cold and hot weather, getting tortured nearly every day and sometimes maybe more than once in a day. A guard led them to a room that turned out to be a public bath for all the new prisoners.

After cleaning themselves, they were given new clothing, which was simple, without pockets, not too thin, not too thick, and then they were taken to what looked like a banquet hall were they could finally eat. Despite being so hungry, they only ate a little, and as soon as everyone was done, the guards led them to a room filled with beds.

## The warden and the five levels of the prison

After an evening that made them feel human again, Kayro and Lurmand woke up early and started a conversation about everything they saw the day before and about the meeting with the warden of the prison that was going to take place soon.

"Grandmaster, was I seeing things before we were allowed to eat or were there some individuals that seemed entirely different races than humans or demons?"

"That would mean we were both hallucinating, my dear boy, and I find it hard for two people to see the same things when their minds are playing tricks on them."

"From what I could see in the distance, some of them had insect features, while others had reptile features. Do you think they might be experiments of the mages or maybe Xorbia's magic changed them?"

"The planet only changes things up to a point, son. The magic makes some individuals stronger, bigger, faster, creates hybrids that are still animals, but never turns them into humanoids. The ones we could get a glimpse of yesterday were more similar to us than to any beast."

"Well, I guess we will soon learn about them since we are all prisoners in this place."

"I am not so sure about that. Compared to the demons and humans they were treated poorly. If I had to guess, I would say they might get each race into a different area. This way it will be nearly impossible for information to be shared and for the humans to find out about the horrors that the mages committed."

"You are probably right. I would definitely try to find out more about them, if I had the chance, and even with nearly no chance to escape from this tomb, I don't think the mages wish for anyone to know the truth about their experiments."

Their conversation was suddenly interrupted by a group of guards and mages that started shouting at everyone to wake up and get ready to start paying for their crimes. As they were taken out of the room, the two men were looking around to check if the humanoids they saw the previous night were still there and if they didn't just happen to hallucinate about the same things.

There was no sign of anyone like that, but at the same time, the number of prisoners was a lot smaller and these were definitely humans. Just as the rest of the prisoners were being taken to an elevator, Kayro and Lurmand were separated from the group and taken to a small room that looked like an office. The room was empty, but, as they were waiting surrounded by six mages and eight guards, a familiar voice started talking immediately after the door behind them opened.

"It is good to see the two of you again. How are you my friends? I hope you enjoyed the treatment you received last evening, because it will be the last time anyone will be kind to you."

The man got in front of them and started laughing as soon as he could see their shock and anger.

"What? Are you still mad that I killed your accomplices or at least that I was the one to give the order for them to be executed?" Ghilod said with a smirk of satisfaction on his face.

"Why are you here, so called healer?" Lurmand shouted while trying to break free from his chains.

"Well, I guess the grandmaster is not as wise as they praised him to be. If you opened your eyes sooner, old man, you could have realised that I was in fact one of the members of the Council of Magic."

"A lowly mage like you? I could easily bite your head off if I wasn't chained right now" Kayro said before growling fiercely.

"It is so good to see that there are still fools who cannot see what is right in front of them. Do you have any idea how hard I had to work to keep my powers in check, but also reveal enough to make me the master of healers at the Mage Institute?"

"I knew that you were holding back, you fiend, but never expected you to be this strong. I may hate you and wish see you dead right now, but only a member of that cursed council could have this much freedom and influence, not to mention that I can sense just how strong you really are."

"That is where you are wrong, grand useless. Even now I am still keeping part of my power hidden. I just wanted to show you how blind you were before."

"Yeah, yeah, you're strong. Let me out of these chains and I will show you just how strong you are not. I swear I will taste your blood for killing Allgos and master Frigus" shouted Kayro.

In a moment of pure rage, Ghilod combined a small orb of lightning with another made of fire and threw them at the young man who couldn't move. Even without the chains, he would probably barely dodge those, but now it was impossible to do that. Just as he was collapsing, the grandmaster tried to protect him by distracting the enraged healer.

"I can see that you are indeed very powerful, but why did you come to Mage Island. Why did you pretend for so many years to be a healer?"

"Because that is what I am, old man. I am the supreme healer. I have been alive for twice as long as you, but thanks to my abilities, I can stay young. Occasionally I allow my body to age when I pretend to be someone else, but I can always restore it. And to answer your question, I came to look for a bride than can finally give me an heir as strong as me."

"But why do this at the Mage Institute? Why not look for one among the children of the strong mages? We both know that only weak mages are sent to the Ardian Continent."

Before answering, Ghilod conjured a barrier around him and Lurmand.

"Now that no one can hear us and you will soon die anyway since I made sure to make it harder for the two of you than for any other prisoner, I guess telling you the truth cannot harm me in any way. You see, with so much time at my disposal, I was able to learn how to read the flow of magic and I knew where I will be able to find the perfect bride, but, just like anyone else that manages to get information about the future using this method, I was not able to see who it will be, where or when will she come from, only an approximate time and that I will meet her on the Ardian Continent.

That is why I made sure to take over as the warden of this prison and, from here, control everything within the barriers. It was hard to convince the others to leave this weak land in my care, because, at the same time I was able to find information about my perfect bride, a crazy rumour started. Something about a half demon, half human with both the powers of mages and the demonic ones, being born here. A saviour for the demons, a friend to all races and the one who will destroy the Council of Magic and steal their powers in order to rule over Xorbia.

Luckily, the demons kept singing praise to a man who was born a human and, after being given blood by the former demon king, became part demon himself and married the princess. With help from the ones opposing the so called royal family, not only did we manage to kill the old king and his wife, but also capture this 'saviour' and the princess and enslaved them. More than that, I was part of the group that stopped him from visiting his human parents and telling them about the secrets we are trying to keep away from our 'free' slaves."

"I remember that I was told to send you there and fight the demons, but I was never allowed to know what exactly happened there."

"I will tell you what happened. We made those creatures suffer. We crushed them in battle and also stopped their lineage. The 'saviour' and his wife are imprisoned deep inside a prison mine similar to this one, only a lot harder to get to, or to get out from. The former king and his wife are dead and replaced by some brutes who act as a council and will not seek to go outside the Blood Lands, which is exactly where we want them to stay. And the last hope, which was the baby who was born from that twisted relationship was killed during the battle when his parents were captured."

"Look at how proud such a powerful mage is for killing a baby. You should be ashamed of yourself."

"From what I heard, it wasn't even our fault. His mother was to blame for trying to hide him in the middle of the battle. It seems she forgot about the animals who saw him as the perfect meal, because all we were able to find was the cloths we was wrapped in and that was covered in blood."

"So, by sending you there, to slaughter innocent people, I gave you the chance to take control of the continent?"

"Foolish old man. You didn't send anyone. The Council of Magic gave you that order and these creatures will never be considered people. Still, you did play a part in this story by not realising who I really was, a thing that allowed me to stay on Mage Island until my bride finally arrived."

"Are you saying that you have found her already?"

"Of course I did. And for that I have to thank this lowly animal next to you. If she didn't have such deep feelings for him before finding out about the evil blood inside him, she would probably not even awaken her powers, but as soon as we tested them, I was certain she is the one. I still haven't figured out how you and your pet craftsman B'dar tricked us into believing that the boy had magic powers, but after the lowly creature defended him following his second trial, I was sure that he is not what he seems."

"So Alyssa wasn't lying to the boy when she told him that you will be her future husband."

"No. She was tricked into loving what this creature pretended to be, but, as soon as she understood what he really was and I revealed my true identity, she became mine and only mine."

"She must be really powerful for you to want her so much as a wife and a mother to your heir."

"When it comes to healing, at the rate she improved her already strong abilities, she might even surpass me."

"And what makes you think that she will not betray you if she gets that strong?"

Just as Kayro was regaining his consciousness and Lurmand was getting ready to say something, Ghilod shouted.

"I had enough of these two. Take them to the elevator and drop them inside the mine. With a bit of luck, they will not survive more than a month down there. At least not after I made sure they will be 'welcomed' by the other prisoners."

Barely staying awake, in a low voice, Kayro made a promise that was carved in his mind.

"One day, I will definitely end your life with my fangs. The deaths of my friends and family will surely be avenged."

As they were lowering the elevator to the last floor, one of the guards started mocking the two men.

"I really wouldn't like to be in your shoes right now. I heard that the warden increased the amount of crystal each floor must collect every day in order to receive food and blamed everything on the two of you making him angry. More than that, everyone on your floor knows about your betrayal, former grandmaster, and about your friend here being a demon. They might not be strong mages, or not as strong as they once used to be, but I am certain they will make sure to torture both of you."

Lurmand was worried after hearing that, while Kayro looked like he might not survive until next day, after taking that powerful combined magic attack from the enraged warden.

After reaching the fifth level of the prison, both men were pushed out of the elevator by the guards and the doors closed behind them quickly.

"Don't worry, grandmaster. Mages or not, we will either make them allies or kill them all. After hearing everything Ghilod said, I will burn down this entire prison if that means I can make him pay for executing Allgos and Frigus and for what they did to my parents and grandparents."

"How did you know about that? Were you able to hear him through that barrier?"

"I heard his entire story. About his real identity, the things he did to get in control of the Ardian Continent and his intentions when it comes to the woman who I now hate after what she did."

"I thought it was impossible to do what you just did. You and your body never cease to amaze me, dear boy. Let's find a place for you to recover and then start working for our meal. I will not survive a whole week of not eating again."

"I just need a few minutes. I will allow my instincts to take over and that should be enough to heal me."

Before the old man had a chance to say anything else, Kayro's body got covered by the demonic aura. He felt it being a lot stronger than it was before his final trial and, in less than ten minutes, not only did his body fully heal, but also he managed to break the chains around his hands and feet. He did the same for the grandmaster allowing them to move freely.

"Once again you did something that I couldn't imagine being possible."

"That meal was able to restore most of my energy and if what the guard said is true, we will need to be able to defend ourselves. Also, after taking down the wolf pack leader and the demon who started controlling it, my demonic powers have grown. Speaking of, I know it's not something pleasant, but you should drink some of my blood again to restore your strength."

Knowing that the young man was right, Lurmand agreed and as soon as he finished they started hearing the voices of men who were coming towards their location. They patiently waited until the men got in sight, since there was no point in hiding, especially in a place where they just arrived.

"Grandmaster, is that you? I heard they imprisoned you, but I was hoping this was a lie."

"Rollio?! You're still alive?"

"Yes, sir. Why would you think I was dead?"

"Oh, how blind I could be for so many years. When you went out on that mission requested by the Council of Magic, I was told that everyone was killed by a beast. And now, meeting you here I cannot even imagine how many times I was deceived."

"I was sure that you were not the one to send us here, despite what all the other mages said."

"Dear boy, I didn't even think mages could ever be brought here. I knew about humans that broke the laws and demons, but after coming here as a prisoner, I discovered the truth, well, at least part of it, because we saw some humanoids that didn't seem to be humans or demons. I'm sorry for not trying to look for you, but the news of your group being killed came from someone I thought I could fully trust."

"Speaking of trust, grandmaster. How much is real of what we heard about you? Is the man next to you really a demon who you tried to use and taken power from the other mages?"

"He is part demon, yes. But also part human. Despite what you heard, he got there by using his own abilities and B'dar or I didn't even know about him."

"How is B'dar? I heard that without help from you and Frigus he would have ended up being executed."

"I cannot say for sure if he is safe, but we did manage to help him get off Mage Island. Sadly, Frigus and the best trainee craftsman were executed instead."

"That reminds me. We should go away from here. While our group doesn't have anything against you, there are ten mages that are quite strong and wish to kill you. In fact, I bet they are getting closer as we speak."

"Let us go then."

On their way to the safe place, Lurmand explained to Kayro that Rollio used to be one of the best fire mages at the Mage Institute, and he was sent by the Council of Magic on a mission in the Blood Lands, or at least that is what he was told. If the mission was going to be a success, than he would be next in line for the title of master of the fire mages at the institute. Unfortunately, two months later, the mission report came in, saying that all the group members were killed by an unknown beast.

Rollio and his group managed to keep the grandmaster and Kayro hidden in a part of the fifth level of the Desert Mine Prison, but after a week he was taken by the mages who wished to kill the ones he was protecting. As soon as they found out about that, the two men became enraged and, remembering what happened to Allgos and Frigus, they swore not to allow anyone else to die for them.

"We will have to trap them somehow. If he said they are quite strong that means they will be very hard to deal with by the two of us and I am not taking risking anyone else's life at this point" Lurmand said.

"I am sorry to do this grandmaster, but you will need to stay hidden. You are far too valuable to lose and with the energy that I have left, I should easily be able to use my demonic aura at a higher level than I did before. In fact, by combining the darkness in the tunnels with the effect the aura has and with my ability to see in the darkness, I could probably rescue him without even being noticed, so you can just stay behind with the others and try to get some crystals delivered. This way I will have some food to recover after using my powers."

"Are you certain you want to do this by yourself? It will not be as easy as you might think."

"I will bring Rollio back, no matter what happens. I can promise all of you that!"

Before Lurmand or anyone else had the chance to say anything else, Kayro covered his body with the shadow-like aura and started moving at a very fast pace. Whenever he could see light from a torch, he was sending strong gusts of wind with small orbs of water ahead to put them off. It took him nearly an hour through the maze of tunnels, but he finally got close to where the fire mage was being held captive. As he got there, he could smell blood and even taste it through his aura. It was Rollio's and it seemed that the man lost a lot of it.

After putting out all of the torches in the room, Kayro used his ability to see in the darkness and he was horrified at the sight of the fire mage's state. He was barely alive and without magic healing he would definitely die in less than an hour. Once again the young man remembered the execution of his friends and his bloodlust was awakened. He growled loudly, just a wild beast might do, which made his demonic aura grow even stronger and then with an incredible speed he started using his fangs, claws and all the body to body combat he learned during Training Camp.

All types of elemental attacks were thrown at him by the terrified mages, but his aura was easily blocking everything. The first three men were laying dead after one minute with claw marks all over their bodies and with their necks bitten.

Surprisingly, Kayro started feeling stronger and stronger after each kill, despite the energy he was using to control his powers. Five of the remaining mages started running away while two earth elemental users stayed behind to block him by conjuring a wall. Part of him just wanted to get Rollio out of there and take him back to safety, but the other part knew that he must end things here and the only way to do that was to kill the other seven mages, before they get the chance to take another hostage.

The wall in front of him seemed strong, and he could sense that the two who created it fled as soon as they finished it, so he had no time to waste here. Using his claws, the young man cut the top of his forearms and by combining water magic with his own blood he easily took down the obstacle.

Since all the mages had at least one cut on their body after he stormed in to save Rollio, Kayro was able to track them by smelling their blood. As he was getting closer to the last two who ran away, his demonic aura was able to taste their magic through their wounds and he knew exactly how much magic power they have left and how strong they were.

He growled again and this time he got as fast and agile as the abnormal gurma which he killed in the Great Forest, allowing him to quickly catch up to the two earth elementals and bite their necks killing them. Knowing that he has no time to waste, after confirming their deaths, he carried on at a fast pace tracking the others.

In about five minutes he could sense a lightning, fire and ice mage waiting to trap him, but as soon as they attacked, two of them were impaled by ice spikes, while the third one's neck was grabbed by Kayro's bloody claws. The young man, who was more of an animal than a human now, snapped his neck and then bit him. To make sure that the other two were dead, he ripped their necks with his fangs as well and then he started tracking the remaining two mages.

Ten minutes later his aura was able to sense a healer and a barrier conjurer very close. These two seemed stronger than the rest and they were trying to deal with their wounds, probably so they could fight him at full capacity of their abilities.

As soon as Kayro tried to put off the light by using wind and water again, a barrier stopped his attack. He could hear them talking about the fact that this barrier cannot be broken or penetrated by any magic from the outside, a thing which he took as a challenge, but they could still attack from the inside. With enough light to see each other, the mages were shocked by the aura around their attacker, but still they tried to kill him with lightning orbs and water blades.

Just like before, his aura was blocking their attempts, but not as easily as it did before, so Kayro felt the need to end things quickly. He initially attacked them by using ice spike, but the mages were right about the barrier and his magic proved useless. Once again he used his claws to make cuts on his forearms, which were already healed and added a little of his blood to the ice spikes. This time they were able to penetrate the barrier, but failed to reach the two mages.

While trying to figure out a way to get to them, the young man started smelling Rollio's blood again and his aura could sense that the fire mage had nearly half an hour left before he would die. With blood on his mind, Kayro remembered fighting the gurma during his Test of Survival and realised that he was using his own blood at that time, instead of the ice or water element like everyone claimed, so he decided to form spikes out of his own blood instead of covering the ice with it.

A minute later, the barrier was easily pierced by his new attack and before having enough time to block or dodge it, the two mages got impaled by the spikes. In a rush to get back to Rollio, Kayro tore their necks out with his fangs to make sure they will not survive and then started running back.

With his instincts taking over, he got faster at both tracking and moving, so he was next to the dying mage in less than ten minutes, but still there was not enough time to take him back to a healer and since the fire mage was unconscious he couldn't give him blood to drink. In a moment of frustration, he punched the wall of the tunnel and he could feel small sparks of lightning coming out of his fist.

"Maybe I am able to control more than what I they discovered I can at the Mage Institute" he thought to himself, before attempting to heal Rollio. Unlike the blue light that Alyssa described coming out from her, after healing the wounds caused by the abnormal gurma, a crimson light was now leaving Kayro's hands, covering the fire mage's body. Ten minutes later, most of the wounds were closed, but with all the energy he used, the young man passed out.

He woke up the next day and next to him was Lurmand waiting impatiently. The grandmaster told him that Rollio somehow managed to drag him back to the safe place and after getting back he fell asleep and was still asleep after so many hours.

"What exactly happened to the two of you?"

"Well, I am not really sure how he managed to bring me back, but I can tell you everything I saw and did."

Kayro told the grandmaster everything as detailed as he could and the old man was left speechless for a few minutes. As impossible as he thought this might have been before hearing all of this, he was now convinced.

"You are indeed the one who could bring all the mages down and take their power. You might not want to do it, but you are able to."

"What do you mean? You know very well I don't wish to do that?"

"Now I understand exactly how your body works and I can tell you, that if you wished that, you would probably be the only being capable of doing it. Not as you are now, but by using the ability that makes you so unique and by training all the powers you now possess or the ones you might get in the future."

"I'm sorry, grandmaster, but I have no idea what you are referring to."

"Well, my dear boy, you are capable of stealing powers that your body and blood seem like a good fit for you. I am not exactly sure how it works, but, thinking about what you told me about this fight, the one from the Great Forest, the one from the Haunted Forest and the ones from you trials, I am certain that you stole powers from the opponents you have defeated. Did you do anything special?"

"No, I just fought, as hard as I could, for my life and to kill them."

"Did you draw any magic out of them or kill them in a certain manner?"

"Well, to make sure that they stayed dead I bit their necks with my fangs."

"That has to be it. Those are the moments when you do it for sure, but I don't know if your fangs are absorbing the magic or if the small amount of blood which you drink at that point is giving you the new powers. Or why not, maybe both of them combined."

"Are you certain about that? It does make sense, but I am still not getting all of their abilities."

"I have a theory about that too. Basically, you body goes for the strongest ability your opponent possesses. If you have it already, it will get stronger, if not, you will get simply get that new one, more likely at a low grade which means you will have to train and improve it."

"But that doesn't explain how I was able to heal Rollio. If what you say is true, I could probably close some of his smaller wounds, but no more than that."

"That is true, dear boy, but you forget about one important thing, which is the colour of the light that covered his body when you healed him. In all my years I have never heard or read about someone who was emitting a different colour than blue, yet yours was crimson."

"And could that be such a major factor?"

"I wish I knew more about the demon race, son. Then I could really give you a proper answer. Still, just think about how much your blood improved your ice magic and even more, how efficient making the spikes out of your own blood was. I wish we had B'dar or your guardian R'mal with us to find out more about your race."

Just as he was finishing saying that, Rollio woke up and they both went to check on the fire mage's health.

"You might be able to find some answers here."

"And how exactly can I we do that? We already know there are demons and humans here beside mages, but I haven't seen any sign of them while looking for you."

"That's because each level is for a certain category of beings. The fifth and lowest is for us, the mages. The fourth is for some beasts , but I have no idea exactly what kind. The third level is where you find humans that found out about the mages or broke the laws of the Median Forests. On the second level there are unknown beasts again and the top level is for the demons."

"Is there any logic behind the way the populated the levels?" Lurmand asked

"There is, grandmaster. They put us here to make sure that it will be the hardest for us to escape as we are seen as the greatest threat to them. On the fourth and second floor they put beasts to make sure that the humans will not try to work with us or the demons on an escape plan, and they kept the demons as close as possible to them in order to act as a wall for anyone who manages to go all the way, because they will try to kill us or the beasts and humans will fear them too much to climb up there."

"It sounds somehow well planned, but that cannot be enough to hold us here."

"Apart from that they have barriers set everywhere that can stop each type of being from leaving their level without being detected and they have patrols of strong mages who check each floor monthly or as soon as the quantity of crystals is not met for more than a week in a row. There were mages who tried digging an escape tunnel at the risk of not getting food, but, while doing that, they attracted the attention of the patrols and they easily got caught and killed."

"So we need to keep up with the crystal deliveries after the ten mages who took you were killed?"

"Yes, grandmaster. If we don't send similar quantities for longer than two consecutive days, a patrol will come down here."

"Wait. I have an idea" Kayro intervened.

"What is it?"

"Well, after waking up, I realised that I can now feel where the magic crystals are exactly. This way, part of us can dig a tunnel while the others make sure we are getting enough crystals delivered."

"We can test that and see if we can keep up. The last patrol checked the level a day before you came so we have almost three weeks until they come down."

With Kayro's help, they were able to find enough crystal deposits to keep a steady flow at least for a month if needed, but still, getting to the next level didn't seems enough to be able to escape the prison, especially not knowing exactly what was waiting for them once they get there, so they had to find a way to check it.

A few hours later, remembering some details from the young man's fight with the ten mages, Lurmand came up with two ideas. The first one was for him to try and detect what exactly are the creatures on level four and how strong they are, by using his demonic aura, and if that didn't work he might have to pass through the barrier hopefully without being detected while being covered in his shadow-like aura.

Since the first idea could only give Kayro a small glimpse of what they might be dealing with, he decided to go along with the second one. It was risky, but, after managing to take down the ten mages, he was certain that he can either kill his way out or simply use his speed to escape. With no time to spare, he started ascending the wall where the elevator shaft was and, with the help of his claws, he was easily able to climb the ten metres between the fifth and fourth floor of the Desert Mine Prison.

Once he got here, he discovered that all life forms started moving away from him, but after an hour, a group was waiting to meet him. Since he couldn't sense any hostility, Kayro gave up the protection of his demonic aura, but still kept using his ability to see in the dark.

As soon as he reached the place where the group was waiting for him, he was so shocked by their appearance that he couldn't say anything for a few minutes. The ones waiting for him had a humanoid shape, but they also had reptile features. What was more surprising was the fact that they were not all the same, with some looking like a hybrid between human and lizards, others like one between human and crocodiles and some like a hybrid between human and snake.

273

Just as he was ready to find a way to communicate with them, the one who seemed to be the leader of the group asked:

"What exactly are you? You are not human, but you don't seem like a demon either? Also I can sense magic in you. Did you come here to kill us?"

"You can speak?" asked Kayro.

"Of course I can, after all part of my race was once human and we kept using the same language. And you didn't answer my questions."

"First of all, I apologise for being rude. Secondly, no. I am not here to kill you and I am half demon, half human, with magical abilities as well."

"And I though the cursed mages went too far when they created us, reptilians. But you seem like something totally different."

"I was not created by them, I was born from a demon and from a human who was given demon blood. The mages had nothing to do with any of that."

"How did you get here then? Only the mages can go up through those barriers, while for any other race it seems impossible."

"I think it has something to do with my blood and the powers I have acquired lately."

As the conversation carried on, Kayro introduced himself and found out that the man who was half crocodile was named Dotropius. He was captured in the north of the Ardian Continent after crossing over the Infinite Sea from the continent called Reptilandia. They talked for a few hours about their past and the history of the land where they grew up and then the young man shared his plan of escaping from the Desert Mine Prison.

Dotropius asked him to wait for some time while he can talk to his fellows reptilians and then a decision to join forces or not get involved will be made. After nearly two hours he came back with an answer and that was an alliance between prisoners.

As soon as Kayro identified the crystal deposits which will allow the reptilians to meet their requested daily quota and dig a tunnel to connect the fourth floor to the third, he started climbing up the shaft wall to the next floor where the humans were put according to Rollio. He could immediately feel where all two hundred people were and started slowly walking towards them. Unlike the reptilians, who could feel magic, the humans were unaware that someone else is on their level and they kept digging for crystals as he got to them.

With torches everywhere, the one that he got close to at first stopped as soon as they saw his shadow on the walls. He chose not to reveal his powers from the start in order not to scare them and carefully approached the two who stayed behind, while another was trying to get away without being noticed.

He introduced himself to them and before they had the chance to say anything, he heard a familiar voice calling his name. As he turned around he saw his former head instructor, Zoss, the man who supported him to become an explorer during Training Camp.

"I would say it is good to see you, sir, but considering the place where we are, I can only say that I am surprised to see you. What happened? Why are you here? Is counsellor Monta here as well?"

"It is a long story, son. I can happily share it with you, but we will need to do that while we dig for those cursed crystals that the mages want. For some reason, around a week ago they suddenly increased the required daily quantity and we can barely keep up with it. If it was just me down here, I would gladly starve to death than do anything for them, but I cannot leave all these people here to die."

Kayro used his powers to detect a crystal deposit that was easy to reach and tested his earth element control to take them out as well. While everyone was scared, Zoss had a suspicions about the young man's powers.

"So, are you one of them? Are you here to check on us?

"I just wanted to test some of my new abilities, head instructor, and also give everyone a break from digging so we can talk quietly. I am a prisoner here too, but along with many others I have a plan to escape."

Since he trusted the man, Kayro told him about his demonic origins, Mage Island and the Mage Institute, how he became a prisoner and about everything that happened since he got to the Desert Mine Prison.

In return, Zoss told him about the fact that all four head instructors from Training Camp taking the blame on themselves for pushing with the training of adventurers and explorers and they claimed to be the only ones involved, as well as they only ones who knew about what happened in the Great Forest during the Test of Survival. All four of them agreed that this was the only way to save everyone else and allowed the Elders to imprison them without trying to run or fight back.

"While we were being questioned by some strange individuals, we started realising that the Elders are not really the ones in charge with the Median Forests, so when we had the chance, we spied on them finding out that they were actually mages.

We told no one about what we found out, so we allowed ourselves to be branded as traitors. Luckily no one else was questioned, which probably means that Monta might now be safe and doing my old job."

Zoss then told him how they were separated at some point, being taken in different directions, and after passing through Tower Town, Port Town and some strange island that was invisible from outside, which was located in the middle of the Grand Lake, he arrived at the Desert Mine Prison.

Kayro gave his former instructor some time to talk to the rest of the humans and see if they wish to join the escape plan. It took the man four hours to explain to them about the other races, or at least what he found out about them, and to convince everyone that this was their only chance to ever escape.

After all agreed, Zoss gave the news to him and asked him to show the people a few of his powers to encourage them. This was the perfect way to test his lightning, earth and healing skills, and, because everyone was in such a bad shape, he uncovered a few more crystal deposits, which they could mine easily and send what the mages asked for.

As soon as he finished doing all of that he headed to the elevator shaft and started climbing towards the second floor where he was immediately surrounded by a different race of humanoids. This time they looked like hybrids between humans and insects, some having bee features, others ant features and some had fly features.

Since the reptilians spoke the language that both humans and demons did, he assumed that this race might also speak it, so he greeted them without hesitation. There was no answer in the beginning, but after pushing him through the tunnels for a few minutes, someone who seemed to be their leader started talking.

"I apologise for my brothers, but we agreed to talk to outsiders only if all of us are present."

Looking around, Kayro could now see that they made him walk to a huge room, which was probably at the centre of all the floor's tunnels, and he was surrounded by two hundred or maybe more individuals. He apologies for his intrusion and introduced himself.

"My name is Agzza" the man with bee features said. "I used to be the prince of Insectum until three years ago, before the rest of my family was killed by some mutated bumblebees."

He carried on, telling how his race came to be, which was again a result of the experiments run by the mages, who only managed to turn the ants, bees and flies into humanoid, while the others were turned into beasts, with the bumblebees and the spiders being the strongest. They were all caught while trying to flee across the Infinite Sea to the Ardian Continent, from the east, where Insectum is located.

After he finished his story, Kayro told everyone about his origins, how he ended up in the Desert Mine Prison and about the escape that seemed to gain more and more members. Since they were all able to hear what he had to say, an agreement to join the escape was reached easily, with the condition that he will try to reveal a few crystal deposits for them too and, if possible, help them release their other brothers who were kept in different shafts or the prison.

"You mean that this is not the entire prison?"

"There are ten shafts in total from what I know" Agzza said. "And there are chances they build at least one or two more since I got here."

"I will do my best to help you, however, I cannot promise in the name of the others."

"We will try to free them with or without help, but having someone like you on our side would help a lot. We all thank you, and hopefully, when all of this is over, most of our brethren will be able to thank you as well."

It was now time for Kayro to go to the first floor, so, once again, he started using his claws to climb up. Distracted by the gap between the first floor and the surface which was around thirty metres, he forgot to use his demonic aura, in order to sense where all demons might be, and he was caught from behind by two of them.

As he was being taken away, he couldn't react since they had their claws ready to take off his head, so he chose to be as little threatening as he could. After passing a few smaller rooms, he reached a bigger one at the end of a very long tunnel.

"Why are you here, cursed mage?" a voice full of rage asked him.

"I am only part mage, and I am also part demon. I came to ask you to join us from the rest of the floors and escape together from this forsaken place."

"You, a demon? You just like a weak human, but I can sense your magic powers. Also, do you take me for a fool? Demons cannot have magic powers."

"Well, as I said, I am not a pure demon. My name is Kayro and I am the child of Larp and V'rca."

"Lies, lies and more lies. And I thought our race was considered evil. But I always forget that the mages are the true evil ones."

"What do you want me to do to prove who I really am? Do you want to see my demonic aura? Will that be enough for you to at least admit that I am part demon?"

"Do you really think that is enough, mage? I know that your kind cand use tricks. Still, if you want to prove yourself so hard, you need to fight and win by using only your demonic powers. Any magic you use, not only it will immediately disqualify you, but will also cost you your life. Do you understand that?"

"I understand, but what about other powers that I gained from killing beasts? Can I use those?"

"As long as they are not the magic used by your brothers, feel free to use whatever ability you wish."

"I agree to your terms. Let us start fighting and stop wasting time then."

Hearing this, made the leader of the demons start laughing for a minute and when he finally stopped he said:

"Do you really think yourself strong enough to face me? First you will need to beat four other fighters."

"Well, bring them all here and I will prove it."

"All right, but don't blame me for being killed. These used to be warriors in the royal guard and I doubt that you could defeat them one by one, let alone all four at the same time, but since you are so eager to die, then I will grant your wish."

Ten minutes later four strong demons surrounded Kayro and from the way they looked at him, he knew they were offended by his request. Still, there was no time to waste so he covered himself with the demonic aura, just like they did. After he growled loudly, giving him the speed and agility of the abnormal gurma, which he killed during the Test of Survival, and the strength of the miskra, which he killed in the Haunted Forest, he began his attack.

By combining all of his gained physical abilities with the hand to hand combat training and his demonic claws, he started taking them down one by one, finishing the fight in less than five minutes. With the demonic aura covering his body and his instincts taking over, he was able to fully heal just before the leader started his attack.

After taking three blows and being clawed multiple times, Kayro growled louder than he ever did and went berserk. His speed, strength and bloodlust increased so much that the weaker demons watching the fight started fearing him, but the one he was fighting didn't show any change of attitude.

Being so confident made the group leader think that no one could ever be faster or stronger than him, but that changes in the next seconds. With a wild look in his eyes, which turned crimson, Kayro started pushing his opponent into a defensive stance. It was too late for the massive demon to do anything about it, but even so, he hoped that by dodging or blocking the punches and kicks, he will tire his attacker.

Just as he was hoping to turn things around, Kayro grabbed his neck with one hand, lifted him a little, despite their big weight difference and threw him on the ground. Immediately after another loud growl he started running towards his massive opponent and as he was getting ready to bite his neck, someone from the crowd ran in front of him and shouted:

"Stop! Please, stop! Leave my father alone!"

Barely managing to slow down, Kayro ended up crashing into the girl who stood in his way. He managed to grab and protect her by putting his arms around her body and making sure that his back will be the one hitting the ground first.

As they were getting up, the massive man gave a desperate cry:

"Please, my prince, spare my daughter. Just kill me if someone has to die. You won already by breaking one of my legs and one of my hand and I now believe everything you said as I am sure everyone else in this room does. Just please let her live."

After getting up, Kayro started laughing and as everyone around was falling to their knees, he headed over to his wounded opponent.

"Now that the fight is over, can I use my magic powers? Or do you need more proof than what happened?"

"Do as you wish, as long as I am the only one you will kill. Just don't hurt the others, please!"

"You know, after refusing to tell me your name and calling me a mage over and over, I couldn't imagine that you can actually be polite."

While kneeling next to the massive demon, Kayro started using his powers to heal him, but, with the wounds being very serious, his energy was finished and he passed out. He woke up the next morning and saw that the girl who intervened in his fight was standing next to him.

"Good morning, my prince. Everyone was worried about your health after you passed out. I will go and let them know you are well."

Since he was still a little dizzy, he just nodded and tried to get up. Despite such a long sleep he still didn't have that much energy.

"It's the food, my prince. Those cursed mages are adding something to keep us weak. They only want us to have enough energy to mine their precious crystal, but not enough to try and escape" the leader of the demons said.

"Can everyone please stop calling me 'my prince'? I am just Kayro, raised by Krysta and Klost in Glade Village. Sure, my mother used to be the princess and her father was the former king, but that was long time ago and doesn't have anything to do with me."

"I apologise my..."

"If you say 'prince' again we will need to start fighting each other again."

"Very well, Kayro it is. My name is D'ram and I used to be one of the leaders of your grandfather's royal guard. I have always been loyal to them as is my entire family, including my daughter, M'nka. Her late mother served your family as well and taught her to always be respectful to any of its members, so it will be hard to make her address you by your name."

"If that is the case, can you please summon everyone, so I can ask them not to do that? I only told you about my parents in order to make you accept my proposal faster. I would prefer if my real identity was kept hidden, because apparently the mages see me as their biggest threat and would most likely do everything in their power to kill me if they knew who I am."

D'ram went away and in less than an hour he got everyone in the room where the fight took place on the previous day. As soon as everyone was there, Kayro came out from the tunnel that lead to the smaller room where he was taken to recover. Seeing that everyone started kneeling and they were ready to call him 'prince' again, he growled loudly making all demons stop.

"As I said to your leader, D'ram, I would prefer if everyone just calls me by my name. There is no royal family anymore and even if there was, I grew up as a regular human, not as the child of the demon princess, so I am asking you to keep my identity a secret and simply call me by the name I was given by my human grandparents.

The only reason why I mentioned the names of my parents was to spare us from fighting while everyone on the lower levels, mages, reptilians, humans and insectoids are working together so we can escape."

The crowd was silent for a few minutes, but then they all agreed to his request. It was hard not to use his title while he went and introduced himself to each of them, but his plan to show them that he is just another individual worked very well. With nearly all demons going back to their activities, Kayro decided to talk to D'ram about the possibly of reaching the surface and about the demons he was leading, and about the drugs the mages were adding to the food.

The massive demon explained that most of the ones imprisoned with him were once loyal to the former royal family and refused to support the "Council" which took over after killing the king and just like them, there were many others forced to work in prisons all across Xorbia. Regarding the drugs in the food, he had no knowledge what it might be, but all demons could smell that something was wrong with it, which made the young man remember that he asked Lurmand and the other mages at first if they too can feel a certain scent coming from it, but they blamed it on the place they were imprisoned inside.

Just as they were ready to start talking about the plan to escape, M'nka joined them and quietly sat next to her father. For a few moments, Kayro forgot where he was and what he was doing and stared at her. Her brown eyes were calling his to look into them, her curly hair made him imagine playing with it, the colour and size of her lips made him think about the taste of her kisses. More than that, her body was very appealing as well and that made him blush and stare at the ground.

"I'm sorry, I guess I am still a little dizzy" he said trying not to let them know about what he was really thinking about.

If D'ram or his daughter noticed what really happened they gave no sign of it and they carried on talking about a way to escape. After many attempts at finding a solution on how to overcome the twenty metres distance between the first floor of the Desert Mine Prison and the surface, they still didn't find an answer.

"I think that the best thing you can do now is to talk to all the other leaders on each floor and maybe one can find an answer to our problem. And if we could find proper food instead of the one the mages give us, or a way to counter the effects of the drugs, it surely will help when we must fight them."

As soon as D'ram finished saying that, Kayro went to the elevator shaft and started climbing down. He made a stop on each floor informing all the leaders about the agreement of each race to work together on escaping and asked them to think about a solution when it came to reaching the surface without alerting the mages.

He decided to look around the fifth floor and check if he can find any type of mushroom that might be safe to eat or at least to cancel the effects of the drugs used by the mages in the food they gave to the prisoners.

After a few days Lurmand had an idea about getting to the surface and for that to work, they needed a solution to their food problem.

"The only way for us to overpower so many mages is to make sure everyone will be in their best condition."

"I agree and based on my what my grandmother taught me as a child, I think I found some Galbana and Astria mushrooms on this floor. I am not sure how well they will work because they seem low quality, but we can make some food by using the first one and try to negate the effects of the drugs by using the second one. To make sure that they work properly, a member of each race must test them, so I will go around each floor tomorrow and check if they are effective."

"That is perfect, Kayro. I needed you to go and talk to each of the leaders anyway. Now that the food problem is solved, we must divide the mages. Even with proper food, we will lose too many people if we don't fight them together. That is why I need you to discuss my idea with everyone else."

The grandmaster's idea was for all floors to stop delivering crystals for a week in a row at the same time. This way, the mages will have to separate into smaller teams and check each floor. Before stopping the deliveries, everyone must get on the first floor so they can easily take down the mages who will check it, as a bigger group. In order for this to work, the demons will have to build traps and places to hide while the others are digging their way to the floor above theirs.

As soon as Lurmand finished telling him all the details, Kayro started climbing through the shaft and stopped for two hours on each floor discussing the plan with each leader. While they talked a volunteer from each race tested the dish he made using Galbana and also the food which the mages sent them after adding Astria to it.

With the food problem solved, he taught a few members of each race how to identify and cook these mushrooms in order to prepare themselves for the week when the mages will not send them any more food for failing to deliver the crystals.

Regarding the plan, each leader found a way to improve it by a little during the next two days when Kayro kept moving from floor to floor, and when they were all happy about it the crystal deliveries were stopped.

The day after doing that, with everyone focusing to break through and reach the floor above, the escape tunnels were ready. Since there was no rush, everyone rested for a day and then started climbing up being helped by the ones on the higher floor.

Moving so many individuals from the fifth to the first floor took an entire day, but everyone was happy with how the plan was working. With two days left before the mages would send patrols to check the tunnels, the leaders decided to organise everyone into teams of five members. Each team consisting of individuals from every race, one mage, one reptilian, one human, one insectoid and one demon, and the only ones who were going to fight by themselves were the leaders and Kayro.

In order to work as a team when the mages come after them, they spent time learning about each other as individuals and as a race. During this time, the leaders were trying to come up with some tactics in order to avoid losing people, or to at least escape with minimum casualties. To Kayro's disappointment, he was told that, along with all leaders, he must preserve his energy for what will happen after they reach the surface, since everyone knew that

Ghilod was very strong and he will not go down as easily as the other mages will.

To distract himself from not being able to help during the fight which will take place on the first floor, he started walking around checking on the teams. As he reached M'nka's, he stopped to greet her and couldn't help from looking into her eyes. Realising that, he came up with and excuse to leave quickly, but, before he got the chance to go too far, Zoss stopped him.

"You seem to be charmed by her and I can see why. Just remember that we must win this battle together first and then think about our feelings for the others. I certainly don't want you to risk your life to save mine and I am sure that all the other leaders will agree with me."

"I understand, sir. I have been in similar situations before and you know it very well. Still there is something about her that makes me forget about everything and just enjoy that moment."

"Then you will have to go along with the plan and after everyone is safe, tell her about your feelings. I think that you might be surprised by the outcome."

"Very well. I will do as you say, after all you always had good advice for me."

# The escape, the way back and the plans for the future

Just as Lurmand predicted, after a week, the mages divided into teams and went down to check each floor. The elevator went down to the bottom floor and the first team got out, then left one team on each floor, before stopping on the first one. As they advanced, Zoss, who was hiding with a small group, at the floor's entrance, made sure that the elevator will not move.

To make sure they will be able to quickly finish this, everyone stayed hidden until D'ram gave the signal to begin the ambush. Not knowing what was happening, the mages had no time to react and soon their hands and feet were chained, while their mouth were gagged.

As soon as they made sure no one can attack them or alert the surface or the teams from the other floors, all the prisoners started making their way to the huge elevator. Since there were more than one thousand individuals and the elevator could fit only two hundred at a time, getting everyone to the surface took nearly two hours.

Because they decided to escape together, the ones who already got to the surface made sure to stay well hidden until everyone was out and then each leader gave the signal to start moving towards the exit of the huge cave. Unfortunately, as they were nearly outside, a barrier was conjured blocking them inside the cave.

"Did you really think that I will not realise that you are trying to escape?" Ghilod shouted before starting to laugh. "Sure you managed to surprise me by getting everyone to work together and I have no idea how all of you got to the first floor, but even so, you are still trapped."

After he finished talking, a group of mages who were hiding close to the elevator was already working on getting back the ones who went to check the tunnels. With no time to spare, D'ram ordered everyone to cover themselves with their demonic auras and each drank something from a small vial.

Lurmand and the other leaders already considered this possibility, so each day, since everyone agreed with the plan, Kayro filled a small vial with his own blood for the demons to drink and hopefully gain at least part of his abilities.

Only a few were able to pass through the barrier, but that proved enough to stop the mages who conjured it. As the demons were busy with freeing everyone Ghilod was already running away. He knew that even with the teams from the tunnels it will not be enough to take on a small army. Seeing him trying to flee, the leaders allowed Kayro to pursue him and promised to check all the other mine shafts and release every single prisoner.

Enraged by all previous events and also by the healer's cowardly actions, the young man growled, covered himself in the demonic aura and was slowly getting closer to him.

After nearly five minutes Ghilod suddenly stopped and faced him.

"Do you really believe you can defeat me by yourself, boy? I am far too strong for a mere demon. I don't understand how you and the other lowly creatures managed to pass through that barrier, since you are stupid enough to run after me without at least the old man to help you. It makes me think that you have no brain at all."

"This is far too personal for me to involve any of the others. Also, I am sure that without my food being drugged, the difference between us might not be as great as you believe it to be."

"Personal?! Are you still in love with my future bride? Do you think that by defeating me she will change her mind about your evil blood?"

"My blood is half human, half demon, and I can proudly say that doesn't make me evil in any way. Regarding Alyssa, I couldn't care any less about her after stabbing me in the back like that, but

I will definitely not forgive you for having my friends executed and for imprisoning my family."

"Your cursed so-called parents somehow managed to disappear before being arrested, or are you referring to the prisoners that you just helped?"

"I am talking about you and your greedy, bloodthirsty council who imprisoned my parents, and after I will bite the life out of you today, I will do so with any of its other members that stand in the way of freeing them."

"We imprisoned countless families, boy. What makes you think they are still alive?"

"They are way too important for you to kill them or let them take their own lives."

As Ghilod was trying to think of who those people might be, Kayro started throwing fire and lightning orbs at him. Seeing that the young man actually had magic powers and it wasn't just some trick, he quickly realised who his parents were.

"But that's impossible! I can only think of one person who might be able to do that, but Larp's and V'rca's baby was killed during the time we were fighting them."

"Well, I guess I forgot to stay dead then."

Before the master healer had the chance to say anything, Kayro used his claws to cut his forearms, conjured ice spikes and coated them with his blood sending them at a high speed towards him. The barrier created by Ghilod to protect himself was penetrated, but still it was enough to stop the spikes from reaching him.

Seeing that his attack didn't work, the young man growled, covered himself in the demonic aura again and used a spike made entirely out of blood. His attack reached its target this time, but it was still slowed down and the mage dodged it partially, suffering only a small scratch.

Realising that the barrier was too strong for any magic or blood attack made Kayro go berserk and without realising how he did it, his aura turned crimson by taking some of the blood from the cut that was almost healed.

"Run! Run! Ruuuuun!" he shouted at Ghilod and while the mage was trying to attack him, the young man shatter his barrier with a single punch.

With higher speed and strength than ever, but also pure rage and adrenaline, Kayro ignored all the attacks easily and grabbed the healer lifting him as if he was nothing. He couldn't hear the man begging for his life, cursing him or his family. All he could sense was the fast beat of his heart and the fear for his life being ended.

A second later, the mage's neck was being ripped off by the young man's fangs, but taking his life was not enough., so he started to repeatedly throw the lifeless body against the outer walls of the cave.

Just as Kayro was punching and kicking the corpse destroying it little by little, M'nka showed up. Despite being shocked by what was going on in front of her, she ran and hugged him from behind telling him that everything was over and to calm down before he reaches the point of losing his mind totally. Initially it seemed like he was gone, but then she shouted an oath to him while crying:

"I swear to help you free your parents and not allow you to turn into a beast until you accomplish that, my prince. I will risk my life to protect yours and promise to keep you sane until your family is finally reunited. After that, if you still wish to abandon yourself into rage and bloodlust, I will even offer myself as a sacrifice, but until then, please stop yourself before it is too late."

Hearing about his family made Kayro snap out of it and a few seconds later he replied:

"I will accept your offer, but only if you stop calling me 'my prince'. Promise to use my name or I will carry on trying to smash this body into nothing."

"I promise my... Kayro!"

A few minutes later just as the leaders of each floor, along with a few of their race following them, got to the place where he fought Ghilod, the young man collapsed.

Two days later he woke up inside the huge cave, with M'nka by his side. He could only see a few people around, most of them demons, and the leaders who were preparing for a journey.

"Please tell me we didn't lose too many people!"

"Relax, my dear boy." Lurmand said, "The only one we found dead was Ghilod, or at least what used to be him, before you went berserk."

"So everyone is well?"

"More or less, yes, everyone is well. As you can see, Zoss is covered in bandages, but still cannot stop himself from barking orders, while everyone else is preparing to leave this place behind."

"Was he the only one who was injured? Allow me to fully heal him."

"He was close to dying while he jumped in front of some magic attacks in order to protect Agzza, but he should be out of those bandages by tomorrow. Meanwhile you should save your energy, because I am certain that you wish to go and check on your grandparents soon."

"What happened after I went after Ghilod?"

"One of the teams of mages from the tunnels was able to get back to the surface, and luckily except Zoss's injuries, everyone else only had minor injuries which we were able to heal. It did take quite a toll on the bodies of the healers, but even so, they were able to wake up after just one day, unlike you."

"I slept more than a day?! Why didn't you wake me up? I could've helped healing the injured."

"I am afraid that was impossible, Kayro" D'ram intervened. "You used up too much blood when you combined it with your demonic aura and nearly killed yourself by doing that. Luckily your healing abilities are way stronger than any of us have ever heard or witnessed, so your body ended up using a lot of energy to fully heal itself, which is why you were knocked out for two days."

As the conversation carried on, Zoss, Agzza and Dotropius joined in talking about their plans for the near future. Lurmand said he will remain in the mine, along with groups from each race, to study the crystals, in order to find a way to use them for the good of everyone just like B'dar was using them to imbue magic equipment, and to see if he can reform some of the mages who were loyal to Ghilod.

The leader of the reptilians planned to go back to his land in the north, but he will send some researchers to help the former grandmaster with his studies and help him turn what used to be a prison into a place where every race would be welcomed.

Agzza and Zoss were going to travel east together, and, while the former insectoid prince will go towards Insectum and try to reclaim it, the man who was Kayro's instructor promised to try and take the humans who still had families in the Median Forests back to their loved ones.

D'ram, along with all the demons wanted to follow Kayro, helping him reach his grandparents, after that try to free Larp and V'rca and then hopefully get them back on the throne of the Blood Lands. Each of them was ready to sacrifice their lives for that goal even before they met their son, but now thinking about what the woman who could read the flow of magic predicted, they were more determined than ever.

"I'm sorry, my friend, but we are not ready for that yet. I could barely take on what was probably the weakest link of the Council of Magic and it nearly cost me my life. Trying to free my parents, will mean suicide at this time, so first we need to get stronger. Let me meet with my grandparents to make sure they are safe. After that, I will seek R'mal, train with him to control my demonic powers better, maybe learn how to combine them with magic without risking too much and then we will be able to at least stand a chance of freeing my parents."

"I agree with the boy" Lurmand said. "After being so easily deceived by Ghilod for more than twenty years, I can only say that we must get a lot stronger and try to keep the Council of Magic from finding out what happened here. I promise to find a way to make them believe that everything is being run just like before, while we slowly start informing the humans about what their actual role is, and then, when the time comes, and all of us are ready, we will take the mages down freeing all races."

"It does make sense and too many have died in the past for me to be reckless, but my people cannot go back to the Blood Lands and we don't have a place where we could live until we get stronger."

"Considering how strong most of you are, I think I might know a place where you might be able to settle without being bothered by the mages, but you will need to fight wild beasts for it. It was so dangerous that the Council of Magic added multi layered barriers around it and decided to avoid it. The only one who could probably open a barrier into that area is Kayro" said the former grandmaster.

"And where is this place?"

"It is on the western side of the Ardian Continent, north of the Great Forest."

"Seems like we can just go there right away an while we take it from the beasts, Kayro can carry on south to get to his parents while avoiding the human communities."

"It is not that simple. You must take only your best warriors if you want to have minimum casualties and then, after you hopefully defeat the occupants of that land, come back and get the rest of your people."

"I have a better idea" said Kayro. "I will go in a straight line south passing through each community while D'ram and his best warriors will accompany Zoss going around the ring mountains. This way we can make sure that everyone will be safe and, after I get to Glade Village and find my grandparents, I will wait for everyone close to the barrier to open it and we can travel together through the Median Forests, leaving anyone who has family in their community. Since my former instructor has no place in any of those communities he can join us while we fight the beasts and claim the land."

The conversation carried on for some time, and in the end, the young man's plan was voted to be the best, with a few alterations. Part of the mages, humans, insectoids and reptilians who didn't have families waiting for them back home would join them on this new land. The ones who could fight were going with Zoss's and D'ram's group, while the rest will wait in the desert until the beasts are either chased away or killed.

The leaders wanted Kayro to be better protected while making his way back to Glade Village, so they proposed a personal guard made of ten people. He immediately refused, because he didn't have the luxury of travelling with such a big group without being noticed as he passed through the communities, so he asked them to choose only one individual.

Before any of them had the chance to say anything, M'nka asked for her to take on that role, because this way she can keep the oath made to him. As they were getting ready to protest, she growled and bared her fangs telling them that she will be more than enough to keep him safe, especially since nothing on the road could be that dangerous, forcing everyone to agree with her.

Since there wasn't much food stored by Ghilod and his men and the desert had no animals that could be hunted, instead of a feast to celebrate the fall of the Desert Mine Prison, they sang and danced, each race displaying part of their tradition. After a few hours when everyone got tired, the mine went silent as they went to sleep.

The next day, Kayro woke up early, he said his goodbyes to each leader at a time and then to all the former prisoners, as M'nka only talked to her father and prepared a small backpack for the travel. Without looking back, they mounted a crafa and started making their way out of the desert. They wanted to avoid meeting anyone before getting to Port Town, so they chose take a longer time before reaching the plains, instead of using a boat to travel on the river.

After two hot days and cold nights, the sand finally ended marking a fist step in their journey and giving them the chance to hunt. Before doing that, they released the crafa, which started running towards the former Desert Mine Prison.

M'nka showed Kayro how demons use their aura to easily stay hidden and managed to impress him, by quickly catching a orren. Trying to mimic her actions, he was also able to catch one too, and, after using the hunting skills gained in Training Camp to butcher them, they started cooking their first proper meal in quite some time.

While the young man was smoking some of the meat to have on the road and curing the hides to craft something out of them later, the demon female was cooking a stew. Since they were not going to stay there for more than a few hours, there was no point in trying to build a shelter, so they used the time to talk about themselves.

Before leaving the area, they made sure to leave it as clean and tidy as possible in order to preserve nature, and then started walking towards the forest between the desert and the Hills of Hope. It was almost dark when they arrived at the edge of the forest, so Kayro proposed for them to sleep on the branches of a big tree that stood there like a guardian watching over the plains.

The next morning, he taught M'nka everything he learned about berries from Krysta and they managed to find high quality arberries, muvaberries and goreberries before entering the forest. While they were getting close to the middle of the forest, they also found a bush of sunberries which were also high quality. The demon female was familiar with these and, this time, it was her giving her travelling companion new information about them.

Apart from what he already knew from his grandmother, it turned out that they helped those with demon blood recover their energy faster when mixed with goreberries and Rozia mushrooms.

Luckily, before exiting the forest they found an area where all known types of mushrooms grew and they also collected some good quality Galbana, Rozia and Astria mushrooms.

Close to sunset, they reached the Hills of Hope and Kayro started looking for a cave where they could rest. Just as the sun was disappearing he found one and they built a fire to cook the abruza and scorm which they managed to catch when they went to get water from the river. Again he wanted to have make extra provisions for the road, so he smoked all the extra fish meat. After eating the young man checked the surrounding area around the cave using his ability to see in the dark. While doing that, he saw what seemed to be five individuals in the distance, but, as he checked again, there was no sign of any being in that area. Thinking it must have been a small pack of wolves that were probably hunting an orren, he went inside and carried on the conversation with M'nka before they both fell asleep.

They woke up well rested in the morning, prepared to climb the Ring Mountains in order to reach the swampy areas on the other side of them, and, soon after they gathered everything and changed into some warm clothes, started climbing. Kayro had a feeling that something or someone was watching them, but every time he turned around there was nothing there.

With the climb being a lot harder than they expected, it was almost night time as they reached the peak and, since there was no place to sleep, the two of them agreed to descend and then sleep during the day. Unfortunately,     as they were getting ready to start going down the mountains, a very loud squeaking sound came from above.

While they were looking up to check what made the sound, four demons appeared in front of them and a fifth behind, making the young man feel like a fool for not fully trusting his instincts.

"What do we have here? Two lousy demon prisoners who managed to escape the Desert Mine Prison? Or was that maniac mage kind enough to let you go?"

"What makes say that? Maybe we are just travellers exploring the world?"

"Don't take me for a fool, boy. Only the demons who have approval from both the Council of Demons and the Council of Magic can travel on the Ardian Continent and that happens to be us. The only other demons are the ones in the Desert Mine Prison, which is in the direction from where you two were coming, and they are all prisoners until they die."

Hearing the squeaking sound again, both Kayro and M'nka looked up again, giving the demons time to start attacking them. The young man asked her to capture the one who was behind them, so they can get more information from him, while he will kill the rest.

As she was covering herself in the demonic aura, he quickly sent four ice spikes which impaled three of his opponents. The fourth one was able to dodge it easily, but he kept his distance instead of attacking. He seemed confident despite seeing what happened to his group members and that made Kayro feel uneasy.

"I don't know who or what you are, and you might be strong enough to kill me directly, but I doubt you can overpower my pet" the demon said before a vuliac was flying at a high speed towards the young man while making the same squeaking sound they heard before.

The creature managed to scratch Kayro, but as it was turning around for a second attack, the young man growled and covered himself in the demonic aura. With his speed and strength growing even more after biting Ghilod's neck, he went after the demon, but, before ending his life, he chanted something that gave a demonic aura to the vuliac.

Knowing from his past experiences that a beast will become a lot more dangerous in these conditions, the young man quickly drew some blood from where the creature scratched him earlier and combined it with the power to create barriers trapping it inside. For a few moments, the growing animal seemed to break the barrier, so Kayro made a blood spike and sent it at high speed towards the vuliac. He cancelled the barrier in order to be able to use his control over wind and managed to impale the beast into a huge rock.

Knowing that it might still escape as it was still transforming, he charged at it and before the vuliac was able to free itself, he bit its neck off taking a lot of power from it. As soon as he made sure that all his opponents were indeed dead, he went looking for M'nka and found her close by making sure that the demon she captured cannot flee.

With Kayro having only little energy to spare, they both covered themselves in the demonic auras and, while he carried their hostage, she took the backpacks following close behind him. They were able to reach the swamps at the bottom of the Ring Mountains in less than two hours and the young man easily found a cave where they could rest and question the captured demon.

Since she barely used any energy, M'nka offered to watch the entrance of the cave and the prisoner while he can sleep and regain his strength. With both the blood from the demon who was leading the group and from the vuliac, he was able to wake up fully rested after three hours. Meanwhile, the demon female used part of the Rozia mushrooms, some sunberries and goreberries to make a potion a few potions giving him one to drink after waking up.

After she went to sleep, Kayro raised a barrier to block the entrance of the cave and a second one around him and the prisoner. The first one should be able to easily keep anything away, while the second one would not allow any sounds outside, which meant that M'nka will not be bothered while she rests.

Seeing the young man's abilities the night before, the captured demon immediately started telling him about their roles and why they started following them.

It turned out that they were a group of assassins controlled directly be the Council of Demons, and also the only team allowed to roam freely on the Ardian Continent. Their mission was to travel around seeking powerful beasts and they were now heading to the desert to get some provisions before going north.

They knew nothing about Ghilod's death or the prisoners being all free, but, after seeing him and M'nka while they caught the fish and got water from the river, the leader decided to have them followed from the distance while he and the other three were going around waiting at the top of the mountain where they can question the two travellers.

His plan was to use the vuliac to intimidate Kayro and the female demon and after getting all the information from them, feed them to the animal before heading to their destination. The plan would have probably worked on normal demons or any other race, but the leader had no idea about what the young man was, so things turned out the way they did.

Fearing that he might be killed after revealing everything, the captured demon pleaded for his life:

"I know that I might seem weak, but I never really wanted to hurt anyone, so I held back against your travelling companion. If you allow me to live, not only will I swear to be loyal to you, but also become you shadow, protecting you from any danger."

"I do seem to be hiding you real abilities, but I don't need anyone at the moment, except M'nka. If you want to prove your loyalty, go to what used to be the Desert Mine Prison and wait there until I come. Right now I am going to Glade Village to check on my grandparents, but, after that, I plan join the former warriors who were freed, in claiming the land inside the multi-layered barriers and get all the former prisoners who wish to join us there."

"Wait. Did you say you are from Glade Village? Do you by any chance know a demon called R'mal?"

"And what if I do? Were you sent to kill him?"

"I apologise, my prince. I should have known who you were from your abilities. My dear friend told me that you can use both magic and the demonic powers, but I thought he was exaggerating."

"Why does everyone keep calling me that? Is it so hard to just call me by my name?"

"I wouldn't dare do that. You see, just like R'mal and B'dar, I was always loyal to your family. I only joined the assassins to train my skills for when we rise against the mages to free your parents and to gain information that would otherwise be impossible to get. My name is H'rir and it would be a pleasure to serve you."

"It is nice to know that you are a friend and somehow I can feel that you are being honest, but please call me by my name instead of some title. Your skills might become very useful to us in the future, so make sure to stay alive until I get back to the desert. I will craft something for you, which you will need to give to Lurmand in order for him to trust you and know that I was the one who sent you there."

While he was waiting for the token of proof to be crafted, the assassin told the young man that R'mal managed to make it look like Krysta and Klost disappeared without a trace and hide them in the Haunted Forest.

After a few hours M'nka woke up and was looking around to see where the prisoner was. Kayro told her the entire story and she confirmed that H'rir was one of the demons who were loyal to his family. She never met him, but her father often talked about him trying to find a way to free Larp and V'rca.

Since it was noon, they decided to talk more on the way to Port Town, which was their first destination, instead of wasting time by staying there any longer. As soon as they packed, both used their demonic auras to cover themselves in order to get out of the swamps faster.

Just a little after sunset, they stopped to get some water from the Grand Lake before looking for a cave where they can rest. Being tired from running, they stopped using their auras, but Kayro was still using his ability to see in the dark while M'nka was getting the water. As he turned his head facing her, he noticed that something was in the lake and it was quickly getting close to her.

He immediately covered his body in the demonic aura again, while shouting at her to do the same, but it looked like it was going to be too late. As he was running at full speed, his body started to lift from the ground and a few moments later he realised that he also grew wings now, not just claws and fangs.

Before the massive crocodile, which was trying to make the female demon his meal, had the chance to get out of the water, Kayro grabbed her by the waist and flew out of there. They were both shocked by the wings which grew on his back, but also happy since it was the only way to save her.

Using his new ability, the young man was able to carry her and improve their travelling speed, but he still needed to rest after flying for an hour. As he was getting ready to land, he saw a cave at the base of the mountains and headed that way. Luckily there were no animals around so they could easily get inside and while testing his control over earth magic, he was able to block the entrance allowing them to rest at the same time.

Having used less energy during the previous day, M'nka woke up early and prepared a few more potions as well as a small feast for breakfast and, after they ate, Kayro forced the wings to grow again and grabbed her by the waist again flying even faster than he did before.

Since they were able to save more time this way, they decided to stop only for a few minutes from time to time. Being able to see what seemed like Port Town in the distance, just as the sun was setting, they decided to rest there for the night and start walking again in the morning. It would probably take an entire day to get there, but if he was seen flying, they will surely attract attention.

They woke up very early and started walking at a fast pace. On their way, they encountered lots of crocodiles, which made sense to him after learning during Training Camp that all the big reptiles were driven away from the area where Port Town was built. Kayro used some small orbs of lightning to scare them off, since he considered killing them without actually needing to a big waste.

Since there was still some light outside, Kayro and M'nka tried to make themselves look like regular travellers and entered the town from the south gate. When asked by the guards at the entrance why are they walking instead of using a boat and without having someone to keep them safe, they claimed to be a poor couple that wanted to trade some of the things inherited from their parents, after hearing they will get a better price here, so they had to leave Tower Town in a small boat which sunk with almost all their belongings just a few kilometres away from Port Town.

Remembering his old friend Laren, the young man made up a story about going to visit the man who he met during Training Camp to ask if he can help them get back to their community. The guards told them how to reach his butcher shop and they started walking slowly towards it.

Seeing it so close, Port Town seemed even bigger than he remembered, for Kayro and M'nka was even more amazed by everything around them. Despite wishing to admire it, the sun was close to setting so they quickened the pace reaching the butcher shop just as Laren was about to close it.

Despite not seeing each other in years, the two men instantly recognised each other and were happy to meet again. After telling him they need a place to sleep, Laren invited his friend, and the woman travelling with him, to his house.

Knowing that Kayro was always with Alyssa and seeing how they acted, Laren asked the young man about her, as soon as they were alone. Since he didn't have the chance to tell M'nka about his former fiancé, he politely asked his friend to wait for his companion's return and he will tell both of them the entire story.

Trusting his friend from Training Camp, completely, Kayro spent the next few hours telling them the entire story of how he got from being a future explorer to becoming a prisoner of the mages. Despite being unaware and a little scared of the things he heard, Laren trusted the young man, especially after seeing his powers, and volunteered to join him and everyone who will settle with him inside the multi-layered barrier. He confessed that, despite liking his butcher role, he wanted to get away from Port Town after Training Camp, but never knew where which community to go to.

"A new village might be the perfect place to start a family and I am sure that Etra, who is now my wife, as well as her brother, Nous and his wife, would like to move there too. Once you start building, let us know and we will be happy to help."

"Thank you very much, for being understanding, dear friend. I know that everything I said might seem crazy, but I promise it's true."

They carried on the conversation while M'nka was talking to Etra in another room, being amazed of how different, yet similar they were. Despite going to sleep a little late, everyone was ready for the new day. Laren and his wife gave Kayro and his companion new clothes to wear on the road and also a small boat which should allow them to travel faster and also stop the guards from both Port Town and Tower Town from asking about the reason they are walking.

After hugging their hosts, Kayro and M'nka slowly went down the river, picking up speed as soon as the guards were out of sight. They avoided using their powers since they kept meeting other boats along the way, but, even so, they reached the dock built on the Great River very close to their next destination.

With their new clothes and some fishing goods gave to them by Laren and his family, the two managed to quickly enter through the northern gate and even got directions on how to reach the market closest to Takya's restaurant.

Initially, Kayro simply wished to pass through quickly after getting some provisions and maybe get on a cart that was leaving for Glade Village at least until they get out of town, but his friend from Port Town asked him to deliver a letter to their senior.

As always, Takya didn't like to talk while she was working, but she asked Kayro and his companion to visit the town and later they will meet and have a proper conversation. The young man gave her the letter and, after eating a delicious meal prepared by his friend, he agreed to stay in Tower Town overnight to catch up.

In his letter, Laren explained to the woman that everything their friend will say might be shocking, but it is real and she can fully trust him. He didn't really need to write the letter, because, just like him, Takya always felt like she can trust Kayro.

A few hours later she met her friend and M'nka, and after she helped them sell the fishing goods and bought provisions, they went to her mansion. Everything she learned during Training Camp proved very useful and she was now one of the most famous chefs in Tower Town.

While they were eating something she cooked before leaving the restaurant, a long conversation started. Just like Laren, Takya first asked about Alyssa, remembering the jealous look in the girl's eyes when they first met, and she was shocked to hear what happened, since she imagined that they will never separate.

As the conversation continued, Kayro and M'nka showed her their powers to make everything they told her believable, even if that wasn't necessary, and before going to sleep she asked if she can also join them in this new community they intend to start. Shocked by hearing that she would want to leave everything behind, the young man asked her about her reasons to go away from Tower Town and Takya said that what she was doing, despite the fame it got her, it didn't feel fulfilling.

After waking up, the young man and the female demon were surprised to see that their friend rented a private cart to take them to Glade Village and also promised that as soon as she gets confirmation that they managed to claim the land inside the multi-layered barrier she will use nearly her entire fortune to buy things that will help the people of the new community.

Kayro and M'nka thanked her and then got on the cart that was going to take them a step closer to meeting Krysta an Klost. As the left, the young man felt sad, because not so long time ago he used the same gate to enter town along with his former fiancé, thinking that their future will surely be a good one. Still, that was in the past and the woman he once loved was nothing compared to the one he was travelling with. Not only was M'nka the most beautiful woman he has ever seen, but her way of seeing life was similar to his. Even so, there was no time for feelings or relationships, because getting to his grandparents, claiming the land which could become a home for a lot of the former prisoners and getting stronger in order to free his parents, were a lot more important.

Three days later, after reaching Glade Village, they thanked the ones who took them there and started making their way towards the eastern gate. As they were passing through the village, Kayro was telling M'nka about the various places where he trained and about the wonderful people who taught him. They even stopped for a few minutes for him to show her where the richest family in Glade Village lives and he remembered his gurma leather vest, which was crafted here, and protected his life a few times before breaking.

Part of him wished to visit each of the people who he felt thankful to, even Alyssa's father, Fargas, but getting to his grandparent and R'mal was the most important thing at the moment.

To make sure that no one could see them going inside the Haunted Forest, Kayro and his companion sneaked inside the house where he grew up and waited until night time. He started telling M'nka about his evening with Klost and Krysta, about everything they taught him and how thankful he was for them raising him so well and loving him, even before finding out that he was actually their grandson.

Two hours after the sun disappeared from the sky, both of them using their demonic auras to hide in the darkness, managed to get out without being seen, despite some howlers trying to alert their owners.

Seeing the green shapes again, reminded Kayro of the night when he found out about his true origins and how curious he was about learning what exactly were these so-called ghosts, but this was just another thing on a long list that had to wait. As they were passing the area were the ground was scorched many years ago, both of them could feel a presence nearby.

Using his ability to see in the dark, the young man saw a figure in the distance and while M'nka acted as a distraction he sneaked behind it getting ready to bite its neck. Just as the individual was turning around, Kayro recognised his former crafting master, B'dar, and released him immediately. After being introduced to the female demon, the craftsman showed them the way to the shelter where R'mal was guarding and hiding Krysta and Klost.

While Kayro was greeting and hugging his grandparents and the man who kept them safe, M'nka was standing outside in order not to disturb them. Realising that she was doing that, the young man went out to get her and after introducing her to them, she was happy to receive hugs as well. She felt ashamed for getting so close to his grandparents and to the demon who her father considered a hero, but, after he praised how reliable she was during their travel, her confidence came back.

A conversation that lasted through the entire night started and, in order for everyone to be there, Kayro conjured two barriers. The first one covered a wider area and it was set to detect any being entering it while the second one was just around the hiding place to keep any sound inside it.

After the young man finished his story, they all agreed that the plan to drive away or kill the beasts from within the multi-layered barrier, claim that land and build a new community, was the best choice to stay safe given the circumstances. Both his grandparents agreed that he should go to the village and, without being seen by too many people, he should talk to all the people who trained him in the past, since they will most likely be able to recommend an apprentice who might want to move from Glade Village and become part of the new community, or at least he might be able to get some goods which could help building it.

During the next week, while they were still waiting for D'ram's and Zoss's group to arrive, Kayro went to the village every day. Just like Klost and Krysta said, each of the people who trained him proved to be not only trustworthy, by keeping his presence a secret, but also helpful. They offered him very good deals on tools, clothing and food, after the young man refused to take them for free, and each of them recommended an apprentice that wished to move away from Glade Village.

As soon as the group of warriors of all races and the humans who were trying to return to their communities arrived outside the Haunted Forest, Kayro created a small hole in the barrier that surrounded the Median Forests and allowed everyone to get in without the mages being able to notice.

In order to trade some of the unnecessary things which they acquired on the road, for something useful, Zoss divided the humans into three large groups and D'ram disguised some of his warriors as human adventurers who were hired to protect the traders. Aside from going inside to trade, these groups were also helping the former prisoners from Glade Village to sneak in and get back to their families.

The first two groups entered the village early in the next morning, one from the northern gate and the other from the western gate, with the first claiming to be from Tower Town and the second from Lumberjack Village. Since some of the craftsmen and tradesmen in Glade Village were told by Kayro about these groups coming to trade, they offered them good deals and encouraged the others to do the same. While they were trading, the former prisoners had time to talk to their families and after telling them what was really happening in the Median Forests, they decided to leave and join the new community even if building it was just an idea for the moment.

The third group went in after three days and everything went on well. This time, part of the apprentices who were recommended to Kayro joined the group as they left Glade Village behind. After two days everyone met close to the Training Forest and, to save time, it was decided that separating into two groups was the best option. Zoss, Kayro and R'mal were taking the smaller one to Lumberjack Village and then the three of them were going to quietly infiltrate Training Camp and see if any of the instructors or adventurers wish to join them, while D'ram, B'dar and M'nka were taking the bigger group to Tower Town and Port Town.

Everyone who wished to join the new community would meet just outside the Great Forest where the final decision on who will go and try to claim the land inside the multi-layered barrier and who will wait behind until they receive confirmation of victory.

The bigger group used the carts and bovri they bought in Glade village to reach their destinations since they had more distance to cover, while the smaller group which included Kayro and his grandparents was going to walk. This was the perfect opportunity for him to talk to them and tell them all the details about what he did when they were apart.

After reaching Lumberjack Village, Krysta and Klost decided to go in with the group and, while Kayro was going to talk to his friend Zodar, they will try to meet her brother, Elyn, and finally talk to him after so many years. A few hours later, when the group pretending to be traders from Glade Village returned to the ones who were waiting outside Lumberjack Village, Kayro was surprised to see that his great uncle and his family decided to join them and help the new community by using his furniture maker skills.

Just like Laren and Takya, Zodar was happy to see the man whom he considered to be his best friend, and volunteered to join as a woodcutter. He was sorry to leave his parents behind, but a new community might just give him the chance to make a family of his own and the chance to help his friend.

Two days later, while the group was waiting outside the Training Forest, just as they planned, Kayro, Zoss and R'mal went to talk to Monta and check if any of the adventurers were willing to join the fight against the beast who occupied the land where they wanted to hide from the Council of Mages and build a new community.

The former counsellor, who was now the new head instructor of Glade Village Camp, was happy to see his friends, but a little afraid of the demon who was with them. He told them that many things have changed since the previous head instructor of each camp were imprisoned, but one of the changes might actually make things easier for them, because the adventurers and the leaders of the Training Camp militia had a camp of their own next to the Quiet Lake.

Despite wishing to join them everyone agreed that the best thing for him to do was to continue doing the role he was given and hopefully, in the future, when the Ardian Continent will be freed from the influence of the Council of Magic, he might join the new community.

The next morning, Kayro, Zoss and R'mal went back to the group joined by a few adventurers who were the strongest among the ones patrolling the Training Camp, and they started walking towards the meeting point. They waited for two days until the group led by D'ram, B'dar and M'nka arrived and after everyone settled in the ones viewed as leaders held a meeting to decide who and how many will go inside the multi-layered barrier. To Kayro's surprise, Takya and Laren, who decided to come earlier than agreed, were chosen as representatives for Port Town and Tower Town.

They told him that as soon as they saw M'nka travelling and trading inside their towns, they talked to her and joined her group along with some of their friends and family. Because of how good they were at performing their roles, not only did people follow them, but also chose them as leaders.

After two hours, the meeting was over and the warriors selected were known. To make sure that the ones staying behind were well protected, D'ram and half of the demon fighters were going to stay behind. Zoss was going to lead the adventurers, the insectoids, the reptilians and a few of the humans who used to be prisoners, while Kayro, despite his protests, was in charge of the demons and the few mages who were sent to fight at his side, as a token of gratitude for freeing them. R'mal and M'nka were going to help leading, but also act as a sword and shield for him, while B'dar, Takya and Laren with Zodar's help, were going to organise everyone who stayed behind.

After two days of preparing their weapons, equipment and supplies, they started walking towards the barrier. It took the group that counted around two hundred individuals almost three days to reach the multi-layered barrier and they decided to rest for the night before going inside and starting the fight to claim the land.

## The battle for the land and the unexpected alliance

Everyone woke up very early to mentally prepare entering the barrier and, with great effort, after nearly fifteen minutes, Kayro was able to make a hole which they used to get inside. The young man was getting better at using this type of magic, so he was wasting less energy now, but he was still carrying the potions made be M'nka to use them as a boost in case it was needed.

Not knowing what to expect both him and Zoss were being cautious when moving forward which proved to be very useful when they reached a wide river and they were able to easily notice that it was infested with crocodiles. A few of the mages who were under Kayro's command were able to use their powers and build a bridge, but leaving all those crocodiles around would still be dangerous in the future, especially since most of them were at least double the size of the ones any of them have seen before.

In order to conserve the energy of their warriors, the leaders of the group agreed that building some traps or trying to lure them out of the multi-layered barrier might be a better option than fighting. R'mal told them that if they managed to find the strongest crocodile who usually acts as a leader, he might be able to control it and have the rest follow him through a hole opened by Kayro in the barrier.

After hearing that, the reptilian warriors in the group decided to take advantage of their beast side and offered to search for the leader of the animals. Their solution seemed risky at first, but, as they advanced, none of the crocodiles saw them as intruders and they were allowed to walk freely. A few minutes later everyone heard a voice inside their heads, which turned out to belong to the leader of the crocodiles.

As the voice was getting louder, a male, four times the size of the others, came out of the river and it looked like a fight was going to start, but the huge reptile proved to seek peace.

"We do not wish to fight against those who share our blood and, from what I could hear, one of you is able to open the barrier which traps us inside, so if you have such a power and can grant us access we will gladly leave this cage to you and join our brothers on what the humans call the Grand Lake."

Kayro approached the beast who could easily swallow him in seconds and looked straight into its eyes. They had a quick conversation during which the young man found out that the reptile's parents were fed magic crystals by the mages and since it looked like a failed experiment, they were released inside the multi-layered barrier. While the crystals did not affect the parents, the new generation started to grow bigger in size and in his case gain magic abilities.

One of these was being able to communicate its thoughts to any being in a limited area and it was able control exactly the group or individual who could hear it.

Kayro agreed to open a hole in the barrier and, at the crocodile's request, the only ones allowed to follow him were the reptilian warriors. While the leader of the crocodiles was waiting for all the others to pass, he gave an warning regarding the beasts who occupied the territory north of the river. Unlike them, who only wished to be free, the three other races inside the barrier wished to dominate the lands and eliminate each other or anything that could be considered a threat.

"I have no idea what they are called or where exactly you can find them, since we always stayed in or near the river, but I can tell you that their leaders have the same ability as me, probably even stronger, because, despite being able to hear their thoughts, when they reached out, I was never able to see them."

"Thank you for everything you shared. I hope life in the Grand Lake will be better for you and that if we ever meet again it will be as friends."

"Thank you for offering us freedom and savings the lives that might have been taken if we fought. We will surely see you as a friend, despite the fact that we have no idea what you are."

As Kayro was closing the hole in the barrier after all crocodiles passed through, his group felt something moving around. Since they were at the edge between the Hills of Hope and the Ring Mountains, he thought there might be some rocks falling from the mountains, but they couldn't see anything no matter which direction they looked. A few moments later, they were surrounded by creatures who broke out from the hard soil and a voice connected to their minds.

"Ground walkers, I am the one leading the ryanjen, or at least that is the name given to us by those cursed mages who trapped us inside their barrier, and I wish to meet and talk to the one who used his power to free the crocodiles. The rest of you can go back and, after I finish talking to him, one of my brethren will bring your leader back without even as much as a scratch."

In order to at least save the rest, Kayro told the ones who came with him to go back to the main group and agreed to meet with the creature behind the voice and see what it wanted from him. One of the ryanjen went back in the ground allowing him to get inside and mount it, while the rest made sure the reptilians were not going to follow them collapsing the tunnels they dug.

Nearly ten minutes later, after moving at very high speed underground through various tunnels, Kayro got to a huge cavern where he found himself surrounded by ryanjen of different sizes. The biggest was five times bigger than any of the other ones and it turned out to be the leader. As the giant was crawling closer, the young man was having a hard time to stop his instincts from taking over, especially after what the leader of the crocodiles told him.

"Relax, strange one, I heard what that overgrown reptile told you, but I can assure you that we mean no harm to anyone unless they force us to attack them. To be honest, I did tell all the other beings that we want kill them and occupy the entire land inside this magical cage, but that was only to stop them from entering our tunnels.

You see, we were different beings long time ago when those who call themselves mages opened what the humans now call the Great Mine. Back then they called us earthworms and we were the same size you are now. While they were searching for the magic crystals which they treasure so much, they saw us eating them and, in order to stop us and have them only for themselves, they used their abilities to chase us away and seal us.

That is how the multi-layered barrier was created and why they never opened it, fearing that we might eat all the crystals. While being forced to live in such a small space, the tunnels my ancestors dug were invaded by the spiders, who lived in the forest next to the hills, and saw them as prey, but with the power given by the magic crystals, my forefathers proved to be a lot stronger. They fought each other for nearly ten years until the hunted decided to become hunters.

A year after the earthworms started eating the spiders, mutations started happening and we were created. When the mages came to check this area for crystals, they were terrified by us and, after giving us a new name, ran away adding two more layers to the barrier."

"So, if you don't want to kill the other, what exactly do you want?"

"It is simple, weird one. We have grown too big both in size and numbers, so the majority of us wants to escape this cage. The old and the children will stay behind, being a lot safer here, but the rest wish to roam freely."

"Why are you calling me that? And if we want to live here, would the ones remaining see us as a threat?"

"I am calling you weird, because you are like none of the beings you came with, or any other I have heard or met. Regarding your second question, my answer is that they could become your allies, if the ones you came with agree and, of course, if you help us get away like you did for the crocodiles."

"I see no problem in that. After all, I aim to create a land where everyone can be free. "

"I already knew that, but I will need a confirmation from everyone who travelled here with you. Only then we will leave the weakest among us behind."

After the leader of the ryanjen finished what it had to say, Kayro was taken to his group and given time to talk to the rest of the humans and humanoids. Everyone was scared when the creature he was riding suddenly came out of the ground in the middle of where they set up camp, but seeing that he was safe, no one attacked it.

A meeting with the entire camp was scheduled in one hour and he told them everything the leader of the ryanjen said. Next morning, the huge creature emerged out of the ground along with ten of the strongest of its species and, after getting confirmation from everyone that they will not attack the ones who were going to stay behind, thanked everyone after deciding to meet with Kayro and a small group that could ensure his safety, near northern side of the barrier, three days later.

As agreed, he went there and this time it was the insectoids who accompanied him, because they were the only ones who could fly. He chose to go there through the air avoiding a surprise like the one after the crocodiles left and also because it would take nearly three days at best any other way. It took several hours for the ryanjen to go through the hole he opened for them and it was already dark when Kayro and the ones travelling with him were going back.

When they were half way between where the group set camp and the northern side of the multi-layered barrier, just around midnight, a voice connected to their minds.

"I need the one who allowed both the ryanjen and the crocodiles to leave the barrier, to come alone and meet me in the middle of the forest."

Thinking of how easy things went by with the other leaders and hoping it might be the same again, Kayro agreed immediately, promising the insectoids that he will get back to camp unharmed even if they cannot accompany him.

Nearly one hour later, the young man arrived at his destination and as he got to a clearing he was intimidated by the creature in front of him. A black wolf with blue eyes and wings, four or five times bigger in size than him, was laying casually waiting for his arrival.

Before he got the chance to greet it, the creature took off and pinned him to the ground howling and growling.

"How could you let the ryanjen and crocodiles leave so easily, you cursed puny being? Do you have any idea what you actions caused?"

Releasing his demonic aura, Kayro grabbed the oversized paw that was holding him down and nearly broke it while trying to release himself. After calming down a little, he decided to try the peaceful approach one more time.

"First of all, no, I have no idea unless you tell me what you mean, and secondly why call me here if you wished kill me, instead of just surprising me as I was going back to my camp?"

"Well that is simple. When I asked you to come, the situation was not as half as bad as it is now. Those cursed leuennas never dared to launch an attack to take a territory, because I was lying to their leader about having an alliance with the crocodiles and the ryanjen. Even after the crocodiles left they were still cautious, but as soon as the ryanjen were out of the barrier, your actions put both my pack and your group in danger.

As we speak a small group of my subjects is helping your people stay alive and the rest are trying to keep those annoying felines out of the forest so we can talk without being interrupted."

"All I can say is that I have no idea what a leuenna is and I have no idea what you want from me."

"It is quite simple, you will fight me right now and, if you prove to be my equal or somehow manage to defeat me, my pack will ally with those worthless being that came with you."

"They..."

Before Kayro had any chance to argue with him about the warriors who travelled with him, the wolf came at him even faster than before. The barrier he conjured in order to keep the beast away seemed only to slow it down a little, but that helped him buy time to cover himself in the demonic aura, grow his fangs, claws and wings and be better prepared for the next attack.

Since his opponent was circling around, the young man decided to be the one on offensive, so he started using all magic elements to test if it was weak to any of them. Surprisingly, only the orbs of lightning proved to be a little effective, but, without being able to perform stronger versions, Kayro was forced to either choose a physical combat or to force things by combining his blood with the magic.

Unfortunately, flying for so long took quite a lot of energy from him, so using blood was not an option anymore. Without that, all he could rely upon were his claws, fangs and the combat practice he did during Training Camp. Despite realising how foolish he was when he gave up on carrying weapons, the young man still believed in his strength, so he growled loudly.

It was hard enough to fight already, when his instincts kicked in, nearly making him go berserk again, but he knew that a future alliance as well as his own sanity would be endangered if he gave in to them, so he was not just fighting the wolf, but also himself.

After receiving a few bites and claw attacks head on, he tried using a little of his blood sending some blades made out of it which barely had any effect on his opponent. Still, he was not ready to give up and tried as hard as possible to find a balance between calm and anger.

Using ice magic and the blood which was coming out from the wounds on his left arm, he created some sort of a shield, and, not only did it stop the bleeding, but also worked very well to block the next attacks. He wanted to make a sword or a spear in a similar way, by using his right hand, but that meant drawing more blood which could make him weaker. Instead, he had the idea to cover his claws with the fresh blood from the wounds all over his body and he was able to wound the wolf.

Ten minutes later, they were both very tired, so they stopped flying and now the fight felt like a twisted boxing match from one of Kayro's memories from his past lives. Each of them had his guard up and only attacked when it felt decisive, but there were almost no openings.

Without any alternative, the young man allowed part of his blood to mix with the demonic aura which gave him enough speed and strength to take down the massive beast. As he was getting ready to bite its neck, he remembered about the possibility of an alliance, so he stopped halfway through.

Using his healing magic and giving the wolf some of his blood to drink, he saved the beasts life just in time, but now he was so weakened that he ended up collapsing. As soon as it saw that, the beast grabbed Kayro, threw him on its back and started flying towards the camp where the humans and humanoids were.

It was already morning when they got there and it looked like a battle just finished. The leuennas were nocturnal animals, so they probably retreated recently, but only to rest and come back with more bloodlust in the evening. Luckily there were no deaths among Kayro's group or the wolves, and, after fighting together against the felines, the wolf leader was allowed to land in the middle of the camp.

Everyone was shocked at its sight, since all the other wolves, despite being bigger than the ones which can usually be found in the forests of Xorbia, were very small compared to their leader. More shocking than its size, was the pair of wings it had, but as soon as everyone saw Kayro they forgot about it and rushed to help him.

The wolf leader told them everything about their fight and how the young man proved worthy of being their ally. More than that, he also won its trust and loyalty by healing it when their fight was over. That was when M'nka started explaining to all who were there that he should be fine after sleeping for a while.

"He just spent too much energy again. The fight would have knocked him down anyway, but it looks like he pushed himself a lot to make sure you will survive."

"He lost too much blood and also his ability to steal powers from other apparently works even without killing his opponent. Just like M'nka said, he should be fine after a good sleep" added R'mal.

Everyone felt more relaxed after hearing that and everything the two demons said was confirmed two days later when Kayro finally woke up. Before he had the chance to say or ask anything, R'mal started telling the young man about everything that happened while he was asleep.

"It's good to have you back with us, my prince! Unfortunately, we can barely keep up, even with the help of the wolves, so you might be the only one who could finish this and finally claim this land. I think sleeping for two days should be enough for you to fight at full power, so let us meet the others and come up with a plan."

"First of all, please stop calling me 'prince', and secondly why did you let me sleep for so long?"

"Well, my non prince, no matter how hard we tried waking you up, you simply couldn't stop sleeping. I guess this is what happens when you use too much magic to heal an opponent that you nearly killed and losing that much blood during the fight didn't really help."

R'mal knew that Kayro would have slept only for a day if not for his ability to steal power from others, but he decided postpone telling this to the young man as he might try to avoid killing his future foes, which was not necessarily a bad thing, but without the proper training it might become a weakness. Unfortunately, now, more than ever they needed him to fight at full strength since the leuennas were getting close to overpowering them, even without their leader joining the fight.

They went to meet Zoss, M'nka and the wolf leader and, after nearly one hour, it was decided that the best way to end things was to kill the leuenna leader. Knowing her intentions of wishing to occupy his forest and how cunning she was, the wolf was certain that she can now be found in the clearing where he and Kayro fought. With his entire wolf pack helping the humans and humanoids there was no way for her to miss that chance, but, in order to fool everyone, she made her subjects circle around a little and pretend that they are coming from the western side.

With Kayro and the wolf being the only ones able to fly they decided to go and fight her together, but everyone else felt like that might not be enough. Each of the other three wanted to go, but M'nka was the one who proved to be the best choice.

Unlike Zoss and R'mal she couldn't really act as a leader for those staying behind and her oath to keep the young man from losing his mind to bloodlust, at least until he was able to free his parents, assured everyone that she would rather lose her life than let anything happen to him. Also she was the weighing less than the others which meant that the wolf will not use too much energy to fly with her on his back at full speed.

Before leaving, Kayro made sure to take some weapons with him, just in case his magic will not work against the leuenna and he enchanted those as well as the outfits worn by him and M'nka. He wished that B'dar was here to do that and by that saving some of his energy, but there was no other choice. They didn't have anything that could protect the wolf leader, but, in case of emergency, the young man would give allow the beast to drink some of his blood to get stronger and recover.

As they were flying, Kayro decided to ask more about what made the leuenna leader so powerful and, at the same time feared by his ally.

"As I said before she is very cunning, but what made her so strong was the fact that she killed and ate all her brothers and sisters immediately after being born."

"And that was enough?!" both Kayro and M'nka asked at the same time.

"I guess it worked similar to how I got part of my power. You see, despite being stronger than most of my siblings, I was just a wolf, long time ago. When I was nearly an adult, I was caught by the mages who experimented on my parents by using crystals before I was born and they forced me to fight against animals who were born in similar circumstances. Initially we tried to pretend that we fought each other, but they caught on to that and started executing members of our families if we didn't do it properly.

For some time it was only to test us, but soon we were asked to kill our opponents, otherwise they will again go after our families. Loving mine so much, I saw no choice but to kill in order to keep them safe. Unfortunately, I was beginning to enjoy the taste of blood and ended up starting to eat the ones I killed.

The stronger my opponent was, the more power I gained, which probably has something to do with those cursed crystals. When I got too strong and grew wings, the mages feared me and tricked me into getting inside their multi-layered barrier by telling me that my parents were moved here, but that was a lie.

As soon as they got me trapped, one of them, who called himself a member of the Council of Magic revealed to me that he killed them soon after I was caught."

Feeling sorry for him, Kayro and M'nka wanted to comfort the wolf leader, but he seemed fine, so they allowed him to carry on with his story.

"I swore to kill that cursed mage, but he is one of the creators of the multi-layered barrier, so I got used to the fact that he will have to die before I can get out of here. Or at least that is what I thought before sensing how Kayro could open holes in it, but that is something we will need to talk about another time.

Getting back to the leuenna leader, she was born here, on the inside of this magical cage, and before her birth, the mages used high quantities of magic crystal when experimenting on her mother who was their previous leader. She gave birth to seven babies, but none survived the hunger of their sister, so my guess is that she absorbed a lot of her power at that time. She was growing faster than any other being inside the multi-layered barrier and, when she was about half my size, her bloodthirst became too hard to control.

While trying to stop her, the former leader was easily defeated and eaten by her daughter who gained even more power following that. That is when I came up with the idea of lying to her that I have an alliance with the crocodiles and the ryanjen, because just like us she could sense the power of the others inside the barrier, and as powerful as she became it was still not enough to defeat all three of us."

"So that is why you were mad at me for allowing them to leave?" Kayro asked.

"Yes, but that is my fault anyway. Instead of lying about an alliance, I should have talked to the others and actually agree to one. Who knows, since you told me that they wanted to be free, maybe we might have killed the leader of the leuenna together, before your arrival."

As he finished telling his story, the sun set and they also arrived at their destination. M'nka was forced to cover herself in the demonic aura before landing, because unlike her companions she couldn't see in the dark, but thanks to this ability she could sense everything around her, allowing her to fight just as she normally would have.

The leader of the leuennas was surprised to see them, but didn't look bothered by their presence, so instead of attacking herself, she just ordered some of her subjects to surround her opponents. After a few minutes all of them proved to be too weak and were unconscious, which forced her to stand up.

Using her full speed she was able to injure all three of her opponents and that made them aware of the difference in strength between the ones they knocked out and their leader. Without wasting time, Kayro growled and covered himself with the demonic aura, M'nka drank a potion to give her more energy and heal the small wounds left by their enemy and the wolf howled as loud as it could.

Being a little worried about facing all three of them at the same time before seeing their real powers, the leuenna roared and less than a minute later three members of her pride showed up. All of them were as strong as the abnormal gurma which Kayro defeated during the Test of Survival and that made the young man and his friends get close to each other and devise a plan of attack.

Seeing their reaction, the leuenna leader connected to their minds wanting to drive even more fear into them.

"Six more of my beloved daughters are on their way to finish off your annoying friends that stayed behind, but I wouldn't worry about them. The three daughters I kept next to me are as powerful as the others and they will make sure you will have the same fate as your followers."

Hearing this, Kayro's anger was triggered. While he knew that the warriors should be able to eventually kill the six daughters of the leader, he was aware that there will be lots of victims as well. Without saying anything to the wolf or to M'nka, he growled loudly and moved at such a high speed that no one realised when he bit the neck of one of their adversaries, killing it instantly.

While their mother roared, the other two leuennas charged towards him, but they were stopped by his companions. Knowing that they will be able to fight equally against the daughters, Kayro focused his attention on the mother and started using magic attacks against her.

Unfortunately, the water blades, ice spikes, orbs of lightning and fire, sharpened rocks, combined with wind to gain more speed, proved to be useless. He tried using a barrier, but the beast had too much magic power inside and easily broke free.

Seeing that magic was not working, and the wolf leader, as well as M'nka, started bleeding and losing energy, he pulled out a short sword and a short spear and charged towards the huge feline. Combining all his skills with the speed and strength gained from training or from killing his former enemies, he managed to give the massive leuenna a few wounds, but, at the same time, he realised this will not be enough to kill it.

Being distracted by the other fights, his spear was broken and his short sword thrown away, but luckily he was able to dodge the claws that were probably going to impale him. Risking themselves by leaving time and space for an attack, both M'nka and the wolf leader shouted at him to trust them, forget about their battles and focus on his own fight, otherwise, all three of them might die there.

Just as he was dodging a bite that could take his arm off, Kayro formed a shield on his left arm and coated his claws on the right hand with blood, just like he did during the fight with the wolf leader not so long ago. This proved to be a good improvement when it came to defending himself, but the claws were simply not getting deep enough to make a difference.

He tried to apply magic on his claws, turning them, at random, into fire, ice, rock or lightning, but only the last one had some effect. Still, he needed to come up with something stronger than that in order to kill his foe, otherwise everything will be lost.

As he was fighting, Kayro remembered that, during Training Camp, Monta gave him a book about beasts, in which he read that the felines on Xorbia had extra thick hide and he will need a sharp and long weapon in order to cause serious damage. He started looking for the short sword while dodging or blocking his opponent's attacks and, as soon as he saw the weapons, started sprinting towards it.

Despite leaving himself vulnerable for a few seconds while grabbing it, he managed to dodge the attack that could cost him a leg and, as he got up, he began moving the fresh blood which was covering his body in order to coat it. Because that was not enough, he used the sharp blade to cut the palm of his left hand and then started attacking. It turned out that what he read in that book was true and now the massive feline was not able to attack as easily as she did before.

While he was doing all of that, the wolf leader and M'nka kept pace with the leuennas, but they started getting tired. Luckily that was also something that was happening to their enemies, so the fights were still balanced. Realising that this way both her and the wolf will probably lose, she pulled out a vial from her pouch and, while dodging the next attack, she drank a third of it.

Immediately after doing that, she gained new strength and got faster, which allowed her to easily block the claws of her foe while she threw the vial at the wolf. He crushed the glass in his mouth and just like her, his speed and strength improved.

The vial had Kayro's blood inside it and they agreed to only use it in case of emergency, but with the demon female not being as strong as the young man, and the wolf leader being weakened by the fight that took place in the same place a few nights before, this was considered a life or death situation.

By doing that, they broke the balance and were able to simultaneously kill their opponents with the next attack. While the wolf bit the leuenna's neck, M'nka drove her claws deep inside its eyes reaching the brain. Just as they were turning around to try and help Kayro, the mother ignored the young man and while charging at, she knocked both of them out.

As she was getting ready to end the life of the female demon, she sensed something that made her freeze with fear. Kayro allowed part of his rage and bloodlust to combine and with even greater speed and strength than before he impaled one of the leuenna's paws to the ground by using his sword. Immediately after that, he sent as much electricity as his control over lightning allowed him to into the metal weapon causing paralysis for a few moments inside the beast's body.

His instincts kicked in and he bit its neck, but that was not enough to convince him that his opponent was dead, so, he grabbed each jaw and pulled them away until the feline's skull split in half. After that he rushed to his companions healing their wounds, before passing out himself.

A few minutes later the wolf and M'nka woke up surrounded by at least twenty leuennas, but they showed no sign of aggression. The leader of the wolves connected to their mind and found out that they had no reason to fight anymore, in fact they never had any reason except fearing that their leader was going to kill them if they refuse to follow her orders.

In order to stop the fight which was taking place between Kayro's group and the remaining leuennas and to save as many lives as possible, the wolf took the top half of the feline leader's skull and flew with it.

As it reached above the camp almost all the leuennas stopped, and the two remaining daughters of the leader, who kept fighting, allowed themselves to be distracted by what the wolf leader was carrying in his mouth and they were killed.

With the battle being stopped, the flying beast dropped the half skull on the ground and flew back to check on the two companions he left behind. Gaining more power after killing one of the strong felines and being healed by Kayro's magic, he was able to fly even faster than before and three hours later he landed inside the clearing where they fought.

Since they were not in a rush, he asked M'nka to get the young man and climb on his back, so he can fly them back to camp. Before leaving, he told the leuennas about the rest of the leader's daughters being killed and they decided to follow the wolf and his companions and join the rest of their pride.

## A new beginning and a new community

Five days after the fight, Kayro finally woke up and before he had the chance to look around, M'nka already wrapped her arms around him holding him in a tight hug. After thanking him for saving her life, she helped him get up and held him while he took his first steps. They went to the middle of the camp where everyone was still resting and after he ate, a meeting was held between all races and species.

It was decided that the best way to honour the dead was for their bodies to be burned except the ones of the former leuenna leader and her daughters. Those would be used up to the last bit, with the meat being shared between the wolves and the felines, and anything else would belong to the humans and humanoids.

A small part of the leuennas asked for permission to remain within the multi-layered barrier and live peacefully with the ones who now were considered the owners of the new land, while the rest asked Kayro to open a hole in the north western side of the barrier so they can be free. Similar to them, the wolves divided, especially since the one who used to be their leader gave up on his title by swearing loyalty to the young man. Part of them wished to be free so they wished to go south of the barrier, most likely join a pack in the Great Forest or simply establish a territory for themselves in there, while the rest offered to stay inside and protect the land and its new owners if the mages ever decided to collapse the barrier or they simply came to invade it.

When it came to the humans and humanoids, they were going to decide where exactly to start building a settlement after the ones waiting outside the Great Forest were going to join them, so as Kayro opened a hole for the wolves who wished to be free, a group led by Zoss and R'mal went to get the others. As a token of gratitude, the leader of the free wolves promised to accompany them and only after everyone will be safe inside the barrier, they will look for a new home.

As soon as they everyone was out, Kayro allowed the hole to close and accompanied by the former wolf leader, who was now named Trex, he travelled with the leuennas to the north of the barrier, leaving M'nka in charge of the camp.

After a day of flying the young man and his companion reached their destination and three hours later so did the leuennas. In case they ever wanted to communicate with the ones that wished to exit the barrier, the rest of them decided to make the north western side of the land their new home and everyone agreed to that during the meeting.

When all the felines who wished to leave where out, Kayro allowed the hole to close and, after saying goodbye to the ones who stayed behind, he challenged Trex to a race back to the camp. A few hours after they arrived, a wolf who was waiting for them humans and humanoids to get to the barrier came to deliver the news and the young man flew south faster than ever,

He couldn't wait to see his grandparents again, after everything he went through, and talk to them about it. Aside from that, he wanted to properly introduce them to his friends and also get to know his grandmother's brother and his family. He wanted to enjoy doing these things before starting to seriously train in order to release his parents from prison.

It took several hours for everyone to get inside and a few more for them to reach the camp. With everyone being tired from the road, it was decided that they will wait until next day to hold a meeting and decide what to do next. Taking advantage of this, Kayro decided to get all his friends and family together and celebrate, but in the end, the entire camp had a big feast.

A few hours after sunrise, the meeting which was going to decide the future was held and it was decided that the place where the camp was will become the centre of the settlement which will be called Everyone's Village, while the land within the multi-layered barrier was called the Freedom Land. The name was chosen as a symbol of their hopes for the future when the entire Ardian Continent was going to be freed from the influence of the

Council of Magic. It was decided that the river in the north was going to be called the Leuenna River, while the one in the south would be named Wolf River. The forest was left without a name for the moment and the mines where named after the ones who build the tunnels Ryanjen Mines.

When it came to how the society was going to work, despite everyone's wishes for Kayro to become their only leader, the young man refused, so he was only given the title of honorary leader, while Zoss, Trex, R'mal, B'dar, D'ram, Laren, Takya, Zodar, Klost and Krysta were going to become pillars of the community. They would act as a council when needed, but mostly as the ones in charge of various aspects of the community.

While Zoss was train everyone in using weapons and creating them, Trex was going to act as an ambassador between humans and humanoids on one side and the animals who stayed inside the barrier on the other side, whether they were wolves, leuennas or ryanjen.

When it came to the demons, R'mal was going to be in charge of checking and keeping the borders safe with help from the wolves and from the leuennas in the north west, B'dar was going to be in charge with the tanners, weavers and all other crafters, teaching them, not only how to improve their quality, but, with help from some of the mages and demons, also how to give them magic properties, while D'ram was going to train everyone in hand to hand combat.

Laren was going to work with the fishermen, hunters and butchers and Takya was going teach everyone how to cook properly in order to make maximum use of their supplies, while Zodar was going to be in charge of bringing a steady supply of wood.

Klost and the reptilians, along with anyone who wished to join them, were going to plan everything that involved working the fields and raising livestock.

Krysta and part of the insectoids were going to work on getting everyone healed and keeping them healthy. They were also going to build greenhouses and fields for medicinal plants with help from some of the mages. The rest of the insectoids along with some humans, were going to enter the mines in search for mushrooms and materials that can be used for crafting or building.

After everyone was given a task, Kayro and M'nka decided to go to the former Desert Mine Prison and see who decided to stay there and who was going to come with them to Everyone's Village. As he was flying above the Grand Lake, holding her tightly, the leader of the crocodiles contacted his mind and offered to get them as close as possible to their destination, helping them save energy and keeping them safe at the same time.

Travelling at high speed, they got to the desert in just four days. After leaving them, the crocodile told them that they are going to wait a week in the forest between the desert and the Hills of Hope in case they decide to go back the same way and their numbers will not be too high.

As soon as Kayro and M'nka reached the huge cave H'rir was the first one to greet them as he was appointed to lead the ones guarding it. The demon took them to Lurmand and they had a small meeting talking about everything that went on after the young man and the warriors left.

The first one to talk was the former grandmaster of the Mage Institute and he had mostly good news. The most important was that he managed to convince some of the stronger mages to join him. Another important news was that with help from some of the demons, insectoids and reptilians, he discovered ways to use the magic crystals which would benefit any community, but that is where all the bad news started.

After sending a few of the mages who used to support Ghilod to Mage Island, they came back with troubling information. Somehow the Council of Magic knew that the former healing master had died and now they were going to send one of their members to see if Alyssa is their best choice to replace him, or if they need to start looking for someone else.

Since that was going to happen, everyone will need to leave, collapse all shafts of the former Desert Mine Prison and someone will need to create a fake trail that will look like whoever survived went across the Infinite Sea to the north, while the rest were going to enter the multi-layered barrier.

Unfortunately, since the mages acting as spies couldn't stay at the Mage Institute, the exact day when the member of the Council of Magic will come to the Ardian Continent, and where exactly he was going to come from where unknown, so they had to leave quickly.

Agreeing that a quick escape was the best option, Kayro chose to postpone telling them of what happened inside the barrier and about the people from the Median Forests who joined the new community. He only confirmed that now they have a new place where everyone can live and that some friends will be able to help them travel faster by water if they had enough boats.

Lurmand had already thought about that and they managed to build some rafts that could take everyone away from the desert, but they will be very slow. He also offered to be the one to mislead the council of magic, and along with some of the mages, insectoids and reptilians he will leave towards the northeast as soon as everyone else was aboard the rafts. He promised to find a way to get to the multi-layered barrier, but not too soon, because there will be a chance of the Council of Magic sending spies to follow him.

While the former grandmaster, M'nka and H'rir made sure that the plan was being properly executed, Kayro flew at maximum speed to get the help from the crocodiles. Considering their size and speed, they should be able to push the rafts to the Wolf River in about four days, maybe even less. He left the desert in the evening and early in the morning he was back with the huge animals. Some of the ones who boarded the rafts were scared by how ferocious they looked, but the leader connected to their minds and assured them that anyone in Kayro's group was seen as a friend and not as prey.

Before saying their goodbyes, the young man asked H'rir to travel with Lurmand and keep the old man safe, not only because he was a dear friend, but also because he had knowledge that was to important for their world to lose.

The demon protested at first wishing to keep Kayro safe, but, after seeing how powerful he got in such a short time, he agreed that the safety of the mage was very important and promised to do everything in his power to get the old man to the edge of the Freedom Land as soon as possible without any harm coming to him or being followed by anyone.

After using their magic to collapse the tunnels, Kayro and Lurmand hugged and each went their own way. The crocodiles proved to be even faster after learning that a member of the cursed Council of Magic was on his way to the Ardian Continent and they rushed to get the young man and his group to safety.

Travelling at maximum speed, they reached the edge of the multi-layered barrier in just two and a half days. Hating to feel trapped again, the crocodiles apologised for not taking them all the way to Everyone's Village, but everyone understood and thanked them for their help. Despite being a lot slower without being pushed by the reptiles, the rafts reached the area where the future dock was going to be built.

While Kayro and M'nka were away, the village began to take shape and, hopefully, once Lurmand and his group were coming, they could use the mage's knowledge to improve everyone's life even if it was just by a little.

A few hours later, a meeting was held, where the pillars of the community were informed about what was happening outside the Freedom Land and, despite the bad news, it was decided that the next day was going to become the annual celebration of Everyone's Village.

Not only did the celebration give everyone a chance to rest after working so hard, but made them forget about the bad news and gave them a chance to focus on the future.

Surrounded by all his closest friends and family, Kayro felt home for the first time in a long time, but he knew that things will not be quiet for a long.

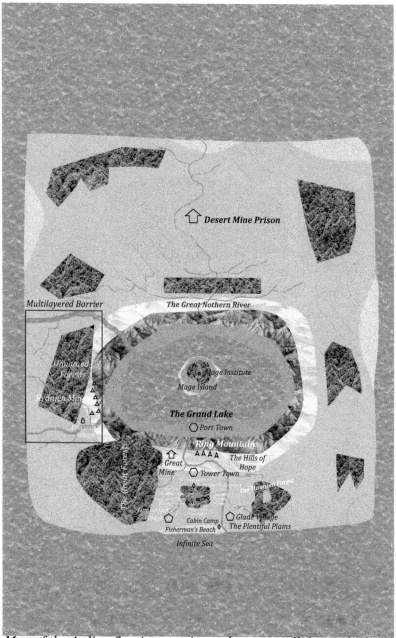

*Map of the Ardian Continent as it was known to all those who lived in Everyone's Village*

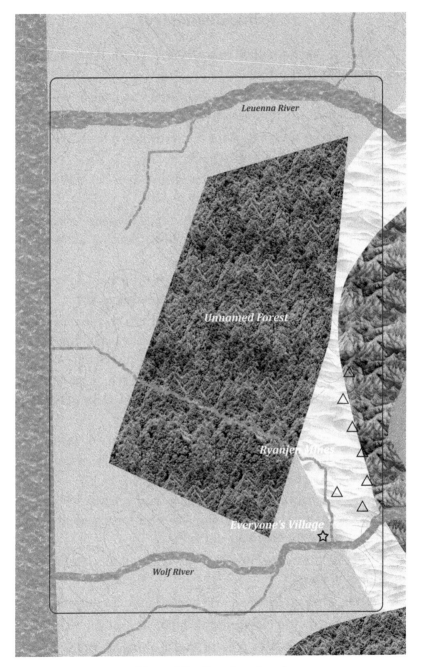

*Map of the Freedom Land*

## Xorbia dictionary

Arberry – a type of plant that grows as a bush. When its fruits reach maturity they are white.

Goreberry – a type of plant that grows as a bush. When its fruits reach maturity they are red.

Muvaberry – a type of plant that grows as a bush. When its fruits reach maturity they are purple.

Sunberry - a type of plant that grows as a bush. When its fruits reach maturity they are yellow.

Galbana – a type of mushroom. Its top is shaped as a star and it is bright yellow in the beginning. When it reaches maturity in becomes dark yellow.

Rozia – a type of mushroom. Its top is round and it is pink in the beginning. When it reaches maturity it becomes red.

Astria – a type of mushroom. It grows as a cluster of smaller mushrooms with round top and it is blue in the beginning. When it reaches maturity white round spots appear on the top.

Bovri – a hybrid between horse and bull. The male bovri is used as a beast of burden and the female bovri is used for breeding and milk.

Glick – a hybrid between a duck and ostrich. Males are usually slaughtered for their meat and some are kept for breeding. Females are used for breeding and laying eggs.

Alpra – a hybrid between a sheep and a llama. Males are slaughtered for their meat and few are kept for breeding, while females are used for breeding and milk.

Horg – domesticated predators used for hunting (welx) or for guarding (howlers).

Welx – a hybrid between wolf and fox used for hunting.

Howler -a hybrid between wolf and bear used for guarding.

Sparus – a common type of metal obtained from melting sparus ore. It is similar to iron, but its colour is yellow.

Horbium – a rare type of metal obtained from melting horbium ore. It is used in a mix with sparus to make objects more durable. Its colour is blue making them mix turn green.

Maxor – a precious metal obtained from melting maxor ore. It is used to make jewellery or to customize the aspect of other metal objects. Its colour is red.

Chrib – a small-sized type of river fish with multicoloured scales

Abruza – a medium-sized type of river fish with blue scales

Scorm – a medium-sized type of river fish with red scales

Falmo – a big-sized type of river fish with golden scales

Orma – a small-sized type of swamp fish with pink scales

Marg – a big-sized type of swamp fish with black scales

Trum – a small-sized type of lake fish with silver scales

Reggia – a medium-sized type of lake fish with purple scales

Lacrom – a big-sized type of lake fish with orange scales

Turen – a hybrid between a chicken and a turkey

Orren – a hybrid between a rabbit and an otter

Miskra – a hybrid between a boar and deer

Gurma – a hybrid between a lynx and a cougar

Flacara – a large reptile that can breathe fire and withstand very high temperatures

Zumzi – a hybrid between a hornet and an ant

Ghetera – a hybrid between a cheetah and a panther

Crafa – a hybrid between a giraffe and a camel

Vuliac – a hybrid between an eagle and a bat

Ryanjen – a hybrid between an earthworm and a spider

Leuenna – a hybrid between a lion and a hyena